ACCLAIM

"An exciting and engrossing second entry into the series, and a worthy successor to *Shadowcast*. Readers will soon find themselves flung to distant realms by this stirring tale."
—THOMAS LOCKE, bestselling author of *Emissary*

"With rich themes of humility, conviction, and sacrifice, *Lightshed* takes a narrative that was already stunning and amplifies it tenfold. As the characters navigate the oftentimes murky terrain between the heart's desires and what is right, Crystal Grant continues her striking tale of a light that can banish the deepest darkness, a love that does not compromise, and a power that makes souls whole."
—ANDREA RENAE, author of *Where Darkness Dwells* and *There Bleeds the Light*

"Compelling and haunting! Grant's second installment in The Gateway Trilogy is a daunting tale about the lure of power and its painful consequences, especially when paired with a soul-staining darkness. *Lightshed* has the perfect blend of pacing, relatable characters, and well-timed twists. This is a story you don't want to miss!"
—RONIE KENDIG, award-winning author of The Droseran Saga

"*Lightshed* was everything I wanted in a sequel! This story reveals the power of unshakable faith and the miracles that can be worked through hope. The question of what will become of Seria and Mason's star-crossed romance will keep readers frantically turning pages. Grant draws the reader in with sophisticated, emotive prose and the current circumstances of the characters sets the stage nicely for the next install-ment. The stakes are high and victory is on the horizon. Readers won't want to miss this spellbinding follow-up to *Shadowcast*."

—ASHLEY BUSTAMANTE, author of The Color Theory trilogy

"Love or duty. Light versus darkness. When lies and truth battle for supremacy on both sides of the Gateway, it can be difficult to discern what is right and what is wrong. *Lightshed* shows us the dangers that come when our loyalties are split in two, with Mason and Seria having to make the most difficult decisions of their young lives so far. But in this world, some choices are not up to them. The end of *Lightshed* will break hearts and yet still have readers begging for the third installment."

—AMBER KIRKPATRICK, award winning author of the Changed duology and *Until the Rising*

LIGHTSHED

LIGHTSHED

Quill & Flame
PUBLISHING HOUSE

CRYSTAL D. GRANT

Quill & Flame
PUBLISHING HOUSE

Lightshed

Copyright ©2024 by Crystal D. Grant

Published by Quill & Flame Publishing House, an imprint of Book Bash Media, LLC.

www.quillandflame.com

All rights reserved.

Cover design by EAHCreative

Dedicated to all those still working to see their dreams become reality. Keep going. You can do it.

CAST OF CHARACTERS

Mason Grey- Shadowman of the Dark Army

Seria Gayle- Mess hall worker/healer in the Gateway Stronghold

Eric Passion- prince of Paladin

Aden Passion- king of Paladin

Braylee Wright- Second Captain of the Steward Army

Dudley Nells- First Captain of the Steward Army

Jervis Planks- Third Captain of the Steward Army

Ollen Knavis- Sergeant in the Steward Army

Lionel Percy- Sergeant in the Steward Army

Lena Carwright- baker in the Gateway

Graulik Jader- Emperor of the New Realm

Bruin Pralus- Commander of the Dark Army

Shon Larson- scout in the Dark Army

Dreeya Faybe- scout in the Dark Army

Areem Kanen- student of Mason's

Hepp Mossen– soldier in the Dark Army

Crue Vancer- Mason's servant boy

Luron Furvor- Physician in the Gateway Stronghold

Larence Shagbut- Bruin's source in the Gateway

Byron Jayes- peasant boy living in the Gateway

Michael and Keeli Jayes- Byron's parents

Kullen Hendrix- Lieutenant in the Steward Army residing in the Gateway

Mavis Derron- Sergeant in the Steward Army residing in the Gateway

Kleff Jaycobs– Sergeant in the Steward Army

Zakkias Pole– Private scout in the Steward Army

Griselle Wright- Captain Braylee's wife

Shayna and Ella Wright- Braylee and Griselle's daughters

Ayna Carwright- Lena's mother

Cal Carwright- Lena's grandfather

Ira Dankton- former client of Seria's

Feegan Hames- Captain and Shadowman in the Dark Army

Nebb Stattler- Steward spy executed by Jader

Liam Grey- Mason's brother (deceased)

Uralis Faunt-former Grand Marshal of the Steward Army (deceased)

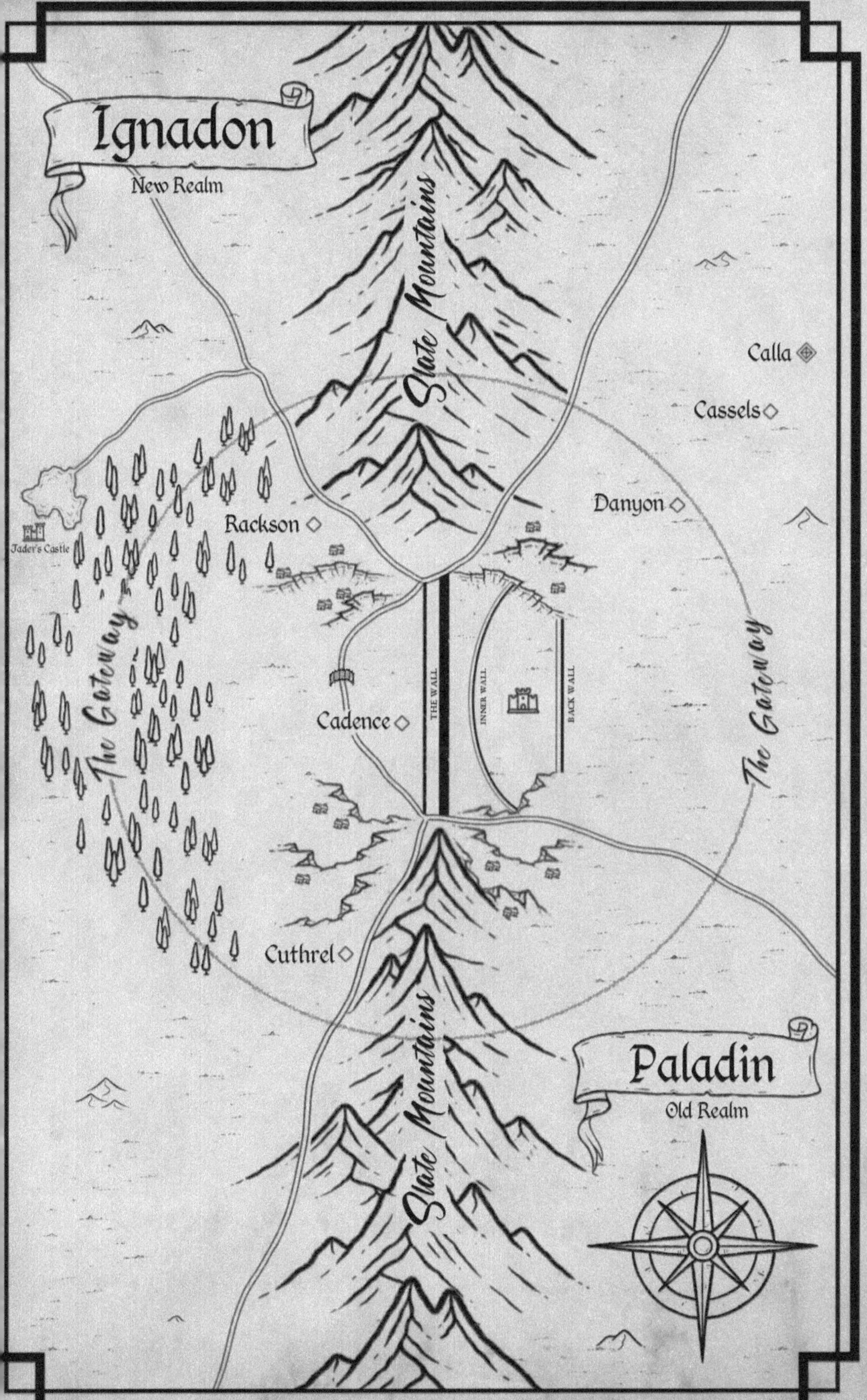

Ignadon
New Realm
Slate Mountains
Calla
Cassels
Danyon
Jader's Castle
Rackson
The Gateway
Cadence
THE WALL
INNER WALL
BACK WALL
The Gateway
Cuthrel
Slate Mountains
Paladin
Old Realm

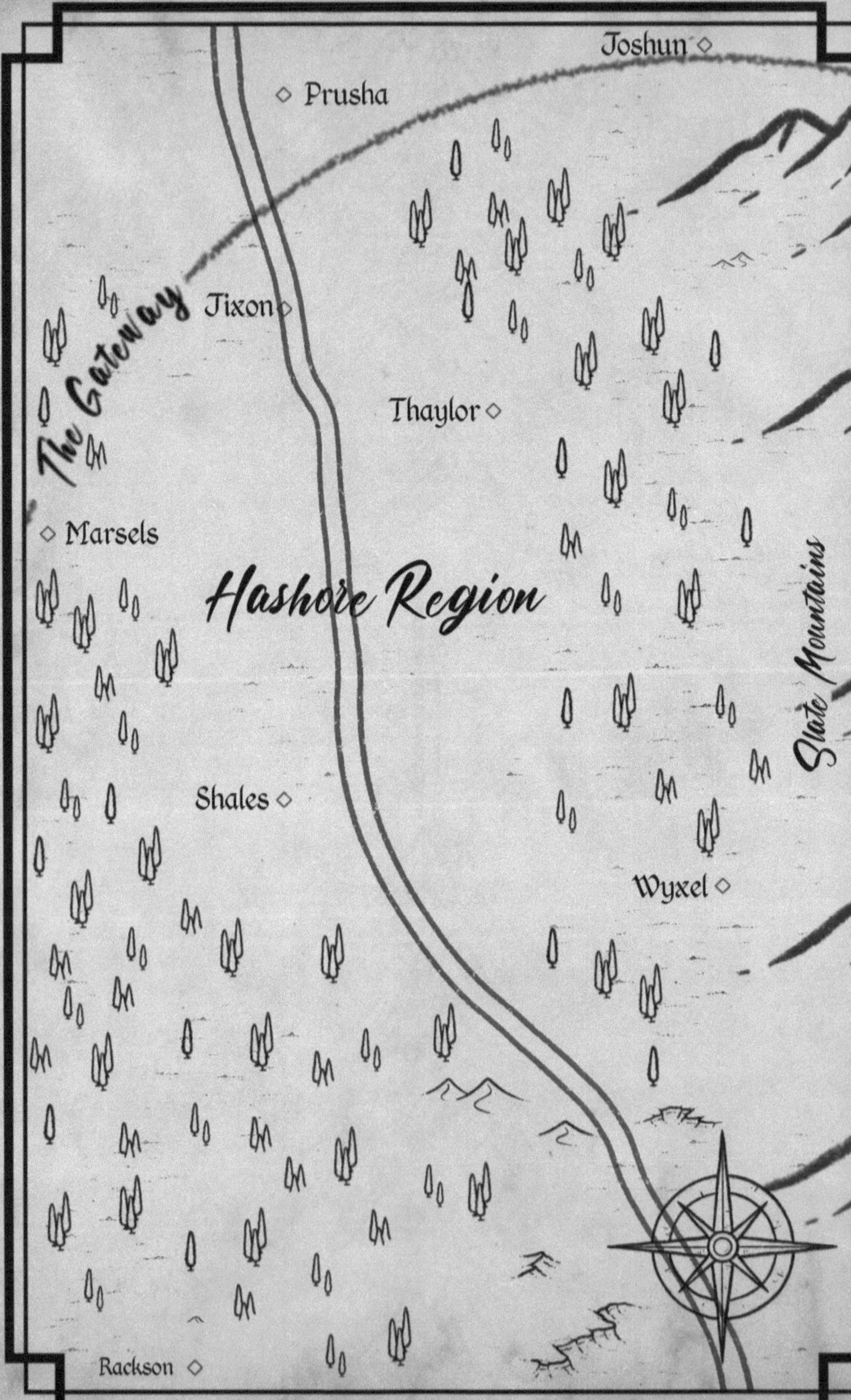

Joshun
Prusha
The Gateway
Jixon
Thaylor
Marsels
Hashore Region
Slate Mountains
Shales
Wyxel
Rackson

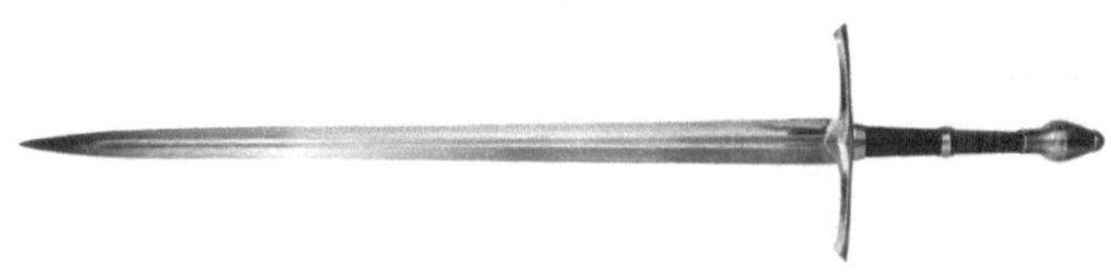

THE MASSACRE

"The Shadowpit is close. I can feel it." Prince Eric Passion bent his head over the map spread out before him and clenched his fist. "I'm not going back until we find it and destroy it."

Captain Hurshel Neems eyed him from across the table in the small tent where they had stopped overnight. "We've been searching for months, Sire."

Eric refused to let the older man's doubt sway him. "Which means we're that much closer."

He sat on the stool, visions of victory crowding his mind. "That pit has caused trouble for the Gateway for too long. It's time we destroy it."

Hurshel exhaled. "I don't deny there would be more peace with it gone, but it may not be as easy as it sounds."

"Nothing is easy." Eric spouted off the words he had heard multiple times from his mentor. "But that doesn't mean it's impossible."

He smiled to himself. Captain Uralis Faunt would be proud to know Eric had listened during one of his profound but long-winded discourses. The man's commencement speeches had become famous among the Steward alumni.

"We'll take a platoon to Morland and check out this last location." He tapped the map before him. "It looks to be promising."

Hurshel did not have a chance to reply before a sergeant called from outside the tent and entered. "Prince Eric, there's been a report of Darkmen activity."

Eric frowned. "Where?"

"Near the small town of Skaller."

In the opposite direction that Eric wanted to go. He grimaced and glanced back down at the map, at the black X that marked where he believed the Shadowpit to be. His pulse skipped in anticipation, followed by a sick feeling in his stomach that would worsen if he walked away from this opportunity. "How serious is this threat?" he asked, drawing Hurshel's gaze.

"We've had three reports of Darkmen being spotted in the woods outside the town," the sergeant said. "One from a prominent Steward loyalist. It's a small band, but they're in the vicinity of the last attack."

Eric studied the sergeant, standing tall at attention, his right hand resting on the Beacon hanging at his belt. He was young and earnest, ready to serve his prince and the Lambient. His lack of experience made him a little too eager at times, which resulted in a few disciplinary actions, but nothing that warranted serious consequences. Eric needed the more experienced soldiers with him.

"Sgt. Mavis Derron, are you prepared to lead a squad to address this situation?"

Mavis's eyes lit up. "Aye, Sire."

Eric stood. "Good, then I'm entrusting this situation to you. Be swift to remove the threat. Do not give these Darkmen room to attack again."

Hurshel spoke up. "Don't you think you should lead this yourself, Sire?"

"Nay." Eric squared his shoulders. "I must pursue this Shadowpit, Captain." How could he explain what it meant? The end of the emperor's quest for power. Peace for his father's kingdom. And respect for Eric, the twenty-year-old prince and newly appointed Grand Marshal of the Steward Army.

His nerves tingled under his skin, sending his heart to pumping. He could not ignore his intuition. It practically screamed at him to get moving. He looked to Sgt. Mavis. "Make haste, Sergeant, and return to us as soon as you can with your report."

Mavis raised his proud head. "Right away, Prince Eric. We won't let you down."

Eric smiled. "I know you won't."

The young officer bowed and hurried out of the tent. Eric imagined it would not take long for him and his squad of newly commenced Stewards to deal with the situation.

"All right, Hurshel. Let's go find that Shadowpit."

Hours later, Eric did not feel so optimistic as they settled down to make camp. Rain had left the forest damp and cool, though the clouds were starting to break apart. They had searched high and low through the bluffs and hills, but there was still no sign of the Shadowpit, despite his hunch.

Eric ground his teeth as he dismounted and handed his black gelding off to a private. He could not go back to Calla without locating this cavern, not after his big talk before his departure. He would look like a fool, a young chap who liked to brag but did not follow through.

He retreated to his tent, looking around for Mavis and his squad. They should have caught up by now. Settling down on his short stool, he spread the canvas map over the block of tree trunk someone had rolled in for him. He scanned the area and scowled. It had to be close. His nerves had buzzed all evening with the sureness of his direction. So where was it?

Captain Hurshel appeared at the open flap. "Prince Eric."

"Aye?" Eric did not bother looking up, sure the captain was about to give his unsolicited opinion on the search.

"Captain Uralis is coming."

Eric frowned, annoyance nipping at him. "Why is he here?"

Hurshel shook his head, looking outside. "I don't know, but he seems to be in a hurry."

The sound of rapid hoofbeats reached Eric then, and he stepped outside just as Uralis reined to a stop and slid to the ground in one smooth motion.

"Prince Eric, I must speak to you."

Eric waved him inside, motioning for Hurshel to join them.

Uralis walked to the middle of the room and faced Eric. He did not waste any time. "I understand you sent Sgt. Mavis Derron's squad to deal with a situation earlier today."

"That's right. How did you know?" Eric glanced down at the map to mask his irritation. Was Uralis checking up on him now?

Hooking his thumbs over his belt, Uralis let out a sigh that made him look older. "I'm afraid the report of Darkmen was incorrect. It turned out to be a group of teenage boys. Orphans from Handan's Home for Boys."

The implication sank in, catching Eric's full attention. "What happened, Captain?"

Uralis looked him square in the eye. "The squad killed the boys."

"Killed..." Eric's lungs hitched, expelling the oxygen he needed. "All of them?"

"I'm afraid so." Sorrow drew deep lines in the veteran captain's face. "The rain was heavy, and the boys all had weapons, so it was hard to make out. Fifteen young men were killed, as well as two Stewards."

Eric groped for the stool, his heart thundering against his chest. This was his fault. It was his order, his impatience and eagerness that had driven those young soldiers to take care of a situation that should have been his to oversee. "What have I done?" he breathed.

Pressing his fists against his eyes, he propped his elbows against his knees, his failure smacking him hard. His fantasies of grandeur had deluded his rationale. His own sense of intuition had tried to warn him, and in his eagerness to be the one to destroy the Shadowpit, he had misinterpreted it. And now, because of his arrogance, his stubborn pride, seventeen lives were lost. It mattered not that he did not lift the sword. He had given the order.

"Where is Mavis?" He hardly recognized his voice, so thin and brittle.

"Not far from the site of the killings."

"I must go there."

Uralis nodded. "I can take you.

Eric stood before the graves, his chest heaving and his eyes burning. Mavis and his squad stood apart from him, their postures broken.

Eric's clothes were coated in dirt, his fingernails broken and encrusted with mud. He had lost count of the hours they spent burying the boys—all so young and lifeless—but it would take much longer to bury the pain.

"I am sorry," Eric whispered to the silent mounds. But the words did not change anything. They were still dead. By his order.

"You've done all you can, Prince Eric," Uralis said. "It's time to move forward."

Eric shook his head. He would never escape this moment, nor would he allow himself another mistake like this.

Turning his back on the graves, he took a shuddering breath and walked away, vowing never to lead the Steward Army again.

1

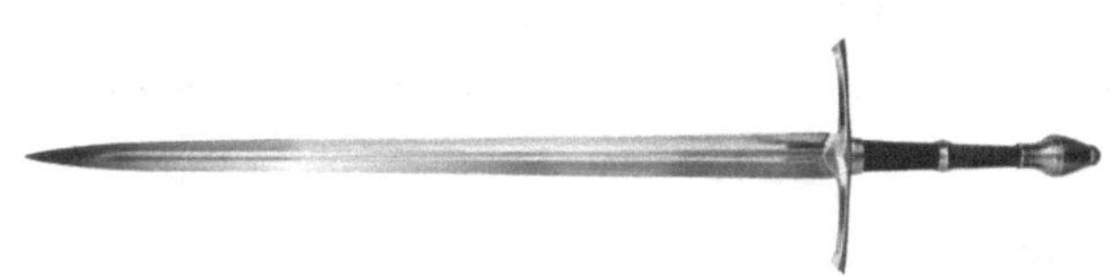

The Gateway
Twelve Years Later

The darkness no longer hindered him. Not with the Shadowstone around his neck.

Mason Grey bit back a curse as he ran on swift, silent feet up the hill, his Shadowstone bouncing against his chest with every step. His team lagged far behind again, unable to keep up with the pace of their quarry, so he went on without them, his ear attuned to the sound of running feet. He did not have time to wait for them. Not tonight.

Tree-covered cliffs cast the area in shadows. The daytime creatures had fallen silent, soon to be replaced by the evening songs of frogs and insects. Mason's breaths came in quick, sharp bursts, forcing him to slow down and fill his lungs.

Heat pressed in on him, though the sun had begun its descent. Sweat trickled down his face, mixing with the whiskers tinting his jaw—a reminder that he needed a shave. He shoved a shock of hair from his eyes with a gloved hand and crouched to study the prints before him. The tracks made a sharp turn to the north.

Blades. Ignoring the stitch in his side, he changed direction, tightened his grip on his crossbow, and moved on. His quarry would be desperate by now. Mason had to be careful. His boots did not make a sound in the soft dirt as he avoided dry leaves and flimsy twigs.

Frustration gnawed at him, time slipping away with every heartbeat. If he missed his appointment because of a team of soft-footed pansies, there would be fire to pay.

He rounded a large gray boulder, too driven by his impatience to check his pace, and came nose-to-nose with a long-legged, very angry grizlon.

Letting out a startled yell, he jerked back. The beast snarled and stood on his back legs to a height of over ten feet. Patches of leathery skin covered his elbows and knees. Two short, thick horns protruded from either side of his head above small, beady eyes that glittered with rage.

Mason swallowed. *Found him.*

They stood frozen for a long moment, waiting for the other to make the first move. Mason still had his bow in his hand, ready to use it if he had to, but as close as he was now, any move he made would only anger the grizlon.

Mason tensed as the animal opened its wide mouth and emitted a deafening roar. He dove out of reach of the razorlike claws, landing in the middle of a thorn bush. "Argh!"

The grizlon lowered to all four feet and went in after him, oblivious to the barbs. Mason scrambled out and spun to lift his bow, which was smacked out of his hands with another enraged bellow.

Not good. The grizlon lunged again. Mason lost his footing and fell flat on his back. He crawled backward several feet, kicking at the massive head, which did not faze it at all. It knocked Mason to the side like a rag doll, his bones rattling until he was sure they would shake right out of his body. Stars flashed before him as he shook his head to gather his bearings.

A grunt drew his bleary gaze back up to where the grizlon charged again.

Idiot, use the stone! Mason grabbed the Shadowstone and willed it to cloak him. The grizlon halted a few feet away and let out a growl, swinging his heavy head from side to side, but unable to see or smell the human right in front of him.

Mason let out a cautious breath and stood to his feet, tightening his control. The grizlon's eyes darted back and forth, his long, lean body tense but immobile under the stone's effect. Mason watched it for a moment, fascinated by its size and build. The grizlons were feared throughout the Gateway for their ferocity and strength, and here he stood mere feet away, unseen and in control, thanks to the stone.

This one—massive as it was—was on the small side, younger than the rest by a few years. It had escaped its keepers while they drove it back to the holding pens after another use. Mason and his team had driven it south during their pursuit, in the opposite direction of its native hibernating grounds.

The grizlon let out a deep sigh and looked north as a rumble sounded deep in its chest. Mason stood still for a moment longer, indecision pulling at him. The emperor needed the beasts to keep the rebellious towns of the Gateway in line. But night was approaching, and Mason had no desire to drag the thing back to its corral. He stepped back into the deeper shadows of the trees and released it. "Go on, you ugly brute," he whispered.

It took a moment for the grizlon to act, its steps slow and uncertain. It swung its massive body around to the north and began its trek. The further it went, the more speed it gained until it loped off into the distance, finally free.

Mason pulled his gloves off, his mind already moving to his next course of action. He would have to report that the animal had escaped, which would not bode well. They had only a few grizlons in their possession as it was. But Mason could not do anything right in the eyes of Commander Bruin Pralus these days anyway, so he didn't care much. Tonight, he had a more pressing matter.

His team was long lost in the woods somewhere, but he did not bother looking for them. Instead, he swiveled and headed for the familiar rock formations that spilled out from the steep stone curtain of the Slate Mountains. He tracked his steps to where his horse was tied safely to a tree, then they took off at a canter for the bluffs. On the other side lay the famed valley everyone knew as the Gateway. So close, yet so far.

Unless...

Tired and hungry, he peered into the blackness, a memory niggling at the back of his mind. *It has to be around here somewhere.* As he approached, he scanned the bluffs until he spotted a small opening, easily missed by a casual viewer. Beyond that was a narrow tunnel, leading straight through the middle of the rocks and saving him miles of travel. Victory surged through him.

Not sure of the size of the passage, he dismounted and secured his horse. After loosening a wrapped package from the saddle, he made his way on foot. At one point, the tunnel veered to the right, and he followed it. A blast of heat from the left made him pause. Another tight crevice opened from that direction, virtually unnoticeable to anyone without enhanced vision. It drew him closer, tempting him to explore its depths. But he had little time, and the heat made exploration undesirable, so he pressed forward, making a note to check it out later.

The tunnel opened up into the valley, just as he suspected. It had been so long since he had first heard of this tunnel, he had almost forgotten it. He stepped out and stood on a slight rise, taking in the spread of the valley before him under the golden evening sunlight. On the other side of the dale, the tall, impossibly steep Slate Mountains continued.

The Gateway.

Mason scanned the abandoned town of Cadence down the hill. Beyond it stood a thick stone wall that stretched from one side of the valley to the other, until it reached the mountains on both sides. Right on the other side of that wall was the Stewards' garrison.

His fingers reached for the Shadowstone at his chest. Taking it on had been everything he had expected and more. His focus was sharper, his vision clearer—both literally and figuratively. Nothing would keep him from fulfilling that goal he made as a stricken twelve-year-old boy watching his brother die at the hands of the Stewards. That day would come. It was what he strove for, *lived* for. And he would fill the deepening hole in the very core of his being.

But something still stirred inside him, as it did every time he looked down at this valley. As if it held a piece he was missing, a vital piece that meant the difference between life or death, hope or despair. He could not shake the restlessness, the growing discontent. It followed him everywhere he went, every turn he took. No matter what he did, there was no joy or satisfaction. Not even the Shadowstone satisfied that deepest part of him.

His chest tightened as he considered the source of his angst. One man—the prince of Paladin.

The gorge sat serene and calm in the golden sunset, but it had become a crucial site for him in so many ways. The only accessible passage through the Slate Mountains. The catalyst for the coming war between the Aged Realms. The location of his ongoing battle with his greatest enemy.

And the home of a green-eyed girl who haunted his dreams.

He stood for a long time, motionless, memories begging to be brought to the forefront again. At the pang that went through him, Mason tilted his head back to look up at the rising moon in the distance. Nightfall was coming. He released a sigh and began the trek down the incline.

He had made his choice, and there was no going back.

2

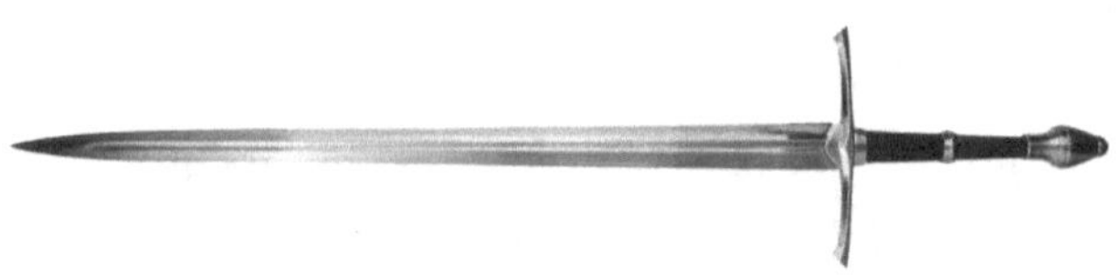

How I long for the nights when Lambient led me by His light. His lamp
shone on my head as I walked through the darkness.
-The Sacred Code

The Gateway Stronghold

The guilt was becoming commonplace.

By all appearances, Seria Gayle had moved on. Her new life here at the Steward fortress was a good one. She had a nice place to sleep, fulfilling work, and dear friends. For all her friends and acquaintances knew, she had learned from the mistakes in her past and looked forward to a new future.

If they only knew.

Sitting on a bale of straw in the large barn that housed the officers' horses, Seria shivered at the idea of anyone seeing past the front she presented to the world. In their eyes, she was a victim of unfortunate circumstances. What if they discovered how she still longed for what was forbidden?

A soft, warm muzzle reached over the bar of the box stall at one end of the barn and bumped her arm. A sigh worked its way from her lungs as she rubbed the old donkey's long gray nose.

Each morning, she put on her brave face that said all was well with her world. But the act was more of a burden every day, following her every footstep, shadowing her every move. She was tired beyond words as she maintained the façade.

Mason. His name blew across her spirit. Why did she keep doing this to herself? It mattered not how busy she kept herself during the day, how many times she told herself that it was over, she still yearned for him. Wished things were different.

It was wrong. She knew it was.

He had made it clear that nothing would take him from the path of vengeance against the prince for the Handan massacre that had taken the life of his brother.

The donkey gave a huff and nudged her again. A soft laugh escaped Seria, despite her gloom. "All right, Sanjo, here you go." She pulled a chunk of carrot from the pocket of her apron and held it before him on a flat palm. He lipped the bite up and chomped it with a contented sigh.

"If only everyone was so easy to please." She stood and dusted straw from her cream-colored gown, and after giving Sanjo another pat on the head, stepped outside. The sun had dropped a considerable distance since she had arrived to visit her furry friend.

The gentle breeze brushed a strand of hair across her cheek, and she wrapped herself tighter within the heavy black cloak she wore. The cloak itself was a stark reminder of what she clung to. Mason had sent it to her through Lena so they could meet in secret away from the safety of the fort. That was when he had told her he planned to take the Shadowstone. And he had admitted his feelings for her.

"Miss Seria, I'm glad I caught you before you headed for home."

Seria jumped at the voice, as if her thoughts had been displayed for all to see. She bit back her anxiety and smiled at the Stewards' gray-headed physician heading her way. "Good evening, Luron."

Luron Furvor caught his breath and put his hands on his hips. "I don't suppose you have time to stop by and make some of your waterstar tea, do you?"

"Tonight?" she squeaked.

"Nay, in the morning."

Seria swallowed back her relief. "Of course."

"I would make it myself, but I still don't have it down right," Luron said, walking leisurely by her side.

"It took me a while to learn it, but it's quite simple once you've got it."

"Well, I'll keep working on it, but in the meantime, I have a patient who could use it, though he's very grumpy about coming in."

"Must be one of our stubborn knights then."

Luron chuckled. "That is correct. I do appreciate all the time you've spent in the infirmary lately. Though I don't know how you keep up with that pace of yours."

"I like to stay busy. It's a little more exciting than cooking." And it beat watching over her shoulder to prevent another uncomfortable encounter with Prince Eric.

She struggled to articulate why she avoided him. Was she justified in holding a grudge against him for something he clearly regretted doing years ago? She had mulled over the question for weeks now and was no closer to the answer. But it made it easier to ignore the truth that she had feelings for the man who had vowed to kill Eric Passion.

Seria glanced up at the moon and sucked in a breath. "I-I better get going, Luron. I'll talk to you tomorrow, all right?"

He waved her off with a "Good night," and she hurried down the path.

The civilians were making their way to their homes for the night. Most of the knights had also gone to their quarters, leaving only those on guard duty. Keeping her gaze averted from any passersby, she did not stop until she reached a small log cabin at the end of a quiet street. She rapped on the door and held her breath. There was a faint rustling inside before the door opened.

"Ready?" Lena Carwright asked, her brown eyes lit with anticipation.

Seria nodded, swallowing her nerves.

Lena called back inside. "We're leaving, Mama!"

Ayna's voice drifted from the back of the house. "You girls be careful tonight."

Lena stepped outside, wearing a cloak that matched Seria's, and closed the door behind her. Together they crept to the edge of the residential area of the stronghold. The inner wall of the Gateway towered above them, and they stood in the shadows until they could make out the guard on top, making his usual rounds. He took a long look around, his face serious. After a minute, he turned and continued on his way.

Something about the sight of him stirred Seria. The knights made her feel secure, yet on edge, like someone was always watching over her shoulder, waiting for her hidden feelings for the Darkman to be revealed. What if the Stewards, whose trust she had worked so hard to win, found out what she was about to do?

"Come on!" Lena tugged on her arm.

After looking both ways, they left their hiding spot and dashed to the base of the wall.

Lena took Seria's hand. "Ready?"

Seria nodded, holding her breath. Putting her free hand on the stone, Lena leaned against the cold stone and passed right through it, taking Seria with her. The sensation of walking through the wall chilled Seria's skin, and she suppressed her revulsion for her friend's Gift of the Moon as they crept through the outer bailey, where they repeated the process.

"Are you all right?" Lena asked after they stepped through the outer wall.

"I'm fine." Seria's voice shook.

Leah gave her an amused look. "It makes my mother sick."

Seria pulled her hood up. "Let's stop talking about it and keep going before I lose my nerve."

They tiptoed along the wall until they reached the shadow of the Slate Mountains, where they were to separate. Panicking, Seria clutched the shorter woman's arm. "What am I doing, Lena?" she whispered.

"You're getting some answers."

She shook her head. "What if he doesn't even show up?" So much could have changed in a fortnight.

"Then that will be an answer."

"But why did he want to wait this long?"

"To give you time."

It all sounded so logical in Lena's calm, no-nonsense way, but something in Seria's middle still shook. "Do you think I'm being foolish?"

"I can't tell you what to do, Seria. That's for you to decide." Lena looked her in the eye under the faint moonlight. "But I do wish someone would have taken time to talk to my father before it was too late."

Seria still did not know much about Lena's father or why he had joined the Dark Army when Lena was a girl. She buried her fingers in her hair that had long since fallen free from the braid she had secured that morning. The inclination to pray to the Lambient rose within her, but fear of what the answer would be held her back.

Lena squeezed her hand. "You don't have to do this."

The reassurance sent strength through her limbs, and she took in a deep breath. "I do have to." She had to see if there was any hope.

"Just take it one step at a time," Lena said. "Get the answers you need tonight, and then go from there."

"I want to see him." Their first few weeks had been far from easy, but they had developed a bond she did not share with anyone else, not even Lena. Her heart yearned for him, despite the chasm that separated their convictions. A sharp pain lanced through her at the memory of his obvious hurt the last time she saw him. When she turned away from him. He had so little love in his life, that she had to give him another chance.

They moved on, each going their separate ways. Lena headed north along the wall to her grandfather's cabin, and Seria moved further into the darkness, toward the empty town of Cadence.

She took a deep breath, her heart beating wildly. All was still and peaceful. The night sky was clear, save for a few drifting clouds, giving her a little more cover, but slowing her down. She picked her way over the rough terrain, careful to stay within the shadows as much as possible.

Stopping at one point to catch her breath, she glanced back at the walls of the Gateway Stronghold. The guards would not be able to see her now. Not with the distance she had put between them and the cloak she wore. *Good thing Captain Dudley's not on guard.*

Licking her lips, Seria tried to get a good look at Cadence. It had been her home for more than two years and held so many memories, some joyful, others painful. There were times she missed it.

Another jolting ache went through her. Even now she could see his devil-may-care grin and his amber-colored eyes that could read her every thought. And the way he chose to serve a lord of darkness and deceit.

Chills settled over her skin, and she trembled. The possibility that he had taken the Shadowstone as he planned was inevitable. Would he even care about her anymore?

Her cabin was ahead, and her pulse quickened. A large cloud covered the moon, hampering her vision. Despite the pitch blackness, however, her whole body itched to rush on.

Sweat beaded her brow and slicked her palms as she crossed the bridge. The cloud drifted by, and her path opened up again. Almost there. Only ten steps from the cabin.

The door opened, startling her to a stop. A figure in dark clothes appeared inside the portal, keeping to the shadows. Seria's feet rooted to the ground.

A masculine voice sounded, rough and curt, sending heat surging down her spine. "Decided to come back, did you?"

She planted her hands on her hips and pursed her lips. "Last time I checked, it *was* still my house."

He stepped closer, the moonlight casting a silvery light over his face—guarded and stiff, much like the first days they spent together in her cabin. Then one corner of his mouth twitched upward, and the mask slipped enough for her to see the hope and relief glimmering in his gaze.

That tentative expression broke through the walls of doubt that bound her in place. Hope illuminated the dark shadows that held her heart in its grip, and her spirit soared with a rush of tears. All her previous doubts and worries flew from her mind as she ran and flung herself into Mason's arms.

3

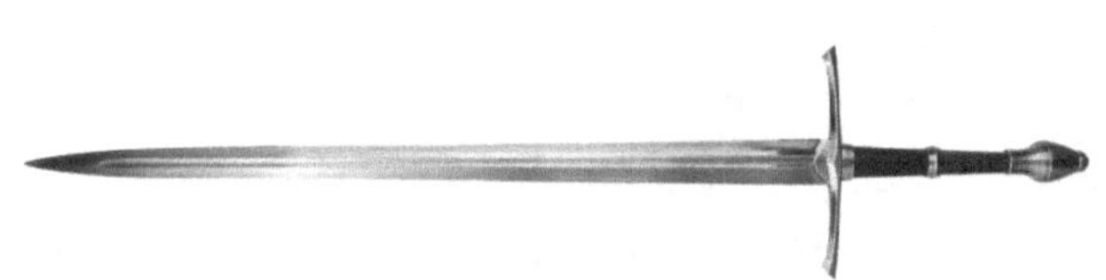

Cadence, The Gateway

Mason caught Seria up in his tight embrace and backed into the
privacy of the cabin. His chest swelled with a dull ache as he held her
tight, his heart pounding against hers.

She was here. This wasn't a dream.

Finally, he set her back on her feet and drew back far enough to stare
down at her. No words were passed for several heartbeats as he mem-
orized every feature, unhindered by the night's veil. The same freckles
dotted her nose. Her eyes, sparkling with unshed tears, did nothing to
hide her feelings for him. The smile she gave him was enough to light
the whole room. His throat tightened around his words. "I'm glad you
came."

She let out a shaky laugh. "I wasn't sure you'd be here."

"I told you I'd wait for you."

"I know, but..." Her gaze skidded to his chest, and he was glad he had
tucked the Shadowstone behind his shirt. Her shoulders hitched. "I was
afraid you'd change your mind."

"Not about you." He grinned to lighten the mood a bit. "By the moon, you are a sight for sore eyes. You got new clothes." Not a tear or stain to be seen on the gown, and the burgundy tunic flattered her figure, rather than hanging on her like a shapeless sack.

A giggle escaped her lips. "Those rags of mine weren't going to last much longer. I declare, I looked like a beggar on the street."

"Oh, I don't know. I kinda liked that cute little beggar." Those ragged clothes had not hidden the radiance of her smile or the light in her eyes.

He could have stood there all night, drinking in the sight and feel of her. But an underlying tension cast an awkward pall over their words.

Moonlight shifted through the sagging shutters, and Seria gasped. "Mason! What happened to you?" She reached up to touch one of the deep scratches on his face.

"Oh, that." He gave a nonchalant shrug. "I had a run-in with a grizlon."

"A grizlon? Are you hurt?"

"No blood loss or broken bones." He caught her hand in his. "I don't need you fussing over me."

She smiled up at him. "Well, it wouldn't be the first time."

"Nay." His eyes drifted to the cot in the corner where she had stood over him so many hours, tending to his wounds, offering him stew, or bathing his fevered face. "It wouldn't be the first time."

"You look like a young scalawag who got caught in the bramble bushes." Her hand slipped from his face to his shoulder, just inches from where his Shadowstone hung.

"Not far off." He cocked a grin and stepped back, out of her reach. "How's that old, broken-down donkey of yours?"

She threw her head back and laughed. "I knew it! You miss him."

"I didn't say that." His denial only made her grin wider.

"You'll be happy to know that Sanjo is thriving."

Mason cocked a brow. "And being spoiled by his mistress, I'm sure."

She shrugged. "What can I say? He's been good to me."

"I hope you're not going out at all hours of the night to check on him." His mind flashed back to the night of the storm, when he had caught one of his own cohorts manhandling her.

"Well, I can't lie." Her tone was light, but from the way she fiddled with the ties on her tunic, he guessed she was thinking back as well.

He cleared his throat. "Um, I brought you something."

Her face brightened. "You did?"

Glad to have something else occupy their thoughts, Mason grinned. "Close your eyes."

"Aw, Mason!" She grimaced. "I hate when someone tells me to do that."

"No whining, Miss Gayle. Now, do as you were told."

"I already can't see much in here."

He cleared his throat, and Seria shut her eyes, sighing through a smile. Mason reached for the large cloth bag in the corner.

"Can I look?"

"Not yet."

"What about now?"

"Nay." He slid the object out of the bag and positioned himself in the light of the moon.

"Now?"

"You're an impatient one, aren't you?"

"I don't like standing here with my eyes closed."

"There you go whining again." He chuckled. "All right, open your eyes."

Seria immediately complied and stared at the slender sword Mason extended out to her. "What's this?"

"It's yours."

"Mine?" She gasped, taking the weapon in her hand. "Where'd you get it?"

"Didn't your papa ever teach you not to ask where your presents came from?" He could not wipe the goofy grin that spread over his face, but her reaction made it worth it. She did not receive gifts often.

She turned the blade over in her hand. "It's so light."

"Just right for a lady's hands. You need something better than your father's old sword to defend yourself should the need arise."

Seria lowered her head with a soft "thank you."

He bit back a curse as the hidden message cast a damper over the moment. Nothing more was said about why she would need a sword, but he was determined she would have a means of protection. "Maybe I can show you a few moves next time."

Her gaze swung up to meet his at the promise. "I'd like that."

Their time drew short, but he could not leave without getting some answers. He drew in a deep breath, taking the sword from her and setting it on the table. Then he stepped closer, cupping her elbows in his hands. When her brows drooped, he hesitated. The last thing he wanted to do was dredge up the past.

"What's wrong, Mason?"

"I need to know something." He did not miss the way she tensed, but he ignored it and spoke through clenched jaws. "Did he... punish you?"

It took a few moments for the question to sink in. Though her shoulders relaxed, her expression remained troubled. His stomach soured as he remembered the day he had left her behind to pay for his deception.

When she answered, she still did not look at him. "It could've gone badly. But they—" Her lips firmed. "He offered me clemency."

His fingers tightened around her arms. "You weren't imprisoned?"

"Nay, Mason. I'm free to come and go about the fort as I please. I'm even working in the infirmary now. And I have a room at the boarding house. It's small, but it's a step up from this place." She waved at the shabby, one-room cabin with a short laugh.

He looked around the room, seeing it clearly with his aided vision. It was in sad shape. Dust had piled in the corners after weeks of no inhabitants. The sagging shutters still had a gap between them. And the table and chairs looked as crooked and crude as ever. But he could not bring himself to criticize it. In the short time he had been here, this was one of the few places that felt like home to him. And that was because of the incredible woman before him.

"I'm fine, Mason." Her hands came up to rest on his chest, right over where the Shadowstone lay. He held his breath as heat generated in the spot. Despite how he felt and what she said, that Shadowstone stood between them like a wall as thick as the one that separated the New Realm from the Old.

Seria's heart sank as her fingers grazed the hard lump under his shirt. She could pretend all she wanted, but Mason wore the Shadowstone.

Silence fell as he glanced around at the worn-out little shack, avoiding her eyes. Her skin prickled as she became very aware of where she was. Alone with Mason—a Shadowman—in the middle of a dark, empty house.

He was so different. Intensity rolled off him. His gaze was sharper, deeper, and she had a feeling it had to do with the stone under her touch.

His features twisted, and he ran a hand through his hair. "I have to go."

"So soon?" Something in her rebelled at the idea of sending him back to his camp. Despite the changes he had undergone, she still caught snatches of the other man, the one she had nursed back to health, butted heads with, and teased until she made him smile for the first time. He was the same man who had saved her life against one of his comrades.

How could something feel so wrong and right at once?

He spoke again. "I'm sorry. I wouldn't have made it here tonight without your tunnel—"

"You found my tunnel?"

"The most crowded, uncomfortable tunnel I've ever been in, but aye, I found it."

She smiled at the grumpiness in his voice. "It got you here, didn't it?"

He sighed. "I shouldn't be, but I had to know…"

"If I would come?"

His gaze grew intense. "I want you to trust me, Seria. I will never take advantage of you again, I promise you that. I'll never read your thoughts for my own advantage."

The reminder of what he could do made her legs tremble as the risk she was about to take weighed on her. But then a flicker of doubt crossed his face at her hesitation. She lay her hand against his whiskered jaw. "I believe you, Mason."

"And you'll come back? Tomorrow?"

Her heart broke at the vulnerability he tried to hide but that still shimmered from his eyes. Remembering all he had lost as a boy, she could understand his fear. "I'll come." Even as the promise slipped out, guilt pierced her for betraying the Stewards. But she could not turn away from him again. He needed her.

If she had to climb the wall with her bare hands, she would be here.

"I meant what I said before." He caressed her cheek with his knuckles. "I love you."

The words lifted the worry and guilt from her heart. "Oh, Mason. I love you, too."

A breath escaped him, mingling with hers. Her pulse quickened as he slipped his fingers through the hair behind her ears and traced her cheekbones with his thumbs. The heat from his touch spread over her skin. His jaw clenched, as if every word he wanted to say, every plan they needed to make was locked in his throat. Instead, he drew her lips to his, letting her feel his promise.

Seria's heart thrilled as his arms slipped around her, and she melted in his embrace. For a girl who had known loneliness and isolation, she had never felt warmer or safer. Despite the stone hanging between them, she had not lost him.

4

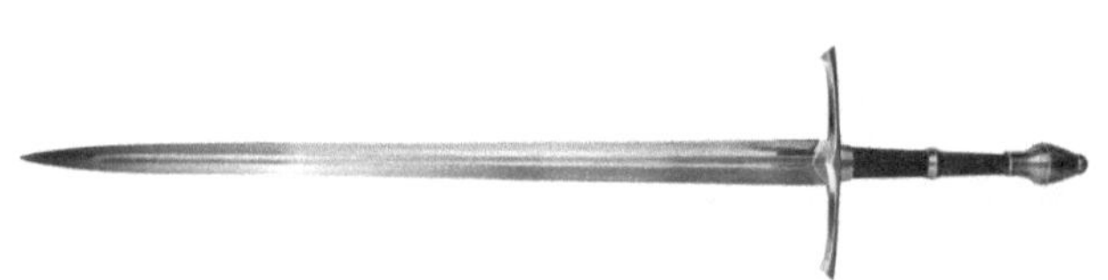

Prince Eric Passion swung his sword, crossing it with his opponent's with a loud clash of steel. His blood pumped madly, sending waves of adrenaline through his body. Panting, he sidestepped the other sword and jammed his own over it, forcing the blade down. The other man came at him again, holding nothing back. Eric inhaled sharply at the wind slicing across his face. He blocked several more blows and ducked one that came too close to his ear.

"If I didn't know better, I'd think you were trying to take my head off," he told the broad-shouldered man before him.

Captain Braylee Wright's lips twitched. "Not intentionally, but you should treat every duel as if it's the real thing."

The real thing, such as the duel he faced with the Reader over three weeks ago. Even as he focused on avoiding Braylee's offense, that night came rushing back to him. The storm that wrecked the fort. The Shadowmen who broke through the gate and into the Old Realm. The face-off that left him at the mercy of the Reader.

His chest hollowed out at the memory of losing all self-will at a few words from Mason.

A quick swipe of Braylee's sword sent Eric back a step. "Hey, take it easy with that thing!"

"You're too distracted." Braylee's dark eyes narrowed at him. "You need to focus."

Eric readjusted his grip on the hilt of his sword, acutely aware of what Braylee did not say. That night would not be the last time he faced off with Mason Grey, and he must be ready.

The pair resumed, both of them a study of determination. Braylee outweighed Eric by a good fifty pounds, but what Eric lacked in weight, he made up for in height and speed. He kept the big man on his toes until Braylee's black hair glistened with perspiration, and moisture streaked down the sides of his tanned face.

But Eric fought to maintain concentration. His sore side complained at the strenuous exercise, the pain a good reminder of how close he had come to losing against the Darkman. He could not afford any more mistakes. His Stewards counted on him.

His leadership had not come easily. For the first few weeks of his command, his army had been split concerning their opinion of him and his ability to lead. Most of their doubt came as a result of his silence of twelve years.

After the Handan massacre.

Braylee smacked Eric's leg with the flat side of his sword. "You're forgetting again."

Eric jumped onto a stump to escape the reach of the sword, his leg and pride stinging. "I remember some things."

"Like?" Braylee challenged, swiping at Eric's legs. Eric reacted with a quick stomp that trapped Braylee's blade beneath his foot.

"Always look for the high ground."

Braylee scowled up at his smug grin and, with a shove to his shins, sent Eric backward off the stump. He landed on his feet, but just barely.

"Good lesson." Braylee rounded the stump to attack again.

He should know better than to underestimate Braylee on any given day. His fifteen-year seniority over Eric's own thirty-two years of age had not slowed him down. If anything, his experience made him an even more fearsome foe. Braylee's mild manner and soft voice concealed a backbone of steel and the heart of a warrior. He was the mentor Eric needed after the Stewards' Grand Marshal, Uralis Faunt, had been lost.

"Are you still with me?"

At Braylee's sharp question, Eric snapped back to the present. "Huh?"

Braylee frowned. "I called your name twice, and you were in a different world. Are you all right?"

"I'm fine. Just thinking."

"About?"

Eric grinned. "You, actually."

Braylee paused. "Me?"

"Aye. About how much I've come to rely on you in the past few weeks."

"If this is your way of softening me so I'll take it easy on you, it won't work."

Eric chuckled. "Wouldn't dream of trying."

"What about the sparring?" Braylee returned. "You still up for it, or do I find another partner?

Eric gave him a light glare. "I don't think so."

And they were off again for several more minutes, jumping in and out, left and right. They kept it up until both were completely spent. Then Braylee took a quick sidestep, and with a jerk of his wrists, flipped the sword from Eric's grasp. Eric groaned loudly.

"Never fails," he mumbled as he bent to retrieve his blade. "That move gets me every time."

Braylee wiped his brow. "You did fine."

"And now you're patronizing me? Please, Braylee, allow me some dignity."

Chuckling, Braylee slapped Eric's shoulder as they fell in step together. "I wouldn't think of patronizing you."

The sun was beginning to peek over the eastern horizon, streaks of orange and yellow staining the dark blue as they made their way from the training fields to the back gate. The stone wall of the Gateway Stronghold rose tall and majestic in the early morning light.

"Let's just hope I won't be so easily outmaneuvered again when it's the real thing." Eric's neck heated at how the Reader had disarmed him of his Beacon the last time they fought, costing him control over his actions, which very nearly led to the loss of his life.

"You're being too hard on yourself." As always, Braylee knew where Eric's thoughts had taken him. "You managed when it came down to it."

Eric held his sword up. "Thanks to Lavrynth." The sword, carrying both the Lambient's light and the blood of his ancestors, had proven to be a shield against Mason's Gift, much like a Beacon. Eric slipped the gum sleeve off the blade and slid it back into the sheath.

"Your mind seems to be elsewhere today."

He could not deny it. His mind was miles away and weeks back.

"Do you care to talk about it?"

Eric pulled his leather gloves off, putting the question off, though it was time Braylee knew.

The captain stopped on the dirt trail leading to the back gate. "What is it, Eric?" he asked, dropping the formalities.

Eric let out a sigh. "It's about the Reader."

"What about him?"

The memories assaulted him, closing his throat off. Guilt and shame hit him, much like they had twelve years ago when Uralis first delivered the news. "He's a survivor of Handan."

It did not take long for the words to sink in. Braylee's stance stiffened. "How can that be?" Even in his obvious shock, his tone remained calm and logical.

Eric shook his head. "I know not. But he was there, told me so himself."

Braylee frowned. "How do you know he's not manipulating you?"

"I feel strongly that it is the truth."

The big man took a deep breath, studying the ground. "That is a shock, to be sure."

"Part of me rejoices that someone survived that senseless attack." Eric squeezed his eyes and mind shut against the memories. "But his brother was killed that night."

"And he is out for blood."

Eric nodded. "He's grown up under Jader's influence, and by now, I fear, has acquired the Shadowstone. Even worse, his Gift will only grow in power and scale. He will not stop until his thirst for vengeance is whetted, and I don't know if I can stop him."

"You forget you do not act alone." Braylee's steady gaze held his own. "You have an army behind you—a united one now. And even more than that." He tapped the Beacon hanging from Eric's belt. "You have the power of the Lambient, who is greater than any Shadowstone the Shreil may use against you."

"But the Lambient is the One who gifted Mason as a Reader," Eric said. "Maybe He did so as penance for my actions back then."

"You know He doesn't work like that. Mason was born with it long before you gave that order."

Eric roughed his short hair with his hand. "I know. I'm just frustrated."

"Understandable, but don't let the mistakes of your past knock you down again. Lambient has a plan. It's time to trust Him."

The words were true, and Eric needed them. But it was hard to let them sink through the layers of regret he had built up over the years. It seemed a cruel twist of fate that his past would come back to haunt him at the same time he reassumed leadership of his army.

"In the meantime, let's get cleaned up so we won't be late for the exit."

"Aye." Eric smiled. In the middle of sending out patrols and searching for Shadowmen, this exit was the highlight of his recent tasks, and he looked forward to opening the gates for families looking to make a new start in the Old Realm.

Just as quickly, his brow knotted. Another group of Gateway citizens had already exited the fort days ago but had instead requested passage back into the Gateway. Some even planned to cross into Jader's Realm to seek their livelihoods there. It disturbed Eric to his very soul to send anyone to live under the totalitarian rule of Graulik Jader and his army of Darkmen, but there was little he could do about it. He could not force the people to stay.

5

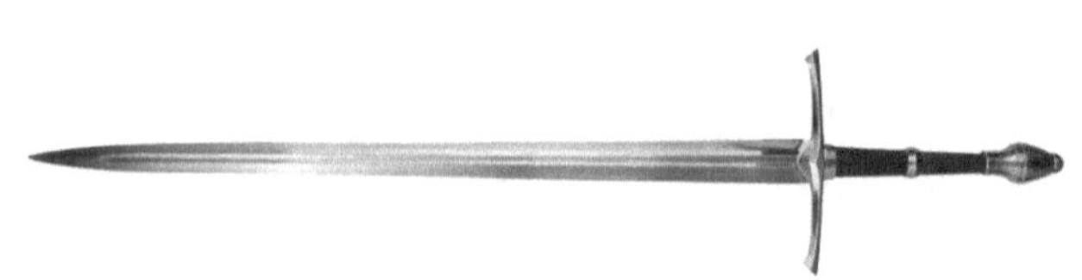

Darkmen Camp, The Gateway

Mason stalked through the camp, his men following silently behind him, sullen since he ripped into them for their lackluster performance. Even with the time spent with Seria, he had waited around a good portion of the night before they finally made their way out of the woods.

Bruin stepped out of his tent, and Mason stopped before him with a nod.

"Any luck?" the commander asked, his voice low and gravelly.

"I'm afraid not."

Bruin's face darkened. "You mean you let it get away?"

"I mean it got away. I'm not the one who let it escape in the first place." His words were clipped, and he held Bruin's gaze, barely bridging the gap between respect and insubordination.

A frown disturbed the dark whiskers around Bruin's lips. "Then you better thank your stars it was the smallest one in the bunch. We can't afford to lose any others."

The rebuke rankled, but Mason knew better than to lash back. One would think earning the Shadowstone would put Mason in Bruin's good graces, but the commander had been hard on his case for weeks.

"I don't know why we're using them anyway," one of Mason's men grumbled from behind. "They're just animals."

Bruin rounded on the man. "Are you questioning the decisions of your superiors, *Private* Hepp?"

Hepp retreated with wide eyes. "Nay, sir."

Mason turned to his team. "In the meantime, you all can take a couple laps around the camp."

Areem Kanen balked. "What for?"

Mason stepped into the younger man's space. "Because had you been able to keep up with me, we might not have come back empty-handed."

Bruin's brows slashed down. "You sorry lot couldn't keep up with an adolescent beast?"

Every man in the group dropped their heads.

"Go on, get," Mason ordered. "And Hepp, you can take an extra lap for questioning orders." A small hint of guilt twinged. Mason had chosen to let the grizlon go on his own, but had the men accompanied him, he may not have allowed himself the weak moment.

Areem's cocky stance drooped as he followed Hepp to the path that encircled the campsite. Bruin frowned but said nothing more as Mason moved away.

Everyone avoided him as he stalked through the camp, his shoulders set in a stiff line and his ever-present frown discouraging any talk. People no longer approached him. He liked it that way.

Weariness weighed his legs down, but it would not do to let Bruin see how tempted he was to fall into bed and sleep the morning away. Instead, he headed for the mess tent where he sat alone for another bland but hot breakfast before starting his duties for the day. A few early diners shot him furtive glances, and he could almost hear their thoughts without reading them. *Mason didn't find his quarry!* His fingers clenched around his cup. They had no idea. He had not failed. He had tracked the grizlon down, all without the help of his less-than-stellar team, and had let it go. But he could never explain why.

It was a stupid thing to do, really. He had never let anything keep him from doing his job. That was how he had climbed the ranks from errand boy to courier to scout and now to sergeant. It was how he had earned the Shadowstone. Hard work, discipline, and dedication. No distractions.

Tired of the stares and whispers no one thought he could hear, he drained the wine in his cup, letting it soothe his nerves. Then he plucked a sweet roll from the table and headed to his tent to ready for his training session with his students. It would be one of the last with this group, and he would not let it go by without giving Areem a hard time. The boy was growing lax in his cockiness. With that kind of performance, he would not pass the upcoming trials.

His hireling was outside, sitting on a stump and gazing up at the sky. A pile of clean tack sat on a blanket at his feet. Upon Mason's approach, he jumped to his feet, his eyes wide.

"Relax, Crue, I'm not going to bite," Mason said. The teen had acted afraid to make a wrong move ever since Mason received the Shadow-stone. "Go on, sit down."

"Aye, sir." Crue gave a nod and perched stiffly on the stump.

"Here." Mason tossed the roll. "I know how you like Cook's sweet rolls."

Crue's face lit up as he caught it. "Thank you, sir!" He sent Mason a grin before chomping a big mouthful.

Mason bit back a chuckle as he retrieved his training gear. "Try not to eat it all in one bite, all right?"

A muffled grunt and a nod was the response he got.

This time, Mason did laugh and smacked the boy's head lightly as he left. "I'll see you later."

"I heard the great Shadowman let the grizlon escape," a snarky feminine voice drifted from a tent as he passed by.

Mason rolled his eyes and kept going.

Dreeya Faybe smirked from the doorway. "Guess that stone didn't make us all as high and mighty as we thought, did it?"

"I didn't hear you volunteer to go after it."

She trailed him with a short laugh. "You didn't either. Bruin had to practically force you to go."

Mason ground his teeth. It was true he had shown a rare reluctance to go after the lousy beast.

"You want to know what I think?"

"Not really," he muttered.

"I think you got that Shadowstone, and now you feel you're above the rest of us. Following orders is too beneath you."

He swiveled to face her. "Get off my case, Dreeya. Jealousy does not become you. You want a Shadowstone of your own, then earn it."

She snorted and opened her mouth to retort back, but he was already down the path, wondering how he had ever been tempted by the brash woman.

Sgt. Ollen Knavis sighed as the fort walls came into view. He and his squad had ridden all night to arrive at the Gateway Stronghold by morning. Behind him, his men were quiet, just as travel-weary as he.

Prince Eric and Captain Braylee met them at the back gate.

"Glad you made it back safe and sound," Eric greeted as the men dismounted. A line creased his brow as he skimmed over the group. "But aren't you missing one?"

"He is well," Ollen assured before turning and dismissing his men. They bowed to him and the prince before leading their horses to the livery.

"How was the trip?" Braylee asked.

"Uneventful, for the most part." Ollen fell into step with the taller men. "We checked out four villages, and there was no sign of trouble. I left word about the threat of Shadowmen so they would be on the lookout."

Eric nodded. "That's the same report I got from the last troop. While it eases my mind some, I know it's only a fleeting relief."

Ollen agreed. The Shadowmen who had escaped into the Old Realm were still out there somewhere, and they would make themselves known soon. "There is one town that left me uneasy."

"How so?"

"Hard to explain." Ollen scratched his dusty face. "The people were standoffish. If the appearance of the civilians is any indicator, the economy is struggling. No one claimed any knowledge of the Shadowman, but the leaders were very abrupt and vague."

Eric frowned. "Did you suspect any suspicious activity?"

"I didn't see any," Ollen admitted. "But it was like all activity stopped while we were there. Everyone watched us, but nothing stood out." He shrugged. "I can't explain it, but I didn't feel good about it, so I left a man behind to observe the goings-on in a bit more of an inconspicuous fashion."

"I'll look into it further as soon as I can. Well done."

"How have things been here?" Ollen asked.

"Quiet," Braylee answered. "There's been no sign of Jader's army since the night of the storm."

"Which, again, is both a relief and a worry," Eric put in. "I still have a few units patrolling the nearby towns, but the further out they go, the more chance of a grizlon encounter."

Ollen frowned. "I'd love to know how they're using those beasts."

"Someday." Eric's voice was soft but firm. He then slapped Ollen's back. "Go get some rest. Anything more can wait until tomorrow."

"Thank you, Sire." Ollen bowed, and they parted ways.

It did not take long for Ollen to wash and make his way to his quarters, where his cot called to him. Stretching out to his full length under the army blanket, he sighed as the tension eased from his muscles.

Now, maybe he could relax. He was back within the walls of the fort, safe, as were his men. Tomorrow, life would resume its usual ebb and flow. He would get back into his normal routine. He would see Seria at her regular place in the mess hall, just like before. Maybe they would even continue their Steward lessons.

His heart lightened at the prospect. But it did not erase the growing anxiety that this respite would be small and the threat would soon be realized. Then Ollen would be pressed to do more than ride around warning about the Dark Army.

He would have to face them.

6

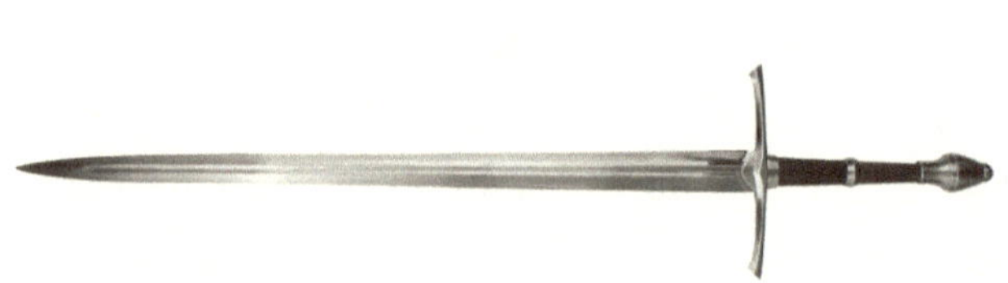

Despite the early hour, the morning sun already heated the air by the time Seria exited the boarding house and took to the street. Spring's mild temperatures and cool breezes were giving way to summer's warmth.

Her shift at the Mess Hall would start soon, but she hurried down the path to the infirmary wherein she had spent hours ever since coming to live in the fort.

She sighed as she walked, her mind too full to pay any attention to anything around her. Her time with Mason played out in her mind again and again. Every time she thought of the kiss, her cheeks flamed. Was this what it felt like to be in love?

On the heels of euphoria, however, came the doubts. The decision to meet him had been grounded in a need for answers and a hope that something had changed Mason's mind. But by the time she told him goodbye, only one thing was clear. Mason had, indeed, taken the Shadowstone. That should have been answer enough. But where Seria should have stood her ground, she fell silent.

He's lost. Mason had no one else to ground him in what was true or good. His almost pleading look was too much for her. She could not turn away from him yet.

The infirmary appeared before her, and she pushed through the doors. The big room was quiet this early in the morning, and no one rested in any of the beds lined up along the walls.

Luron exited his small office and greeted her. "I didn't expect you so early."

"I was already up and awake, so I thought I'd stop by on my way to the Mess Hall." She waved at the empty beds with a laugh. "But it doesn't look like you need me."

He smiled. "It's been pretty slow lately, a fact I'm glad of, to be sure. I only have one patient that I know of coming in, and I already picked the flowers for you."

She hurried to the supply room next to Luron's office and washed her hands at the basin on the table by the hearth. Then she grabbed all the items she needed from the small cupboard in the corner. The older man studied her movements as she pulled the pink and white petals off the stem.

He straightened. "Well, you don't need me watching. Bring it out when you're done, if you don't mind. He'll be here any minute."

Seria smiled as she stirred the pot over the hearth, waiting for the water to heat through. A short time ago, Luron had all but chased her out of his clinic. Now, he requested her assistance.

After crushing the flower with the mortar and pestle, she tied the bits into a clean cloth and then dropped it all into the mug. She measured the last of the herbs and then poured the hot liquid into the cup. Her mind wandered back to Mason's kiss. Some of the water from the pot spilled over into the fire as she dipped it into the mug, letting out a hiss.

"Girl, it's time to pull your thoughts back to the task at hand." She wiped the moisture off and carried it out to the big room where a patient waited.

To her surprise, it was Lionel Percy who sat on the cot, his arms folded at his chest. His usual positive demeanor was displaced by a scowl and slight pallor to his skin.

"I'm sorry you're unwell, Sir Lionel," Seria spoke when she reached them.

"It's nothing," Lionel grumbled, then covered his mouth to hide his cough.

Luron took the cup from Seria and handed it to the Steward. "Now, young man, you just take this and drink it all down. It'll get you feeling like new before you know it."

Lionel did not look at Seria as he blew over the top of the steaming tea. She held back a sigh. Even after all the weeks of her living in the fort, Lionel still treated her with indifference.

"It's not serious, is it?" she asked Luron as Lionel frowned into his cup.

"Nay. He'll be back on duty in a day," Luron said. "I never saw anything cure a cough like that tea of yours."

It was ironic, hearing that from Luron. This tea had been the source of contention at their very first meeting. And now he requested it each time a patient came in with a cough or congestion.

Lionel grimaced and tipped the mug up. Seria muffled a laugh as he downed the contents of his mug in one sitting.

Luron wiped his hands on a towel. "I wager you'll wear your cloak next time you stand guard in the rain. You Stewards must believe yourself invulnerable to the elements, the way you all act."

Lionel handed the cup to Seria. "Duty comes before comforts."

The physician huffed. "Well, go on and get some rest. That's an order. And remember your cloak next time, you darn fool."

Lionel gave them both a single nod and left without another word, eager to escape the infirmary.

Seria carried the mug back to the pot over the fire to wash it before heading over to the Mess Hall to help Nola with the morning meal.

If only she could save everyone with a cup of tea. But some people could not be saved, no matter how hard she tried. And others chose not to be.

Seria spent the morning running back and forth from the kitchen to the dining hall with plates of steaming food until her feet ached and her ears rang with requests. It would not be so bad if her heart did not twitch in her chest every time the door opened.

These days, she spent most of her time in the kitchen instead of waiting on tables. It was easier that way, as she didn't have to worry about awkward encounters. But she could not bring herself to make such a request today. Nola was stretched to the limit with what few workers she had. The large room was already near capacity, and people were still coming in. It seemed everyone wanted their breakfast at the same time.

She raised her head when the door to the mess hall opened yet again, her breath catching.

But a smile lifted her features when Braylee and Dudley entered. After depositing the plates she carried to the proper table, she made her way to their table.

"How are two of my favorite diners today?"

"Hungry," Braylee said. "I worked up a good appetite in the training fields."

"I just hope there's enough food for us by the time everyone else eats." Dudley looked around. "Pretty busy, eh?"

"Very." Seria blew a strand of hair off her face.

"Not surprising. We've got more folks leaving the fort today."

She looked around. "Are all these families moving out?"

Dudley chuckled. "I'm sure most of these are nosy spectators. But we do have a good number of travelers heading out this afternoon."

Braylee clasped his hands together on the table. "This is not exactly where most people want to be right now."

Seria swallowed. The Gateway that had once known peace would soon be overrun with war and violence. The whole concept left a knot in her stomach. "Any word about Sgt. Ollen?"

Dudley nodded. "He got back in early this morning."

"Good." She missed her friend's quiet presence when he wasn't around. "He's been teaching me all about the Steward ways."

"Those are good ways, to be sure." Dudley smiled.

"Well, anyway, even with this crowd, I'll make sure you two get your fill."

Dudley gave Braylee a wide smile. "Cause we're her favorites."

"I wouldn't let that go to your head." The big man's tone was dry. "She says the same thing at every other table."

"Not true." Dudley sent Seria a teasing wink. "Right?"

"Of course not." She patted his shoulder. "Only three or four other tables, at the most." She laughed at his scowl and, after assuring them she would be back soon, hurried to the kitchen to fill their plates. She found Lena there, delivering a bag of flour from the bakehouse.

"Thank you, dear." Nola plucked the bag from Lena's arms and scurried off. "I was afraid we'd run out this time."

"That's the second bag Mama has sent over," Lena told Seria. "I guess it's been pretty busy."

"Oh goodness, I've never seen it like this. I'll get the dishes all washed, turn around, and they're all piled up again." Seria laughed and swept her hair off her brow. "There are a lot of people leaving the fort today."

Lena nodded. "It's a great chance to get a new start, away from the threat of the Dark Army."

It sounded so easy, but Seria had tried twice to make a new life for herself, and she still sometimes wondered where she belonged.

Nola cut between them, setting some plates on the table. "Here, Seria, take these on out."

"I'll help for a bit," Lena offered. "Then I better get back before Mama misses me."

Seria gratefully accepted the offer and returned to waiting on tables. The lines were unending, and the people kept coming. The chatter was full of hope and eagerness, as well as curiosity from those who came to see the travelers off.

On her umpteenth trip out to the hall, she carried the captains' plates, but at the sight of the tall form of the prince entering the hall, she spun to Lena, who was empty-handed at the moment. "Would you mind delivering this to the captains and serving the prince?" she asked, hoping her calm image hid the way her hands trembled.

Lena's gaze found the table where Eric had joined Braylee and Dudley. "Nay, I don't mind."

"Thank you."

She handed her friend the plates and rushed through the doors before anyone could call out to her.

Eric did not miss Seria's hasty retreat as he joined the captains. Her friend, Lena, strode up to the table with two loaded plates and an easy smile. "Good morning, gentlemen."

He squinted up at her. "Aren't you busy enough with your bakery business to be working for Nola now?"

She gave an airy laugh as she set the plates before Braylee and Dudley. "I came by to bring some flour from the bake shop and stayed to lend a hand. The kitchen staff is running ragged."

"Aye, they're certainly running," Eric said with a sigh, glancing back at the swinging door.

"How is your mother doing these days?" Braylee asked.

"She's well, thanks to you."

He gave a chuckle. "That was weeks ago, Miss Lena."

"Nonetheless, we will never forget it."

Eric would not, either. The fire at the home Lena shared with her mother had gone up quickly. The older woman had been trapped inside, compelling Braylee and Ollen to enter the burning building to find her and Lena, who had somehow managed to get inside to look for her mother. Eric had been forced to stay outside, holding the burning beams up with his Gift to keep the house from collapsing.

"Prince Eric."

Lena's voice startled him from the memories. "Aye?"

"I never got a chance to thank you for tending to that matter we discussed that very day."

"Ah." Eric thought back with amusement. After he had pardoned Seria and found her a place to live, Lena was quite adamant that Eric consider her friend's clothing needs.

"It was my pleasure and handled with great tact and subtlety, as you requested."

Her brown eyes lit up. "I appreciate that, sir."

Eric found himself smiling back. The young woman had a quiet maturity and charm that made her a favorite in the fort. It was no wonder she and Seria had become friends.

"Now, what can I get you?"

He ordered Nola's special, and she moved away with a quick, graceful step, promising to return soon.

"What was that all about between you?" Dudley asked.

He almost told him but thought it unfair if too many people knew of Seria's clothing needs. "She reminded me of a duty I was overlooking. Since then, it has been corrected."

The grizzled captain gave a slow nod. "Mmhmm." He took a sip of his ale and said nothing more, though he winked at Braylee.

By the time Eric left the hall and headed for the back wall, the morning sun promised a beautiful, clear day. A squad of soldiers was already there, and the knights parted so Eric could pass through the midst and climb the stone steps at a brisk pace. Once at the top, he looked out over the wall into the Old Realm and took in the distant hills of Paladin, his kingdom.

He drew in a deep breath and turned to the crowd of people standing at the gates. They waited for him to give the order that would open the gates and allow them passage into the Old Realm to begin their lives anew.

The faces looking up at him were as diverse as the stories behind them. Some were young men and women, ready for adventure and hoping to find it in Paladin or beyond. Others were worn down by the cares of life and just wanted to find a place to settle down. Some faces showed the fear of leaving all they knew to go to unknown territories. But all wanted to leave the Gateway, where Jader's power had drawn a little too close for their comfort.

Meeting the gaze of the gateman, Eric gave a single nod. The sound of creaking hinges filled the air, and a collective breath sounded from the group of travelers. Eric straightened and spoke to them one last time before they left the fort.

"Best of luck to you all. May the Lambient keep you well as you search for a new life in the Old Realm."

There was a murmur as the people responded in one manner or another. Then, one by one or in small groups, they began filtering out of the Gateway Stronghold.

A crowd of citizens waved flags and banners as they left. Cheers and laughter rose in the air. The entire mood was jubilant and optimistic, as it should be. Eric's men gave a salute with their Beacons, then the gate was closed, and the knights went back to their duties.

Eric exhaled. Life would not be easy, no matter where anyone went. The business of keeping food on the table and clothes on one's back would never slacken. But at least they would have a chance to do it somewhere where they had the freedom to live in peace, under the promises of the Sacred Code.

If only everyone would take that opportunity.

7

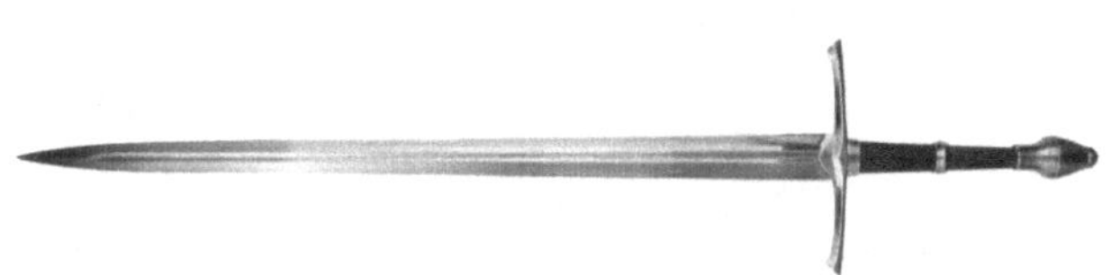

Ollen took a deep breath of the warm afternoon air as he stepped out of the barracks. After sleeping through the day, he headed straight to the mess hall. The days of dried meat and fruit had grown wearisome, and he was ready for a hot meal.

The room was almost empty when he arrived, and Nola took his order promptly. To his disappointment, however, Seria was already gone, off to some other task for the day.

He ate with gusto, thanking Nola before heading back outside. The temptation to seek Seria out was great, but he feared that would be too obvious. Their paths would cross soon enough.

Despite his pep talk, his stroll led him to the officers' barn where she kept her donkey. And there he met her coming out, an empty bowl tucked under her arm.

"Ollen!" Her face lit up. "I heard you were back this morning. It's good to see you."

Her delight was genuine, but it did not match the way his heart sped up at the sight of her. "You mean, you haven't forgotten me?" he quipped, trying to mask his pleasure.

She laughed. "Not at all. Who else is going to tell me the history of the Stewards?"

He kept his smile in place. "I'm sure there are others around here much more versed in Steward lore and history."

"But they wouldn't be as fun." She motioned for him to join her as she walked back up the street. "How was the trip?"

"Not as productive as I would have liked, but safe, so I can't complain."

She nodded but did not press for more like she used to. Her lips pursed in thought as she walked beside him.

"But I have the whole day off now, thanks to the prince's thoughtfulness."

This time, her smile lacked its usual spark. It was not the first time he noticed her tension when Prince Eric was mentioned, which was a complete switch from how it used to be. When they first met, Ollen was the one who had issues with the prince, and Seria had called him out on it.

He considered her profile for a moment before plunging ahead. "Can I ask you a question?"

"Of course."

He bumped her shoulder with his. "What do you have against the prince?"

"Oh." Surprise silenced her for a moment, but at his wink, she let out a chuckle. "I suppose the tables have turned a bit."

He recalled how caught off guard he had been when she had asked him the very same question. "Do you care to talk about it?" he asked, serious now.

A sigh preceded her answer. "I know I'm being unfair, but..." Her smooth brow furrowed. "I learned something about him, and it disappointed me."

"Ah." He tilted his head back. "It's always a tough tumble into reality when you discover someone you believed infallible to be only human."

"Aye, but I'm afraid this is a bit more complicated."

"Maybe." He clasped his hands behind his back. "That was my whole problem when the prince took the position of Grand Marshal." When she looked up at him questioningly, he explained. "I put Uralis on such a pedestal that I resisted Prince Eric unfairly. Had I not given up my stubbornness, I would have missed out on the good he brings to the fort."

"You think I'm being stubborn?"

He put his hands up with a chuckle. "I didn't say that. I'm only sharing my own experience."

Her lips quirked up. "How kind of you."

"How about a change of subject?" he asked, eliciting a laugh. "I'm free today if you would like to resume our sessions."

"Oh." She faltered.

Another "oh." He was not doing well.

"I'm sorry, Ollen." She stared at the ground as she walked faster. "I have so much to do today, and tonight..." She bit her lip. "I have plans with Lena."

"I see." Before he could say anything more, she went on.

"I've been trying to get everything done today so I have time to spend with her. I didn't even get to do more than toss Sanjo some carrot scraps just now. And Luron asked me to show him how to make the waterstar tea again. I wish—"

Ollen put a hand up to stop her, chuckling at the speed with which she talked. "It's all right, Seria. I understand. We'll plan another time."

She searched his face, so he hid any disappointment that tried to show itself.

"We will," she said. "Thank you for seeking me out. I was hoping to see you today."

He hid a grimace at how obvious he had been. "Of course. I had to check and see how my friend fared in my absence."

"Pining away the entire time," she said with a dramatic flair. "I am truly glad you're back safe. I best hurry to the infirmary now, but I will talk to you soon."

He returned her wave as she dashed up the street, trying not to feel so deflated. She had been happy to see him, and it wasn't her fault if she was busy.

There was plenty of time to talk later.

Outside Cadence, the Gateway

"Where are we going?" Seria asked as she followed Mason through the thick woods, her fingers clasped firmly in his.

They had met at her cabin as before, when Mason had suggested they take a walk. It was not until he stepped off the worn trail and into a thicker, darker part of the forest that she questioned him.

"I want to show you something."

"What is it?"

"You'll see.

Her foot caught on a fallen branch, and she tugged his hand. "Mason, would you slow down? I don't want to walk into a tree."

"Oh, right." He slowed down. "Sorry. I guess I'm used to these woods now." He said nothing about the stone he wore that helped him see in the darkness.

Seria swallowed and grasped his hand with both of hers, her shoulder brushing against his. It was on the tip of her tongue to ask him about it, force him to admit he wore it.

"I've never been in this part of the woods," she said after a few minutes. "Never had any reason to."

"I think you'll find it worth it. Watch out." He lifted a low-hanging branch so it wouldn't smack their faces. The trees were closer together here.

She tripped again and laughed as he caught her. "I hope so. I'm not usually out traipsing about in the middle of the woods."

Mason snorted. "Says the girl who goes out by herself to go fishing in the middle of the night."

"That's different."

"How so?"

"It's not in the woods, and I use my tunnel to cut the distance."

"It's still a bit of a walk."

"I usually have Sanjo with me."

He poked her side. "Aye, I'm sure that old beast is a great help."

"He is!" She poked him back, making him flinch. "Mason Grey, are you ticklish?"

Mason swung to a stop and pointed at her. "Don't."

She bit her lip to quell her amusement. "Of course not."

He groaned, taking her hand again. "You're not going to let that go, are you?"

"I didn't say anything."

"Uh-huh. Liam never did either."

She glanced over at him at the reference to his brother. Mason had not mentioned Liam since revealing he had died at Eric's order.

"Was he older than you?" she asked hesitantly.

"By four years."

"Ah, so he took his role of teasing his little brother seriously?"

He swallowed and nodded. "He used to get me down on the ground all the time."

"I'm afraid I wasn't much better with my siblings." Her voice was light but soft with remembrance. "I liked to tease."

"Oh, surely not."

Seria laughed, but Mason put his finger up to hush her.

"We're getting close."

"Close to what?" she whispered.

Mason crept closer to a thick bramble of brush, pushing back a few branches so they could enter. Then he stopped and pointed. The trees here thinned out enough to allow some moonlight to shine down. There in front of them was a bed of twigs and leaves. In the middle of the nest was a bundle of black fur and pointy ears.

Seria covered her mouth with her hands and let out a soft gasp. "Oh my goodness, what are they?"

"A litter of black foxes," Mason answered with a grin. "A week old, I'd say."

One little fox raised its head and blinked sleepily, before opening its tiny jaws in a huge yawn. Its pink tongue hung out, and a contented groan ended in a little squeak.

"They are so adorable," Seria breathed, leaning into Mason. He wrapped an arm around her shoulders.

"I thought you'd like them."

They watched them for a few more minutes as they woke up one by one, stretching and shaking their little heads. After a while, Mason tugged Seria back. "Come on. I think mama's getting nervous."

A sleek, black fox stepped out into the edge of the clearing, her ears and nose twitching. The cubs caught sight of their mother and yelped for her.

"Oh, let's leave them now," Seria said. "They want their mother."

They traced their steps back, both quiet now, Seria's hand back in his. As they stepped out of the thickest part of the trees, she pressed her cheek against his shoulder. "Thank you for showing me. You're right. It was worth it."

He pressed a kiss to the top of her head. "You're a lot like Liam, you know."

"Really?"

"He loved anything that walked or flew. Sometimes, he dragged me all over the place, pointing out birds' nests and tadpoles."

"I was like that as a child, too. My mother forever tolerated me bringing her critters with hurt wings or bleeding paws. But she always patched them up for me."

"I didn't really appreciate anything like that until he was gone." He stopped and faced her, a crease formed between his brows. "I think it makes me feel closer to him, somehow."

Her throat tightened as Mason met her gaze. Talking about his brother was not easy. Maybe this outing was more about sharing Liam with her than showing her the foxes.

The losses they had shared connected her more deeply to him than to anyone else. "Thank you for sharing Liam with me."

"Thank *you*, Seria," he whispered, drawing her close. "For..."

He struggled to finish his statement, but Seria caught the grief that he still wrestled to control. She lay a hand against his clamped jaw. "You're welcome, Mason."

He was so different from the man she had gotten to know in the cabin. This Mason was willing to bare his soul to her, to let her see the scars that made him into the man he was. And it gave her hope that there was still a chance he would see the truth. She could not give up on him.

Even if it meant betraying the prince.

The forest was still, save for the calls of the night creatures. A slight breeze rustled the leaves, cooling the air. Mason hardly noticed the chill, sitting at the base of a large ancient tree, his chin resting on Seria's head. She lay back against his chest, her fingers entwined with his. Their words were hushed and few so as not to disturb the peacefulness of the moment.

"What about that one?" Seria motioned towards a constellation. "What do you see?"

"Mmm, a lion."

"Me, too."

"There's an interesting one." He lifted her hand with his to point.

She lay her head back against him. "Looks like a tree."

"More like an arrow."

Silence fell as they lost themselves in the scope of the star-studded sky. Mason could stay this way all night. The serenity of the moment blew peace across his weary soul. He tightened his hold on her, wishing he never had to let her go. "What are you thinking about?"

There was a quiet chuckle. "That's a strange question coming from a Reader."

He nuzzled her ear. "I can't see your eyes."

"I was letting my mind wander a bit."

"Where to?"

She shifted to a more comfortable position before answering, settling deeper in his arms. "Byron Jayes."

He recalled the young boy Seria had troubled herself to help. "And here I was hoping you were thinking about me."

"His family left the fort."

"Really?" Mason put his cheek against Seria's temple. He wasn't much interested in Byron's family, but she cared about them. Maybe too much, but that was just her. And besides that, he enjoyed the mere sound of her voice. "That might be good for them to get back on their feet."

"That's going to be a bit hard for a couple who can't even *stand* on their feet very well."

He bit his tongue. His sentiment of Byron's parents was the same as it always was. People needed to stop relying on soft hearts and handouts. If they had no other choice, they'd be sure to find ways to survive and support their family. "I'm sure they'll be fine."

She turned her head to look up at him. "You still believe people should take care of only themselves, don't you?"

"I think a lot of people will take advantage of those with giving spirits, like yours. People get by a lot better with their own two hands and willpower."

Seria frowned and turned back around. "I worry about them. Things are so crazy right now, it's hard for anyone to get a good start, much less someone with six kids." Her sigh was quick and shallow. "But it's not just them. Lena's worried about her grandfather."

Lena. The girl who passed through walls—the reason Seria was able to sneak out and see him. "What's wrong with her grandfather?"

"He won't leave his home. Lena's worried to death he's going to get hurt or worse, but he refuses to go the fortress."

Can't blame him there. The old man must have his reasons for not wanting to be surrounded by Stewards.

Seria sat up and shifted until Mason found himself under her scrutiny. "Regardless of your view of the Stewards, Mason, the fort would be safer than an open valley when war does come."

He winced. Another Reader could not have been more accurate. "I know. And I'm sorry you're worried about your friends. It shows the kind of person you are." Heaviness pressed around him. "We'd better get you back before Lena leaves you out here." He held his breath, holding on to a wild hope that she would decide not to go back at all.

But Seria sighed and nodded. "I suppose."

A painful band squeezed around his chest. The thought of sending her back to the lair of his enemies felt like a punch in the gut.

Then don't. The thought would not be denied. *Control her into going with you. You could convince her to leave the Stewards and join your side.*

Even as the idea formed in his head, he rejected it. As much as he wanted to, he could not do that to her. It would not be fair. No more than if she could force him to join the Stewards. The very thought of that made him recoil in disgust.

"Why are you getting so tense?"

He blew out a sigh through his teeth. "I don't like the idea of sending you back there."

"I'm perfectly safe, Mason."

"What if they find out where you've been?" His tone sharpened. "You think they'll be so willing to forgive and forget then?"

"And what about you? Will your leaders be so glad to know you're spending time with a Steward loyalist?"

So that was how she still saw herself after learning about Handan. "You still don't believe Eric's responsible for killing my brother, do you?"

When her face blanched, he fought to keep from reading her thoughts. "What is it, Seria?"

She licked her lips and fiddled with the hem of her tunic. "He admitted his responsibility for Handan."

An icy blade pierced his heart, swiftly turning to a raging fire that swept over him. He punched to his feet and paced a few steps away, clenching his fists.

For years, there had been nothing but silence as the prince hid behind castle walls and tried to pretend Handan's massacre didn't happen. And now to hear that he calmly admitted that he was the reason Liam and fourteen other boys were dead, it brought that day back to the forefront of his mind. Suddenly, he was twelve years old again, watching a Steward kill his brother.

"And you would go back there?" He spun around and scowled down at her, still sitting on the ground.

She drew back, her face stricken. "He said it was a mistake—"

"Nay." He jabbed a finger. "I do *not* want to hear you defend him."

"Then what do you want to hear from me, Mason?" She scrambled to her feet, her face flushed now. "You've long known my loyalties."

There was that spirit she displayed every so often. "Aye, but I thought—"

"That I had changed my mind?" She shook her head. "I still believe in the Lambient, despite what man may do. I can't change that."

His nostrils flared. "Then what are you doing here with me?"

"Maybe I shouldn't come back." Her chin raised in stubbornness, but her voice caught.

The words chilled Mason's anger, and he stepped closer. "Nay, Seria, I don't want that." Desperate to erase the last few minutes, he clasped her hands in his own. "I'm sorry. I should not have reacted like that."

He hardly recognized himself at that moment. Who was this man, apologizing, and to a Steward loyalist, at that? But the fear that she would leave him dug its cold roots in his heart. "Let's not talk about this again."

"Oh, Mason," she murmured and leaned against him. He wrapped her in his arms, a sharp, sweet pain piercing him.

"We better go," he whispered, releasing her to intertwine his fingers through hers.

The walk back to the cabin was quiet and pensive. But the feel of her fingers clinging to him gave him hope that he had not ruined the night. They reached the door and stepped just inside. Seria gazed up at him, her heart in her eyes.

"Will I see you again?"

Her question let loose the tension building in his chest. He had not lost her.

"Nothing can keep me away from you." Resting his forehead against hers, he stood there for a long moment, drinking in her sweet scent. Then he kissed her, long and unhurried, storing up the bank of memories for when they were apart. With a slow, deliberate move, Mason pulled her hood back over her head and opened the door. She gave him one last, longing look before heading out into the darkness.

He stood in the doorway, watching her leave. With every step she took away from him, his heart sank further. By the time she was out of view, he was made aware of one painful detail: the hole in his soul was back.

8

Braylee climbed the stone steps at a brisk pace, his chest tight with the report he had received only moments ago. He found the prince standing at the wall, looking out over the valley, deep in thought. At Braylee's approach, he turned.

"You look like you bear bad news."

Braylee inhaled. "Ollen heard from his man in Danyon."

Eric shifted so that he faced Braylee. "What is it?"

"Seems some of the town leaders got suspicious of him and forced him out of town without credible cause."

"Which only makes their actions more suspicious." Eric led the way to the stairs. "There must be a reason they don't want strangers around."

"Captain Jervis has also made contact. There are rumors of growing disorder in the outlying towns of Calla. Whispers of revolution against the king's reign. It's only a matter of time before some openly revolt. While unrest in the land has been increasing for some time, this chaos has only made itself known in the last few weeks."

"When the Shadowmen escaped into the Old Realm." Eric frowned. "Which towns?"

Braylee repeated the ones Jervis had given him.

Eric sighed. "You must be relieved that Cassels is not among them."

Surprised that Eric's mind had moved to his family, Braylee nodded. "Very much so. I would hate for my wife and girls to face this kind of madness without me. But at the same time, while I want my family sheltered from the turmoil, dozens of innocent families across the land are facing it."

"You're right." Eric straightened. "We cannot sit by and allow the communities of Paladin to be swept up in a cloud of deceit and darkness."

"What will you do?"

"I don't feel that it is a good time to leave the Gateway unprotected, even with Jader's recent absence from the area. We both know he's biding his time."

Braylee agreed. There was a strategy for Jader's supposed withdrawal. The dark lord would not accept defeat so easily.

They strolled through the outer bailey, passing by people going about their daily business. A few greeted them, to which they responded, but did not slow their pace.

Eric spoke again. "As soon as we pull our forces from here, Jader will use that time to strike. But I can't make a fair decision or assumption unless I know for sure what exactly is going on and how they're working." He grimaced. "If only we could get those prisoners to talk."

They had apprehended several Shadowmen the night of the storm and placed them deep in the dungeons under heavy guard, but of course, they refused to talk, not even to ease their sentence.

"That would be too easy," Braylee said. "Besides, we would not be able to trust anything they said anyway."

"That's true." Eric twisted his lips in thought. "Danyon is less than a day's ride from here."

Braylee could already guess what Eric was considering. "Are you thinking of leaving the fort?"

"Only temporarily. I will not be able to rest until I know the Shadowmen are apprehended and not causing us more damage."

"Could be pretty risky. There's no telling how far the Shadowmen will go to turn people against the crown."

"Aye." Eric acknowledged the truth with a grim nod. "And that's exactly why I need to go."

"So, your mind's made up?"

Once again, Eric did not answer right away. Braylee could see him working through the options. But after a long moment, Eric nodded once. "Aye. We'll take a squad and leave as soon as possible."

"Will you take Ollen's squad?"

"Nay." The answer was immediate. "They've only been back a few days. They need the rest."

"How about Sgt. Kleff then?"

Eric thought about it for a moment. "He's one of our newer ones, right?"

Braylee gave a single nod. "That's right. He was the last one Lt. Draven promoted before his death."

"Aye, he'll be a good man to have along. Young but sharp."

"Very well. I'll let him know as soon as I can." Another thought struck him. "Speaking of Draven, we've yet to fill his position."

A sigh preceded Eric's answer. "I know. I haven't put enough thought into it. If we were at Calla, we'd put a few candidates through the trials. But we don't have the privilege of time to do so here and now. We need to select one and make it official."

"You know who I recommend."

"You still believe Ollen Knavis to be the best candidate?"

"I do."

Eric's look became thoughtful. "He's young to be given that much responsibility, especially over a platoon comprised mostly of men not much younger than himself."

Braylee could not deny that, but he also knew better than to underestimate the younger man on any given day. Ollen would go far as a Steward.

Ironic how much his thoughts had shifted. Only weeks ago, Ollen had shown his stubborn side in resisting the Stewards' new commandant. Although he never out and out rebelled, he had made his position clear. He still felt strong ties to his former mentor, Uralis, a great man in his own right who had been shot down in Rackson. In Ollen's mind, Eric Passion had not earned the right to lead the Stewards.

Until the night the Shadowmen had broken into the fort, and Eric had been almost killed by the Reader in his attempt to stop them.

Eric's voice cut the memories short. "He's a good man, though, and a good Steward. I think Kleff and the other sergeants in Draven's platoon would respond well to him."

"If it helps, Dudley is also in agreement with him receiving the promotion."

"It does." Eric dipped his chin once. "It's decided then. We'll make the announcement and hold the ceremony when we return. In the meantime, prepare to leave for Danyon."

It was good to see Eric like this—decided and unhesitant to move forward. This was the prince who had been absent when Eric had first taken the command of the Stewards after Uralis's death. "When do you wish to leave?" Braylee asked.

"Tomorrow at dawn."

The dinner rush was much more lowkey than it had been all week. All the families who had requested leave were gone, many to forge new lives in the freedom of the Old Realm, while some had chosen to move closer to Jader's authority, as Byron Jayes's parents had done.

Her spirits soggy and leaden, Seria pushed her way through the kitchen doors again, bearing a tray loaded with dinner plates and mugs. After delivering the plates to the correct diners, she moved to the next table, where a lone man sat looking out the window. She drew up short at the sight of him. "Oh."

Her soft exclamation drew Eric's attention from the dusky scene outside. He gave her a small smile. "Is it all right for me to eat here?"

There was no judgment or anger in his expression, so she stepped closer. "Of course, Prince Eric. I just didn't expect to see you." She fumbled with her apron. "Wh-what would you like?"

"I'll take Nola's daily special. I've yet to eat something I didn't enjoy."

Tongue-tied and tense, she nodded and backed away. "All right. I'll, um, go get your dinner."

"Thank you."

The weight of his scrutiny sent her hurrying back to the kitchen. By sheer force of will, she managed to keep from running to escape his presence.

His order was prepared quickly, and before she was ready to face him again, she moved back out into the hall with his dinner. Eric was still alone, staring down at the table with furrowed brows. But he gave her another smile as she approached.

"Here you are." Seria set everything before him. "Nola made sure you got a fresh piece of meat."

"Give her my thanks." Weariness darkened the edges of his eyes and tightened the lines around his mouth.

"I will." She slid her agitated hands up and down the edges of the empty tray. "Well, enjoy. I-I guess I'll see you in the morning."

"I'm afraid not."

The soft-spoken words halted her retreat, and she blinked. He always came in to break the fast. "What do you mean?"

"Something's come up, and I'm leaving for a while."

Concern sprung up within her. "Is your father unwell?"

"Nay, he's fine, although I appreciate your asking."

"Then why must you leave?"

Eric took his time in answering. "There's been some trouble."

Her insides clenched. So, this was Steward business. Her curiosity begged to know what was happening, but her lips remained stiff. "I'm sorry to hear that. Do be careful, Prince Eric." With that, she turned and left him to his meal.

In the kitchen, she excused herself for a moment and stepped outside, gulping deep lungfuls of clean, fresh mountain air. Her knees shook so that she leaned back against the wall.

Self-loathing squirmed inside of her.

Who was this person she had become? She could no longer talk to Eric—someone who had been nothing but good to her. Could not even express concern over his leaving. Did her love or loyalty to Mason mean that she had to harden her heart to anyone else?

He is responsible for the death of Mason's brother. The reminder left a bitter taste in her mouth. It was true. Eric himself did not deny it. But did that give her leave to harbor unforgiveness toward him?

It was Mason's choice to hate Eric. Seria could not hate anyone, much less the compassionate prince of Paladin. But did that mean she was disloyal to Mason?

Amid all the confusion and questions, one fact stood out. She did not want to lose Eric's friendship, regardless of her feelings for Mason. Eric was the first person to offer her grace when she had been arrested for aiding the enemy. It was his thoughtfulness that allowed her to make a new start and build a new life here. She had witnessed his caring and wisdom time and again. In truth, the thought of not having his goodness and light as a standard in her life scared her.

And now, he was heading out on a mission, maybe a dangerous one. What if she never saw him again?

She stared up at the stars, silent and serene above a world falling to chaos. The stillness fed peace into her troubled spirit, and she straightened again. The least she could do was tell the prince that she would be praying for him.

But when she peeked into the mess hall, ready to swallow her pride, she was disappointed to find an empty table.

9

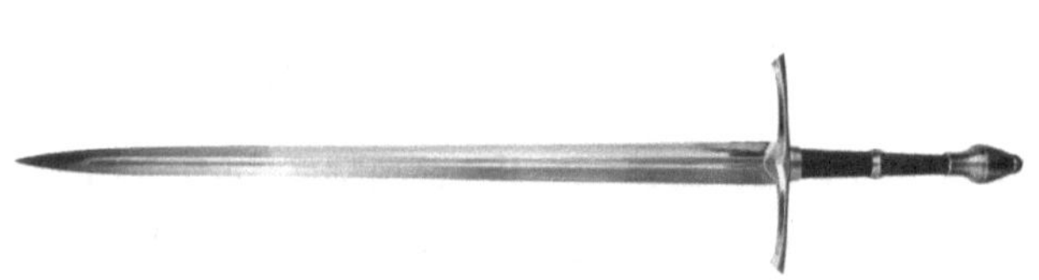

"Take no thought of the Beacons or the weak soldiers who bear them. The Shreil will show his power, and the Beacons will fail before the dark one."
-Pre-battle speech by Graulik Jader during Calla's War

Graulik Jader held himself tall and straight on the back of his black stallion. The reins rested loosely in his hands, the horse submissive to his control. With his good eye, he swept his sharp gaze over the camp and gave an acknowledging tilt of his head to those standing at attention on both sides. He spotted Mason in the line and sent a personal nod his way.

"Thank you, ladies and gentlemen." He raised a hand. "Go on about your business."

The ranks all bowed and fell away. Soon, only the gray-eyed commander stood before him. "Emperor Jader, it's good to see you."

Jader swung down off the horse, letting his assistant lead the animal away. "Commander. You seem to have everything in order."

Bruin inclined his head, stepping aside so the emperor could precede him to the large tent set aside for Jader's frequent visits. "I was unsure you would be able to get here so soon."

"A traitor in our midst is not something to put off."

"Will you deal with it before the ceremony tonight?"

"Nay, we shall take care of the matter in the morning. Let us not spoil the celebration."

Anticipation hummed over the camp as barrels of beer and ale were rolled out to the clearing in the center. Black and gray flags and banners flapped in the cool breeze of the evening. A chance to put aside the work to feast and drink did not come along very often, and the soldiers would not miss it.

"Mason's group will be included tonight, correct?"

"Aye." Bruin swept the tent door aside and offered Jader a chair. "His cadets took the highest marks."

"He looks well, I notice."

"Seems so."

"Have you had problems?"

Bruin shrugged. "Not with his work, so much."

Jader tilted his head back in understanding. "He has slipped away?"

"The past two nights."

Jader watched as Bruin tried to conceal the misgivings he had about the young scout. "Is there something on your mind, Bruin?"

Bruin's mouth hardened. "I realize you know what you're doing concerning Mason. But what if he continues to fraternize with this girl from the fort?"

"I understand your concerns," Jader answered calmly. Bruin's honest feedback had proven beneficial more than once, even if the tall man overstepped. "But tell me, friend, what good would we do in forbidding him from seeing her?" At Bruin's frown, he continued.

"You see, Bruin, I have never kept Mason from doing what he wants. That is the beauty of my rule. The people have freedom of choice. I doubt they would have that option on the other side of the mountains. Eric would be mortified if he knew one of his own people was keeping relations with a Shadowman. And he would forbid it."

Bruin nodded. "True."

"By allowing Mason free rein, he will have no reason to distrust me. I see only good coming out of this." He held up a finger to count off the ways. "First, she could grow tired of the Stewards' laws and revert to my kingdom, which would make Mason very content in his present state. Or she would feel forced to break things off with him, which would upset him, turning him even more against them."

"So...you're not concerned?"

Jader scoffed. "Mason is trying his wings, living dangerously. When it all comes to a head, he will see I never prohibited his actions."

"And his loyalty will only strengthen."

"Exactly." Jader straightened in his seat. "Now, my friend, let us make plans."

The music grew in volume and fervor, echoing off the forest around them. Firelight danced off the broad tree trunks, casting an orange glow to the scenery. Voices rose and fell in merriment, coarse laughter cutting through the air. Wine flowed freely as the celebration continued into the late night. No one was quite willing to end the festivities, despite the early hour they would rise the next morning.

Mason sat on an overturned log, staring into the flickering flames. In the midst of the loud merrymaking, the stillness of the night rested deep within him. A few stars blinked down on him, and a cool breeze teased his hair. Crickets sang in the distance, while frogs croaked their approval of the world around them. In the distance, he could hear the lonely cry of a wolf. Someone threw in a log, and the sparks flew up and disappeared into the darkness.

At another bout of laughter from the crowd, he raised his head. He would have been welcome to join the festivities but had no desire to throw himself in the middle of the ruckus. Not even for his own students.

All but one had passed the final trials and were now officially part of Emperor Jader's Dark Army. The hard work and criticism he had put them through had paid off. From here on out, they would be instated as Darkmen, and he, their mentor, had helped get them there. The student who had not passed would return to his home city, disgraced by his failure. Life would move on without him.

Mason watched Areem fill his mug once again from the foaming barrel. The young man was louder than usual, almost giddy with his accomplishment. Of course, he had passed every trial with stellar marks, which would do nothing but feed his arrogance. Mason could imagine what shape Areem would be in the morning when he awoke, but he would carry out his usual responsibilities, regardless of how he felt. Bruin would see to that.

Dreeya Faybe sauntered over to where a morose-looking Hepp sat by himself. She perched beside him, leaning against his arm, and tried to engage him in conversation. Hepp shrugged her off and continued to stew. Dreeya rolled her eyes and found another willing companion. The pair whispered in each other's ears, giggling at whatever they shared.

Mason considered Hepp's moodiness. The younger man had been very apathetic in his work lately. Mason would have to have words with him soon, he was sure.

Restlessness stirred within him. Social gatherings had never been his forte. He preferred action to sitting around visiting. He had always been that way, but even more so since receiving the Shadowstone.

Mason caught the stone in a light grasp, running his thumb over the smooth surface. Sometimes, he still marveled that he had finally earned it after working toward it for almost half his life. And yet, here he sat, partying instead of working toward the next phase of his goal of tearing down the Steward Army.

He didn't like it when things stood in the way of his goal.

A frown settled over his brows, and a long sigh heaved its way through his chest. He raked his hand through his hair, then left it to massage the nape of his neck. Someone stepped in front of him, blocking his view of the fire. Mason looked up to see Jader staring down at him.

"Emperor Jader." He jumped to his feet.

"You seem a little quiet tonight, friend."

"I was thinking."

Jader nodded. "Your students did very well. Especially Areem. You should be proud."

"I am. Except for James's elimination."

Jader waved it off. "Not everyone is cut out to be a Darkman, Mason. Do not assume responsibility for his shortcomings."

"Aye, sir."

"I wonder if I could pull you away for a time?"

"Certainly." He was done with the party anyway.

The two made their way through the crowd of drunken men and women, toward Jader's tent. Mason caught sight of Bruin, sitting on the other side of the bonfire, observing the activities in his quiet manner. He looked up as they passed and gave Mason a subtle nod.

"Areem seems to be enjoying himself." Amusement tinged Jader's voice.

Mason glanced at the new Darkman and let out a snort. Areem stood on top of an empty barrel, laughing hysterically. "He'll be fun to wake in the morning."

"Let him have his fun," Jader said as they left the light of the fire. "Then it is back to business."

"Sounds like you have something in mind." Mason followed him into his large tent.

"I do." Jader motioned for Mason to take a seat. He took the chair on the other side of the table. "I received word from Feegan."

"How are things going for him?" He had heard nothing of the gray-haired captain since Mason had helped him slip through the Steward fort and into the Old Realm.

Jader smiled. "Seems the people are ripe for a change in the regime. It has taken very little effort for him to raise a following. And the news he receives from the other Shadowmen is the same."

Mason nodded. "That's good."

"We have you to thank for that. You are the one who got them through."

That was the night he had come face-to-face with Eric Passion. His shoulders tensed at how close he had come to carrying out his vow of vengeance for his brother.

Jader's soothing voice cut through his musings. "I know you still carry regret for not fulfilling your personal objective that night, but it will come."

"I hope so," Mason said, thankful Jader understood him so well.

Jader scrutinized him for a long moment with his one dark eye. The pale one twitched slightly under the vicious scar running down the right side of Jader's face. "You have carried such a weight with you these last few years." His voice was heavy with empathy. "I look forward to the day you will be rid of it and find some peace."

Peace. The word pulled at him. Was that what he was missing? Ever since his brother died, there had been a churning in his spirit, and lately, it seemed to grow, ready to devour him. It followed him everywhere he went, no matter what he did, driving him to work from sunup to sundown. It kept him from feeling truly settled or content.

These days, peace only came in the form of a green-eyed girl with long, blonde hair.

Drawing in a sharp breath, Mason straightened and turned his attention back to his mentor. "Thank you, sir." His words sounded too casual to his own ears. "I appreciate your understanding."

"Aye, well, back to the matter at hand." Jader did not seem to notice Mason's strange behavior. "I believe that when the time comes for a full assault from our Dark Army, Feegan will have built up a strong militia on the other side."

"Trapping the Stewards in the middle."

"Correct."

One corner of Mason's lips raised slightly. "Sounds like a good plan." Except he needed to first find a way to get Seria out of there.

"Aye, but one that, unfortunately, will take some time. I am afraid I have no choice but to raise the tolls of my people." Regret tinged his statement. "My toll collectors have been overrun with protests and complaints. It has delayed the army's movement to the Gateway. I sent more men to provide a little *persuasion,* if you get my meaning."

"I do, sir." Mason leaned forward. "But it seems like a lot of effort for taxes."

Jader raised a brow. "Pardon?"

He rushed on. "Oh, I don't mean to criticize your move, Sire. I am just surprised you would concern yourself with this now. When we're so close to a breakthrough at the Gateway, I mean. Seems that's where we should be putting our focus and energy, not on seeing our people pay a few extra tolls."

"I can understand your doubt. And I appreciate your candor. But our soldiers still need to be fed. And all the energy that we are directing at the Old Realm requires more resources. They must come from somewhere."

Mason nodded. "I see your point, sir."

"Good."

Even with his royal position, Jader always took the time to explain things and allow Mason to speak his mind. It had been that way since the very beginning when Jader first took him in. The emperor was more of a father to him than anyone else he could remember.

"There is more." Jader folded his hands on the table. "As I am sure you know, I have been in conference with Bruin."

Mason nodded. There was no one in the camp who did *not* know.

"We have come to a very crucial moment, and while we expect to soon see victory in Paladin, we cannot neglect our place in the New Realm. Which is why I have decided to instigate a series of pickups."

"Pickups?"

"Aye." Jader sat back in his seat, in no hurry. "Up north, my loyal people are very generous with their funds, their time, even their children. Many have offered their offspring to be trained to serve in my army. These offerings assure peace and prosperity to the cities, while their children have a future of security and purpose. It is a positive situation for all sides."

Mason nodded. He knew of this practice in the outer New Realm cities. He had even helped train the youngsters when they grew older. Many of those recruits became loyal, skilled warriors.

"Unfortunately, it is not always that simple." Jader let out a sigh, his good eye darkening. "Some of my people near the Gateway have begun to revolt, which requires me to take much more assertive measures. If they will not pay the agreed-upon price, I must take it. The process might be a bit painful, but I believe in the end, it will work out in a positive fashion for all concerned."

Understanding dawned. "You're requiring their children."

Jader studied him. "Aye. It is not as I wish it, but necessary. The children are being fed a doctrine of rebellion and legalism, and the leaders of the towns are breaking agreements. It is harsh, but being a leader is not always easy. Sometimes, it requires assertiveness."

Mason mulled over the concept. Jader had won the entire New Realm with patience and ingenuity. Sometimes, that meant taking something by force, but most of the time, he was able to gain control peacefully.

That meant agreements and contracts had to be made. And if they were broken, there must be consequences.

"Do not worry about the recruits, Mason. They turn out the better for it. Consider your student, Areem, and where he would have been had he not been one of those recruits."

More than likely, he would have grown up poor and helpless. Now he stood out as Mason's best graduate. Dreeya had also shared how fortunate she was that her family had offered her to Jader's service.

"You're right, of course," he said. "I wasn't aware of the need, that's all."

Jader looked relieved. "These young recruits play such a big role in the future of our Dark Army. There are still some details to work out, but as soon as everything is in order, Bruin will ride with a company to carry the plans out. Hopefully, within the week."

Mason listened without interrupting. Jader must have a reason for telling him all this, though he had trouble staying focused on the conversation. Jader's next words arrested his attention.

"You will accompany him."

Mason started. "Oh, I see."

"Will that be a problem?"

"Nay, not at all. I only assumed I was needed here more."

"Your weight will certainly be missed at base camp," Jader said. "But I believe you being a part of these pickups would be beneficial, and not just for your own good. You would be a great asset to Bruin. There are very few we can rely on as we can you."

"I'll be glad to help." The unease that crept over him had nothing to do with the nature of the assignment, distasteful as it sounded. Nay, it had more to do with the fact that this assignment would take him away from Seria. This would not be a short job.

Jader sat back with a satisfied smile. "We will start in Hashore."

"Hashore. In the Gateway?"

"That's right. The towns in that borough which have long been loyal are starting to revolt, much like Rackson did. I think the recent involvement of the Stewards has made them bold. But I would rather not have to take such extreme consequences again, if at all possible."

The town of Rackson had been demolished by Jader's forces, despite the Stewards' attempts to interfere. It was during that fight that Mason had been injured. Where Seria found him and took him in.

He pressed his palms to his knees. "Sounds like we're winding down to the end of the wait."

"Oh, we are. But we must be cautious as well. We do not want to get overconfident, or things will unravel." Jader paused. "So, am I correct to assume that this meets with your approval?"

Mason set his jaw, picturing again the chance to meet Eric in combat. Maybe the war could end before it ever reached the fort, which would keep Seria safe from being caught in the middle. "Very much so, sir."

10

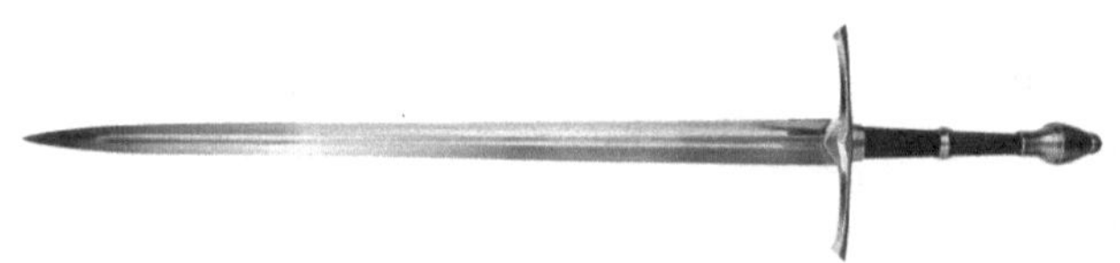

The moon still hung low in the sky as Eric sat astride his gray stallion, Oakley, and met Sgt. Kleff and his squad by the back gate. He greeted each man, appreciating their readiness. Kleff responded with eagerness brimming, but he carried an air of maturity that eased Eric's mind.

Soon Braylee joined them on his big bay, his face shuttered. Knowing better than to push the bigger man so early in the morning, Eric held his tongue.

There was no goodbye crowd to wave them off as they ventured through the gates and began their journey. His plan to leave early kept the majority of the citizens from even knowing about his exit.

Stroking Oakley's mane, Eric glanced back up at the great wall, then did a double take. One figure, blonde hair blowing in the slight breeze, stood watching them leave, waving a scarf over her head. Much like she had the very first time he saw her in Cadence so many weeks back.

Recognizing it for the olive branch it was, Eric raised his hand, and Seria waved back. Even with the emotional distance between them, she had risen at this early hour to see them off. Her silent support did much to lift his spirits in this uncertain time. And it gave him hope that her friendship was not lost.

The company rode in silence for a while until Eric glanced over at Braylee attempting to keep his horse from nibbling the tall grass. "Is it safe to talk now?" he asked, fighting a smile.

Braylee frowned at him. "Of course it is."

"Good. Because I need you to know that whatever we find in Danyon, I plan to ride on afterward to see my father."

"I see."

"There are some things I need to understand about why this war is happening." Remnants of a conversation about Aden's past dealing with Jader bothered Eric. It was time to get some answers. "And I don't want to talk about it through a pool."

Braylee nodded. "I understand."

"You don't think I'm using this as an excuse to visit my father while so many are cut off from their families?"

"You would never take advantage of a moment out of selfishness. However," he slanted his gaze at him, "very few would begrudge you an opportunity to see your father if the opportunity arises. These are uncertain times. We know not what tomorrow holds."

Appreciating the big man's understanding, Eric let a smile loose. "Good. Because I want you to accompany me part of the way and take the time to see your own family."

Braylee blinked. "What's that?"

"Your hometown is on the way to Calla. We can stay the night in our own beds, then get an early start and meet up the next morning."

Braylee opened his mouth as if to refute it and then closed it. "How am I supposed to argue with a chance to see my family?"

"You're not. It's already settled."

The bay ducked his head for another bite of grass, and Braylee sighed as he checked him. "If I can get this beast of mine to focus on traveling rather than eating."

Eric chuckled. "Rumor had it that Uralis spoiled him."

"I believe it."

Danyon, Paladin, Old Realm

The sky was streaked with the colors of the evening sun by the time Eric's company topped the last ridge that allowed them to look down into the town of Danyon. Braylee pointed out the lone man who waited for them there.

"How goes it, Gann?" Eric asked as they approached.

Gann jabbed his chin at the town below them. "Two nights ago, I heard rumors about a liberty meeting from some of the locals. I asked the storekeeper about it, but he refused to give me any information, called me a spy. A little while later, a few of the town leaders showed up at my inn door and requested I take my leave."

"Requested?" Eric asked.

"Aye. With swords in their hands. I left peaceably, then found the closest stream so I could contact Sgt. Ollen."

"Good work." Eric fingered the rod hanging at his belt, sending up a silent plea for wisdom. The men had already been given their orders, so he motioned them to proceed. Two by two, they began making their way down the ledge.

"Private Gann, you can join Sgt. Kleff. Stay on the outskirts so no one sees you. We don't want to arouse suspicion."

Gann nodded and followed the young sergeant to the east.

Eric waited until he could no longer see any of them; they would be in position just within or without the perimeter of the town.

He looked to Braylee. "You ready?"

Braylee raised his wide chin. "I am."

With careful steps, their horses descended the hill, heading for the main entrance into the town. Eric kept his head low as they entered, his eyes moving, Braylee's comforting presence to his right. Their colors were covered by large dusty cloaks to keep from drawing any attention. They meandered about some, trying to blend in while familiarizing themselves with the streets and keeping an eye out for anything suspicious.

The town was bleak and plain. Civilians cast them suspicious looks as they passed. There was a restlessness in the air, as if everyone was on edge, waiting for something to break.

"One thing's for sure." Eric kept his voice low.

"What's that?"

"Something's not right here." His discomfort grew as they went on.

They came to the front of a small trade shop. It looked rather run-down but hosted a great deal of merchandise. Barrels of corn and flour sat against the wall, and various items of tack hung from hooks on both sides of the door.

"You stay here. I'll try to dig up some information," Eric said as he dismounted. Angry voices greeted him from within when he pulled the warped, wooden door open.

"Come on, Hank!" A woman screeched.

A man replied, "Ain't gonna do it, Nonnie."

Eric entered the store, squinting through the gloomy lighting. A tall, thickset man with a bushy black beard stood behind a crude counter, glaring at the bedraggled woman on the other side.

She crossed her arms across her thin bosom and scowled right back at him. "I'm down to my last coin. How do you expect me to feed my young'uns with you jacking the prices up so high?"

"That ain't my problem."

Nonnie slammed her hand down on the counter. "Dad blast it, Hank! I've already given my oldest for the cause. Don't that count for something?"

The mention of the cause piqued Eric's attention.

"There ain't nuthin' I can do 'bout it, Nonnie. I gotta pay the dues, too."

As far as Eric knew, there were no dues required from the Gateway towns on this side of the Slates.

Nonnie let out a loud breath and tossed some coins on the counter. "Fine, there ya go, ya thief!"

Hank scooped the change and counted it over. "That'll cover your dues." His voice was cool. "You still owe thirty-two pence for the flour."

The woman's eyes bulged. "What the blazes…? Hank, that money *is* for the flour."

H shook his head. "Dues come first."

Nonnie's face went blotchy. "I don't have a blasted thing in my cupboards!"

Hank leaned forward. "If you can't feed your young'uns, maybe you should consider turning the rest of them over to someone who can."

Eric had heard enough. "Would you allow me to pay for what you need today?" he asked the woman.

She gave him a suspicious look. "Why?"

"I want to know your kids won't go to bed hungry, that is all." Looking to Hank, he said, "Give her the flour she needs, and throw some beans on there, too." He would do more but feared insulting the woman's pride.

Hank gave him a black look but moved off to fill Eric's order.

Nonnie gave a huff. "Well, ain't you just a do-gooder! I thank ya kindly for yer help. Things been pretty tight here since my Joel's gotten caught up in this aut'n'mee business."

"Pardon?"

"Aut'n'mee. You know, independence."

Eric tilted his head back. "Oh, autonomy. Forgive me."

"I don' do well with thosen fancy words, ya know? But, my husbin's been spending every cent we make on our liberashion, you know? Don't leave a lot for kibbles."

"Seems wrong to sacrifice your children's welfare for a cause." When Nonnie blinked up at him, he said, "I'm sorry to hear you lost your oldest child."

Nonnie shrugged. "Oh, she ain't lost. She training."

"Training for what?"

"Nonnie!" Hank slammed the bags on the counter. "Don't you go telling a stranger our business." He glowered at Eric. "You owe me seventy-three pence."

Eric held his gaze as he pulled out the coins and handed them over, fully aware Hank had charged him more than the signs showed. He turned and gave Nonnie a slight bow. "You take care, ma'am." He inclined his head respectfully, then turned on his heel and stalked out before he said something else he would regret.

"What on earth happened in there?" Braylee asked, causing Eric to wonder what his face must look like.

He rested his elbows on Oakley's back and shook his head. "Someone's stirring up trouble, that's for sure." He paused as Nonnie left the store, giving her a wave, then filled Braylee in on what little he had heard.

"What are they training their children for?"

Eric sighed. "I wish I knew, but none of the options that come to mind bring me any comfort at all. Let's leave the horses here and see what we can find."

He caught many a wary look as they made their way through the streets. His neck tightened the further they entered the small town. It was clear by the frowns he received that he was not welcome, though they could not possibly know his identity.

"We're being watched." Braylee motioned to a young boy of about twelve watching them. He was the first child Eric had seen since entering Danyon.

"Maybe we'll get a little further with someone who won't suspect anything from two lost strangers." Braylee followed him to where the child stood.

"Excuse me, lad," Eric spoke, his voice cordial. "Could you help us?"

The boy jutted his chin. "I ain't helping you. Now leave me alone."

Eric faltered at the heat of the boy's words.

Braylee raised a placating hand. "We're not going to hurt you, son. We need—"

The boy rounded on him, his eyes blazing. "I ain't your son, and I don't want to help you!" With that, he kicked Braylee square in the shin.

Braylee let out a grunt and grabbed his leg, gaping at the fleeing boy's back. "He kicked me!"

Eric gripped the big man's arm to stop him from going after the kid, biting back his humor. "Easy, Captain."

"Sure. He didn't kick you."

"Nay, but it won't do any good to go after him." Eric released him.

"It would do *me* good." Braylee rubbed his shin. "The little brat."

Eric chuckled, then shook his head, looking after the boy. "What a sad day when war poisons the minds of children as well as everyone else."

Braylee followed him back to the street. "I'd like to poison his backside."

Eric sent him a wry smile over his shoulder. "That would certainly draw some unwanted attention, don't you think?" The hairs on the back of his neck stood up at the small crowd following them.

"Don't look now." Braylee moved to Eric's side. "But we've already drawn some attention."

Eric kept his eyes forward. "I noticed."

They maintained their casual pace. With every turn, Eric caught glimpses of the growing throng trailing them. The feel of their stares made his skin crawl.

Up ahead, another group formed, blocking their path back to the horses. At the forefront was a cocky-looking young man with a sneer on his face.

"This doesn't look good," Braylee murmured through tight lips.

"Let's see what they want."

The man crossed his arms. "You mind telling me whatcha doing in our town?"

"Not at all. We're taking a journey up north and just stopped by for a while on the way."

"Then why were you harassing one of our boys?"

Eric raised his hands. "I'm afraid the boy misunderstood our intention. We meant him no harm."

"That's not the way he tells it. He says you threatened him."

Eric could feel the tension rolling off Braylee. "I assure you, we would never bring harm to a child."

The man did not look convinced. "While you're here, you'll have to abide by Danyon's laws."

Eric nodded. "Absolutely."

"Hand over your arms."

Giving a quick look to Braylee, Eric reached down to pull his sword out. The air was charged with animosity, and he did not relish being without his sword when it did, but they still had their light rods, safely hidden under their capes. Still, he took careful note of the man who took the weapons—a rough-looking character who, despite the apparent law, carried his own sword.

"May I ask your name?" Eric asked the young man before him.

He threw his shoulders back. "I'm Mick, one of Danyon's appointed peacekeepers."

"I hear you've had some trouble around here," Eric said.

Mick frowned. "Who'd you hear that from?"

Before Eric could reply, there was a shout not far off. The crowd parted as a tall, skinny man shoved his way to the center, his face flushed.

"You!" He pointed to Eric.

"Do you know this man, Joel?" Mick asked.

Joel cast him a quick look. "Nay, but he apparently opened his big mouth and filled Nonnie's head with doubt. She's questioning whether our cause is worth the sake of the kids or some such nonsense."

Mick put his hands on his hips. "Is that so?"

"I was only trying to help."

Joel's face turned almost purple. "By sticking your nose where it don't belong?"

Eric looked him square in the eye. "I'm only concerned that this cause of yours is taking precedence over more important things."

"What do you know of our cause?" Mick stepped forward. "You don't know anything about us."

Another voice cut in. "I wouldn't be so sure about that, Mick."

Mick lifted his eyes to someone standing behind them. "Lord Arthen." He bowed his head.

Three men moved through the shifting crowd. One man, whom Eric assumed to be Arthen, cut an impressive figure in his long robe that labeled him as someone of importance. Hank stood at Arthen's right, a smug expression on his face.

The third man hung back, his white-blonde head rising above most of the men around him. His icy gaze locked onto Eric, making his skin crawl.

Arthen spoke again, approaching with his hands behind his back. "You see, he might know more about our cause than you think." He stopped before Eric. "In fact, he might be the problem."

11

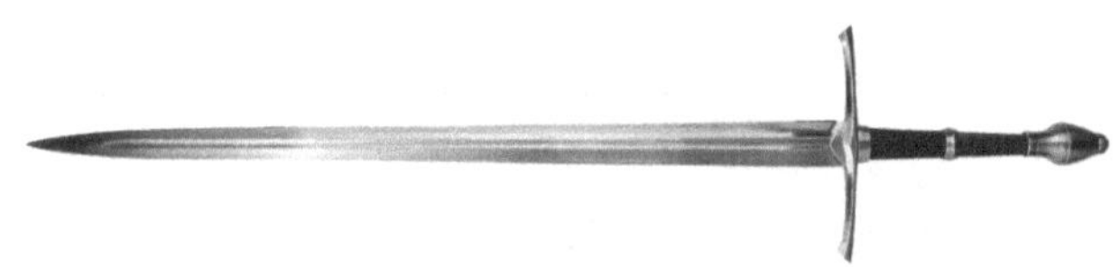

For those who make friends with the terrors of darkness, midnight will be their morning.
-The Sacred Code

Braylee straightened at the implication in Arthen's words.

"It seems you've caused quite a stir for someone just passing through." Arthen glanced back at the bearded man. "Hank, here, tells me you were interfering with his business."

Hank nodded. "That's right."

"And he's got Nonnie all confused, too," Joel added. Others quickly chimed in.

"He harassed Huger's boy."

"And he's been wandering around town like some useless drifter."

"I had no intention of causing trouble," Eric said.

Arthen crossed his arms and began to circle them. His pale-headed companion took his place in front, his eyes never leaving the prince. Braylee kept his focus on him, his stance alert and wary.

"We've been warned about people like you." Arthen's voice was low and cool. "People who come in here and throw around their lofty ideals and try to tell us what's best for us."

He brushed Eric's shoulder as he came around him. "Those who would force us to live by some ancient creed. Men like that self-righteous prince of Paladin," he added as he came up beside his companion.

Braylee's breath caught in his throat.

"Isn't that right, Thane?" Arthen asked the white-headed man.

Thane's cold eyes glittered. "That's right," he said in a thin voice.

Arthen turned his head to study Eric again. "And then you come in here, with your lordly airs and your fancy sword." He motioned with his chin. The man holding Lavrynth gave him a gap-toothed grin.

"If I didn't know any better, I'd think you were Prince Eric himself. I heard he's come out of hiding. Thinks he's going to *save the world.*" He punctuated the words with his fingers, then scoffed. "As if we need saving."

Braylee shifted his jaw. Arthen's speech was a little too forthright, and Thane grinned as if keeping a secret. Eric did not move or speak.

"But now, Eric Passion is *special*, see." Arthen addressed the crowd. "Not only is he a part of the lordly Passion bloodline, but he's been Gifted of the Moon." He waved his hands around mystically. "Can move things with just a thought. Never has to lift a finger, from what I hear."

A muscle in Eric's jaw jumped. Braylee gave a subtle look around. This would be a good time for Kleff to show up.

"Now wouldn't that be exciting?" Arthen put his hands on his hips with a sardonic sneer. "To think the great prince himself would visit our humble dwelling to set things aright. Wouldn't we love the opportunity to speak with him face to face? What a welcome he would get, such as no one had ever before received!" Laughter rolled through the crowd around them.

There were so many people pressing in. If a fight broke out, Braylee and Eric would be seriously outnumbered, even if they were able to get their swords back. *Lambient, see us through this.* The desire to see his family hummed through him.

Eric stayed silent through it all, his features set like stone in the face of Arthen's scorn.

"But I suppose we don't have to worry about that, do we?" Arthen continued. "Prince Eric is too much of a coward to set foot anywhere without bringing a whole slew of precious Stewards with him, now isn't he?"

Braylee stiffened when Arthen's eyes landed on him.

"You're awfully quiet, big guy," Arthen said. "What are you hiding under that cloak?"

Eric spoke again. "We never meant to cause problems."

"Oh, but didn't you?" He stepped closer until he was inches from Eric's nose. "You started with a poor, uneducated woman who doesn't know any better. And then you tried to use an innocent child. You thought you could come in here, flash your pretty smile, and pull us back from the brink of darkness, right?"

A cold feeling went over Braylee. *He could be the Shadowman we came looking for.* Who else would know so much about what Eric was doing these days?

"Just like a prince, aren't you? Come here to save the day." Arthen's face hardened. "Maybe *we're* not the ones who need saving."

Thane tilted his head back, his eyes shifting for the first time from Eric's face. Braylee followed his gaze to a bristly man standing several feet behind them. The man pulled a long dagger from his belt.

Arthen smirked. "Maybe *you're* the one who needs saving."

"Eric, look out!"

At Braylee's call, Eric spun to halt the flying dagger in midair, inches from his chest. The crowd reacted with a gasp as he reached out to take the weapon in his hand. The murmuring grew in volume. There was no denying who he was now.

Arthen stepped back and drew a sword from the folds of his robe. He used it to point to Eric. "This here is Eric Passion of Paladin! He's come to take over Danyon and take away our liberty!"

Mayhem broke loose. There was a roar in the throng around them as they surged forward. Eric stretched his arm out again; his sword and Braylee's flew out of the surprised keeper's hands. Braylee caught his as Eric closed his hands around the golden hilt of Lavrynth.

Several horsemen rode into view, led by Kleff, their crimson breastplates shining from underneath their cloaks. Relief washed over Eric as his Stewards plunged into the midst of the angry mob.

Fights broke out on every side as the knights worked to keep the furious crowd from reaching Eric. He was barely aware of Braylee facing off with Arthen nearby. Blocking a blow from Mick's blade, Eric drove a hard kick into the young man's stomach, sending him sprawling on the ground. Looking around, his attention was drawn to Thane, standing stock still in the middle of the chaos. He wore a satisfied smirk, unmoved by all the fighting around him. Eric stared as Thane backed his way through the crowd, receding until he reached the dark shadows of the simple structures on both sides of the street, then disappeared from sight.

Shock rippled through Eric's body. Thane was one of the Shadowmen who had broken through the Gateway Stronghold. Now he fed this town lies and deceit, single-handedly turning the majority against the truth of the Sacred Code.

Eric set his chin as anger burned within him. *No more.*

A trio of townsmen came before him with clubs and farm tools. Not wanting to harm civilians any more than necessary, Eric lifted a whirlwind of dust from the ground and sent it flying into their faces. Shouts rose as they stopped to grab their stinging eyes. Eric skirted around them and resumed his pursuit.

Running deep within the gathering shadows of the small town, he slid around a corner and stopped. The street was dark here, and he proceeded with caution. With the cloaking aid of his stone, Thane could be lurking anywhere.

Holding his sword before him, Eric made slow and careful steps, eyes and ears ever vigilant. He could still hear the echoes of the riot behind him and hoped Braylee and the Stewards would gain the upper hand without too many people getting hurt. His main focus now was bringing in the Shadowman responsible for all the turmoil.

The street corner was so still, so quiet. At a familiar quickening of his spirit, he swallowed and tightened his grip on the hilt of Lavrynth before moving on. His senses were on full alert, his intuition at its height. Pausing again, he tilted his head. He could hear or see nothing unusual, but still, there was something. Something that prevented him from taking another step. He stood motionless for a moment, taking in the very feel of the air. Then he tensed and took a quick step to the side.

From a roof above, Thane dropped down, missing Eric by a hair. Eric spun around and raised his sword to block the other man's. He narrowed his eyes into the cold face before him. The Shadowstone swung out from the folds of the man's shirt, buzzing and glowing.

Eric scowled. "You should have kept running."

Thane smirked. "And miss the chance to kill the legendary prince of Paladin?"

"Do it first, then talk about it."

In response, Thane pushed Eric's sword down and swung at his head. Eric blocked it and jabbed at Thane's torso. Thane jumped back, just out of reach.

"You're not welcome here." Thane taunted him, his lips twisted in a cruel grin.

"What's not welcome is you and your dark lord's lies," Eric said, his voice tight. "You've already destroyed enough lives. You will not take my kingdom."

"Your kingdom?" Thane mocked as their swords clashed again. "Spoken like a true tyrant."

"Nay, that's the difference between me and Jader." He strained against Thane's attack. "I'm willing to take a risk in order to save my people. What has Jader ever done for you, outside of his own interests?"

"He's given us freedom." Thane's speech sharpened in his fervor. "Freedom from serving a defunct law, freedom to live as I choose."

"Yet in this freedom, you're spending your life in service for Jader's cause." He stepped back to catch his breath.

Thane glowered at him. "Do not try to twist my words against me."

"I don't have to twist them. Jader has you just as deceived as you have those people back there." He pointed over his shoulder with his chin. "He cares nothing of you or his followers, interested only in seeing his power grow."

"Aye. He will see his power grow." Thane's face twisted, and he wrapped his fingers around the Shadowstone at his chest.

Cold, darkness pierced Eric's chest, taking his breath away. The sensation was quickly followed by righteous rage. Lavrynth's handle heated in his hand, breaking Thane's hold.

The Shadowman snarled and swung his sword again. The two men traded several quick, vigorous blows. Eric stumbled back to miss a close swing, breathing hard.

"He's done nothing but bring chaos and devastation to the New Realm, and he will stop at nothing to do the same in the Old. And you will be just as responsible for the destruction if you continue following."

Thane bared his teeth. "If that's the way you want to look at it."

"But it doesn't have to be that way." Eric paused with both hands on the hilt. "I'm giving you a chance right now."

Thane narrowed his eyes.

"Give yourself up. Denounce Jader and his hold on you. And I promise your sentence will be reduced."

Thane made a face. "To what? Lifelong imprisonment rather than a quick execution?" He scoffed. "No thanks. I'd rather die seeing your brand of supremacy destroyed. Your pathetic pieces of light will be overpowered by Jader's dark power, and your Code will be crushed. That's what I choose to live for, and no fancy words from you will deter my mind. I'm a Shadowman until the day I die. A Shadowman does not change, does not go back on his belief." He was practically spitting with every word.

Eric gritted his teeth. He had assumed as much, but hearing it said out loud drove the truth in deeper. "If that's your decision." He brought the blade of his sword before his face. "So be it."

Thane gave a roar and stepped forward again. Eric waited the space of a heartbeat before making a move. They had no restraint, no hesitation as they came at each other in determination to be the victor. Their swords crossed between them, the sound ringing out in the still air.

12

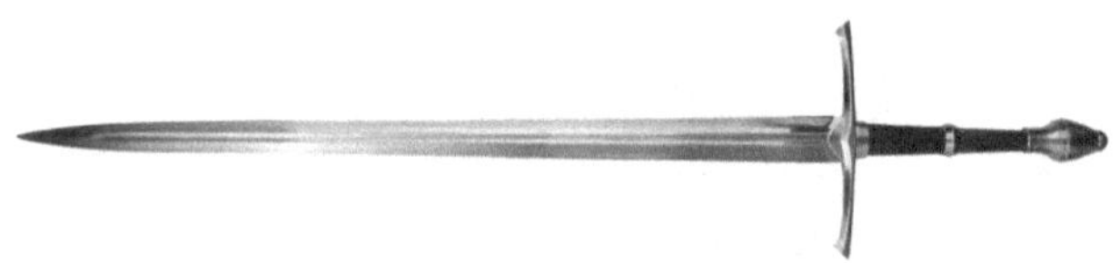

Mason returned to the campsite with a freshly killed buck slung over his saddle. After depositing the venison at the mess tent, he noticed a large crowd gathered outside Jader's tent.

"What's that about?" he asked Crue as he dismounted.

A wrinkle creased the boy's smooth brow. "A trial, sir. They're requesting your attendance."

"A trial?" A trace of alarm heated Mason's chest. "For what?"

"I'm not sure, sir, but I think it's pretty serious."

It certainly seemed so. He approached the group, meeting up with Areem. "What's going on?"

Areem stood with his arms crossed. "I'm not sure, but Hepp was arrested." Indeed, Hepp stood between two guards, his hands bound.

Mason's brows rose. "For what?"

Bruin Pralus exited the large tent, his face mottled in his rage. Hepp straightened. "Commander—"

Bruin sneered. "Shut him up."

One of the guards reached out and backhanded Hepp across the face.

"You will speak when spoken to, and no other time." Bruin's eyes shot gray sparks; the muscles around his lips clenched.

Areem shuffled his feet. "I've never seen the commander this angry."

Mason snorted. "His temper is nothing to take lightly."

Bruin caught Mason's eye and waved him forward. Mason adjusted the bracers on his wrists and joined him.

Jader stepped out. "Ah, there you are, my boy."

Mason gave him a slight bow, appeased by the pleasant greeting. "I apologize, Emperor. I didn't realize you were asking for me."

"No harm done, I assure you. But I wonder if you could assist us with a small matter."

"Certainly, if I can."

Bruin turned his chilly glare on Mason. "One of your men was found socializing with a Steward spy."

"What?" Mason snapped a hard gaze at the man in question.

Hepp blanched. "Nay, sir!"

Jader spoke up. "We have witnesses we could call, Mason, but we thought it would be much simpler to have you confirm the story."

There was a brief, panicked moment as Mason considered Jader's request. What was he implying? Then it hit him. Mason could use his Gift to find the truth.

"The Steward spy has already been dealt with. All we need to know now is if Hepp here has indeed fraternized with a man who is a known enemy of the Dark Army."

Breathing deeply to settle his heartbeat back into its usual rhythm, Mason nodded and looked Hepp straight in the eye, seeing past his wild, terrified stare and into the thoughts he could not hide from Mason's Gift.

He saw Hepp sitting at a table in a pub, across from a gray-headed man with a sword hanging at his side, their manner casual and familiar, even friendly. The Beacon half-hidden behind the man's cloak made it clear what he was.

Mason's lips drew tight as he pulled back to the present and scowled at the white-faced Hepp trembling before him.

The moment weighed on Mason as he stood there. His words would condemn a man to death. But the Darkman had served Jader long enough to know the penalty for fraternizing with the enemy.

"Well?" Bruin demanded when Mason did not speak.

The stone at his chest burned hot. There was only one thing to do. "It's true."

Hepp slumped in defeat, burying his face in his hands.

Jader stood tall, his dark eye sweeping over the crowd. "My loyal army. It is with deep regret that I must announce that our own Hepp Mossen has been found guilty of treason."

Angry mutters rose in the air.

"I am not an unreasonable man," Jader said. "I rule as fairly as I can. I am tolerant of those who do not see eye to eye with me. But there are those who want nothing but to see our beautiful land overrun with tyrants and a law that chokes the very essence of living. And we cannot abide by that."

Mason stepped aside amid the loud murmur of agreement. His mind wandered back to the memory of his brother dying at the end of a Steward's sword but then landed on the visit with Seria the night before. His shoulders tightened.

"There are rules that must be abided by," Jader continued. "And befriending the enemy is not to be endured."

The gathering grew louder in their support.

"Would you see our freedom stripped from us?"

"Nay!" The answer came in perfect unison from the dozens of on-lookers. Mason's mouth went dry.

"Would you have our empire overtaken by a Code that kills rather than brings peace?"

"Nay!"

"Would you be kept in the iron grip of the Stewardship?"

"Never!"

Mason's breath quickened at the zeal being unleashed. His Shadow-stone hummed against him.

"Would you be governed by the House of Passion?"

Everyone around him raised a fist and shouted, "Never!" But Mason stood frozen.

Jader turned his piercing glare to Hepp. "You, Hepp Mossen, have been found guilty of treason. Thus, you are sentenced to death by hanging, to be carried out immediately."

There was a loud cheer as Hepp was shoved to a grove of trees. Mason barely heard Hepp's protests over the shouting. Jader and Bruin stood where they were, allowing the Darkmen to carry out the execution.

A rope was tossed over a thick branch. Someone led a horse over, and Hepp was forced onto its back. Dreeya was the one to tighten the noose over Hepp's neck, a cold sneer on her fine features.

The shouting grew in volume once more. And then it was over.

A chill settled over Mason as he stared at the still body, not hearing the cheering going on. Only last night, he had assured Seria he had nothing to fear about seeing her. But now the risk weighed heavily on him. How quickly would his cohorts turn against him if they knew he was in love with a Steward loyalist?

But this was a different situation. Seria was not a Steward. She was an innocent girl deceived by the Stewards. Hepp had committed a serious offense. He had betrayed Jader and allowed the enemy to thwart his code of ethics. His actions could have destroyed all that Jader had built. Now the man had paid for it with his life.

Somehow, the contrast did not bring him comfort, and he turned away from the death scene, back to where Crue tended to his horse. Glancing over his shoulder, his heart lurched when he met Bruin's stone-cold stare. The older man's face was unreadable, his thoughts unreachable. But something about the look caused Mason's stomach to tighten. He gave a respectful nod. After a long moment, Bruin returned it with a curt one of his own.

Then he turned and followed Jader back into the tent.

"Kleff, have you seen the prince?" Braylee asked.

The other Steward mopped his brow and shook his head. "I have not."

Braylee grimaced and ran a hand through his damp hair, scanning the area.

The outburst had been reined in. The Stewards had the most prominent antagonists bound hand and foot. Some were still on horseback, their Beacons casting light across the moonlit street, holding the rest of the townspeople in place. The bodies were lined up along the street.

A murmur rose from the crowd, drawing Braylee's gaze up. A wave of relief washed over him at the sight of Eric walking towards them, a limp Thane draped over one shoulder.

Eric stalked to the middle of the street, where everyone could see him, and dumped the body on the ground. He inhaled deeply as he took in the subdued scene. He soberly skimmed over the bodies of Arthen, Mick, and the rest. Then he raised his head and swept the people with a sad look before calling out, "Citizens of Danyon, you have been deceived."

A hush fell over the square, every eye turned on Eric. Bitterness still lingered on many faces, but no one made a sound as the prince went on.

"The House of Passion has never come here and thrown our demands around that you live a certain way, or even that you believe in the power of the Lambient. We've never demanded your children or dues. All that we ever asked was that you respect the Code that we live under."

He pointed down at Thane. "This man would have you believe that Jader has your best interests at heart, that he fights for your freedom. But it's all lies."

The Stewards did not move as Eric spoke, but they kept their focus on the crowd. Braylee took a deep breath. Would anyone even hear Eric's words?

"Graulik Jader is only looking out for his own advantage. He will plunder and devastate any town between him and his quest to control the Old Realm, bringing nothing but destruction and tragedy to your lives. Jader does not want the best for you, he wants *your* best for *him*."

"That's not true!" someone shouted.

"Isn't it?" Eric took a step forward. "Look around, friend. Your town is but a shadow of what it used to be. He's already taken the best of your resources to fund his agenda. He's taken the best from your families, leaving them desolate while you put his cause before their own welfare. He's demanding your *children*."

A flash of shame appeared on Joel's face as he dropped his eyes.

"He's taken your integrity in business and benevolence."

Hank scowled in Eric's direction and spat on the ground. He was on his knees, his hands bound behind him.

"And it won't stop here," Eric continued. "It won't get better. He won't stop until he has bled every last drop from all those naïve enough to think he is looking out for you. He'll sacrifice your children for his cause until you've lost everything, and he's left you with nothing but bitterness and emptiness. All in the name of freedom."

Eric paused, letting the weight of his words sink in. "That is the price Jader demands for his loyalty. All he wants is everything you hold dear."

The words were powerful and compelling. But would it make a difference in a town already twisted by the Shadowman's lies? The silence was thick with feeling. Sober faces looked back at Eric; a few still looked angry but not as many as before. Some of the townspeople exchanged uncertain looks.

Eric took a deep breath. "Danyon is a part of Paladin, and we will defend it with every ounce of our strength. We do not wish to be your enemy. We've only ever wanted your peace and prosperity. But we cannot help you achieve that goal if you harbor enemies of the Code."

A throat cleared, drawing Braylee's gaze to where Joel stood, looking back at Eric gravely. "Is it too late for us?"

Air filled Braylee's tight lungs as Eric answered.

"Absolutely not. You were deceived. That's what Jader's Shadowmen do best. I will do all I can to see Danyon reborn."

13

"Can I ask you a question?" Seria asked Lena after they were a safe distance from the fort, their pace unhurried.

"Of course."

"Why do you visit your grandfather at night?" She had always been afraid to ask, lest Lena decide to change the time. But curiosity finally got the better of her.

Lena brushed a strand of hair off her face. "If I do go check on him during the day, it's more likely he'll be asleep than if I try at midnight." She let out a chuckle. "He blames that on the years he spent working as a night guard in his younger days."

"Well, that makes sense. Maybe someday he'll agree to live in the fort with you, and you won't have to worry about taking care of him out here." The very idea made her flinch, though, because then she would lose her only way out of the fort.

"That's my hope." A look of concern crossed her face. "We both know what's coming to the Gateway, Seria. If he doesn't agree to move to the fortress..." Her words faded.

Seria understood her fear. They were taking a big risk leaving the safety of the fort. The day would come when their nighttime jaunts would no longer be an option. What chance did one old man have should war break out all around him?

They walked without talking for a few minutes. Then Lena spoke. "Can I ask you a question now?"

"You know you can."

Even with the assurance, Lena did not rush. "How long do you think you will be able to continue with this?"

Seria's head jerked to her friend. Was Lena already tired of sneaking her out of the fort?

Lena lay a hand on her shoulder. "I will help you as long as I am able, Seria. But you and I know this...arrangement cannot last forever."

The statement brought back all the uncertainty she had dismissed earlier. And though she wanted to get angry at Lena for bringing it up, she could not. Because she was right. "I don't know, Lena. It's only been a few nights."

Lena nodded, but her brow wrinkled. "If I'm ever discovered and questioned, I have very little risk. I am simply going to see my elderly grandfather. But I'm afraid you have more to lose."

A cold feeling prickled over her at the truth. If the prince or one of his Stewards found out what she was doing, she could only imagine what the consequences would be. Her breath caught in her lungs at the very thought.

"I can't leave him, Lena," she whispered. "Not now. Maybe not ever."

Lena studied her seriously before she nodded. "Just be careful with your heart, Seria. It can be an untrustworthy leader."

"What do you mean?"

"My father believed in his heart he was doing the right thing when he joined the Dark Army. But in the end, that belief cost him."

Blinking back tears of frustration, Seria turned back to the path before them, where they were to separate. Lena squeezed her hand before slipping down the trail on the right, leaving Seria alone with her fears.

But she put them all out of her mind at the sight of Mason waiting for her outside the cabin. She dashed her hand across her eyes and conjured up a smile for him.

"'Bout time." His voice was light as he pulled her into his embrace.

"Hey, I'm early." She clasped her hands behind his back.

"I know. It just seemed like forever."

Seria caught the note of relief in his words, though he tried to hide it with a cocky grin. No matter how many times she came, he still worried she would change her mind.

"How have you been?" she asked.

"Nothing but lonely." His answer came instantly. "You?"

Guilty. The word popped into her mind without warning.

"Seria?"

Realizing with a start that she had not answered his question, she buried her head against his chest so he could not see into her eyes. "Same as you," she said. "Nothing but lonely."

You're a liar, Seria.

This was wrong. Even now, wrapped in Mason's arms, her mind was plagued with the same guilt she struggled with all day. Only that morning, she had watched Eric leave on a mission with his Stewards, with no idea where he was going or why.

And now she stood in the arms of his enemy. All it would take was an unguarded moment for Mason to learn that the prince of Paladin was absent from the Gateway Stronghold. A slip of the tongue...or a glimpse into her thoughts.

She squeezed her eyes shut, trying to dismiss that chance. Mason had promised her.

But how do you know he hasn't read your thoughts every time you were together? The question popped unbidden into her mind. *It's not as if you would ever know.*

She swallowed back a cry. Nay. Mason loved her. She knew that as surely as if she could read his mind. He would never use her, take advantage of her like that.

Like he did the first time you met?

"You all right?" Mason's voice fell in a whisper in her ear.

She drew her arms tighter around his waist. "I just...have a lot on my mind."

"You and me both. Anything wrong?"

"Only everything." Her response came out flat.

Mason did not answer.

A well of pain opened up within her while questions hammered at her again and again until she wanted to cover her ears and flee back to the fort. What was she doing? How could she betray Eric like this while he was out risking his life for the well-being of the entire Old Realm? How could she claim to stand for the Sacred Code while she secretly met with one who hated it with all his being?

"You're trembling."

She swallowed. "I'm sorry. I'm being lousy company tonight."

"I'm happy just to be with you. You always make my day better."

His words washed over her, stilling the troubling echoes in her mind. Despite her doubts, she knew one thing for certain. Mason loved her. It did not matter to him that they stood on opposite sides. He accepted her, loved her, *needed* her. Surely that was all that mattered for now.

And maybe someday, she could help him see a better way.

She pulled back and smiled up at him. "Thank you for saying that. I needed to hear it."

A tendril of unease wrapped itself around Mason's heart at the shadow lingering in Seria's eyes. It was so tempting to read what troubled her, but he refrained. He would not take advantage of her like that. Not like he had when he had first awakened in her cabin and thought only to use her to get back to his base.

She raised her brows. "What?"

"Just thinking about when we first met."

"Oh, you mean when I was an annoying little chatterer?"

"Aye." He touched her cheek. "You put up with a lot from me, didn't you?"

She shrugged. "You were no worse than Ira."

He released a bark of laughter. "I like that! Compare me to a fat, fussy drunk."

Her eyes sparkled with mirth now. "Well, you've got a few points up on him."

"Like good looks?"

"Maybe." She drew the word out.

"Maybe? Seriously?" At her impish grin, he bent his head and nuzzled her ear. "I hope you at least consider me the better kisser."

She cocked her head. "Hmm. Not sure. I've never given Ira the chance to—"

He covered her mouth with his own, burying his fingers in her hair. Sparks lit from his hands all through his chest.

"Aye, you are definitely the better kisser," she murmured dreamily when they broke away.

He cleared his throat and stepped back, his heart racing at the feel of her against him. It was time for a distraction. He glanced down at the sword hanging at her hip. "Come on. Let's get some practice in."

"Hold it up higher."

"Like this?" Seria's face twisted in utter concentration as she lifted her sword.

"Aye, like that." He bit back a chuckle. She always made him want to laugh.

"This feels awkward."

"That's because you're not used to it. Now, take a swing at me, like I showed you."

She tightened her lips and arced her sword at him, her movements slow and unsure, but in decent form. He blocked her easily, impressed when she recovered with an instant defensive strike that he ducked.

He grinned. "Perfect." He was rather surprised at how quickly she picked it up, though she would never be a master. But maybe she would have a chance to defend herself.

"Be honest with me." She put a hand on her hip. "Am I a slow learner?"

He shook his head. "Not at all."

"You look like you're having to stay on pace with a snail." Seria chuckled. "Every move you make takes me four times as long."

"You're learning, but you've already got a good grip."

She swung it in slow arcs before her. "My father was no swordsman, but he tried to show me a few things. He always laughed at my stroke."

"It takes practice. I've used mine a bit more than you have."

Her face paled, and she dropped the weapon, spinning to walk away a few paces.

"Seria, What's wrong?"

"I'm fine." The tremors in her voice belied her words.

Mason cursed under his breath and circled around her, stopping when she averted her face. "What is it?"

"Nothing."

"Then why won't you look at me?"

Seria winced and covered her face with her hands.

Hurt rolled over him. "Do you believe I would read what you're thinking if you didn't want me to?"

"Not intentionally. But even you've admitted that it takes concentration on your part. One little slip, and you know everything on my mind."

He crossed his arms. "So, what is on your mind that you're so adamant I don't know?"

"Does it matter? We're both lying to ourselves."

"What's that supposed to mean?"

She still did not look at him. "Do you realize how wrong this is? For both of us?"

Mason ground his teeth. "Wrong? For two people who love each other to be together?"

Seria finally faced him. "Like this? We're deceiving the very ones we claim to stand with. How long do we think we can keep this up?"

A myriad of emotions rumbled in his stomach, a wave of uncertainty battling to take precedence in his heart. Seria's eyes were clouded, and he fought to keep his Gift under control. Something had triggered her sudden doubts, but he had promised. He stepped closer to her, anxious to alleviate her sudden attack of fear. "For as long as we want this to last."

"And what about when the war hits?" Her questions were relentless. "Regardless of our viewpoints or beliefs, we both know one side is going to lose." Her voice caught.

Mason did not want to think of it. "I'll find you." He clenched his teeth. "Nothing is going to keep me from you."

Her eyes shone with unshed tears. "And what if you're killed? Or taken captive?"

The very idea of being in Steward custody was repulsive. "I won't let that happen. Justice *will* be carried out, Seria, whatever your feelings on the matter."

At her flinch, regret knifed through him. He took her hands, working to sound calm. "I'm sorry. I'm not sure what brought on these doubts.

But I love you, Seria, and I'm willing to do whatever I have to do to be with you."

"Except leave the Dark Army."

He clenched his jaw. "You know why I can't. Why I won't."

Mason hated this huge canyon that stretched out between them. If only Seria would come around to what he already knew—that Eric Passion was not a man to be trusted. That the Stewards were not the noble warriors she believed them to be. That the Sacred Code was not a principle to guide men, but a chain to bind them.

Seria sighed and lifted her head to look at the midnight sky. "Have you ever stopped to think of how different things would be for us if we'd never met? If I hadn't found you in the field, if we hadn't had the chance to get to know each other..." Her voice faded. "You would be nothing more to me than a soldier of the Dark Army. I would know only fear for you, and you would care nothing for a simple peasant girl."

He grasped her shoulders. "Seria, stop it. We *did* find each other. That's all that matters."

Seria met his gaze again, looking up at him in absolute trust. Mason's heart turned over. Never had he felt for anyone the way he felt for Seria Gayle. He would do almost anything to convince her of that.

"I'm sorry," she whispered. "I just...I don't want to lose you."

"You won't. We may not...agree on everything, but I love you anyway. And that won't change."

The slightest of smiles eased the worry lines on her face. She allowed herself to be drawn into his arms once more, and Mason felt a measure of relief. When they were together like this, it did not matter how uncertain their future looked. Indeed, he could almost forget what it was that kept them apart. They had their obstacles, but they were making it work. She would need time, but someday, she would see the Stewards' true colors. The rest would eventually fall into place.

14

Calla, Paladin, Old Realm

The king's palace stood resolute against the wind, its white and scarlet flags waving from their lofty positions. Six turrets surrounded the largest tower, their black roofs reaching for the sky like eager fingers. The red-stone structure rested on a high hill, lush with fescue and shrubbery, the greenery broken here and there by white boulders.

Eric breathed in the familiar scent of lilac. It had been weeks since he had last laid eyes on the place of his childhood, but this was home. His heart quickened at the prospect of seeing his father again.

The call to open the gate was given. Captain Jervis Plank's dark face brightened upon seeing him.

"Your Highness." He bowed his head. "This is an unexpected pleasure."

Eric exchanged handshakes with the man who had faithfully guarded his father and the castle for the last decade. "Thank you, Jervis. How is your wife? Last I heard, she was climbing the ranks of the Stewardesses."

His chest swelled. "She's now a lieutenant, and let me tell you, her platoon is a force to be reckoned with."

"That comes as no surprise. She always excelled at what she set her mind to. Much like the man she married." He sobered. "How is my father?"

"Quite excited since your arrival was announced, Sire."

Leaving Oakley with the stableboy, Eric thanked the captain and left to find his father.

Aden rose to his feet as soon as Eric crossed through the double doors into Aden's private suite. "Eric! Come here, my boy! Let me look at you."

Eric allowed Aden to wrap him in his arms. "It's good to see you, Father."

Aden pulled back, holding Eric's face in his weathered hands. "Are you well?"

"For the time being, aye."

"Come, sit." Aden drew him to the sitting area. "What brings you all the way out here? I must say I'm surprised you made the trip."

Eric exhaled as he lowered his tired body into an ornate stuffed chair, relieved at how his father looked. Tired and worried, but he still walked upright, with shoulders straight and chin held high.

"I came from Danyon, where I found one of Jader's Shadowmen."

Aden sat back in his seat. "What happened?"

Eric spared no details in the account.

"So he managed to turn the entire town against us."

"It's a small town."

Aden shook his head. "That makes little difference. The next time it could be a larger one. Or a city. Or even Calla."

Eric did not reply. It was true. There was very little limit to the deception that Jader's Shadowmen could wield. They had learned from the very best in manipulation and treachery.

The king sighed. "It sounds like you got there in time, but surely you don't expect to go traipsing all around Paladin, following every rumor of turmoil."

"Nay, but I had to see for myself what was happening. Jader won't stop there. He's gathering strength on both sides of the Gateway now. That's why it's vital we protect it. And it's also vital that I stop his power at the source."

Aden's lips pinched. "You mean to resume your search for the Shadowpit, then?"

"I've let it go unchecked for far too long." The very thought of stepping outside the fort left his skin crawling, but Eric would not hide any longer.

"Any signs of the Reader?"

Eric shook his head, trying not to let his father see the dread that always hit him with every mention of the Reader.

"How long do you plan to stay?" Aden asked.

"Just for the night." Already, Eric wished it did not have to be so soon. But he did not feel right staying away from his people in Cadence.

Aden gave Eric an accepting smile. "I figured as much. But as I plan to journey to the Gateway Stronghold soon, I shall be content with the short visit."

His father's pronouncement snagged Eric's attention. "Why do you plan to come to the fort?"

"You don't expect me to miss my son's birthday, do you?"

Eric let out a short laugh. "Father, I do not expect you to travel all that way to celebrate me turning another year older. If truth be told, I'd almost forgotten."

"We cannot celebrate as we used to, but I fully intend to spend the day with you anyway."

There was no point in arguing with him, so Eric shrugged. "If you insist. I'm afraid the quarters are not very fitting for a king."

"You forget, son, that I oversaw the building of the fort. I know very well how accommodating they are." The deep lines around his face softened. "When will you leave?"

"I'm meeting Braylee in the morning. He's on his way to see his family tonight."

"Good. I'm glad you convinced that captain of ours to take the night as well. At least you'll both have a full meal and a good rest tonight."

Eric chuckled. "It did not take a lot of pressuring. It's been too long since Braylee has seen his family."

Cassels, Paladin, Old Realm

Three months. It had been exactly three months and six days since Braylee had stepped foot on his property, since he had left to fulfill his duty with Grand Marshal Uralis Faunt.

He stood before his cabin and drank in the sight, ignoring Beast as he munched on the grass at his feet.

Humble as it was, it was home. Full of love and laughter, thanks to his wife and daughters. His wife knew how to make the four rooms into a place of comfort and safety. Where Braylee could come after a long day of patrolling and find his pillow on his favorite chair and dinner simmering over the fire.

Even now, a hint of spicy meat met his nostrils, and he smiled at his fortunate timing. His wife was cooking his favorite dish of roasted pheasant.

The door creaked open, and a young girl stepped out to dump a bucket of dirty water. As usual, she did not take it as far as her mother preferred but turned it upside down right outside the entrance. Water splashed up and soaked her hem.

Braylee's throat grew tight as he stared at his sweet, precocious little Shayna, so tall and gangly now at eight years old. She groaned at the mess on her dress before she looked up and spotted Braylee. An unearthly shriek erupted from her small body before she tossed the pail and ran headlong for her father.

Chuckling as he braced himself for the wild hug, Braylee swept her up into his arms.

"You're here, you're here, you're here!" she squealed, her arms wrapped around his thick neck like a vice.

Ella ran through the doorway next and let out a squeal. Braylee held out his arm to her, and she swiftly joined them. He hugged her close, stunned at how grown up she looked.

"Girls, what on earth? Are you trying to put your mother into the ground?" A familiar, breathless voice greeted Braylee before his wife made her appearance. Upon seeing what had caused the commotion, she stopped short and brought her hands up to her mouth.

Braylee smiled and set Shayna back on the ground. "Hello, Griselle."

She burst into tears and approached him as if in a dream. Unwilling to wait for her, Braylee met her midway, embracing his wife for the first time in too long. She cried against his chest, and he rocked her back and forth, gently hushing her.

"Come now, you don't want to spend what little time we have crying, now, do you?"

Griselle shook her head against him and pushed away, sniffling and wiping her eyes. "Nay, I do not. I'm just so surprised!"

Shayna giggled and jumped up and down as if the idea had been hers.

"How long can you stay, Papa?" Ella asked, always the inquisitive one.

He rested his hand on her dark curls. "Only for the night, I'm afraid. I'm fortunate I was able to get away at all."

"Then come in, come in!" Griselle took him by the arm, and he dropped a kiss on her cheek as Ella claimed his other hand. "Dinner is done now, so let's all sit down together for once!"

"Just as soon as I take care of my hungry beast."

Once the bay had been stabled and fed in Braylee's small barn, the evening passed in a flurry of laughter and hugs. The girls caught their father up on all the latest gossip and their most recent accomplishments. Braylee could not keep up with it all but basked in the sound of his daughters' lively voices.

"Have you seen the prince, Papa?" Ella asked too casually, not looking at him.

Braylee's mouth twitched even as he caught Griselle's amused look. "I have seen the prince. We've become good friends, in fact."

The thirteen-year-old's eyes widened. "You have?"

"Of course, they have, silly," Shayna jumped in. "They both live at the fort, and everyone's friends with Papa."

Braylee chuckled at the little girl's confidence, even as her words nestled into his heart and stayed there.

Ella, however, ignored her sister. "What's he like?"

Braylee thought of all the obstacles Eric had weathered in the past few months. "He's a fine man and a good prince. He even saved my life once."

Ella sighed and sank back into her chair. "He's so handsome."

Shayna snorted. "He looks like mud next to Papa."

"Now, now," Griselle spoke up before Ella could argue. "It's late, and you two need to be getting to bed."

"But Mama," Shayna whined.

"Your mother's right." Braylee fell back into his role as if he had never left. "It's past your bedtime, and you need a good night's sleep if you want to be up early enough to see me off."

That silenced her complaints, but both girls held on to Braylee a little longer before they made their way to their room. Braylee swallowed thickly as they closed the door behind them. Maybe coming back home tonight was a bad idea. It was going to make it so much harder to leave them again in the morning.

Despite the need for rest, Braylee and Griselle were awake far into the night, enjoying one another's company and sharing what they could not share while separated. Griselle lay beside him, her hair scattered over the pillow. He stretched out on his side, his head propped up with one hand.

"So, truthfully now," Griselle said. "How is our young prince doing?"

Braylee drew in a deep breath. "For a while, I worried. The Stewards were divided, and he didn't seem to know how to lead them. He's come a long way in a few short weeks, but I think he's still letting his past hold him back. I fear he's trying to make up for what he's done."

Griselle's face filled with compassion as she brushed a curl from Braylee's forehead. "He's got a lot of weight on his shoulders."

"Aye, he does that."

"What do you think will happen?"

Braylee frowned. "I think war is coming. Sooner than we may be ready for it." He rubbed his tired eyes. "And I think I'm getting too old for this. I should be home with you all, keeping you safe."

Griselle let out a soft chuckle. "Braylee, we couldn't be safer here than if we had a whole army stationed next door. Your Stewards are always dropping by to check on us."

"That so?" His load lifted, just a bit, to know that others were looking after those he loved.

"Besides, you and I both know you would never rest easy if you left the prince in his most trying time." She patted his whiskered cheek. "You need to be there. It's your duty. I understand that. And so do the girls."

He caught her hand and kissed her palm. "That doesn't stop me from missing you."

"You'll be back home soon enough. In the meantime, you're serving a greater cause for the Lambient. None of us would think of holding you back from that."

He stared down at his wife of twenty years, wondering how he was so blessed. Griselle never chafed at his position as a Steward. Though he knew she worried about him, she put her faith in the Lambient and encouraged him to do the same.

"I do love you, wife of mine," he whispered.

The fine lines at the corners of her eyes deepened as she smiled up at him. "And I love my big-hearted knight."

He kissed her softly then lay back down, pulling her to his side. She nestled against his shoulder, and he held her close, thanking the Lambient that Eric had insisted he come home.

15

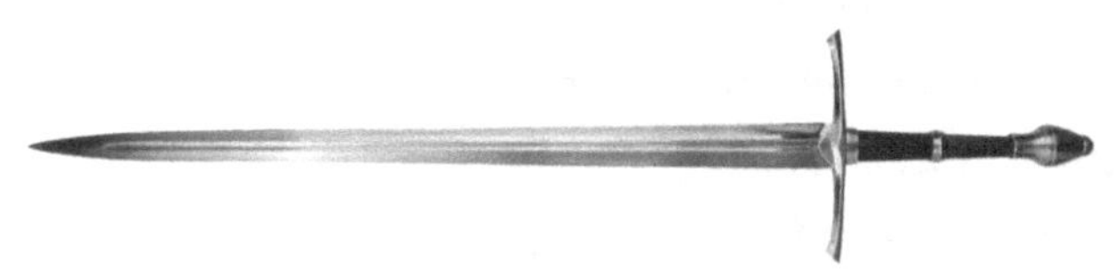

"Hey, girl!"

Seria spun around at the voice. Ira Dankton approached her on the path to the barn with short, wobbly steps. Her heart sank at the storm clouds on his face that let her know what was coming. It seemed he had brought his rum with him to the Gateway Stronghold.

He stopped right in front of her, jabbing a finger at her face. "You owe me!"

Hiding a sigh, Seria took a step back to avoid his sour breath. "Ira, I don't think this is the best place to hash this out again."

"Don't you go thinking that just because you've gotten in good with these Stewards that I'm gonna let you get by with stealing from me!" Spittle flew from his mouth.

"I didn't steal, Ira." She took another step backward. "Why don't you go home and get some rest? You're drunk." She turned to resume her walk to the barn.

He grabbed her arm, jerking her back to face him. "Don't you patronize me, wench!"

She tried to pull away. "Let go of me." Now would have been a good time to have her strap.

"I want my money!" He gave her a hard shake.

"That's enough, sir." Ollen's stern voice sounded from behind Ira, who started and let go so fast he stumbled. Ollen came around, his manner calm, but his jaw set.

"Nothing good comes from manhandling a lady," he said softly, stepping between Ira and Seria.

Ira pointed at her. "She stole from me! I wanna see justice done!"

"Justice does not condone physically assaulting a woman. If you have a complaint, let's take it to the Council."

"They won't believe me!"

"Let's go talk about it." Ira looked too surprised and drunk to argue. Ollen took the older man's plump elbow and glanced back at Seria. "Are you all right?"

Seria swallowed and nodded.

Ira scowled and swayed slightly, but he trotted dutifully next to Ollen's long strides, his legs moving so fast that Seria let out a giggle. Then she sighed, remembering the last time Ira had accosted her. If Mason had witnessed the drunken man's actions just now, she would not have been able to keep him from reacting a bit more aggressively.

And in truth, she wasn't sure she would have wanted to. She was so tired of Ira's constant harassment. In the two years she had known him, he was nothing more than a drunk, and that did not seem likely to change, which meant she would be stuck with dealing with his fits whenever the mood struck him.

Ollen caught up with her later after breakfast. "He didn't hurt you, did he?" he asked, scanning her arm where Ira had grabbed hold.

She waved him off. "I'm fine. I'm used to Ira's ranting."

"Why did he threaten you?"

"I tore a garment of his when I was doing his laundry. I repaired it as best as I could, and I even gave him his money back, but..."

Ollen took a seat at an empty table and waved her to sit across from him. "And he's still unhappy?"

She shrugged as she sank onto the wooden bench. "I thought when we came here, he had let it go. But some people never change."

Ollen shook his head. "Well, that's a shame." His smooth brow furrowed. "He's spending some time in the brig for assault."

Seria couldn't say she felt bad. There were plenty of times she wished she could throw him in the brig herself.

"I don't want you worrying about him, so I'll do what I can to make it stop. But if he bothers you, please make sure to tell me."

Guilt tugged at her for comparing him to Mason earlier. He still looked out for her, even if his method was quite different.

He caught her look. "What?"

"Are you sure you can handle Ira?" she teased.

His brows relaxed as his frowning lips turned up slightly. "You doubt me?" He straightened up and raised his chin. "I can get pretty mean."

She laughed. "Oh, can you? Is that why Lionel beats you on the dueling field?"

Outrage crossed his features. "Who said that?"

"I may have overheard him bragging about it one day, but don't tell him you heard it from me."

"You just wait until I see that..." He shook his head, then sobered. "Are you truly well?"

"Aye, I am. I appreciate you stepping in."

His fingers fidgeted on the table. "I...ah...I suppose you're still too busy to have another Steward lesson?"

"Oh." With a jolt, she realized she had never gotten back with him on that. Her nights had been tied up with her short secret meetings. She had another one that very night. "I am so sorry, Ollen. I did not mean to abandon our lessons."

He smiled back at her, though the light in his eyes seemed to dim. "I understand. I tell you what, we'll leave off for the time being. When you're ready, you let me know. That way I won't keep bothering you," he added with a chuckle.

"You could never bother me, Ollen Knavis," she scolded. "It's just...life is a little complicated right now."

"Aye." He let out a sigh and stared at the table. "It is that."

She cocked her head. "Is everything all right?"

He looked up and shrugged. "It's fine. We got word that Prince Eric will be back in a day or two, but it seems things are getting a little tense in the Old Realm, thanks to the Shadowmen."

Her stomach tightened. "How bad is it?" She bit her tongue. The less she knew, the better.

Ollen sat back. "It's hard to say. The Stewards ran into some trouble but were able to deal with it pretty easily. But we know that's not the end of it."

Seria clasped her hands tightly on her lap, remembering the night the Shadowmen slipped through the back gate of the fort into the Old Realm. And Mason helped them do it.

Ollen slapped the table and stood. "Anyway, I better get back. Let me know if you have any more issues with Ira."

She licked her dry lips and nodded, staying in her seat long after he was gone.

Sometimes it was so easy to forget what Mason was and what he had done. Their brief snatches of time together were spent in deep conversation, sparring, and even laughter. But at the end of the day, Mason was still a Darkman. A Shadowman.

She took a deep breath, trying to shake the fears that settled over her. Her time spent with Mason showed her a different side of him, a good side that treated her like something special, enjoyed watching baby foxes, and wanted her to be able to defend herself. This was the real Mason that he wrapped under a cover of vengeance and pain. But she needed more time to help free that part of him.

16

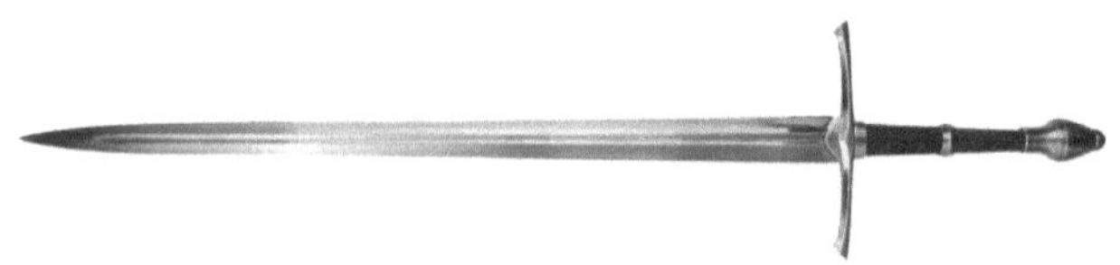

"I see you are up before the sun again, Mason."

Mason stopped sparring with the padded pole and turned to bow with his fist over his bare chest, panting and sweating. "Emperor Jader."

Jader dismissed his salute. "I did not mean to interrupt your morning workout."

Wiping his face with his discarded shirt, Mason shrugged. "I'm finished. I like to get it done before the day starts." He didn't bother telling him he couldn't sleep for chafing about his coming departure. Jader would not understand why he was not more excited. But all Mason could think about was how long he would be gone from Seria. Which bothered him. He was not one to drag his feet on a mission.

"It is certainly busy these days with the impending move from camp. There is a lot of energy."

Mason pulled his vest over his shoulders. "Aye. Everyone's pretty excited about the pickups."

"It is a big undertaking that requires a lot of thought and effort. It can be a disconcerting experience the first time. But I have confidence you will do fine." Jader cocked his head. "You were not much older when we met than some of our new recruits will be."

Mason's mind went back to those early days when he was the youngest in the camp. What a frightened, angry boy he was, refusing to speak to anyone and getting into all kinds of trouble with his Gifts. "Took me a while to settle down."

Jader chuckled. "You were a lively one. But then again, you had a lot to deal with."

That was certainly true enough. Watching your brother's brutal murder at the hands of coldblooded Stewards, and then being left for dead with an arrow sticking out of your chest, was enough to traumatize any twelve-year-old.

The emperor sobered, his good eye becoming distant. "That day seems like such a long time ago, does it not?"

The memories crowded in Mason's head again, reminding him of the bitterness and rage that had consumed him for so long. Being with Seria had made him almost forget. But he couldn't forget. Not now, not when he was so close. The prince of Paladin and the Stewards would pay for their crimes.

A sudden cramp drew his gaze down to his white knuckles gripped around his shirt. He flung it down to the ground. "And sometimes it feels like yesterday."

"I understand." Jader clasped his hands together. "It is a hard day to remember, especially considering how the king sent those same Stewards back into the New Realm to flaunt their brutal acts."

Mason jerked his eyes to Jader. "What's that?"

Jader's lips turned down as he shook his head. "A travesty. The very same Stewards responsible for the Handan massacre were allowed to infiltrate my domain. It was meant to be nothing more than a slap in the face. And yet the army stands guard in the Gateway as if they own it."

His hands trembling, Mason turned away so Jader would not see the turbulent emotions on his face.

Stewards. In the New Realm. And not just any Stewards but the very ones who had killed all the boys from Handan. The memory of Hepp's Steward friend made more sense now.

Mason clenched his jaw, trying to quench the red-hot rage surging throughout his being. But it grew until spots appeared before his vision. Finally, he swung a fist as hard as he could at the padded pole. Pain sliced through his knuckles, but it helped rein his emotions back in.

"I am sorry I never told you before, Mason." Jader's voice was soft, regretful. "I thought it too much for you to deal with in the beginning. And then, over time, I did not want to burden you with the knowledge."

Sucking in a deep breath, Mason dipped his head once in acknowledgment. Jader was not the one he was angry at.

"Is it not ironic, however, that you were able to do the very same thing against them?" A hint of a smile could be heard in the statement. "You managed to get some of our very own Shadowmen through the fort to infiltrate their kingdom. What a sweet twist of justice."

It was true, and Mason grasped that victory now, allowing it to pull him back from the churning hole that threatened to suck him in.

"But there is something else you should know. Something that might bring you even more comfort."

Mason gritted his teeth and turned to face the emperor, still unable to speak.

Jader's dark eye was lit with satisfaction. "I took it upon myself these past twelve years to seek out those very same Stewards and bring them to justice."

"You have?"

"I promised myself that what happened to you and your brother would not go unpunished. It has taken time, but many of those killers have been found and executed. In fact, I tracked one down during your absence a few weeks back. A Nebb Stattler. The coward even surrendered his children in an attempt to spare his life."

He should be thankful. And he was, but it was a lot to process, and Mason did not know how he felt. There were too many memories and emotions.

"It is all right, Mason." Jader placed a hand on his shoulder. "Do not feel you need to say anything."

Mason sighed and nodded, grateful for Jader's understanding.

"I have fought Aden's Stewards for many years now." Jader's brows pinched. "And though I would never compare my experience to yours, I have also suffered at the hands of the Stewards."

At the quiet fervor with which the words were spoken, Mason managed to pull his focus off himself and to the older man standing before him.

Jader stroked the scar on his face. "I faced the cruelty of the Stewards long before you were born. Back when I realized what kind of men they were that they would even stoop to massacre a bunch of adolescent boys."

Mason's curiosity simmered at this glimpse into Jader's past.

Straightening his shoulders, Jader turned his eye to Mason. "The Stewards are notorious for betraying those who get in their way. Even those who considered them friends at one time."

"Friends?" Mason's brows shot up. "You, sir?"

A sad smile touched the other man's lips. "Aye, even me, many seasons ago." A heavy sigh seemed to deflate him. "I fought alongside them, though I was never considered good enough to be accepted into their elite Stewardship."

The shock rolled over Mason. Jader had fought alongside the Stewards? "How...how could that be?"

"Because I was young and naïve, like so many of their followers. I worked hard as a Reservist to earn Aden's favor, sat at his table many times, and led my men to victories for his cause. But when it came down to it, I was nothing but a pawn in his greater game."

"What happened?"

"I offered another source of power that would have benefited their army to no end. Their Beacons were impressive, of course. But I knew Shreil's power would make Aden's army virtually unstoppable." Jader paused, a shadow falling over his face. "But when I suggested it, they turned on me as if I was their enemy. I was violently expelled from the army and turned out of their kingdom."

Mason shook his head. He had always guessed Jader's history with the Stewards ran deeper than mere competition over the Aged Realms, but he had never expected his emperor to have once been in the middle of them.

Jader let out a soft chuckle. "But they overestimated their army. I had acquired an army of faithful militiamen who stood by me. It caused a civil war within Paladin that left a smear in their history books that they tried to blot out. Even some of their own Stewards turned against their king and fought for me."

"The Stewards fought each other?"

A slow smile spread over Jader's face. "But of course. The Stewards differing over the prince taking command was not the first time the Passions led a divided army."

Eric sat at the large oak table in the familiar dining hall early in the morning, breaking the fast with his father, but he did not have much time. He could not put off the conversation with his father any longer.

"Father."

Aden set his goblet down and turned with a slight smile. "Aye, son."

Eric's insides squeezed at the contentment on the old man's face. If only they could forget about the threat that drew ever closer to their kingdom.

"I need to know."

Aden's expression dimmed a bit. "Know what?"

"What is the history you share with Jader? Why is he so bent on destroying us?"

"What kind of question is that?" Aden looked into his mug. "He wants to rule. That's his motivation."

"Father, stop." Eric swallowed. "You spoke of a personal vendetta Jader has against you. I need to know what is driving this mad pursuit of control."

A frustrated breath blew past Aden's lips, stirring the white hairs on his chin. "I had hoped to put it behind me."

"Perhaps that was your hope, but Jader is not allowing it."

Aden grimaced. "It almost worked on this side of the Slate Mountains. There aren't many who remember those days. Certainly, no one ever speaks of it."

"I need to know."

"Of course, you do." Aden sat back in his seat, looking shrunken against the high back. "It happened when you were very young, but to this day, 'tis hard to speak of, for it is not something I am proud of."

"Nothing will change how I feel about you, Father. You know that, right?"

Aden nodded, then took a deep breath. "The fact is, Graulik Jader used to be one of us."

Eric blinked. "One of us? You mean a Steward?"

A sudden snort lightened the mood for a moment. "Hardly. The Lambient has more sense than to entrust Jader with that kind of honor. But he was a member of my Reservists. For some years, in fact."

"Is that so?" Eric tried to imagine it, but try as he might, he could not picture the emperor dressed in the grays of the Militia Army. "What happened?"

"He climbed as far up the ranks as he could in the Reserves, and he was a good soldier. But he had his sights on higher levels of leadership. And he could not understand why we would not give it to him."

"So he never understood where the Stewards' authority came from."

Aden shook his head. "More like, he wouldn't accept it. He grew resentful about it and stirred up animosity in the militia ranks. But even then, I did not expect what came next."

Eric held his breath as his father gathered himself to continue.

"Jader came to me with an idea. A suggestion for growing the Stewards' power. I knew he was hoping to earn my good graces just so he could earn the Stewardship, but I heard him out anyway. Turns out, he had discovered a source of power, all right, but it was nothing I wanted anything to do with. He had found a direct connection to Shreil, the dark one himself."

Eric resisted a shudder. He could almost predict what happened next.

"When I realized what he was suggesting... that he actually believed we would take on the Shreil's power was beyond me! Of course, I refused, and he grew angry. I warned him about playing around with any kind of darkness, told him there was no power that would ever be greater than Lambient's light. Not even the Shreil. But by that time, his mind was made up."

Aden sighed and rubbed his eyes. "Jader had garnered enough support among the militiamen to start a small civil war. It took the kingdom by surprise, devastated Calla at the time. But that wasn't the worst of it."

"What could be worse than a civil war right outside your window?"

"The way he manipulated our Stewards."

Eric sucked in a breath. "He had Stewards fighting for him?" How could they be so blind as to support a man who would choose darkness over light?

"Remember, son, he is the master of manipulation. He knew he would never get the Stewards over to his way of thinking. But he could manipulate and deceive them into doing his bidding. Somehow, he managed to engineer an entire platoon of Stewards into a blind position. And that's when our army first experienced Jader's dark powers."

He paused and folded his hands on the table, his face pensive. "Our soldiers were surrounded by a black cloud. It disoriented them and put them in a panic. And then, to make matters worse, he somehow shaped it into monstrous beasts. The Stewards went on the attack."

Eric held his breath. "I've never heard of Jader wielding such a power."

"While those Stewards thought they were defending themselves against shadow creatures, they turned their weapons on their allies. Dozens of Stewards were killed."

A chill settled into Eric's bones. "Why have I never heard this before?"

"It was a devastating and humiliating blow to the Steward army. Those who had been manipulated were shattered that they had allowed themselves to be so overcome by darkness and fear that they killed their comrades. It was a scar they could not get over. A blight on the Steward record."

"So, what happened?"

"Eventually, Jader and his new army were defeated. I fought him myself at the gates of the city. Nearly killed him, too." Aden's finger grazed the side of his face.

Eric's jaw slackened. "You left him scarred."

One corner of the old man's lips turned up. "He got a little too close to Lavrynth. But it was a hard victory. The Steward army ran Jader's men out of the Old Realm. It wasn't long before I heard he was gaining power in the New Realm, and I knew then that he would come back. That's when the Gateway Stronghold was built."

A long, heavy silence fell as Eric went over this new revelation. Then finally, he asked the question that would not be ignored. "Whatever happened to the Stewards?"

Aden's blue eyes darkened. "Devastated and ashamed, they felt they had disgraced the Stewards and wished to be removed from the army. So, I quietly dismissed them and did everything I could to hide their role in the war."

"Where are they now?" Eric asked hoarsely, though he already knew.

"While they wished to leave the army, no one but Lambient could take their Stewardship from them. Their loyalty was still strong, and they desired a chance to redeem their mistakes. So, they went to the New Realm, where they could serve as spies and informants."

Massaging his temples, Eric remembered the days after the Handan massacre. As the one behind the order, he could relate to those feelings of shame and brokenness. The Stewards responsible for the death of the boys had felt the same.

"That's where the Handan Stewards are now, isn't it?"

"Aye." Aden's voice was tired. "Just like their predecessors, those Stewards wanted to right the wrong they had committed. I knew the veteran Stewards would help them make a new start."

Leaning forward, Eric braced his elbows on the table and clasped his hands in front of his face. "I knew we had Steward contacts across the Gateway, but why did you never tell me why they were there?"

"Because I promised myself no one would ever know. I did not want to cast shame or doubt on the Stewards."

"So you hid it all these years. Just like we hid what happened at Handan."

"Are you disappointed in me, son?"

Eric rubbed his face. "Nay. I understand why you did it. The same reason I was so willing to hide the massacre." He looked up. "But in hindsight, I'm not sure it was the best thing. In either case."

Aden shook his head. "No good would have come from the public knowing about the Stewards falling for Jader's deceits. They need to know they can trust the Stewards to protect them."

Eric was not so sure, especially now. But he recognized the stubborn set to his father's chin and knew the conversation was drawing to a close.

"Well, at least I know why Jader hates us so much."

"It's more than hate, son." Aden scowled as his gaze went distant. "He stood before me and swore that darkness would always overpower the light. And now he will stop at nothing to prove it."

17

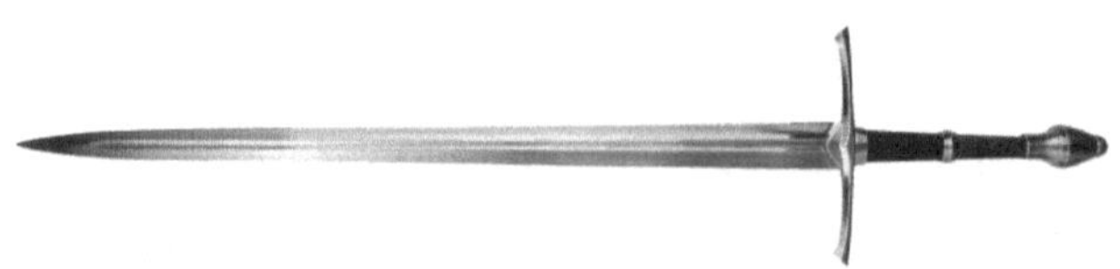

Mason sat outside the cabin door, waiting for Seria to make another appearance. Moonlight cast silvery shadows all around him. The silence of the night was broken by an occasional hoot of an owl.

He peered through the darkness with clear vision, trying not to worry. She wasn't late. Not yet. She just wasn't as early as usual.

Leaning back to rest against the cabin wall, he straightened his legs out before him where he sat on Seria's overturned wash bucket. His foot wriggled in his impatience. He would have to tell her tonight that this would be their last visit for a while. Jader's plan would take him away, and he could not say for how long.

He crossed his arms at the thought. Frustration coiled within him, tight and tense, ready to snap. Their time together was already so brief, though he cherished every moment. Almost every moment. He did not like when their differences got in the way. Seria's doubts and her long-held faith in the Lambient still hindered her from choosing her own path. But most of the time, it was good.

A smile loosened his stiff lips as he thought back to their conversations. She was every bit as talkative and curious as ever. After years of feeling nothing but emptiness and anger, she was his reason to laugh, his source of joy when he thought he was past that.

Which was why the idea of leaving left such a bitter taste in his mouth. He wasn't ready to go back to the work he had been so committed to for so long. For the first time, he was tempted to abandon his obligations.

Guilt buffeted him. Liam's death still hung over his head, unjustified and unresolved. Eric Passion had to pay for the massacre, despite the pitiful lies he fed Seria.

Someday, she would know the truth. Someday, this war would be over, and they would be free to live their lives together, without worrying about the Stewards destroying them. Someday, but not yet.

A soft footstep reached his ear and he tensed, ready to blend into the shadows if he had to. But it was Seria's blonde head he spotted crossing over the bridge, shining like gold under the moonbeams.

His chest warmed at the way her face lit up at seeing him. Every night, he worried she would not come. That she would change her mind about being with a Darkman and choose the Stewards over him. But here she was, which told him more than anything that his hope was not in vain.

He stood and held his arms out to her. As she tucked herself against him, he decided to wait until their parting before telling her he had to leave. There was no sense in ruining the whole night.

They stood there, quiet and unrushed, for the space of several heartbeats.

"Sorry I'm late," she murmured, tilting her head back to look at him.

"You're here now. That's what matters." He squinted at her. "But you look tired."

She sighed. "Rough day."

Protectiveness reared its head. "Are you having problems?"

"Nay. Unless you want to count Ira."

His arms stiffened. "Is he still bothering you?"

"He's been taken care of, so don't you worry your handsome little head about him."

He blew out a breath. "I should've had him walk into a lake. And stay there."

"Mason!" She smacked his arm. "Don't let one man's flaws bring out your own."

Feigning a gasp, he gaped at her. "I have flaws?"

She narrowed her eyes at him. "I'm serious. Just because one pathetic man takes a low road, that doesn't mean you have to follow him."

Her words clanged through his mind, and he held her gaze for a long moment before giving her a nod. "You're right."

The scolding look melted into a smile, and she kissed his cheek. "But thank you for wanting to look after me."

Cold fingers of unease slipped around his shoulders and down his spine as visions of war flooded his mind. Stewards pitted against Darkmen. And Seria trapped between them. He cleared his throat. "I'll always look out for you, Seria." Even against his own men, if need be.

The night was clear, so Mason suggested a walk in the woods. Seria agreed without hesitation, and they strolled, hand-in-hand, and talked. He told her a little bit more about his brother, and Seria shared stories about her family.

There were moments of laughter, but there were times they walked in silence, the peacefulness of the sleeping forest wrapping them in a cocoon of peace. Mason could sense Seria's contentment as she walked beside him. His heart responded in kind, sighing within his chest with a painful squeeze.

How he hated to break this moment.

As their time drew short, they turned back and walked to her cabin under the moonlight, enjoying their last few minutes.

"I wonder if Lena was able to talk her grandfather into coming to the fort with her." Seria spoke softly, as if to herself.

"I'm sure the old man will be fine."

She gave him an exasperated look but did not reply. Mason was reminded again of how much she worried about everyone around her. He brought her hand up to kiss it.

"How's your little buddy?" he asked, trying to appease her.

"I don't know. He's somewhere in the Gateway." Her flat voice made her feelings on that matter clear.

"Oh, right." Mason winced. "He'll be all right, Seria. He doesn't need you to take care of him now."

"I miss him."

Mason slid his arm around her shoulders. "Not as much as I'm going to miss you."

Her eyes snapped to his face. "What do you mean?"

They were almost to the door, so he waited until they were inside before he brought her in front of him. "I have to leave."

Seria's face fell. "When?"

"Tomorrow."

"When will you be back?"

"Not sure."

"So, we don't know when we'll see each other again." Her face paled. "I can't believe this. I mean, I always knew there was a possibility something like this would happen, but I had hoped..."

He did not want to consider what she had hoped. "Hey, this is a temporary thing. We'll see each other again."

Seria bit her lip, not appeased by his assurance. "And what happens if the war hits the Gateway before you get back? I'm scared, Mason." Her words picked up speed in her distress. "I'm afraid this might be the last time we'll be together like this. That maybe the next time we see each other, our whole lives will have changed. Maybe too much."

Her words stirred the same kind of fear within him. How could he know what would happen between now and the next time they met?

The Gateway was a powder keg, ready to explode with war and violence. The Stewards and Darkmen were poised to come against each other with everything they had.

Stepping closer, he brushed her hair behind her ears, and then he kissed her, soft and gentle. The prospect of the next few days or weeks filled him with dread and longing. How could he leave her? She completed him, more than any mission or stone ever could. Deepening the kiss, he slid his arms around her, holding her tight against him. Her kiss was a sip of cool water to his dry spirit, and he wanted to keep drinking.

At a whimper from Seria, he released her and backed away. "Did I hurt you?"

She shook her head, brushing her disheveled hair back, her cheeks flushed. "Nay, Mason. You did not."

He clasped his hands over his head. "I scared you then."

"Mason—"

"I'm sorry, Seria. I didn't mean to. I would never—"

Her soft chuckle brought him to earth. "Mason, would you quit trying to talk for me now? I was overwhelmed, that's all. I think we both let our emotions get the better of us. Not knowing..."

Seeing she spoke the truth, he dropped his arms to his sides and took a deep breath to settle his racing heart back into a semblance of its normal rhythm. When he was sure he was in control, he took her hands. "I really wish...things were different. I'd rather be here with you."

"Then stay."

Her wide green eyes beseeched him, pulling him in. The hope that sparked in them killed him. At that moment, all he wanted to do was forget everything to stay with her. But he could not. Not after what Jader had told him. Mason had worked too hard and come too far to go back now. His mission was still unfinished, his vow unfulfilled. Liam deserved more than to be forgotten.

The Stewards had to pay for what they had done.

"Listen to me, Seria." His voice was low and heavy with feeling. "No matter what happens, I *will* find you again. I promise you that."

Her lips trembled, but she held her chin up and nodded.

He framed her face and wiped her tears away with his thumbs. "I love you," he said thickly. "Like I've never loved anyone in my whole life. And nothing will change that."

They were not just pretty words he spoke to win her heart or ease her mind. He meant them. His brother was the only other person he could ever remember loving, but what he felt for Seria was beyond anything he had ever imagined or expected. And he would fight to the death to keep it.

18

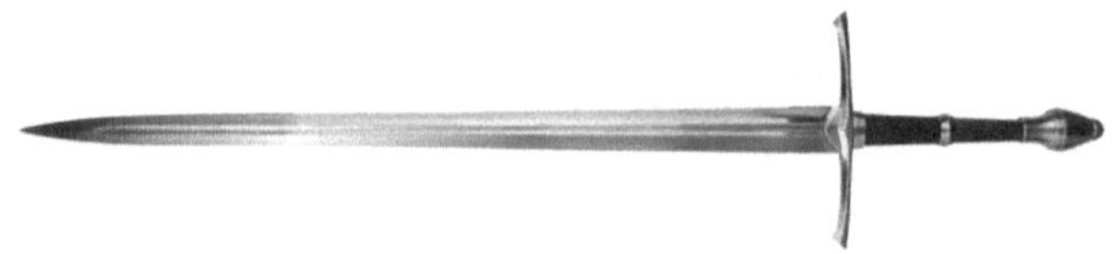

Seria wandered around on top of the outer fort walls, too restless to go to her room for the night. The day had kept her too busy to think ahead, but now she could not ignore the fact scratching at her spirit.

Mason was leaving tonight. She had no idea how long he would be gone. The reason for his departure frightened her too much to put a lot of thought into it.

But hope clung tight, despite the fear. Mason's face last night as he clung to her had betrayed him. He did not want to go. Maybe it had nothing to do with his changing convictions, but it was a start, and Seria would take it.

She exhaled, hating the way her stomach always felt tied up in knots anymore. When was the last time she had truly been able to relax and not worry?

What do you expect when you stand between two mortal enemies?

Not willing to evaluate the truth in the thought, she walked faster, welcoming the cool breeze on her face, and caught sight of Captain Dudley, alone on the wall, leaning against the stone ledge and gazing out into the night.

"Mind if I join you?" she asked.

He looked up at her with a ready smile on his weathered face. "I can't imagine any better company."

"What were you looking at?" She rested her elbows on the ledge beside him.

"Oh, I was just watching two squirrels fighting over a nut in that far oak tree out there." His drawl carried a hint of teasing.

She glanced at him from the corner of her eye, not sure if he was serious. "Really?"

He winked. "Would I lie to you?"

Shaking her head, she scoped out the distance between where he stood and the nearest tree. It was clear on the other side of Cadence. She had forgotten about his Gift of long-distance sight. "I would love to be able to see as much as you can."

Dudley's lips turned up. "Maybe so, miss, but even my eyesight doesn't allow me to see what I'd really like to see."

She cocked her head. "And what's that?"

His face softened. "The sight of my wife's smiling face every morning."

"You must miss her." The crisp air prompted her to pull her shawl tighter.

He confirmed with a slow nod.

"Where is she?"

"She's gone, miss," he said with a sigh. "Been gone close to ten years now."

"Oh, Dudley, I'm so sorry."

"Thank you, miss, but I'm closer to seeing her now than I've ever been before." A look of contentment settled on his grizzled face. "I've got more years behind me than I do ahead. One of these days, I'll be walking into that High Light, and I'll see my sweet Anna again."

Seria's throat tightened at the words and the sincerity with which he spoke them. "I'll be happy for you when that day comes, but is it selfish of me to hope it doesn't come for some time yet?"

He chuckled. "That's mighty sweet of you, miss." His eyes twinkled down at her. "I expect to still be kicking for a few good years yet. I've got to help Prince Eric win this war, you see?"

She returned his smile and turned with him to stare out into the lovely night once again. Several minutes passed in peaceful camaraderie before Dudley stirred and stood up straight.

"Hmm. Someone's coming."

Seria's heart jumped as she strained to see movement, but of course, she could see none.

"Moving kind of slow." He glanced at Seria and began moving away. "Excuse me, miss. I've got to see about this."

Seria was in the courtyard by the time the gate was opened, holding on to an irrational hope that the visitor would be Mason. But it was an elderly man. Two Reservists assisted him, supporting him on both sides. The old man was huffing and puffing, carrying a small knapsack with him.

Dudley asked his name and business, his voice brisk, but polite.

"My name's Cal Carwright, sir."

"Oh!" Seria's eyes widened at the name, and she hurried forward. "I know this man! Or rather, I know his family. They're staying here at the fort."

Dudley looked back at Cal. "Is that why you're here, sir?"

"That is." Cal bobbed his head. "They've been wanting me to come since they first moved in."

Seria clasped her hands together. "They'll be so happy you're here!"

Cal gave her a long look, as if trying to place her.

"Oh, I'm sorry, sir. I'm Seria, a friend of Lena's."

He gave a soft snort. "Another friend of Lena's, huh?"

"Well, I'm sure you're tired after all that walking," Dudley said. "My men will escort you to your family's residence."

"I'd appreciate that, young man," Cal said. He squinted at Seria again. "You said your name was Seria?"

"That's right."

"You like watching the stars?"

Caught off guard, Seria gave a slight laugh. "I suppose so, aye. Why?"

The old man looked up at the night sky. "The same stars you see here tonight are the same ones others are watching. No matter where they're at."

Wondering if the man was talking out of his head, she sent Dudley a confused shrug. The captain took over, directing his men to assist Cal to where Lena and her mother lived so he could get some rest.

Hands on her hips, Seria watched the small entourage move away. After all of Lena's pleading and cajoling, what had caused him to change his mind and walk all this way on his own?

And what on earth incited such a random question about the stars? She sympathized with his apparent confusion. Nothing a good night's rest would not cure.

Tilting her head back, she took in the millions of sparkling lights, her lips curling up at the sight. She did love watching them. They always made her think of Mason and the times they spent under a star-studded sky.

She let out a gasp. Looking over her shoulder, she could barely see Cal being led away by the Stewards. Her heart skipped a beat as she thought again of his sudden arrival and strange words.

Lena had told her more than once of his stubborn refusal to join them in the fort. Nothing she said or did could convince him. But something had abruptly changed his mind tonight. Or someone.

Could it be? Had the random message about stars come from Mason in one last attempt to remind her they would be together again? That they were not that far apart?

Seria bit her lip and swallowed back tears. There was no way to know for certain, not now anyway. But given the peculiarity of the whole situation, Seria had very little doubt Mason had had a hand in convincing the man to seek safety with his family. And that he had managed to speak to her once more only reminded her why she could not give up on him.

19

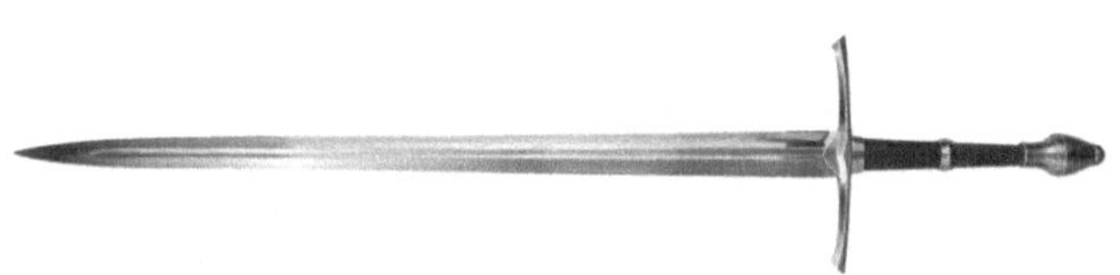

Eric woke up and sighed in contentment as the plain walls around him came into view. He and Braylee had arrived at the fort late the night before with Sgt. Kleff's squad, greeted Dudley, and then Eric had promptly retired to his familiar, though lumpy, bed.

Despite his extreme weariness the night before, some habits could not be broken, so Eric rose early and readied for the day. Not bothering to stop by Braylee's room, he stepped out into the cool morning air. The big man had to be as tired as he had been.

Besides that, he was a bear in the morning.

It lifted his spirits to be back at the Gateway Stronghold. Though not the safest place for anyone to be at the moment, with the threat of war looming ever closer, it was home, and for the time being, it was still safe. It also housed the people he had come to care a great deal for in the past few weeks.

He had a meeting with Dudley later to catch up on all the happenings of the fortress during his absence, but first, his stomach growled for breakfast. He had not gone far when he saw Seria heading his way. The way she brightened upon seeing him did his weary heart good.

She ran to meet him, and for a moment, he thought she would throw her arms around him. "Eric! You're back!"

He smiled at her delight. "It's good to see you again, too."

"I was worried about you. Did...everything go well?"

"I appreciate your concern." He was careful with his answer. "We accomplished what we needed to. That's the important thing, I suppose."

She looked as if she wanted to ask more but refrained, which was out of character for her. From her first day at the stronghold, she did not hesitate to ask questions or to learn as much as she could to satisfy her thirst for knowledge. Until recently.

Then she swallowed and straightened her shoulders. "I need to apologize, Prince Eric, for the way I've been acting toward you lately. It was unfair of me to blame you today for something you did years ago."

"So this was about Handan?" he asked carefully.

Her eyes darkened. "It was, aye. I had heard about it when I was younger, and I was shocked you had anything to do with it. But I realize that the man I know today is different from the man who must have been responsible."

"Aye, that is true. But it doesn't make it any easier to deal with."

"Especially when foolish girls behave like they've never made a mistake in their life. I declare, my mama used to say she didn't know what to do with my knack for talking myself into trouble."

A chuckle broke the tight lines on Eric's face, and Seria's expression lifted.

"How have you been?" he asked, feeling a weight slip from his shoulders.

"Oh, just fine." She waved the question off and gave him a cheeky grin. "I kept myself out of trouble. Didn't want to answer to the prince when he came back, you see. I hear he can be a real pain to deal with."

Eric chuckled. Now this was more like the Seria he had come to know—teasing and lighthearted. "I've heard the same thing."

She waved at someone over Eric's shoulder. "Good morning, Captain!"

Seeing Braylee rested and in his usual good humor, Eric could not help but tease him. "Hold on, Seria," he whispered loudly. "Don't speak to him until we know if it's safe or not."

A begrudging smile worked itself on Braylee's broad face. "Funny."

Seria frowned at him. "What did I miss?"

Eric sent Braylee an unrepentant grin. "Let's just say our good-natured captain does not always start his days well."

Braylee gave a huff. "I'm not that bad." At Eric's raised brow, he shrugged. "Sometimes."

Seria shook her head. "I can't believe the captain could ever be anything but the gentleman he always is."

Eric snorted. "Try waking him up one morning."

Braylee turned his back on him and held his arm out to Seria. "Who's ready for breakfast?"

She lifted her chin and took his offered arm. "I would love breakfast, Captain Braylee."

Eric chuckled as they walked off, leaving him behind. It felt good to be back, to laugh with his friends and see Seria more like her old self. He wished every morning could be so carefree.

Dudley met him outside the mess hall after the meal. Seria was working in the kitchen, and Braylee had taken to the training fields.

"Ah, there you are," the older captain greeted. "I was looking for you."

"Something on your mind?"

"An old man showed up at our gate late last night, half-blind and talking out of his head. Turned out to be a relative of a family who already lives here. According to Miss Seria, they tried to get him to come here since you first opened the doors to the civilians."

Eric frowned thoughtfully. "Cal Carwright?"

Dudley bobbed his head. "Aye. How did you know?"

"I've talked with him myself on more than one occasion. He refused to move." He cocked his head. "So, what changed his mind?"

Dudley shrugged. "Not sure, but he seems content enough. His family was happy to see him."

Eric nodded in understanding. "Well, he's safer here than out there. I'll talk with him as soon as I have a moment."

They parted ways then to fulfill their errands for the day. Eric had to put off his visit with Carwright until late morning. The family's rented house was not hard to track down, though not as conveniently located in the center of the civilian square as their last home had been. He knocked on the door and gave a polite smile to the middle-aged woman who opened it.

"Oh, Your Highness!" Ayna gasped.

He bowed his head to her. "I apologize for coming unannounced, ma'am."

"Oh no, you're most welcome any time." Her hands fluttered around her hair and her dress. "Please, come in."

Eric stepped inside and took in the room's simple but comfortable furnishings with a quick glance. "I am glad you were able to acquire new lodgings."

"Thank you. We are grateful."

"I understand you had an unexpected visitor last night."

Ayna nodded. "Aye, Papa Cal, my late husband's father."

"Would it be possible for me to see him?"

"Of course." She motioned to another door. "He's not feeling well, but he'll be glad to see you."

"I hope it's nothing serious."

The woman shook her head. "I'm not sure what it was, really. He was quite disoriented when he woke and didn't even remember coming here. I was afraid he would insist on leaving, but he is very faint and has a terrible headache. I don't think he could go if he wanted to."

The description stopped him in his tracks. "A headache, you say?"

"Aye, he's never had one this bad, he says. But it seems to be passing." She must have caught the strained look on his face. "He's already feeling some better."

Eric forced a smile, his mind spinning. *Surely not.* "That's good." He followed her into the spare bedroom.

Cal was still in bed but looked alert enough. He squinted up at the tall prince as Ayna excused herself. "Well, I guess you're happy now, huh?"

Taking the chair beside the bed so the man did not have to strain to see him, Eric said, "I'm happy you're safe and back with your family, aye."

Cal nodded, a knowing look on his face. "I never intended to, you know."

Eric leaned forward, resting his elbows on his knees. "What changed your mind?"

With a casual shrug, Cal said, "A friend of Lena's convinced me."

"Who?"

"Never got his name."

"Can you tell me what he looked like?" Eric hated to sound as if he was interrogating the man, but he had to know.

Cal shook his head. "Nay, sorry." He winced as he adjusted positions on his bed. "Couldn't see too good last night. He was just a big blur." As he talked, a hand came up to massage his temples.

Eric asked a few more questions, but Cal's account was vague, so there was no point in continuing. "I'm glad you're here, Mr. Carwright. I hope you get to feeling better."

Cal gave him a tired wave, not even looking at him as he left.

Eric stood outside his door. *Headache. Disorientation. Extreme weakness.*

"Is everything all right, Prince Eric?"

The soft voice jerked him back to the present, where he discovered not Ayna, but her daughter, Lena, watching him.

"Oh, pardon me." He gave her a small bow.

She answered with a nod and handed him a cup of hot cider. "You looked like you were lost in thought."

Eric accepted with a soft thank you. "I'm trying to understand what happened to bring your grandfather here." His brow furrowed as he regarded the young woman before him. "He said it was a friend of yours?"

Lena shrugged and offered him a seat at the small table. "Grandfather wasn't exactly clear with the details."

Settling into the chair, Eric decided to be frank. "The symptoms he is displaying are very similar to what happens after the Reader controls someone."

She cocked her head, a wrinkle furrowing her brow. "I don't know why the Reader would be concerned with a little old man living by himself."

"True." Eric frowned. "Unless he had ulterior motives," he murmured, thinking aloud.

Lena cocked a thin brow. "Are you suspecting my grandfather of being a spy, Prince Eric?"

He jerked. "What? Nay!"

At her soft laughter, heat climbed up his neck, and he chuckled at himself. "Maybe I'm overreacting." He took another drink and stood, ready to end the awkward exchange. "Thank you for the drink, Miss Carwright."

"It was my pleasure. Come by the bakery later, and I'll make sure you get your favorite."

He paused. "My favorite?" Did he have a favorite?

Lena crossed her arms, her brown eyes twinkling. "Well, considering you can never pass up a honey tart, I assumed."

His mind immediately ran over all the times he stopped by the Carwrights' bakery. Sure enough, he always left with a honey tart. "I never even realized."

She laughed and crossed the room to open the door for him. "I make it my business to know what my customers like."

He thanked her again and fled the house, certain he must have come across as a bumbling, adolescent prince.

Trying to dismiss his embarrassment and needing more answers than Lena had given, he sought Dudley out in the training field. "What did Cal do when he arrived?"

"After we questioned him, we took him home."

"Did he do or say anything to anyone when he got here?"

Scratching his head, Dudley tried to remember. "I was the one who spotted him coming. Sent a couple of men to escort him in. Then I met him at the gate and talked with him for several minutes. I confirmed his story with others in the fort. His daughter-in-law and granddaughter run their bakery business from their home."

"Aye, we've met," he said dryly.

"Many of our men are familiar with them. His story checked out on all sides, so I figured he was harmless." He frowned. "Was I wrong?"

Eric put his hands on his hips and sighed. "Not that I can see. What about after he got home? Did anyone come back out?"

Dudley scratched his head. "Nay. I didn't want to take any chances with a stranger who showed up out of nowhere, so I posted some extra guards. They said it was dark and quiet all night long."

Eric nodded, appreciating Dudley's care.

"Anything wrong?"

Not sure he wanted to explain his suspicions, Eric smiled and said, "Nay, I'm being paranoid, I guess. You covered everything just as you should." Slapping the older man on the back, Eric thanked him and moved on.

Now he was really confused. Cal showed all the signs of having been controlled. But why? What motive did Mason have? What could he hope to accomplish with a half-blind old man?

Stopping where he was on the hill, Eric stared at the ground. The symptoms Cal displayed this morning made it clear that the effects of Mason's control had passed. There was no fear of Cal acting outside of his own power now. So, what was the point? What game was Mason playing?

20

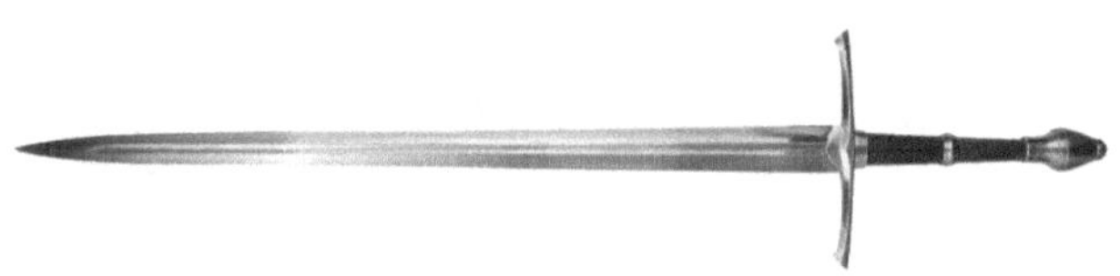

When they hope for good, evil comes; when they look for light, darkness falls.
-The Sacred Code

The Gateway

"Hashore gives us the advantage of distance," Bruin explained to Mason as they slowly made their way across the rocky terrain. "Its location in the bluffs shields it from the eyes and ears of the Stewards, which allows the region a bit more freedom to live outside the rigid expectations of the Old Realm. The emperor still has a loyal following there, despite the Passions' efforts. But, as with any kingdom, there is always the threat of rebels."

Mason shifted his position on his saddle, his back growing weary from the long ride. "Which is why Emperor Jader is targeting it for pickups."

Bruin's dark brows lowered. "He's not *targeting* anyone, Mason. This is part of being a leader."

"Aye. Of course." Mason winced at his poor choice of words.

"Hashore has a very—shall I say—*assorted* population. There are always those who think they know what's best for everyone around them. Technically, Hashore is a New Realm region, but a few leaders got the notion they could start a resistance movement and even declared they were seceding from the New Realm. You'd think the fools would know by now the idiocy in even attempting it." Disgust colored his voice.

He cast a glance at Mason and went on. "Despite the opposition of a minority, we have a very faithful following in Shales, including a reliable contact who always knows what is happening in the surrounding areas. He's very good at uncovering potential uprisings. We'll stop by his place first."

Mason nodded but had trouble generating much interest. Silence fell, and he settled in for a quiet ride. The moon was hidden by clouds, and only a few stars dared to make an appearance. The wooded hills around them were still, save for an occasional call of a night bird or croak of a frog. The perfect night for a midnight stroll with a special someone.

Except there would be no stroll. Not on this night. And maybe not for many more.

Mason sighed deep within his spirit, taking care that Bruin did not see his shifting disposition. Stirring in his saddle, he looked behind him. Dreeya and Areem rode without a word, both looking lost in thought. The rest of the band was just as quiet, no one daring to disturb the stillness. For some reason, the quiet bugged him. It gave him too much time to think.

If Seria was here, she'd be talking my ear off. His lips twitched. It was a trait he had found irritating at first. But now he enjoyed hearing what she had to say. She was very open with her feelings and just as direct with her beliefs. Even if she knew someone would not agree.

Mason's brows lowered at the extent of their differences. What kind of future could they hope for if they stood on opposite sides of an impassable chasm?

Not liking the direction of his thoughts, Mason straightened his shoulders and gave himself a mental shake. Now he was acting like Seria with all her doubts. He had no idea what their tomorrows held, but he was sure of one thing. That canyon would not keep him from her. Somehow, he would build a bridge between the two.

He wondered how long it had taken the old man to reach the fort the night before. Smart as she was, it would not take Seria long to figure out Mason was behind it. He wished he could have seen her reaction, though. It was a small thing he could do for her, as well as an act of appreciation for Lena. But it felt right.

Shales, the Gateway

The town of Shales was nestled deep within the territory of Hashore and, at their unhurried pace, took Bruin's company all night to reach. By the time Mason saw the outline of the settlement under the rising sun, he felt as if he had traveled forever. All he wanted was to get off his horse and sleep in a real bed.

Their arrival was met with a lot of curious stares and a few resentful ones. There was a dramatic drop in the noise level as they rode through the main street to the business section.

Bruin tossed him an arrogant grin. "Can you smell it?"

"Smell what?"

"Respect." Bruin motioned with his head. "These people know the consequences of turning against Jader. Very few would try it again." Bruin drew in a long, satisfied breath through his nostrils. "You can feel it every time we pass through their borders. They respect us, to the point of fearing us. They'd hand over their own kids if we asked. Many of them have."

Mason's stomach squirmed at Bruin's pompous gloat.

The commander sat tall in his saddle, leading the way until they came to a stop before a small, well-built structure with a flatwood roof.

"This is the home of Larence Shagbut," Bruin said as he slid off his horse. He handed his reins over to a Darkman named Greggor. "You all stay out here and keep an eye on things."

Mason exchanged looks with Areem, who only shrugged and slouched into a more comfortable position, resigned to a long wait.

The morning was already warm, drawing beads of sweat that ran down the sides of his face. He waved a fly away and squinted at the sunshine, gauging the time. Off-key singing sounded from a nearby house and a couple of dogs fought somewhere out of sight.

Bored, Mason hooked a knee around his saddle pommel and looked behind him at the small crowd accompanying them, spotting Crue among the servants. The boy seemed to have handled the rigors of the trail quite well. Mason had debated whether to bring him or not, as this was far from a pleasure trip. But several brought their servants along, and Mason was not sure how Crue would fare with him gone.

A few short months ago, he would not have given Crue a second thought. Dreeya had very nearly had him kicked out of the camp for some mild damage to her saddle. Mason offered Crue a chance to work for him, a decision he had not regretted once.

More than a half hour went by, and Bruin did not make an appearance. Mason rested his chin on his hand, absently studying the mild activity taking place on the street. A few people moved about, casting furtive glances at the small company of Darkmen waiting outside the house. Bruin was right; the people here did fear Jader's authority. Some of those passing by opened their eyes wide at the sight of the band of Darkmen, then dropped their gaze and moved quickly on by.

Letting out a soft sigh, Mason watched a stooped figure make his way across the street. The man looked to be in his early thirties, but his pace was extremely slow and painstaking. His worn face seemed permanently etched in a wince, and he held one hand against the small of his back. His stance was so awkward and stiff, that Mason hurt just to look at him.

Boy, he's in bad shape.

With nothing else to do, Mason watched as, inch-by-inch, the man made his way across the road, a few impatient horsemen railing at his slow pace as they bypassed him. He was almost to the other side when a small blond boy hurried to him, putting one arm around the man's waist. The man braced himself against the boy's shoulder, though clearly trying not to put too much weight on the small frame.

Mason's attention was drawn to the boy, shaking shaggy hair from his thin face. He straightened in his saddle with a jolt. Byron! He observed with more interest as the pair made it to the door.

So that's Byron's father. Seria had not exaggerated about his condition. There was no denying the man's agony with every step.

Byron moved aside to let his father enter, then paused and glanced back, as if he somehow knew he was being watched. His eyes widened when they met Mason's, who shot him a warning look and a barely detectable shake of his head. Byron dropped his gaze and disappeared into the house, but not before Mason read the boy's pleasure at seeing him.

Bruin finally returned, looking quite satisfied. "We'll leave everyone at the campsite to set up, but we're riding out."

"Are we starting the pickups today, Commander?" Dreeya asked.

Pulling himself up on his horse, Bruin settled in and nodded. "Tonight. Seems the town of Prusha is in need of a little visit."

Prusha, the Gateway

The time drew short. Mason could sense the excitement in the riders around him as Bruin gave a few last-minute directions. Dreeya tightened up the girth on her saddle, and Areem practically bounced in his excitement.

"Are you ready?" Bruin asked him.

"Sure." Mason's heart rate began to pick up. They were perched at the edge of Prusha, ready to make their move. Though he had never assisted before in a pickup, he had been to the secret location of Joshun during the training process of the subjects. He would do what was necessary.

Bruin nodded. "You've got a lot of greenhorns in your troop. Get them ready."

"Aye, sir." Mason turned his horse and trotted the few steps to where Dreeya and Areem, among others, waited for him.

"We're going in on the east side. Bruin's taking another band around the west."

Areem nodded, while Dreeya gave him a bland stare.

"For a lot of you, this is your first big assignment." Mason looked at Areem. "The important thing to remember is to follow orders. Don't go off on your own, or Bruin'll have your head." He looked around to make sure his point had been taken.

"Okay, we're looking for sturdy targets between seven and ten." Mason went on. "Get in and get out. Keep it as simple as you can, and watch out for one another. I'll be holding the east end. You'll meet with some resistance, so react as needed, but we're not looking for an all-out war. We already have that in the Gateway. These are Jader's people. They'll know what this is all about."

"What are we waiting for?" Areem asked, ready to burst with anticipation.

Mason studied him briefly. When was the last time he had displayed the same enthusiasm? "We're waiting on Bruin's signal."

It came a few minutes later, a single bugle blow from the far end of town. "All right, let's go." Mason led his group of twelve into the town. He could hear the startled yells from the people ahead. Bruin had already made his presence known.

There was chaos in the street. It was getting dark, but not so late that everyone had retired to their homes yet. Not that it mattered. Darkmen stormed the streets and broke through doors, searching for their targets. Most kids were promptly released if they were not deemed fit enough. Some were kept.

A scream drew Mason's attention to the side, where Greggor dragged a young boy by the elbow from his home. The boy fought and cried, but Greggor moved on, his grip firm. A man with a bloody face and a weeping woman burst from the house, but Dreeya, on her horse, cut them off until Greggor threw the sobbing boy on his horse and mounted up behind him. And then they were gone.

Men and women darted from out in the open, sheltering their youngsters against them, and dashed for safety. Screams and cries erupted on every side as boys and girls were snatched from the street, ripped from their parents' arms.

Mason held his position at his end, struggling to keep his roan under control. He kept a careful watch, noting the number of kids that had already been pulled onto the backs of the Darkmen's horses. Muscle memory kept him moving, guarding his location, driving back the adults who tried to follow their children. His Shadowstone warmed his breastbone, numbing him to the emotions of what took place before his eyes.

He was here to do a job.

Bruin maintained control in the middle of the pandemonium, his cold gaze alert, always watching. At one point, he kicked his horse's flanks to cut off a young boy running across the street to reach his parents. Bruin reached down, took hold of the back of the boy's shirt, and lifted him in the air. The parents screamed and ran after him, but Bruin ignored them. He held the boy against his horse until he came up alongside Dreeya, then swung the child carelessly up to her. Dreeya grabbed him and hauled him onto her horse.

The scene played out before Mason in a matter of seconds. A strange knot began to form in his gut. With his mind's eye, he saw Seria kneeling before Byron, her hand gently touching his shaggy blonde hair. Mason shook his head. Touched his Shadowstone. Reset his focus. This was not the time.

Areem pursued a young father, holding tightly to the hand of his daughter. Pushing his horse between them, Areem forced them apart and snatched the girl, throwing her in the saddle in front of him. The father reached out for her, hollering out his pleas. Areem kicked at him until the man flopped down on his face, sobbing and pleading.

Mason swallowed. Areem had come a long way since the day he had been taken from his northern village ten years ago.

"Move out!" At Bruin's order, they all fell in line, thundering out of the town together. Mason could hear the wails and moans over the hoof beats.

They ran on, the horses pounding a steady beat as they left the town behind them. Bruin sent a few riders with no kids to mask their trail.

Night fell before Bruin brought them to a walk so they could pass through a thick grove of trees. Jagged rocks and outcroppings broke through the ground all around them, closing them in.

Mason recognized the setting and sighed. They had arrived at Jader's secret location of Joshun.

Unbeknownst to most people, Joshun was not a town, but a small clearing tucked into the Slate Mountains. Built against the Slates was Stonehard—a massive structure of three stories and housing nearly a hundred rooms, not including the dungeons. There were few windows, leaving much of the interior of the castle shrouded in darkness at all hours of the day.

The building had been used by Darkmen to train their young recruits. Very few knew of its exact location, making it a secure spot to hold their young subjects until they were ready to graduate to a more permanent position.

"Good work!" Bruin called out as they approached the tall doors.

Dreeya wrestled with the boy in her grasp. "Can we get these little monsters where they belong?"

Mason watched the kids. Some struggled in their captors' hold, like Dreeya's boy. Others sat huddled in the saddle, afraid to move. Every one of them wore wide-eyed expressions of terror and dread. These kids had no idea what was ahead. The adjustment would be hard, but it was all for a greater purpose.

Even so, he tried not to think of how Seria would react if she knew.

Bruin appeared before him. "You all right?"

"Sure."

Bruin scrutinized him. "A first-time pickup can be a bit rattling if you're not used to it."

Mason snorted. "Not for Areem."

Both men looked to see Areem sitting astride his horse proudly. The girl he had taken sat frozen in his arms, pale white and trembling.

Bruin chuckled. "He seems to be taking it all in stride. Let's get these kids inside."

Mason stayed outside to tend to his horse, trying not to think about what was happening inside. He checked the saddle and gave the horse a friendly pat on the shoulder. The animal had unbridled energy and an almost belligerent expression on his face, as if looking for the right moment to leave his rider in the dust.

Taking a deep breath, Mason stepped back and looked up at Stonehard. Certainly, the next few months would be difficult, but in the end, the youngsters would be better citizens for it. Both Dreeya and Areem were stronger and harder, unmoved by the usual trifles of life, more focused and driven. Dreeya could act a bit childish when she did not get her way but never when she had a job to do. And Areem had already thrown himself into his work despite his age and inexperience. He was the youngest Darkman chosen to be privy to the location.

And those were the kinds of people the world needed. Life was harsh and unfair. Mason knew that better than most. Weak-minded persons would only drag everyone around them down and make their way of living more difficult. The world needed more hard-nosed, practical men and women who could get things done.

That's what the pickups were all about. Taking children from environments where they would grow up uneducated, vulnerable, and unprofitable, and turning them into strong, useful members of society. And that was something for which he need feel no shame in taking part.

It would get easier with time. He was sure of it.

Stonehard, Joshun, the Gateway

The pickup in Prusha had gone off without a hitch, much to Bruin's satisfaction. In all, seven boys and girls had been acquired. And everyone would hear about it. Not bad for a virgin run.

Bruin sat in the main room as the kids were transported to their dark chambers. They would spend the first night sleeping on cold, hard floors, without meals. Then they would receive enough to sustain them as the drilling began, for which he would assign new trainers.

Mason had always been effective with the kids in their later phases, but Bruin doubted Jader would want to leave him at Stonehard indefinitely. There was still hope the Reader would face off with Eric again.

Dreeya could probably run the place. The young woman was cold and no-nonsense, just what the kids needed. His mind made up, Bruin began to carry out his next plans. He would leave Dreeya here, along with a small company, to manage the place and keep the kids in line, freeing him to move on to other places of interest.

Once the arrangement was in place, Bruin headed back outside, where the rest of his team waited for their next assignment.

Mason mounted up without a word, the big roan dancing about underneath him.

Bruin watched the horse for a moment. "He's raring to go."

The gelding tossed his head and tried to bolt. Mason spun it back around in a tight circle. "Always."

"Just make sure you don't get left behind." His voice was low and heavy with unspoken meaning.

Mason caught it and met his gaze with a hard one of his own. "That won't happen, sir."

"I hope not." Bruin gave the call to move and led the men and women from Stonehard back to the main camp.

The young Shadowman did his job without hesitation, and he did it well. But there was a distance that left Bruin unsettled and wary.

But Jader trusted him, so Bruin had no choice but to leave things be. He would, however, keep a sharp eye on him.

21

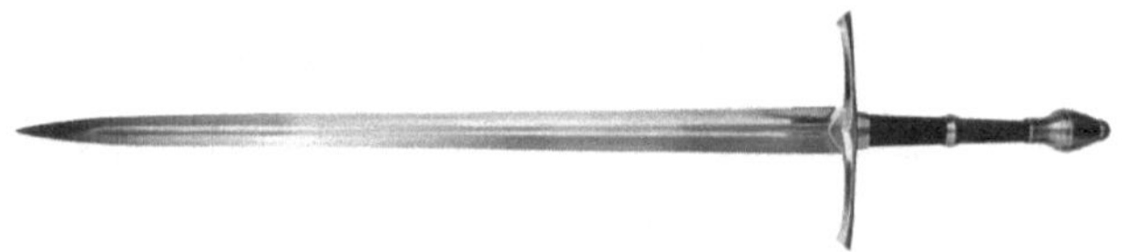

Mason's parting gift of sending Lena's grandfather to the fort had lifted Seria's spirits, so she determined not to wallow in his absence and went about her daily tasks as usual. There was always plenty to do, and she was glad to stay busy. It kept her from worrying about what he might be doing out there under Jader's order.

The morning had already seen her back and forth between the mess hall and infirmary, thanks to a small—but not serious—outbreak of croup. She hoped to get a quick visit to Sanjo, who had been sorely neglected lately. Fortunately, she had no worries about his care, thanks to the gruff but kindhearted blacksmith. But before she knew it, it was almost dinnertime, so she hurried back to the mess hall.

Eric's voice reached her ear, and she paused, looking about her before realizing it was around the corner of the Great Hall ahead. Not sure who he was talking to, she cautiously peered around.

He stood over the stone pool in the courtyard, staring down with his Beacon tilted in the water. A sad smile lit his face. "'Tis just another birthday, Father."

King Aden's voice sounded from the well. "Nonetheless, I wanted to spend it with you."

"It's more important you get well. I don't want you pushing yourself and making yourself more ill."

There was a deep sigh, followed by a raspy cough. "I hate to admit it, but you are right. It would not be wise to travel in this condition. But if you were home, we'd celebrate as we always have."

"There will be other birthdays."

There was a long pause. "You take care, son." Aden sounded choked up.

Seria turned and walked the other way at that point, but what she had heard rang in her ears. Eric's birthday! And if she knew him, he had no intention of letting anyone know and would let the day pass as all the others.

She frowned. Surely something could be done for the prince's birthday. Her friendship with him lately had been so strained, that it seemed right to do this one small thing for him. Especially since his father was unable to come. Eric gave so much of himself every day to the people around him. Couldn't they give something back to him?

It took all day for her to come up with a plan, but as soon as she could, Seria set out to find Dudley or Braylee, her mind made up. She found them both talking to Ollen outside the Steward quarters.

Dudley saw her coming first and sent her a wide smile, assuring her it was all right to join them.

"To what do we owe this pleasure?" he asked.

She hesitated only a moment before plunging ahead. "Did you know the prince's birthday is coming up?"

Surprise flashed across his face, and he looked to Braylee. "Goodness, it is coming, isn't it?"

Braylee shook his head. "I'd almost forgotten. And of course, he wouldn't say anything."

Dudley scratched his whiskered chin. "It used to be cause for a big celebration in Calla."

"I think we should celebrate it here," Seria spoke up.

"Celebrate it how?" Dudley asked.

"Like a dinner or something. I know it won't be anything grand like he's used to. But we should do something." She held her breath as the three men exchanged looks.

"It's a nice thought," Braylee said, "but I'm not sure it's the best time."

"Of course, it is!" She was not to be put off. "What's the point in a war that protects the right of people to live freely if we're not free to even live? Surely it can't hurt to set aside a few hours to honor someone who's set aside his whole life for the sake of his kingdom."

Dudley let out a chuckle. "Well, when you put it that way..."

Braylee winced. "It sounds good, but we'd be hard put convincing Prince Eric to let us go through all that trouble for him."

"True." Dudley rubbed his chin.

Seria jumped in. "We'll surprise him!"

"Hmm." Dudley turned to Ollen, who had been very quiet through the exchange. "We could use your promotion as a cover."

Seria's eyes flew to the younger man. "Promotion?"

"That's right." Dudley smacked him on the back. "Our young Steward here has been selected to become our newest lieutenant."

"Ollen, that's wonderful!" She clasped her hands together. "Or should I address you as Lt. Ollen now?"

Ollen smiled. "That's not necessary. I'll still answer to plain ol' Ollen."

"You wouldn't feel you were being slighted, would you?" Braylee checked with him.

"Not at all. I'd be happy to have a reason *not* to be the focus of attention, as well as play a role in pulling the wool over the prince's eyes."

"It could work, then," Dudley said. "We wouldn't have to make a big shindig out of it."

Seria agreed. "All we'd need is a couple of hours to eat and visit."

"Might be good for the men's morale, too," Braylee added. "I think all this waiting and wondering has some of them discouraged."

"We'll do it." Dudley pointed to Seria. "This was your idea, so you see what Nola can have for us. I'll arrange to have the hall ready."

"I'm sure Ayna and Lena would be happy to help as well."

Dudley looked at Braylee. "You might be the best one to get him over here without letting it slip what's going on."

"You want me to hide the truth from a man who can sense when something's not right the moment he steps into a room?" he deadpanned. "Great."

Ollen winced. "I don't envy you. Now, if you'll excuse me, I need to relieve Lionel at the wall." He gave them all a bow before taking his leave.

Seria's conscience smote her as he walked away. She had neglected this friend of hers lately. Maybe with Mason gone, she could resume their Steward lessons.

But her heart soared as the captains bid her goodbye and moved away to see to their tasks. It was going to happen! Eric would have his celebration. It may not be the kind he would receive at home, but it felt good to be able to give in some small way to the man who had done so much for her.

As much as she hated to admit it, there was a bit of a release in knowing that her meetings with Mason had come to a temporary stop. Lena was right. She was taking a huge risk in meeting with him. For the time being, she could stop worrying about it and focus on the present.

Of course, she still missed him fiercely and longed for him. And while she was beyond touched that he had sent Lena's grandfather into the sanctuary of his family and the fort, she also worried about what that meant for any future visits.

But for now, she would continue to build a life for herself at the fort. And that meant repairing some of the friendships she had set aside.

Starting with Ollen.

Ollen stood at the top of the wall, barely listening to Lionel as he filled him in on everything he had witnessed while on guard duty.

The news of his promotion had taken him by surprise. It was everything he had worked for the last few years, but the timing seemed off. He wasn't as excited as he should be. Maybe because he knew that with the title came more responsibility. Was he up for that?

He leaned his elbows against the wall and let out a breath. The idea of war never frightened him before. It was not as if he had never seen battle. He had been to Rackson. He had fought the night of the Shadowmen infiltration.

So why did the very idea of fighting again make him freeze up inside?

If only Uralis Faunt was still alive. Ollen wasn't quite comfortable talking to the prince or one of the captains about this, but the former marshal had always made time to listen to him.

"Ollen, you're not listening."

He tossed Lionel a glance. "What makes you say that?"

"Because I just told you I watched a grizlon dance with the prince in the courtyard."

Ollen snorted. "Really?"

Lionel frowned. "You're no fun to talk to anymore, you know that?"

"Sorry, friend."

"What's she doing here?"

Ollen turned to see who Lionel was looking at and straightened as Seria approached. He was vaguely aware of Lionel moving off down the wall before she stood before him, looking hesitant.

"I wanted to make sure I gave you a proper congratulations on your new promotion," she said, clasping her hands behind her. "I'm very happy for you."

"Thank you. I hope I'm up for the job."

She gave a decisive nod. "You will be."

For some reason, her simple statement lit a spark of hope that she was right. This was what he had always dreamed of, working up the ranks of the Stewards. What Uralis had trained him for.

"I feel like I've neglected you lately."

"You make me sound like a forgotten puppy."

She laughed. "That's not what I meant at all. It's just I've had so much going on that we haven't had a chance to talk for a while, and I've been missing my Steward lessons. But I would love to plan another time to talk."

"So, your time has become a little more free?"

Her gaze flittered to the valley outside the wall they stood on. "Aye. For now." She took a quick breath. "But only if you are available."

"Well, I don't know." He stroked his chin and waited long enough for her brows to bunch. Then he winked. "How about tomorrow afternoon?"

Her face relaxed. "Tomorrow would be fine. Should we meet in the mess hall as usual?"

An idea hit him. "How about the training field?"

"The training field?" She blinked at him.

"Aye. I think it's time you see how the Stewards train for battle."

"Oh, that sounds wonderful!" Her smile lifted his spirits.

"Good." His mind failed with what more to say.

She exhaled. "Well, I'll let you get back to your duty, and I'll talk to you tomorrow. Good night to you both." She raised her voice to include Lionel, who waved in response.

Ollen watched her descend the stairs and disappear into the fading light.

"I don't know why you bother spending so much time with her."

His neck heated, and he sent his friend a dark scowl. "What's that supposed to mean?"

"For someone who gave Prince Eric such a hard time, you're awfully willing to forgive and forget all she's done."

"That's not fair," Ollen responded testily. "You know that wasn't all her fault. Besides, it was Seria who got me to thinking about my actions toward the prince."

Lionel huffed. "She gives you the cold shoulder for weeks, and now suddenly she has time for you?"

"That's funny coming from you, considering you still give her the cold shoulder."

"I don't trust her." Lionel frowned. "I think she's stuck on that Darkman."

The words settled on him like a rock, heavy and cold, but Ollen could not deny that there may be a small measure of truth in them. He suspected Seria had had her heart broken by the Darkman. If so, one could not expect her to recover without any scars or trust issues. "She's a friend," he said, quieter now. "For me, that's enough."

Lionel shook his head. "It's your time, your choice." He stood and smacked Ollen's shoulder as he passed by on his way to leave. "I just hope you don't regret it someday."

Ollen let out a big sigh. *So do I.*

22

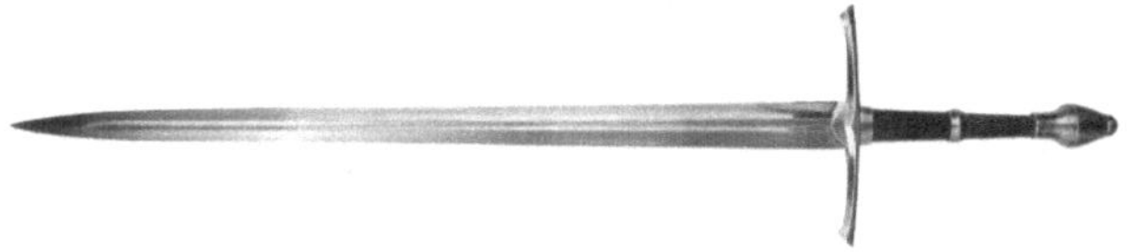

Darkmen camp, the Gateway

Mason jerked awake, disturbing dream remnants lingering in his memory. Pictures flashed before him in the darkness of the tent. The streets awash with frantic parents. Kids screaming as they were snatched.

Sitting up with a low groan, Mason covered his face with his hands, trying to dispel the images. The pickups had followed him into his sleep.

"Sir, are you all right?" Crue asked from the other end of the tent.

"I'm fine. Go back to sleep." He winced at the curtness of the order. There was no need to bite the kid's head off. The dream was not his fault.

After Crue settled back down onto his cot, Mason threw his blanket off and grabbed his shirt and his sword.

No one else was up, save for the night guards. Mason gave one a slight wave as he passed by, muttering something about needing some air. He walked on, not caring where he ended up. Had he been home, he would have found his ledge that overlooked the valley, from where he could see the village and remember the precious times he managed to share with Seria.

But he was far from Seria now, and for some reason, thinking about her tonight made him uncomfortable. Because no matter how hard he tried to convince himself she would understand, he knew the truth. He could only imagine her disappointment if she learned he was a part of taking kids from their homes and families. She would never understand. In her mind, what he did would be no better than what the Stewards had done.

But the kids they took were still alive. His brother and the other boys at Handan were dead, killed by the bloody hands of the Stewards.

Wandering around the woods without aim, he lost track of the time. He really should be using this time to rest up. After the rigors of the nightly pickups, he was exhausted.

A headache began to form, and he stopped to rub his temples. Dawn approached. It would be best to get back before Bruin missed him. He turned to retrace his steps and then heard a snap in the woods ahead. Tensing, he reached for his sword and waited. There was another rustle. Whoever it was, they were not very careful.

Tightening his hold on the hilt, Mason moved forward, eyes and ears open. Pausing at the base of a huge tree trunk, he listened. Mason waited until they were close, then stepped out, his blade at the ready.

Byron's head bobbed in surprise, and he took a faltering step back.

Mason scowled, his blood racing. "Blades, boy! What are you doing out here?"

Byron didn't answer, his attention fixed on the sword. Mason slid it back in its sheath, out of sight. "I asked you a question."

"I was hunting." Byron dropped his gaze.

"You're a little ways from town, aren't you?"

Byron shrugged and squirmed, his eyes flickering up once.

"You got lost?"

The boy raised his chin. "I just got turned around."

"Hmm." He looked down at the skinny wild rabbit hanging on Byron's belt. "I see you got something. How'd you catch him?"

"Slingshot."

Mason raised his brows. "Good shot. But this isn't the time or place for you to be wandering out in these woods, kid." He did not even want to think what would have happened had Bruin or Areem come upon him. "You should've waited for your father to go with you."

Byron bit his lip and stared at the ground again. Remembering the state Bryon's father was in, Mason sighed. The man was far from being able to move around in these woods.

"Let's get you back before you have your folks worrying."

Byron's eyes lit up at his words.

It was a quiet walk through the woods, as Byron was not a chatty kid. Mason caught him glancing over at him every now and then, eyeing his height or the length of his stride.

Mason spoke after they had walked for over an hour. "Boy, you really did wander far."

"I didn't mean to. I was chasing the rabbit, and I didn't notice."

"Well, at least you got your rabbit."

A small smile appeared, gone almost as soon as Mason had seen it.

The stillness was broken by a loud yip in the woods and Byron tensed, stepping closer to Mason.

"It's just a black fox somewhere, looking for its mate," Mason said.

Another silence stretched, then Byron asked, "You can read people's minds, can't you?"

Mason sent him a sharp look, but Byron did not look at him. "What makes you say that?"

He shrugged. "You always react to things like you know more than what people are telling you."

The boy's perception impressed him. "Aye. I can read people's thoughts."

Nothing more was said about it.

As they neared the town, Mason was tempted to send Byron on the well-worn path and head back. Instead, he walked alongside him as they broke through the woods and entered the sleepy town of Shales. Byron led the way through the quiet streets until they approached his cabin.

"Oh, Byron!"

Mason looked up to see a rail-thin woman standing in the doorway. By the look of relief on her face, Mason guessed it was Byron's mother.

Byron quickened his pace to meet her, allowing her to fold him in her arms. Mason watched them for a moment, then turned to leave.

"Please, don't go!" The woman's call surprised him. "Won't you come in for a little bit?"

"Nay, that's all right." He lifted his hand.

"Oh, but you must let me at least get you a hot cup of tea on this chilly morning."

Her offer caught him off guard. "That's not necessary."

"I insist." She opened the door wide to let him in.

"But...I..." One glance at Byron's hopeful face, and his feet moved towards the rundown shack.

"I'm Keeli Jayes, by the way." The woman held her hand out to him. Her hand was thin, with dark veins crisscrossing under her gauzy skin. She was so slight and pale, a big gust of wind could up and carry her off.

"I was so worried about Byron this morning." Keeli pulled out a worn chair for him to sit at the table. "He's always going out and about, but I didn't expect him to go out so soon. Or so long." She sent him a scolding look. "When he didn't come in for breakfast, I knew something was wrong."

"I got lost."

At least the kid was honest.

"And you helped him find his way?" Keeli sent Mason a warm smile.

"Well...aye, I guess."

Byron swung the rabbit up on the table. Keeli brightened. "Good job, son!" She made no mention of how little meat was on the animal. "We'll have us some rabbit stew for dinner!"

His face glowing at his mother's approval, Byron moved away. It was only then Mason saw the other children sitting on a cot in the corner of the room, watching him. Five of them in fact, all younger than Byron. How could that many kids be so quiet?

"Please, won't you join us?" Keeli motioned to the chair he still had not taken. "Michael will be back in just a moment."

The door opened, and the stooped-over man from the street entered. He moved about a little easier this morning, though still slow and stiff. Byron immediately rose to help him to a chair. "Well, look who decided to join us for breakfast!" His voice boomed as he ruffled the boy's hair. "You had your mother worried, son."

"Michael, we have a guest," Keeli spoke up. "I'm sorry, I don't even know your name."

"It's...ah...Mason." Awkwardness invaded his veins, and his mouth went dry.

Michael immediately put his hand out. "Glad to meet you." With slow, careful movements, he lowered himself to a chair. "Pass him the biscuits, Mama. We don't want our guest going hungry."

It only took a sweeping glance to see there was not much food on the table. A plate of biscuits and a pan of some dark gravy. "There's no need," Mason said. "I need to be getting back." At the flash of pride in Michael's eyes, he fell silent. These people would not send a guest from their home without sharing what they had, no matter how meager.

Feeling more and more uncomfortable, Mason allowed Keeli to dish him up a plate; she did not spare him. "Thanks." The word fell short to his own ears. He glanced around at the rest of the plates. No one had a full serving.

"Eat up." Michael waved a hand at him. "And tell us how you came to find our Byron this morning."

"I just happened across him in the woods." Mason talked around a bite. He was surprised at the lightness in the biscuits and the flavor of the gravy. Keeli Jayes may not have much to cook with, but she could cook what she had. "Thought I'd walk him back so he wouldn't get lost again." He looked over at Byron, who gave him a wry grin.

"Appreciate that." Michael nodded. "We moved here not long ago, and Byron isn't real familiar with these woods yet."

Keeli shook her head. "I don't like him going out by himself. But Michael says he's as capable as a grown man."

Mason did not doubt it. In the little bit of time he had spent with him, he could see wisdom beyond his years in the boy.

"Besides that, there's very little that could harm him out here," Michael added.

Thinking of the Darkmen camped less than an hour outside of Shales and the grizlons contained a little further than that, Mason gave him a small, tight smile.

"Mama, I want some more," a little girl of about four whispered.

Michael asked where Mason was from, as if trying to cover the conversation at the end of the table.

Keeli, meanwhile, turned and spoke in low tones to the girl that she had had enough. Mason found it suddenly hard to swallow his bite.

"Um, I come from up north. I've lived in Ignadon for the last seven years." Mason watched Byron discreetly tear off part of his biscuit and hand it to his sister.

"I see." Michael rested his elbows on the table. "So, what brings you to Shales?"

Mason gave him a quick look but ascertained that the man had no idea he was a part of the Dark Army or that he had any connection to Seria. "Business, so I may not be here long."

He squirmed under the other man's gaze. This was the most uncomfortable meal he had ever shared with anyone, yet he could see these were decent, honest people. Their kids were quiet and polite at their side of the table, none of them complaining over the meager meal. The shabby house was clean and orderly.

"Speaking of business, I better get to work." Michael painstakingly pushed himself from the table, and Mason wondered how he could handle working a whole day.

"It was nice to meet you, Mason. Feel free to come by anytime."

"Ah, thanks." He stood and shook the man's hand again.

"You working late today?" Michael asked Keeli.

Mason had to work to keep from gawking at them. This frail woman was holding down a job? Then a quick glance into Byron's knowing eyes told him why. Keelie Jayes was forced to take on work so they could pay the new tax. Jader's new war tax.

"Only for the afternoon," she said, receiving Michael's kiss on the cheek.

After charging his kids to be good for their mama, Michael left. Keeli smiled at Mason, her pride in her husband shining from her face.

"I, um, I better go, too." He could hardly wait to flee the room.

"I'm so glad I had a chance to meet you." Keeli's tone was gracious. "Thank you again for helping Byron find his way."

Mason looked at Byron again. "Just don't get lost again."

"Aye, sir."

Glancing around at the group of youngsters staring up at him, Mason gave Keeli another nod, then made his escape.

He stood on the porch, mulling over what he had witnessed. Seria had said Byron's family was hard-working and proud. He could see now that it was true. They were both willing to work to provide for their family. Looking for a handout was the last thing on their minds. On the contrary, they were more concerned with sending him away fed than they were about themselves.

And Byron. Mason could not believe how wrongly he had judged the kid. Byron had given up the last of his breakfast, scant as it was, for the other children. He was up before dawn to provide his family with food and took whatever job was offered to him to help his parents in whatever manner he could.

Mason shook his head, feeling very small. *I owe Seria an apology.*

23

In the Lambient can be found truth, hope, and love.
-The Sacred Code

"Are you too busy to talk to me now that you don't need me?"

Seria stopped at the sound of Lena's teasing voice behind her. "I'm sorry. My mind's in the clouds." She hugged her friend tight. "It seems like forever since I've seen you."

Lena raised a brow. "It's been what, four whole days?"

"Aye, but..."

Lena winked. "I know. After getting together every night or so, it feels like it's been a while."

"How is your grandfather?"

"He's doing well, thank you. Settling in better than I thought he would, to be honest."

Seria looked around and lowered her voice. "What do you think made him change his mind?"

Lena laughed. "As if you and I don't both know. Mason is the only one who could have convinced my stubborn grandfather to leave his cabin." Her face softened. "And I'm very appreciative to you both."

"I'm glad he's safe and sound with his family."

"Me, too." Lena crossed her arms. "Mama sent me to talk to you about party business."

"Oh. Well..." Seria hesitated, not wanting to put Ollen off again. "I was just heading to the training fields to meet someone. You want to sit with me until they finish?"

Lena tapped her chin. "Hmm. Have a legitimate reason to watch the big, strong men in their element? I suppose I could suffer through it."

Seria laughed out loud and took her arm. "I hope it's not too much for you."

They set off for the back gate, already deep in conversation by the time they reached the guardsman. He tipped his head to them both, his attention lingering on Lena as they passed.

"Someone's taken notice of you, Lena," Seria teased after they were beyond earshot.

Lena chuckled. "In case you're not aware, there is a shortage of females in the fort. They notice anyone wearing a dress who is unattached and under the age of thirty."

The afternoon was warm and breezy, the blue sky streaked with feathery white clouds. Seria picked a spot in the grass to sit and shaded her eyes against the sun. "Looks like they're still at it."

Lena gazed down at the group of Stewards clad in green leather training suits. "It's been a while since I've sat in on a training session."

"Oh, you've done this before?"

"Sure." Lena batted her eyes. "Where else is a girl supposed to get such a display of manhood?"

Seria laughed. "Don't tell me a Steward has caught the attention of the fort's very own baker, Lena Carwright?"

Lena smiled, though her mood darkened some. "I can't deny there is some definite appeal, but I doubt any Steward would give me a chance after learning about my papa."

The words made something in Seria go cold. She had almost forgotten about Lena's father. She bit her lip and then broached the subject she had been afraid to ask about.

"Can you tell me what happened with your father?" When Lena turned to look at her, Seria put her hands up. "Unless you don't want to. Then tell me to mind my own affairs or slap my face or whatever pleases you."

Lena rolled her eyes with a grin. "Do you honestly think I would slap a friend for a genuine question?"

Seria shrugged. "I just didn't want to overstep."

"You've never overstepped, Seria."

"Even when I asked you to visit your grandfather more often so I could see Mason?"

"That's what friends are for. When you learned about my Gift, you continued to treat me as you always did."

Seria threw her arm around Lena's shoulders and gave her a squeeze. "Which is why I don't want you to feel you have to share if you're not comfortable with it."

Lena cocked a brow. "Even if you're—"

"Dying to know," Seria said, wringing her hands. When Lena threw back her head and laughed, she relaxed.

"Well, dear Seria, I have no qualms about telling you." Lena's gaze became distant. "I was about ten when he decided to join the Dark Army. We were living in a city in the New Realm at the time, and while we felt safe enough, times were hard, and Papa struggled to put food on the table. Grandfather was never a Steward loyalist, and they both believed Jader had been judged too harshly. Our life was pretty peaceful at that time."

Seria tried to imagine Lena as a young girl living somewhere other than the fort.

"He was in the army for two years before things started bothering him. He would never come out and say what it was, but even I could tell something had changed." Lena shifted her position and brushed a strand of brown hair behind her ear. Every move was graceful and assured, even here, sitting on the ground. "He and Mama spent hours talking late into the night. Finally, they told me they had decided we would leave the New Realm and go to the Gateway to live. Grandfather was not happy about the decision, but he didn't fight it. He even surprised us by deciding to join us."

Lena frowned and hugged herself. "But we never had the chance. The emperor found out that Papa was no longer as loyal as he once was. Had Papa arrested and tried for treason."

Seria held her breath at what would come next.

"He was hung on the spot."

"I'm so sorry, Lena." Seria squeezed Lena's arm. "That had to be awful."

Lena nodded. "Grandfather was devastated at the loss of his son, and Mama became frantic about leaving the New Realm. I remember her saying over and over that she would not allow Jader to use me." She shrugged. "We fled that very night."

The end of her story was so similar to Seria's last day in the New Realm that she shuddered. Her parents had also talked about going to live in the Gateway, but they never got the chance before they were murdered by greedy landowners.

"So," Lena spoke again, "while my father was wrong to join the Dark Army in the first place, I knew his motives and his heart. And that's why I firmly believe that while there are plenty of no-good soldiers carrying out Jader's mission, there could also be a lot of misguided ones."

Seria swallowed. Surely Mason was one of the misguided ones. Did he know that Jader executed his soldiers just because they chose not to follow him anymore? She bit her lip, surprised at the tears that suddenly gathered at the corners of her eyes.

Lena reached out and took her hand. "I don't know much about Mason or his past. All I know is that he won your heart, and you're the kindest, sweetest person I've ever met. So, be careful, all right?"

Trying not to take offense at the caution, Seria blinked her eyes dry. The Stewards were finishing up their training by this time, and she did not have time to press for the meaning behind Lena's words.

The knights gathered their tools and made their way up the hill back to the gates leading into the fort. A few waved and called out greetings as they passed. Prince Eric was the first to approach them, inclining his head in a polite bow. "Ladies, I hope you are well this evening?"

"Aye, we are, Prince Eric, thank you," Lena replied.

He gave a small smile, swept his gaze over both of them, then nodded and moved on.

Lena chuckled. "Our prince is sometimes at a loss for words when it comes to talking to the fairer sex."

The statement struck Seria as odd. Eric had never had trouble talking to her. Unless she was being a brat, but she was trying to do better. That's why she was adamant that his party go without a hitch.

Ollen greeted them then, bowing much like the prince had. "Ah, what a bright spot for the Stewards to find after a grueling day of training and work."

Seria laughed. "You certainly seemed to hold up just fine down there."

"I had to save my strength for my student."

"Is Sir Ollen trying to turn our very own Seria into a Stewardess?" Lena teased.

"Not at all. He's been teaching me about their ways. Do you want to join us?"

Lena dusted her hands. "As intriguing as it sounds, I need to get back home. You let me know how it turns out." Ollen offered her his hand, and she took it, rising gracefully. When Ollen stretched a hand out to Seria, she felt as clumsy as Sanjo trying to get up off the ground.

"I'll get with you tomorrow about those pastries, Lena," Seria assured as Lena followed the trail of knights filtering into the fort.

"Ah." Ollen tilted his head back. "Party business."

"That's right, so don't say anything to the prince."

He held his hand up. "I will say nothing." Then he gestured to the field below. "Shall we begin?"

The next hour was spent in the weapon's shed, talking about weapons and fighting styles. Seria found it fascinating and peppered him with questions. Remembering Lena's teasing about Stewardesses, she asked, "Are there female Stewards?"

Ollen gave an immediate nod. "We have a very strong Stewardess army."

The idea was amazing to her. "I never knew there was such a thing."

"Well, that's probably because their army is smaller, and they tend to stay close to Calla. But they've been around for years. They're fierce fighters and excel at archery."

Seria caressed the smooth wood of one of the bows on the makeshift table Ollen had set up. Although she would never tell Mason, if given a choice, she preferred archery over swordsmanship. She never got tired of watching the arrows shoot through the air and make their marks on the canvas.

"You want to try it?"

She stopped, her pulse skipping. "Could I?"

"Why not?" He gave her a wink. "I'll make sure I stay behind you."

She looked back at the bow. Could she? "I must confess, I've always wanted to."

"Then let's go." Before she could object, he led her outside to the shooting range, then jogged away to adjust the target for her. Seria bit her lip, trying to contain her eagerness.

"This might not be a good idea," she said when he returned. "I might hit something."

He chuckled. "That's the point."

Seria giggled, her fingers itching. "All right, show me what to do."

Ollen licked his lips and put an arrow to the nock, trying to ignore the way Seria's scrutiny heated his skin. He faced the target and raised the bow to his shoulder, pulling the string back.

"You hold the string steady and hold your elbow up."

"Right." She sounded so serious, taking in every word.

His throat went dry, hoping beyond hope he would not miss the board. He would have appreciated the prince's Gift of moving things with his mind right about now.

"And then you let it go." There was a long pause while he took careful aim. He released the arrow and breathed a sigh of relief when it hit the bull's eye.

"That's amazing! I don't know how you do it."

He grinned. "I just told you." He held it out to her, demonstrating where to position her hands.

"I hope I don't regret this," she said as she placed her hands where he pointed.

"That's good. Now lift it even with your shoulder."

"Like this?" She raised it higher.

"That's right." Ollen stepped behind her, took hold of her shoulders, and shifted her to face the target. The smell of her windblown hair—sunshine with a hint of something flowery—hit his nostrils, and he sucked in a breath. "Um. A little higher." He put his fingers under her elbow, tilting it up.

She tensed at his touch at first but then relaxed. He brought his other hand up and positioned it over hers. "Don't grip the arrow so hard. Just let it slide between your fingers."

His heart thudded against his chest at her nearness, the feel of her hand under his. This was a bad idea. It was too tempting to forget that they were only friends. He cleared his throat and reined in his emotions, pulling his hands back. "You ready?"

Seria gulped and narrowed her eyes at the target. "Ready."

"Then let it go."

Her hand trembled, then tightened around the bow. She hesitated a brief second, then released the arrow. It zipped straight to the canvas, burying itself right outside the biggest ring.

"I hit it!" She bounced up and down. "I never thought I'd get that close." She spun around to face him.

Ollen jerked back a safe distance and plastered a wide grin on his face. "That was great." He crossed his arms over his chest. "You, uh, you got pretty close for your first try." Did his voice sound as strained to her as it did him?

Seria chuckled and tucked her hair behind her ear. "I don't know about close. I'm surprised I hit it at all."

Her smile almost blinded him, and he busied himself with retrieving the bow she had dropped in her excitement. "Wanna try again?"

"I better not. I've still got to check in at the infirmary."

"Sure. I'll see you later."

"Ollen?"

At her soft voice, he braced himself and looked into her face, hiding a wince at the uncertainty on her face at his strange behavior. He forced another smile. "Aye?"

She relaxed. "Thank you. This was amazing."

He gave her a nod. "Sure. I'll see you later." He watched her go, calling himself every kind of fool he could think of. As soon as she was out of sight, he dropped his head back and groaned, his heart still hammering in his chest. "Good going, Ollen."

What did you think you were going to do? He grabbed at his things, stuffing them into the quiver. *Kiss her?*

Just the thought made his ears burn. What if he had followed through on his desire? He could have ruined everything.

An arrow snapped in his hold, and he brought himself up short. His bow lay carelessly on the ground, arrows scattered haphazardly at his feet. One glove was on, and the other was in a crumpled heap by his bag.

Ollen took a deep breath. "All right, you need to calm down before you break something else." He spent the next few minutes meticulously cleaning up his area, forcing his mind on his task of returning all the items to the shed. When he was done, he swung his bag over his shoulder and trekked up the hill.

From the day he had met her, he sensed a kind and generous spirit, one that would do him good to nurture. And it had paid off. Their friendship had grown, but in all that time, he had denied what was going on in his heart.

At the top of the knoll, Ollen stopped and pinched the bridge of his nose. He took a minute to study the sky, as if expecting answers. There were none, of course. He was left to deal with his painful situation on his own.

He sighed as his brow furrowed deeply. Seria had never given any indication that she wanted anything more than friendship. After having her heart broken by the Darkman, Mason Grey, he could hardly blame her for being hesitant. The last thing he wanted to do was bring her confusion or hurt.

A heavy cloud settled over him, despite the sunshine pouring over his body. The confused look on Seria's face hung heavy in his mind. His heart sank even further as he hoped he would not ruin what he had come to consider a precious friendship.

24

Follow the Light or be swallowed by darkness.
-The Sacred Code

"Mason!"

At Bruin's brusque call, Mason set aside the polish and carried his sword with him. "Aye, sir?"

"We're going to Jixon for another pickup."

"Now?"

"Now." Bruin frowned. "We're not waiting for nightfall. Word will spread, and the people will try to prepare for our coming. We're leaving as soon as we get everything packed up, so don't waste time." He stalked away, barking out orders.

Mason turned to gather his clothes. *Boy, he's in a mood today.* He shoved the last of his things into his sack and hurried out.

They were mounted in record time and followed Bruin to their new destination. The brooding commander did not say much as he led the way. Mason tried not to think about the task ahead. It was just another pickup. As soon as they had their objective number, they would move on to something else.

Bruin fell back from his position in the front to ride alongside him. "You know what to expect up here, right?"

"Of course." He had already done this three times before.

"I want to see you take part this time, Mason."

Mason snapped his gaze up. "Sir?"

Bruin's thick brows lowered over cool, gray eyes. "You have yet to acquire a subject yourself."

"You told me to hold the east end," Mason said with a frown. He had guarded his team as he had been asked.

"Aye, but I didn't mean that you didn't have to do anything more, Mason." Bruin's face was hard. "Everyone's got to pull their weight. Don't let squeamishness keep you from doing your job."

"I don't intend to." The insinuation heated his blood. He had never had any trouble getting things done.

"Good. Then I'll see you in Jixon." He raised his voice. "My party, follow me. We're going in the west end."

Mason held his eager horse in place while half of the band thundered away, swinging to the left to circle the town he could now see in the distance. Remembering Bruin's order, he set his jaw. Another picture of Seria surfaced in his mind, but he pushed her away.

Don't let her interfere with your job.

His team watched him, waiting for orders. He hardened his expression. "No slackers." The reminder was as much for him as any one of them.

They spurred their mounts to the eastern end of town. The town was already in an uproar by the time they got there. He took his position, calling out to his followers to spread out.

The streets were overrun by panicked citizens. The dust rose from the dirt paths. It was the same scene as before. Not a pretty sight, but he would do what needed to be done.

Bruin was right in that the parents were more prepared. A few put up a fight, albeit in vain. They had not gotten as many kids in the last pickup, most likely because the civilians took to hiding sooner. Hitting

Jixon while the sun was up changed the routine and caught some of them off guard.

Mason anchored himself at his post, watching out for any opportunities. The noise was deafening as parents fought, cried, or struggled for their children. He caught sight of a young mother, clutching her small boy to her diminutive frame. She somehow managed to dart in and out of the chaos unnoticed by the riders.

His muscles tightened as she headed for his end. One touch of the Shadowstone eased the thundering of his heart. He moved his horse, blocking her path, and waited.

He spoke firmly when her wide eyes met his. "Hand the boy over."

"At once." She stepped to his horse's side.

"Nay, Mama!" The boy kicked his feet and clung to her.

Ignoring the pleas, Mason took hold of the child's arm. Just as he started to pull him up in the saddle with him, a sharp pain struck between his temples. Sucking in his breath at the intensity of it, he dropped both the boy and his reins to grab his head. Unfortunately, the roan took advantage of the moment and sidestepped. Already disoriented, Mason fell out of the saddle and hit the ground with a hard thud. As he lay there groaning, the woman blinked and shook her head, her expression clearing. She took one look at him on the ground and shrieked. "You're not taking my son!" She kicked at him again and again.

Other civilians saw what was going on and jumped in to assist the mother. Paralyzed by the pain in his head, Mason could only shield his face from the blows by the enraged crowd.

An arrow shot by, and one man fell over on his back.

"Get back!"

A sharp voice cut through the noise around him, and the attack let up. Mason looked up through bleary eyes to see Bruin, his face a thundercloud, brandishing his sword. Greggor was nearby, preparing another arrow. The civilians cowered from them; the young mother fled, her child safe in her arms.

"Get on your horse." Bruin's sword held them at bay.

Mason pulled himself up on his hands and knees and tried to shake the ache that lingered. One of his men led the roan back to him. Stumbling to his feet, Mason grabbed the reins and painstakingly drew himself up on the saddle.

"Move out!" Bruin called. He cast another glance to make sure Mason was upright, then he kicked his horse and started out at a gallop. Squinting against the dim sunlight, Mason moved his horse to follow.

After they had put some distance between them and Jixon, Bruin slowed. "What happened?" he demanded.

"I'm not sure, sir." Mason massaged his temples against the fading pain, still dizzy. His whole body ached from the civilians' assault. "Everything was going fine, and then I got this...pain in my head, and I couldn't do a thing." He took a careful breath. "Then my horse dumped me in the dirt, and they all took advantage of my weak moment." His neck heated at his vulnerability.

Bruin stared at him. "A headache?"

"That's right, sir." He did not flinch at the skeptical scrutiny.

A muscle in Bruin's jaw twitched. "How are you now?"

"It's letting up," he replied stiffly.

Bruin looked around at the gathering around them. "We still got a fair number, though not as many as I'd hoped."

Mason caught the jab. Rather than try to make excuses, he lowered his head. "I apologize, sir."

"I just hope it doesn't happen again."

Mason pinched the bridge of his nose, the lingering effects of the strange headache hanging over him.

Me, too.

25

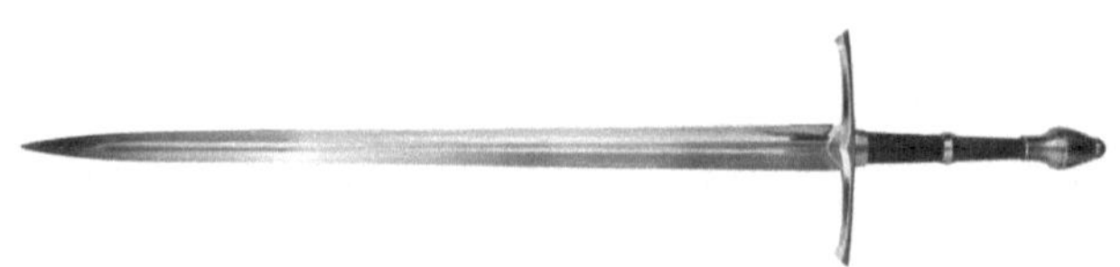

Despite the last-minute notice, the plans for Eric's birthday celebration had taken off with a fervor that surprised Seria. Everyone pulled together with gusto preparing the food, sending out the announcements, and making sure the prince was oblivious.

Seria felt as if she were running in all directions at the same time, determined that Eric would have a nice celebration, a chance to forget his troubles for a few hours. Lena was a great help, pitching in wherever she could. All was in place and ready for the next evening. Now everyone could turn their thoughts to dressing their best and enjoying an evening of food and fellowship.

Lena walked Seria to the mess hall for her morning shift as they went over last-minute party details. They met Dudley and Braylee coming out of the hall. Braylee seemed cautiously optimistic, but Dudley's eyes twinkled with anticipation.

"I think we're going to pull it off after all," he said. "Won't the prince be surprised?"

"Oh, I hope so." Seria felt herself beaming. "I do want it all to turn out nice."

"It'll be great," Lena said with a smile. "You put in too much work for it to be anything otherwise."

"It wasn't just me!" Seria corrected. "So many people have been involved. It's been wonderful watching everyone come together for the prince."

Dudley lifted his arm in a wave. "Ho, there's the new lieutenant."

Ollen approached and gave the captains a bow, and then a brief nod to the ladies, his gaze almost hesitant as it reached Seria.

"Have you got your Lieutenant suit all pressed and ready?" Dudley asked with a grin. "The prince is most anxious to see you promoted."

"Aye, sir. It's all ready for tomorrow." His smile looked strained, leading Seria to wonder if he did not look forward to the party like everyone else did. She had not had a chance to speak with him since the archery lesson two nights before.

"Good. I want you all to enjoy yourselves. Parties are scarce around here, and you're all too young to grow stale like me and Braylee."

Braylee cocked a brow at him. "Coming from the man who has been unable to talk about anything but this party since it first came up."

Dudley shrugged. "Can't say I don't still enjoy a good romp now and then." He turned his focus on Seria. "Now, you make sure you don't spend your time working. I want to see you out and about with the guests."

Seria blinked. "Oh, well, this is for Eric and his Stewards. I planned to work the tables."

"Not acceptable." Dudley's voice turned stern. "You have just as much right to enjoy the night as anyone. Any man worth a grain of salt would be more than happy to escort you like a proper lady, *not* a servant girl." He turned and pinned Ollen with a pointed look.

"Of c-course. I was thinking about that on the way over here." He cleared his throat. "I'd be happy to escort you, Miss Seria, if you would let me."

Her face warmed that Dudley had cornered him into asking. "I didn't—I don't...surely that's not necessary. It's not even for me." She turned to Lena, who stood by watching it all. "You don't have an escort, do you, Lena?"

Lena's lips twitched up. "As a matter of fact, I do."

"Oh." Why had it not occurred to her to have an escort? She had never been a part of an event like this.

Ollen's soft voice cut into her awkwardness. "None of us meant to put you on the spot."

Dudley crossed his arms, not looking the least bit remorseful.

Seria fidgeted with the strings of her apron. "I know. I just didn't expect such a fuss. But, if you're willing, I'd be happy to go with you, Ollen."

"Certainly."

She forced a small smile.

Dudley clapped his hands together. "Now that that's settled, I'll see you all tomorrow." He and Braylee, who quirked a brow up at Ollen, left the younger people and headed for the Steward quarters.

"Well, I need to go check with Mama on that batch of honey tarts," Lena said.

Seria gave her a distracted look. "Honey tarts?"

Lena smiled as she left. "Aye. I wanted to make sure we had plenty for tomorrow."

"Of course." Seria yanked on her strings like they were responsible for her tension and waited until the other woman was gone. "Ollen, I know Dudley sort of tricked you into asking, so don't feel you have to escort me. I'm happy to help with the staff, and—"

Ollen stopped her with a laugh. "As long as you don't mind going with me, I'm more than happy to be your escort. I intend to see you have a good time."

She gave a sheepish shrug. "I've never gone to a party before." Gracious, she sounded pathetic. "I mean, I planned this party. I didn't expect to actually…participate." Would she never learn to stop talking so much?

"This will be my first formal party as well."

Her eyes shot to his. "Really?"

"Mmhmm." He looked down at the ground. "I was pretty poor growing up, and we didn't get invited to many fancy events. In fact, I don't remember ever going to one, other than my own commencement ceremony."

His admission cooled the flames of her embarrassment. "Then I guess it wouldn't be inappropriate for friends to attend their first party together."

"Of course not."

"Good. I appreciate you asking. Even if Dudley initiated it."

Ollen waved in Dudley's direction. "Captain Dudley is a fine man who loves to get involved in other people's affairs."

Seria laughed and relaxed. "I suppose it comes with the job of being captain?"

"I suppose."

Her shoulders lifted as she retied the strings of her apron. "Now, I best get inside. Nola threatened to fire me the next time I was late."

He snorted. "That woman would sell her own children before she would fire you."

Mason let out a groan and rolled over on the narrow bed. He opened his eyes and frowned up at the gray walls surrounding him. Stonehard. Bruin's company had arrived here late last night, and Mason had been assigned the first watch duty. By the time he had fallen into bed, it was well past midday. No wonder he was so tired.

Swinging his feet down to the cool floor, he plodded across the room to the window. He could see streaks of color across the sky as the sun prepared to make its bed for the night. Bracing his hands against the windowpane, Mason stared down at Areem, now on duty, walking around on the ground. The newest Darkman had taken on his job without hesitation, accomplishing what he set out to do.

Unlike me recently. He rubbed his face, remembering the severe head pain he had in Jixon. He had shrugged it off, but it perplexed him. What could cause a headache so extreme that he couldn't even stay in control of one woman? In his work, he could not afford one moment of weakness. One second of losing focus could mean the difference between life and death.

It was just one instance. Probably something he had eaten come back to torment him. There was no use in getting all worked up over something that more than likely would never happen again. There were plenty more important things to dwell on.

He ached to see Seria again, to hear her infectious laugh. She had a way of making him see things in a different light, to want to be a better man. He had spent so much time looking out for himself, especially after Liam's death. Now he found himself trying to see the world through other people's perspectives.

Drawing in a long, slow breath, he let his body rest against one side of the window. If only Seria would do the same for him, to understand why he held to his convictions. He clung to the hope that someday her eyes would open to the truth.

Time was running out. Jader was making preparations to enlarge his army at the Gateway. The Dark Army would soon break through the stronghold and get into the Old Realm. Mason was counting on it, but he knew the process would be long and hard. Not to mention dangerous. He had to get Seria out before then, make her see the dangers of the Stewards' control.

The sun began its descent. He watched it in anticipation, waiting for the satisfaction of watching the darkness fall, smothering every remnant of light left. His eyes stayed fixed on the golden orb. Shadows lengthened as the sphere touched the distant horizon. A hush fell, all of nature acknowledging the day had ended. Only the night creatures would dare to be heard now.

Mason chewed the inside of his cheek. The sun still sent out rays of fading light, attempting to shine until the very last moment. It smoldered and glowed as it dropped further and further. A curtain of darkness fell over the land, covering Stonehard and everything else in its path. The sun hovered, still fighting to keep from being hidden. Then, with one last ray of dying light, it sank into the black skyline, once again subdued by the growing darkness.

Mason held his breath, awaiting that sense of peace and gratification that always came at sunset, confirming what he always knew. There was nothing to fear in darkness, and there was nothing more powerful. He waited for the assurance. Several minutes passed before it hit him, bringing his brows down in a confused frown. For the first time he could remember, the sunset had not done anything for him. He felt nothing.

All was still, save for the chirping of one brave swallow. A flutter of wings and the screech of a night owl. Then silence.

26

Truth and light create laughter in the heart of the believer.
-The Sacred Code

Eric straightened the collar of his blue tunic and made sure Lavrynth hung securely at his side. It was a nice gesture for the Stewards to hold a dinner in Ollen's honor. The young man's formal promotion would not be until noon the next day, but it seemed Ollen had many friends who wished to celebrate tonight.

Braylee waited for him at the large double doors of the main building, all decked out in his formal captain wear, complete with red cape and black boots.

"Well, it's nice to see you haven't forgotten how to clean up," Eric teased.

"You, too." Braylee returned, but his smile looked a little tight. In the next instant, he looked fine, so Eric shrugged it off.

With time to spare, Eric set a leisurely pace, the coolness of the evening beckoning to him. "Nice night." He stared up at the purple sky.

Braylee nodded. "Aye, it is."

"Makes a man wish for more peaceful times so we could enjoy more evenings like this."

"Mmhmm."

Eric glanced over at the bland response. Maybe his friend missed his family. A distraction would be good for him. "How about we take to the dueling field again tomorrow?"

"You and me?"

Eric grinned. "Why not?"

"Sure."

Satisfied, Eric clasped his hands behind his back, ready to resume their companionable walk. They passed by the gates, and he waved to the lone guard.

"Is he going to make it?" he asked.

Braylee blinked at him. "What?"

Eric pointed to the guard. "Is Frakes going to make Ollen's dinner?"

"Oh." Braylee let out a tense chuckle. "Someone will take his place in an hour."

"Good. Are you all right, Braylee?"

"Huh? Of course. I'm great."

Eric's brows lifted at the speed of the words, almost overlapping in Braylee's hurry. "You seem...distracted. I thought you must be missing your girls again."

Braylee gave a jerky nod. "Always."

Eric studied the big man as they neared the mess hall. He would have to catch him after dinner. If something troubled his dear friend, Eric would do all he could to ease the load.

Just before they reached the stone steps, Eric heard the distinct call of a nightingale and paused to take it in. "Isn't that pretty?"

"Pretty," Braylee repeated flatly.

The bird sang with all its might, and Eric's lips turned up. It had been a while since he'd heard a songbird. All the turmoil of the valley seemed to have affected nature itself. He glanced over at Braylee to find him staring at the steps, tapping it with the toe of his boot. Eric sighed and moved for the steps.

Braylee brought his head up and moved aside.

Eric waved him forward. "Go ahead."

"Ah, nay, you go." Braylee backed up a step. "I want to listen to that bird again."

Eric cocked his head at the man. *Boy, he is acting strange.* His second captain must be working too hard. It was beginning to affect his behavior.

When Eric reached for the large door handle, Braylee followed on his heels. So much for the bird. Pulling the great door open, the darkness caught him off guard. "Isn't this where we're supposed to meet?"

The room lit up with numerous Beacon lights as the air exploded with shouts of "Surprise!" Dozens of shapes stood around him, and he caught sight of a large cloth banner that read, "Happy Birthday, Prince Eric!"

Eric's head bobbed. "What is this?"

Braylee chuckled behind him. The light from the Stewards' Beacons was replaced with lantern lights, and Eric stared at the scene before him. The banquet hall was filled with Stewards, Reservists, and civilians. Laughter rose as they all took in his surprised face.

"I thought this was supposed to be for Ollen," he protested.

Ollen grinned at him from his position. "Nay, Sire. That was just a cover-up."

"But you are being promoted." Eric wanted to make sure that was clear.

"Aye, and I'm still honored beyond words."

A beaming Seria stood nearby, her hands clasped under her chin. "I suppose you were in on this, too?"

"It was her idea," Braylee said.

Eric turned to the captain. "At least I know why you were acting so out of character now."

Braylee let out an exhale. "You didn't make it easy." He looked to Seria in exasperation. "I don't know how I held it together. Everyone was here waiting on us, and he decides to stop and talk about anything and everything that came to his mind."

Eric laughed, relieved to know all was well in Braylee's life. "I was about to give you some time off, friend. I thought the stress was beginning to get to you."

There was another round of laughter, then everyone headed to the tables laden with food and drink.

Eric sat at a table with Braylee, Seria, and Ollen, still stunned that they had managed to pull this off without him knowing. Considering how strained things had been when he first arrived, his gratitude knew no bounds.

"You shouldn't have done this," he said at one point.

"Which is the exact reason we didn't let you know we were doing it," Braylee said.

"You spend so much of your time worrying about everyone else," Seria spoke up. "It was time to let us do something for you."

Eric smiled at her. The tension between them the last few weeks seemed to have lifted. He was pleased to see Ollen with her; the two young people looked very at ease with one another.

His throat tightened as he scanned the people around him. Dudley and Braylee. Seria. Ollen, who had gone from resenting his command to helping him celebrate his birthday. And Lionel, with a lovely, serene Lena on his arm.

Eric swallowed, wishing his father could be there. It would have done the old king a world of good to see the kind of company his son had been blessed with.

It did not take long for the evening festivities to fall into full swing. The minstrels picked up their instruments on one side of the hall that had been cleared for dancing. In the middle of the room, a table groaned with the abundance of good food: roast mutton and a suckling pig; cooked cabbage and carrots; fresh bread. The potent smells of black pepper, cinnamon, sage, and mint rose in a warm, pungent mix. In another corner, groups were drawn into games, already calling out challenges to one another. There was laughter and conversation at every turn.

Ollen bit back a chuckle as he glanced over at a glowing Seria. "You're feeling very pleased with yourself, aren't you?"

She lifted her chin. "I am. He deserves a nice party." She brushed her skirt of invisible dust.

"I'm glad it's a success after all the work you put into it." He took a sip of ale. "And you look lovely." Indeed, he found it hard not to stare at her. She wore a dark green gown that suited her fair coloring. The square neckline was modest but flattering, and golden thread trimmed the sleeves, hem, and bodice. Her hair cascaded down her back in a mass of ash-blonde waves with a few tendrils framing her face.

"It belongs to Mallie's daughter. I didn't have one of my own." Her cheeks turned a delightful shade of pink at her admission.

"Nice to have friends who share, isn't it?"

She smiled and nodded. "It truly is."

The music changed to something fast and upbeat. Couples stood and formed a line to dance the saltarello, their faces brimming with excitement. Ollen caught sight of Lionel and Lena laughing as they took their spots in the line.

"That looks like a bit of fun," Dudley commented. He poked Ollen in the back. "You know how to dance?"

"I do, in fact," Ollen said. "Despite my poor background, my mother made sure I grew up a decent and cultured gentleman, even if I didn't attend any parties."

"Then what are you doing sitting here with us old fellas?"

Ollen faltered. "Oh, right." He looked to Seria. "Would you like to dance?"

Uncertainty froze her to her seat. "I'm afraid I was *not* raised to know all the dances."

He gave her an encouraging smile and held his hand out. "It's pretty repetitive, and the steps are simple. I think you'll get the hang of it."

She tucked her lip between her teeth but allowed him to pull her to the dance floor. Her fingers trembled in his, making his heart turn over. Determined to make sure she would not feel awkward, he positioned them at the end of the line, away from so many eyes.

"Just follow my movements," he whispered. When her gaze flickered to him, he sent her a wink. "And hold on."

Her hand tightened in his, just like the cord around his heart. He took a deep breath and began slowly hopping and kicking his feet in beat to the music of the pipes and drums, tugging her along with him.

The steps were simple, but her movements were hesitant at first. At one point, she shook her head and mumbled, "I move like a plodding donkey."

"You're doing fine."

Her mouth pinched as her expression became a study in concentration. Soon, her steps began to match his. Delight lit her face, taking his breath away.

He cleared his throat. "Now kick in the opposite direction as me." Seria did, and then it all fell into place. Their steps synced, and they moved as one in time with the music. The lilting tones of the trumpet and lute swelled, filling his ears. She laughed out loud in pure joy, and Ollen felt like he could hop, skip, and float right up to the sky if it meant holding on to this moment.

He grinned back at her, holding her hands securely in his. Seria's gaze locked onto his, and his stomach flipflopped. Everything else faded away, and it was just the two of them, moving in sync, as if they had been doing this for years. Her cheeks flushed, and hope stirred within him. Then she tripped and stepped away, halting the dance.

"Leave it to me to mess it up." She laughed, shaking her head. "I think I'm danced out."

He forced a smile and dropped her hand. "I need to catch my breath, too."

She chattered about the other dancers as he offered his arm and led her from the floor, her hand burning through his sleeve. Before they rejoined the captains at their table, she looked up at him. "Thank you for teaching me. Just like our Steward lessons."

"Of course." His throat tightened as he motioned to an empty seat. "Sit here, and I'll bring you some cider."

She thanked him again and turned to join Dudley and Braylee's banter. Ollen walked away, his heart throbbing.

Holding her hand and dancing with her had felt right. But to her, it was nothing more than a fun moment with a good friend.

27

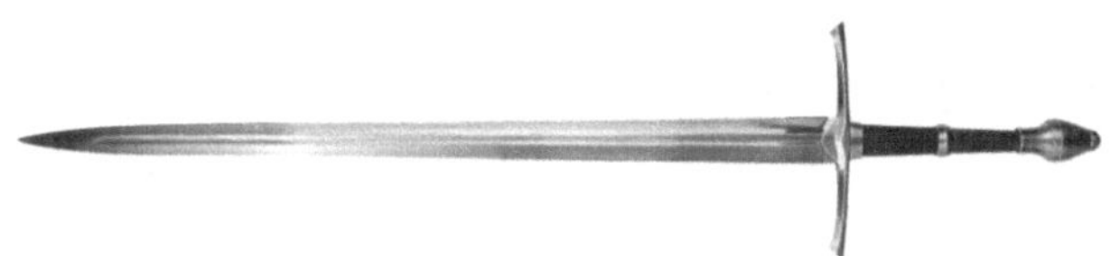

Marsels, the Gateway

Bruin spurred his horse through the southern end of Marsels, some of his soldiers already breaking through doors and dragging their targets out. The rest of his team would be at the other end of town, doing the same.

Hardened against the cries, Bruin called out orders and stayed alert for trouble. The adults had become more resistant to the pickups, which sometimes resulted in more unnecessary engagement.

An arrow whizzed by, and he whipped his horse around, searching for the archer. Another one shot past him and hit a Darkman in the shoulder, landing him in the dirt.

Bruin finally spotted him ducking behind a wooden post. A man with long, shaggy hair and ragged clothes. He looked like a common civilian, but there was no mistaking the skill with which he took aim or the sword that hung from his belt. The strong set of his shoulders and the challenge in his narrowed eyes set him apart.

"A Steward spy!" he barked, urging his horse out of reach of the shots. "Greggor, take him out!"

Greggor lifted his bow and fired. The Steward pulled back behind the post.

"Kill him!" Bruin shouted. "*Now!*"

Other Darkmen took up the order and turned their focus on the man. Arrows shot out, most of them hitting the post or the walls behind him. But finally, one hits its mark, high up on the man's leg. He jerked and fell out of sight behind a barrel.

Bruin reached for his sword, but there was no time to make sure the man was dead. The town was rallying, raising their makeshift weapons, even throwing rocks. The Steward had prepared them to put up a fight, pitiful though it was.

"Ride out!" Bruin ordered, his blood hot and raging. "To the north!"

Three kids screamed as they were carried away. Not as many as Bruin had hoped, but a smirk lifted his lips at what this pickup had unearthed. He would reassemble the rest of his Darkmen and come back to take care of that Steward.

Dust rose with every hoofbeat, swirling around and clogging the air. Mason's chest burned beneath the Shadowstone as he waited for Bruin at the edge of town. A boy sat shivering before him in the saddle, but the purpose that throbbed through him shoved out any remorse Mason might have felt.

Screams pierced his ears. People ran in all directions as the Darkmen swooped in to grab their intended targets. Soon, this mission would be over and Mason could resume his former duties. Maybe even go back to see Seria.

Unease coiled inside him like a snake ready to strike, pulling his focus from the chaos around him. Seria would never understand. Her compassionate heart would not allow her to accept what he did. Not while she was still under the influence of the Stewards.

His whole being longed to see her, but would she see him the same way if she knew? The answer was already clear in his head, which led him to the next conclusion.

She could never know.

He ground his teeth and looked around.

Almost done. Just a few more.

"Liam!"

The name cut through the noise, snapping him out of his focus. He jerked around, his lungs seizing.

A little boy of six or seven ran across the street, his sturdy legs pumping, his face stark white. On the other side, a frantic teen boy waved him over. "Hurry, Liam!" he cried.

Mason's mouth went dry, his skin clammy. The name sank its talons into his memory, drawing up images of his brother's last moments.

Dreeya, her face cold as a stone, cut her horse between the boys and yanked the younger one—*Liam*—up on her horse. The older boy cried out and grabbed Liam's arm, fighting to pull him off the horse and into his arms. A swift kick of Dreeya's boot to his face knocked him loose. The boy jumped to his feet and lifted a makeshift bow, an arrow already in place between his shaking fingers.

Mason sat still on his saddle, watching the incident unfold like a slow-paced nightmare. The arrow flew, the shot lacking good form and missing Dreeya. But that didn't stop the boy from trying again.

"Don't do it, kid," Mason breathed, hot blood pounding in his ears. The boy was young, maybe fifteen, and clearly in over his head. But a look of grim determination crossed his face as he aimed for Dreeya again.

Bruin and his men thundered into view, Greggor's crossbow already loaded and raised.

"Stop!" Mason threw himself from the saddle as Dreeya galloped by with a wailing Liam.

The dart was released and hit the teen square in the chest.

"*No!*" Mason bolted for the boy, but Bruin's horse blocked his path.

"Get on your horse," Bruin spat, his gray eyes smoldering.

His chest heaving, Mason glared up at him. But it was too late to do anything. The townspeople were regrouping. Rocks and arrows flew through the air. The rest of the Darkmen had already headed for the edge of town.

Pivoting, Mason grabbed his roan's reins and swung up. The boy he had taken was gone, but he no longer cared. With a kick to the flanks, he followed the throng of Darkmen.

Nothing was said as they made their departure, but as soon as a halt was called, Bruin dismounted and rounded on Mason, who had already landed on the ground to face him.

"Don't you ever interfere like that again."

Mason did nothing to restrain the rage that erupted from his lips. "You didn't have to kill him!"

Bruin's face reddened. "He threatened our soldiers."

"He was a kid."

"A kid with a weapon." Bruin stepped forward and snarled in Mason's face. "That makes him a threat."

Areem chose that moment to chime in. "You're the one who said anyone who stands in our way becomes the enemy."

Mason turned on him with fists clenched. "*Back off.*"

Retreating with his hands up, Areem fell silent.

Bruin grabbed Mason's shoulder and pulled him back around. "What's wrong with you?"

Mason swung his arm up, breaking Bruin's hold.

"Do you realize what you cost us?" Bruin demanded, his nostrils flaring. "While you're bellyaching over a kid who tried to kill one of us, you lost us a Steward *spy*."

"What are you talking about?" Mason rasped.

"One of Aden's filthy spies was back there. He was the reason that boy had a weapon in the first place."

Turning away before he swung a fist at the commander, Mason struggled to rein his emotions in, but there were too many for him to control. His gaze landed on the whimpering boy who had just watched his older brother die.

Pain racked his head, and Mason closed his eyes, trying to erase the memory of the scene. It looked too familiar.

"You see the difference?"

At Bruin's challenge, the image of his brother dying at the edge of the Steward's sword played out in his mind. Over and over. Reasoning tried to break through the wall of pain. The Stewards had attacked unprovoked. They killed every boy of Handan. The Steward in Marsels was the reason young Liam's brother was dead.

"Aye," he ground out. "I do."

"Then get a hold of yourself, and don't let this happen again."

He gave a curt nod, acutely aware that he had drawn everyone's attention. He felt their speculation like stinging needles on his skin. Areem's puzzlement. Dreeya's scorn. His jaw hurt from the tight way he held it, and he flexed his throbbing fingers.

It didn't feel right, but he couldn't change it. The loss was tragic, but it wasn't his fault. Or Bruin's. Areem was right. Mason had made that same statement to his students. They could not let anyone—regardless of age or name—stand in their way. Mason knew this. And he would abide by it.

Because his cause was too big to let sentimental feelings hinder what needed to be done. Even if he hated it.

28

In the face of darkness, light is ever present.
-The Sacred Code

Eric sat at a table and observed the merriments around him in contentment. He might have been the guest of honor, but he had more fun sitting back and watching his friends have a good time than putting himself into the center of attention.

Dudley proved to be the opposite. The grizzled captain regaled anyone within listening range with stories of his younger days. He did not hesitate to poke fun at anyone close enough to fall prey to his teasing, though it was all in fun.

A trencher and a mug appeared before Eric.

"I figured you hadn't fed yourself yet," Lena said from across the table.

"Too busy taking it all in." He glanced down at the plate, his stomach rumbling. A honey tart rested on the edge, tempting him with its buttery sweetness. He looked up. Lena's lips twitched in amusement as he shrugged and reached for the sweet first.

Dudley passed by and smacked him on the back. "You know what you need, Sire?"

"What's that?" Eric lifted his mug for a drink.

"You need to find yourself a lady companion for your own birthday dinner."

Eric snorted just as he tried to swallow and ended up choking on cider.

Dudley went on as if he did not notice Eric's fit. "I'd be happy to help you find someone."

Eric held up his hand, still trying to catch his breath. "I, ah, appreciate the help, Captain, but I think I'll pass."

Dudley's eyes twinkled with merriment. "Are you sure? It sure beats sitting by yourself."

"You know, I'm kind of used to it by now." The words were meant in jest, but Eric's mind jumped back to his younger days, when he thought he had his future all planned out. But he only chuckled and pointed to his chin at Braylee. "Not everyone can be as lucky as Braylee, here, married to the love of his life."

Braylee gave a satisfied shrug. "What can I say? I'm a blessed man."

The attention shifted from him at that point, to his relief. He took a deep breath and stared down at the food before him, trying to dredge his appetite back.

"People don't always understand, do they?"

He raised his head at Lena's softly spoken words. "What's that?"

Her head tilted. "Sometimes our pasts get in the way of our futures."

He stared at her, speechless.

"I'm sorry. Maybe I jumped to conclusions, but I somehow got the impression that something once held you back from settling down with a bride."

Eric glanced around them, but everyone else was involved in various conversations. "I don't suppose you happen to be a Reader, would you?" he asked with a chuckle.

She joined in the brief chortle. "Nay, I believe Readers are too scarce to have two in existence at once."

Surprise that she would know that sobered him. "That's right."

"Living in the fort so long, you learn things about the Lambient and Gifts and such."

"I see." Eric wrapped his hands around his mug. "Well, it happens to be that you are right." His brows furrowed. "I made some reckless decisions as a young man that carried over through the years, and I never felt the time was right to bring a woman into that situation."

Lena's face softened in compassion. "I'm sorry. And I certainly didn't mean to bring up such a sore topic on what is supposed to be a happy evening."

He waved her apology away. "No need to feel sorry. I'm working through it."

She nodded. "It takes time."

"You sound as if you speak from experience."

"Mmm..." She wagged her head from side to side. "Let's just say I've seen my share of bad decisions."

"Then I am sorry for that." Eric marveled that he was having this conversation, but it did not feel uncomfortable. Lena's personality exuded warmth and security. He believed he could tell her anything, and she would hold it safe.

Seria laughed out loud from across the room, breaking his reverie. She listened in as Dudley and Braylee debated about the merits of cider versus ale. Ollen stood by, his eyes riveted on Seria's flushed face.

Eric nodded toward them. "They make a fine pair, don't they?"

Lena turned to observe them. "Aye. I dare say, Sgt. Ollen would be good for her." Her words were soft, as if meant for her own musing.

"You've certainly been good for her," Eric said without thinking. His neck warmed when her regard landed on him. "I mean, you two are obviously close. Friends. I've seen you." Good grief, he was rambling. What was it about this woman that turned him into a blundering idiot?

But she only nodded with a soft sigh. "I'm blessed to know her. She's a strong woman, though I worry about her compassionate heart."

"She's blessed to have you, as well." He held his breath, hoping he did not sound too forward. But when a soft smile brightened her eyes, something he thought he had given up stirred within him. Lena was a good woman, the kind he would want to know better if times were different. But war was looming, and this was certainly not the time to lose his heart or drag someone else into the mess his choices had created. Maybe someday he could take that step. But not yet.

He swallowed the last bit of his cider and nodded to the corner where some of the Stewards were locked in a game of chance. "What say you we go see who wins?"

She agreed readily, and they joined the growing crowd of onlookers.

There was no gambling in the Steward ranks, but chance was a popular game among the men. Lionel argued with Ollen about his calculations, and Dudley kept up a constant stream of grumbles about his low score. All the while, Braylee filled the front and back of his parchment with tallies. True to character, he never bragged about his success, but with each turn, he added more points to his card with a satisfied gleam in his eyes.

It was nice to see Eric's Stewards so carefree. For this night, at least, they did not worry about Jader's Dark Army or Shadowmen or war. Their biggest concern was seeing how many points could be won, or catching up with old acquaintances, or knowing the steps to a dance.

"You just lost eighteen points," Ollen pointed out.

Lionel growled at him. "I can deduct." He shook the cup wildly and called out a twelve.

"Thirty." Ollen crossed his arms. "Eighteen off again."

"How about you keep track of your own points instead of calling mine."

Ollen shrugged. "Just trying to help."

Seria tittered nonstop throughout the entire conversation until Lionel scowled up at her. "What are you laughing at, Giggles?"

"Sorry." She covered her mouth with her hand.

Ollen rolled and earned twenty-five points, earning cheers from the crowd.

Braylee took the cup. "Nice to finally have some competition."

Dudley put his chin in his hand and tossed his scorecard over his head. "I give up."

The comforting roar of laughter filled the room. Eric slapped him on the back. "That's a fine example to all these knights that look up to you."

"Hmph."

In the midst of the gaiety, one of the double doors opened, and a guard entered. He gave Eric a casual bow before he eyed the table where the knights played. Approaching Dudley, he bent and whispered in the captain's ear.

"What is it, Captain?" Eric asked as Dudley stood to follow the guard.

"Going to go check on something outside," Dudley said as he passed. "I'm not doing any good in here anyway."

The game continued, but Eric's focus was gone. He stared at the table, not seeing or hearing the numbers that were passed around. Neither the guard nor Dudley had acted as if something was amiss, but Eric's skin prickled with awareness. Finally, he looked to Braylee and tipped his head to the door. Braylee caught his message.

"I think I'll pull out while I'm ahead," he said, handing the cup over to Lionel.

"Where are you going?" Seria asked as they headed for the door.

Hating the tense silence that fell, Eric turned with a smile. "No cause for alarm, ladies and gentlemen. I hope to return shortly. Please, continue to enjoy yourselves until we get back." But even as he turned to leave, he had a sinking feeling that the party was over.

The night guard met them outside the Council Hall. "I was just coming for you, Sire."

"What's happening, Hiram?" Braylee asked.

"A messenger's arrived, sir. A Steward messenger."

Eric's breath quickened. "From where?"

Hiram pointed west. "From the New Realm."

A Steward from the New Realm. One of his father's spies.

"He's inside with Captain Dudley, Sire. He insists on speaking to you right away." Hiram opened the door and stepped aside so they could all enter, then slipped away. Eric immediately spotted the stranger, his gray head bent over the table. Upon hearing their approach, he quickly stood to his feet.

"Your Highness." He bowed. "I am Lt. Kullen Handrix."

Dudley spoke up. "He fought with your father in Calla's War."

"I apologize for coming to you unannounced."

"No apology necessary, sir. Stewards are always welcome here." Surprise rattled around in Eric's chest as he introduced Braylee and motioned them all to sit. "I am honored to have one of my father's Steward spies."

"There's not many of us left, I'm afraid."

"I'm sorry to hear that."

Kullen sighed. "It's nothing more or less than what we expected when we chose to live in Jader's domain. But he has been relentless in searching us out. A third of our division has been executed. There are even fewer of the Handan Stewards left, and we lost track of another one a few weeks ago."

"Would that be Nebb Statler?" Eric asked.

"That's right."

Braylee spoke up. "Jader boasted a few weeks back of Nebb's death."

Kullen's gaze sharpened. "What has become of Nebb's family?"

Eric's stomach turned as he shook his head. "We have no idea. But Jader made some kind of vague reference to the children's new location."

"That's what we were afraid of. Which brings me to the reason I'm here." The lines around the older knight's mouth deepened. "Are you familiar with Jader's pickups?"

Eric straightened, his mind going over all that he knew. "Aye. His subjects from cooperating villages in the northern cities of the New Realm offer their children for his service."

"They're not always offered peaceably, as the reports say, but, aye, that's how it's been done for years. Families and communities who surrender strong, healthy children of the right age are promised grace and benevolence from his harsh governing hand. The people there are too scared and beaten down to fight it. Those of us working behind the lines cannot even figure out where the children are kept. I'm sure you've heard the rumors that it's in a place called Joshun." At Eric's nod, he continued. "But no one knows where that is."

Eric ran a hand over his eyes. "How in the world does a whole realm fall prey under one man?"

"One unsuspecting town at a time."

The words hit him like a splash of cold water, and he returned Braylee's sober gaze. Jader's Shadowmen were already working to turn towns like Danyon in the Old Realm. They were even training their children to fight for him.

"Mercy," he whispered.

Kullen drew in a deep breath. "Now, he's doing it in the Gateway. And he's taking them by force."

Heat surged through Eric's frame, red and raging. "He's kidnapping children in neutral territory?"

"That's right. Several communities have been hit. Over a dozen children taken at the last count. People are getting nervous and guarded, but they have very little defense against the Dark Army."

Eric ground his teeth together. *Lambient, give me direction.* The options flew through his head, too fast to snag one. The mistakes of his past roared to the forefront of his mind and doubts assailed. But one thing was clear. He could stay in the fort no longer.

It was time to defend the Gateway.

29

Only through light can righteousness and justice reign.
-The Sacred Code

Seria held her breath when the doors to the hall opened again, the mood remarkably different than what it had been only moments before. She sat alone at a table while everyone else stood about in small clusters, talking nervously about the prince's abrupt exit. Plenty of assumptions and theories were tossed around.

But silence fell when Braylee stepped in and spoke. "All Stewards convene in the Council Hall immediately."

Seria's heart jumped to her throat at the seriousness on the big man's face. Something was wrong, and could it only be a coincidence that trouble began mere days after Mason had left on assignment?

Of course not. He's a Darkman. He serves the Dark Army.

The reminder was a slap in the face, making her eyes sting. As the Stewards stood to file out of the mess hall, she attempted to rein in the panic that threatened to engulf her. She was not ready for this. She needed more time. Mason needed more time.

What was happening?

Ollen was slow to stand to his feet, his face pale and his lips thin. But he gave Seria a steady look before he left.

Seria rose as well, unable to sit still. A loud ringing sounded in her ears, and her hands shook as she looked for Lena.

What if this messenger brought news that involved Mason? What if the war everyone knew was coming was upon them? *Where was Mason?*

Lena stood off by herself, her arms crossed in front of her, staring at the door the knights had exited. At Seria's approach, she gave her a wobbly smile. "I guess the party's over."

"Lena, I have to know what's happened," Seria said, her voice shaky.

"I wish I could know, too."

Seria shook her head and drew closer. "Nay. I *must* know. Please, help me get into the Council Hall." Her heart pounded in her chest as she waited for Lena's assent.

But Lena stared at her, her lips parted in silence for several moments. "You want me to sneak us into a meeting we are not permitted to attend?"

"I need to hear what this is all about." Seria took hold of Lena's arm, desperation making her breathless. "I have to make sure he's not in the middle of it."

Lena's shoulders stiffened, even as her expression cooled. "I won't do that, Seria."

"What? Why?" Seria dropped her arm. Lena had never refused her.

Lena shook her head and retreated a few steps, leading them both further away from the crowd. "Seria, listen to yourself. You are asking me to go against trust and principle. Is that really what you want?"

"Nay, but—"

"But nothing." Lena's brows pinched. "I think it's time you decide if this relationship is worth it."

Seria gaped at her. "I didn't expect this from you, Lena. You were the one who said you wished someone would've done the same for your father. You encouraged me to give him a chance."

"And you did." Lena's tone softened some. "Yet, after all this time, he still has not changed."

"I just need more time."

"And what is he doing while you're waiting?" Lena lowered her voice. "Don't fool yourself into believing this timing is a coincidence. Whatever it is that the Stewards are about to be called to, Mason is already a part of it."

Hurt washed over Seria. Of all people, she never would have believed Lena would let her down like this, that she would change her opinion so quickly. "So, you won't help me?"

"I can't. Nay—" She closed her eyes briefly. "I won't."

Seria pressed her trembling lips together and turned before Lena could see the tears brimming. Betrayal stung like a hundred needles as she pushed through the double doors into the quiet evening. She gulped in the cool air, her breaths escaping her body as soft sobs. With no other place to go, she headed for the barn, paying no heed to the way the green gown trailed in the dirt.

After all this time, Lena did not understand. Seria could not give up on Mason. There was still a chance for him to see the error of his ways. But how could she show him that now? Would she even get a chance to see him again before war erupted all around them? What if he was killed? Or killed someone else?

By the time she reached the barn, her lungs burned and her throat ached. The horses all nickered at her, but she passed them for the large stall at the end. The little gray and brown donkeys all huddled at the wooden bar when they saw her. All except the sway-backed donkey in the corner. Sanjo stood with his rump to her. Even when she called him, he glanced at her over his shoulder, flicked his tail, and turned away.

"Not you, too, Sanjo," she groaned, leaning against a post. Was everyone bound and determined to turn away from her?

The fears and anxiety from the last few minutes pressed in on her. Her mind sped with all the facts. The Stewards were being called to the Gateway. The Dark Army was on the move. Mason was out there. Eric would lead his men out into danger. Braylee would go. And Ollen.

Seria could not stand by and do nothing.

"Are you sure you won't let us put you up for the night?" Braylee asked as he escorted Kullen to the gate. "The journey will be easier after a night's rest."

"I appreciate the offer, but I have a family I want to get back to as soon as I can. Things are a bit tumultuous for me to be away from them for too long."

"I certainly understand that. I wish I did not have to be absent from mine." The news of the pickups had sent Braylee's heart and mind in a whirlwind of worry as he considered his daughters in Cassels and the Shadowmen manipulating towns like Danyon to surrender to Jader's will.

Please, Lambient, don't let it come to that in the Old Realm. Even as he prayed, he was reminded that other families lived with the terror of losing their own young ones. His prayer changed direction as he sought help in ending the pickups.

They reached the gate, and Braylee motioned the guard to open it. Before Kullen could leave, however, Braylee spoke again.

"I didn't want to say anything before, but there's something I think you should know."

Kullen's brows lowered. "And what's that?"

"Jader has a Reader in his employ. One who may very well be a Shadowman by now."

Kullen's mouth turned down. "Gracious. The last thing we need to worry about." He rubbed his jaw. "There were rumors, I must confess. Rumors of a power that Jader wielded that controlled the wills of others. But I never attributed it to a Reader."

"This one has already stirred up quite a bit of trouble."

"Unless I'm mistaken about my Reader history, he's only going to get worse." Kullen crossed his arms and stared at the ground. "Legends tell of their power growing so that no one can withstand their control. Whole crowds of people can be manipulated with a single word." He brought his head up and looked Braylee in the eye. "Or whole armies."

The thought was a chilling one. "This Reader was also a survivor of Handan."

"A survivor of Handan?" Kullen whistled. "Merciful... That means he's got an ax to grind."

"And he's meaning to sharpen it on the prince, but I don't believe he aims to stop there."

"Which is going to be all the easier when his Gift fully develops." The Steward pulled a small piece of canvas from his pocket. "This is my location, should you ever need it. But I would appreciate it if you could keep it between you, Captain Dudley, and the prince. The fewer who know where we are exactly, the better. I've already had too many close calls with the emperor."

"Of course." Braylee took the map and stretched his other hand out. "You all be careful out there."

Kullen returned the handshake with a firm one of his own. "There's not many of us left, but we're out there if you need us."

"I speak for all of us when I say we appreciate everything you're doing in the New Realm, as well as the Gateway. I hope someday you will be able to come out of hiding."

Kullen gave him a nod, then went on his way, his tall form disappearing into the deep shadows of the night.

The gates swung shut behind him, but in a few short hours, they would open again, and Braylee would ride out of the fort at the prince's side. His Stewards would head out into the Gateway to face Graulik Jader and his army of Darkmen and Shadowmen, as well as Bruin Pralus who could control the weather at his will.

And a Reader whose power would soon be unstoppable.

Unease pooled in his gut as he headed for his quarters to pack. Jader had the upper hand as long as Mason Grey rode with him. And Mason would stop at nothing until he killed Eric.

Unless someone stopped him first.

30

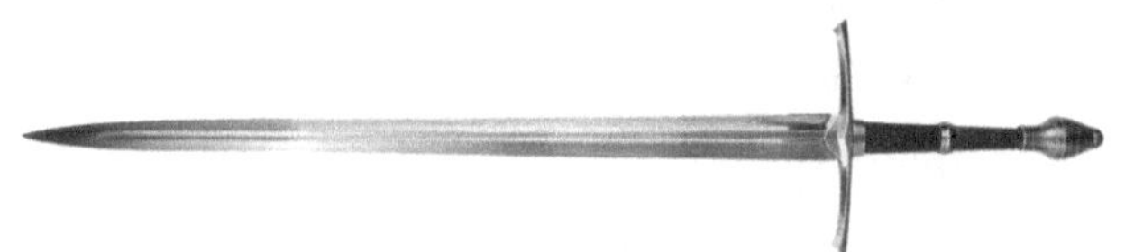

The light reveals the true nature of all deeds.
-The Sacred Code

You're an idiot, Seria Gayle. An absolute idiot.

It was the same thing she had told herself since the night before, but the self-reproach had only grown more intense with every passing hour.

What were you thinking? How are you going to explain this? Do you have any idea what you've done?

Seria bit her lip against the whimpers that wanted to escape her lips. Her bones ached from her cramped position, and her feet had gone numb. Her sword pressed into her side, and the cloak grew heavy and hot with the rising of the sun.

But it was the guilt that brought on the tears. It was only a matter of time before she was discovered. And then what?

Everything happened too fast, even though the winds of war had been blowing over both sides of the Gateway for years. It was bound to happen. No amount of resisting or crying or denying could stop it. But it was so unfortunate the man she loved had to stand on the other side.

Every time she closed her eyes, the sound of war filled the quiet spaces of her thoughts. Screams. Swords. Death. There was no avoiding it. Seria shuddered at what would happen when Mason stood face-to-face with Eric. Her worst nightmare come to pass.

If she could just get to him, make him see reason.

Maybe that's why she did what she did. But it had not taken long for her to regret her actions. Sneaking into the Steward supply wagon had seemed like a good idea at the time, but the prodding of her conscience and her reasoning would not let her rest. And now she could not undo what she had done.

Dear Lambient, please forgive me! Even the prayer made her feel wretched. Lately, she had not talked with the Lambient as much as she used to. Maybe if she had shared her worries with Him, she would not have made such an idiotic move.

The cart creaked beneath her, jostling over the rough trail. The clopping of dozens of hoofbeats filled her ears. Leather, dust, and herbs tickled her nostrils as she shifted her position so her feet could regain feeling.

Then, at long last, there was a shout, and the bouncing stopped. Her heart pinched within her chest at what she had to do now. There was no excuse for what she had done. She had to talk to Eric, make her confession.

Seria wiped her face dry and raised up a bit, pulling the cloak off her head. Trees surrounded the wagon, casting a welcome shade across her hot face. Men moved about in the wooded area, checking their horses and supplies. Eric was nowhere to be seen.

Taking a deep breath, Seria sat up fully and slid out of the cart. The young driver drew up short with a surprised shout. "What—how did you get in there?" He gawked at the sight she must make. Her father's tunic, covered in straw, fell to her knees. His trousers were too baggy and too long, the bottoms stuck in a pair of floppy boots she borrowed from Mallie.

She swallowed. "I need to see the prince."

"What are you doing here?"

The voice was familiar but not friendly. Seria turned to see Lionel stalking up to the wagon, his eyes wide.

Seria clasped her trembling hands in front of her. "I kn-know I shouldn't be here—"

"Nay, you shouldn't!" Lionel's face darkened. "How could you even...?" He shook his head. "I don't believe this."

"Lionel, I need to see the prince."

He gave a sharp nod. "Aye, you do." He took her by the elbow and led her through the midst of the Stewards, who had all stopped to stare.

Seria's cheeks burned as she tried to match Lionel's pace. What would these men think of her now?

Someone called for Eric, and he appeared in the crowd. His jaw unhinged at the sight of her, and he strode forward.

"Sir Lionel, what is the meaning of this?"

Lionel released her elbow and stepped aside, as if he could not stand to be near her.

"She was hiding in the supply wagon, Sire."

Eric gaped at her, his brows crashing down. "You were *hiding*?"

"Prince Eric, I'm so sorry. I—"

"Get the driver up here."

Seria started at his bark, his face turning a deeper red than she had ever seen.

The young man hurried forward. "Aye, sir?"

"How is it you did not check the wagon before we left?"

The soldier's face paled.

Seria gasped and stepped forward. "It was not his fault. He did check it, multiple times. I was watching. I snuck in while he was tending to the horses." She did not add that the cloak helped to camouflage her in the darkness.

Eric's glare pinned her to her spot. "How could you do such a thing?"

She gripped the cloak tighter. "I-I don't know. I'm sorry."

"That's not enough, Seria." His voice, always so soft and gentle, hit her in the stomach like a rock. "Do you realize the danger you put yourself in? The position you put these men in? They can't afford to have any distractions, not right now." He paused, his lips thinning. "What were you thinking?"

"I just…I wanted to help." The excuse sounded lame to her own ears.

"You made it worse." He turned away, raking his hand through his hair. "Mercies, you've made it worse."

Seria took in the expressions around her. Braylee stared at her, his tan face frozen in outrage. Ollen's shock was laced with a great deal of concern.

Eric spoke again, tension rolling off him like waves. "Sir Lionel. Take her back to the wagon and see that she stays there until I can deal with the matter."

She could not walk away without trying again. "Eric—Prince Eric, I really am sorry." Her throat closed up at the way he would not even look at her.

"Let's go." At Lionel's clipped order, her shoulders slumped, and she went with him without argument.

The walk back to the wagon was torture, worse than when she had been arrested by the Stewards for harboring a Darkman. At least then, she had been unaware of what she had done. This time, she had known all along that the ramifications would be profound. And she made the choice anyway.

"Sit here and don't move." Lionel motioned for the wagon and waited for her to sit on the edge before positioning himself a few feet away to stand guard over her. As if she was a criminal.

Despite the heat, she clasped the rough material of the cloak close to her, a poor substitute for the man who had given it to her. Tears slipped down her cheeks, and she did not bother to wipe them away.

What a mess she had made of everything.

"I can't believe she did this," Eric ranted to Braylee as he paced in the privacy of a grove of trees. "To put herself at risk like that. To put everyone—" He stopped and ran his hand over his face.

Braylee's voice was little more than a growl. "She's always been impulsive, but I never expected a move like this."

"But why did she do it?"

The captain crossed his arms across his chest with a frown. "I'm sure she thought it a good idea at the time, but I don't know what she was hoping to accomplish, besides putting herself in danger."

A knot formed in Eric's middle, tightening with every question. Just how well did he know Seria?

He stared at the ground for a moment, thinking out his next move. "Would you have Lionel bring her to me?"

Braylee gave a single nod and left him alone. A few minutes later, Lionel escorted Seria to the spot. Eric could see that she had worked herself up to a fine state of emotion.

"Thank you, Sergeant. You may go."

Lionel looked disappointed, but he bowed and made his exit. Eric pointed to a felled log. "Sit, please."

Seria lowered herself to the seat, silent and wary.

Eric sat across from her on a stump, trying to figure out where to start. "Seria, I have always strived to be an understanding friend to you and hope you see me as such. However, I am not speaking to you now as a friend, but as your prince. And what you've done is—"

"Foolish." She nodded. "I don't know what I was thinking."

"Not only foolish. It was selfish. You put—"

"Selfish indeed. Thinking only of myself."

"Your being here has put not only yourself at risk but my men as—"

"So many at risk! You and Braylee and Ollen and *all* the Stewards *and* the workers—even the poor cart driver!"

Eric stared at her before nodding. "It was indeed foolish, and while I'm sure—"

Seria stomped her foot. "I'm so *ashamed* of myself!"

"I'm sure your intentions were not meant to harm anyone. However, actions like this cannot be ignored. So, there will be consequences."

Seria threw her hands up. "There *must* be consequences!"

Startled at her fervent response, he paused and regrouped his thoughts. "Aye, there will—"

"I deserve it." Seria sniffed and squared her shoulders. "I was wrong."

"I'm glad you see that, but—"

Her voice cracked. "I'll go to the brig when we get back."

"All right, stop." Eric put his hand up, finally stopping her verbal wave of regret, tempted to smile for the first time all day. "I'm not putting you in the brig."

"But Eric—"

His upraised hand halted her again. "How about you let me talk now?"

Seria snapped her mouth closed and covered it with both hands.

Eric cleared his throat. "What you did was wrong, and I'm glad to hear you acknowledge it. Not only did it put you at risk, but it does compromise our situation."

Her head dropped.

Eric softened his voice. "I've already contacted Dudley. By now, he's probably already assured Lena that you are safe, as well as everyone else."

She swiped at a tear on her cheek. "Thank you."

A moment passed, the silence thick. Eric cleared his throat. "I'm at a loss with what to do, Seria. We're hours from the fort, but I can't justify taking you along for what is sure to be a dangerous mission. Which means I will have to send some of my men back with you."

Her shoulders slumped. Then she brushed her hair off her face and straightened in her stool. "I don't want to cause you more trouble than I already have. I'll go back alone."

"That's absolutely out of the question. I won't risk your safety like that."

"But you'll be short men if you send them back with me."

"That's right."

She chewed her lip and wrung her hands. "I have no right to make any requests, but if you let me stay, I will do all I can to help. You may need a healer."

He shook his head. "I'm sorry, I cannot allow it. While you are right in that we could use a healer, I will not risk your life. Nor do I want my men to be distracted in their concern for you."

Seria's eyes slid shut. "I can't undo what I did," she whispered. "But at least let me attempt to make it right."

"Tell me why you did it."

Her eyes flew open and then darted about before landing on her hands. After a long moment, she finally spoke. "I wish I could tell you it was done in complete selflessness, but I can't." She drew in a shuddering breath. "I realized the start of the war was upon me, and I somehow thought I could do something to turn the tide. A fool's hope, I know." Her gaze lifted back to his. "I've heard so much about how terrible Jader's rule is and all the harm he is inflicting. I guess I needed to see it for myself."

There was no doubt in his mind that she was not telling him the complete truth. Maybe she did need to see for herself what Jader was doing, but that wasn't what drove her to hide in the supply cart.

Regardless of her reasons, it did not change the situation she put him in. "All right, here's what we're going to do, Seria. You will travel with us until we find a safe room for you. You will remain there unless your services are needed."

Her eyes brightened in hope, but he was not done.

"But we have to have an agreement." He hardened his voice so she would grasp the gravity of the agreement. "You are to abide by my orders. Under no circumstances are you to act without Steward supervision, approval, or knowledge. Is that understood?"

She nodded. "Aye. Completely."

"You may be traveling with the Stewards, but you are not a soldier." He glanced down at the small sword strapped to her side. "I have never been given any reason to believe you can wield a weapon like that with the skill of one. Am I wrong in that assumption?"

"Nay. What little instruction I've received would certainly not save anyone on the battlefield." Sadness tinged her words.

"Very well. We don't have much longer to go." He stood and motioned for her to precede him. She moved to do so, but her demeanor was so downcast that he stopped her with a hand on her shoulder. "I do forgive you."

Her expression lifted briefly before falling again. "Will you tell Captain Braylee that I'm sorry?"

He offered her a small smile. "I will do that."

"Thank you, Eric. For giving me another chance. Again."

His lips twitched. "That seems to be a habit of mine."

They moved back among the men, and Eric turned her back over to Lionel. The young knight did nothing to hide his displeasure at being assigned Seria's guard, but he quickly acquiesced and led her away.

Eric watched her follow Lionel through the middle of the midday meal preparations. Seria may have had innocent intentions in stowing away with his company, and she may be genuine in her regret and sincere in her desire to help. But he could not shake the feeling that there was more to her actions.

31

The Gateway

"I'll ride with her for a while."

Seria looked up to see Ollen urging his sorrel mare even with Lionel's horse.

Lionel arched a brow at him. "I'm not sure that's a good idea."

"What, do you think I'm going to help her escape?" He sent Lionel a light glower. "Don't make me pull rank on you."

Rolling his eyes, Lionel tugged on the reins and left his position from beside the wagon where Seria rode.

She offered him a tentative smile. "Are you sure you want to be seen with me? This is the second time I've ostracized myself."

"You certainly surprised everybody."

"I surprised myself." She sighed, letting her feet swing off the back of the wagon.

"Can you tell me why you thought it was a good idea in the first place?"

Her cheeks flushed, and she couldn't bring herself to look at him. How could she explain that she thought she could stop Mason from doing something terrible and keep him and Eric from killing one another? "I had this wild idea that if I came along, I could somehow keep a bad situation from becoming worse. Instead, I made things worse anyway."

"Your intentions were good."

"Were they, though?" She shook her head, thinking back to her recent actions. "All I've done lately is let my friends down. I left Nola, Mallie, and Luron all without any word. I took advantage of my friendship with Lena. I've been angry at Eric for something he did years ago. I've not been very fair to you." Her shoulders drooped. "Even Sanjo is unhappy with me."

"And everyone you mentioned will be more than happy to forgive you. Especially that old donkey."

Her lips curled upward just a bit.

"You're human, Seria. You're bound to make mistakes. I've made my share, as you may remember." He added, quieter, "Lambient knows I've got my own faults."

"Well, you keep them well hidden," she teased, glad when the tension eased from his face enough for him to give her a grin.

"I didn't know there were Stewards in the New Realm." She had caught that much about the visitor to the fort.

"The history is vague, but they're there. I don't have any information as to why they're there or how long they've been there." Curiosity set Ollen's eyes to glowing. "But I do know the New Realm was once led by strong men and women of honor, determined to uphold the same Sacred Code we follow in the Old Realm. Maybe they were Stewards."

"What happened?"

"People grew tired of following what they considered to be a list of rules. Many began neglecting the Sacred Code; others flat-out rebelled against it. And that's when Graulik Jader swept in, convincing scores of people they were better off without it."

Seria bit her lip; the same story would sound quite different coming from Mason. Had the people been within their right to forsake the Sacred Code? Were they better off living as they wished, rather than having to live up to a standard expected of them?

"Looks like you're about to get another visitor."

Her stomach tightened as Eric approached. They had not spoken since their meeting earlier.

"Lt. Ollen, Sir Braylee wishes to speak with you up front."

"Aye, sir." Ollen gave her a reassuring wink, then moved his horse onward.

Eric took his spot, silent, but relaxed. The wagon bumped beneath her, and she shifted her weight, trying not to disturb the supplies stacked around her.

"Would you like a horse?" he asked.

"I haven't done a lot of riding," she admitted, looking at Oakley's powerful form.

"We brought a couple extra horses. I'm sure we can find one that will suit you."

"Thank you, Prince Eric. I would appreciate that."

"We're almost to our destination," Eris said. "I'll get you a room so you can rest a while."

"What about you?"

"It depends on what I learn."

She opened her mouth, then shut it. Eric would not welcome her questions. But she still had no idea what urgent request had called him from the fort with a whole platoon of Stewards.

"What's on your mind, Seria?"

"I'm afraid to ask, especially after already causing such a stir."

"If I decide it's not for you to know, I'll say so."

Fear silenced her a moment longer. Was she ready to learn what had led Eric to leave the fort? But the need to know finally drove her to ask, "What's happening?"

Eric drew in a deep breath, his face thoughtful. "The Dark Army has been seizing children."

"Children?" Seria gasped. "Why?"

"For future soldiers."

The blood drained from her face. "But why children?"

He gave her a steady look. "Because they're easily molded. Brainwashed. It's a sick, twisted ritual that Jader has used in the New Realm for the past twenty years. Only there, the parents usually offer them freely."

Horror washed over her. How could anyone give up their children?

"But now, he's taking them from the Gateway by force."

"What do they do with them?"

The answer was long in coming. "I can't answer for certain. No one's ever been able to find the location where they hold them. They're very good at hiding." He cleared his throat. "All I know is that the next time the children are seen, they're no longer the innocent boys and girls snatched from their parents' arms. Instead, they are hardened, driven, skillful members of Jader's army."

Seria squeezed her eyes shut to block out the images. "And when did it start happening here?" she asked, her insides shriveling.

"About a week ago."

Oxygen failed her for a brief, horrifying instant. Her limbs went cold and limp, her heart thumping numbly.

The abductions started right after Mason had left her.

Oh, Mason, please tell me you're not a part of this.

Mason could see his brother, standing in the midst of the fallen bodies. His young face was frozen in shock and fear as the Stewards thundered all around him. He raised his crossbow in a feeble attempt to save his life.

A Steward approached the teen, raising his sword high. Liam's eyes widened as the blade lowered, aimed straight at him.

"*No!*" Mason screamed, unable to move from where he stood, unable to help his brother. "Liam!"

As if the name triggered it, the image changed just before his brother fell. Two boys, brothers, stood huddled while Darkmen circled round them. The older boy valiantly tried to shield his brother from the outstretched hands reaching for him.

Mason's breath froze in his throat as he watched the anger and terror on the young face. One Darkman managed to reach the younger brother, jerking him from the ground and onto the back of his horse.

"No!" the older boy cried as the Darkmen charged away, the child firmly in their grasp. "Liam!" Before Mason could make a move, the boy looked at Mason, his expression twisting into one of anger and hatred. "It's your fault!" His fists shook. "*Why?*"

Then an arrow flew through the sky and cut his cries short. The boy fell to the ground.

Mason jerked awake, his breath coming in quick gasps. His chest burned for air. Throwing the blanket aside, he swung his feet to the side and held his head in his hands.

If only the dreams would stop! And the crushing feeling of self-reproach every time he awoke.

He could rationalize his actions, could defend Jader's practice to anyone bold enough to challenge them. But in the dreams, there was no distinction between his actions and the Stewards.

And the name! The way it elicited painful memories of Handan only made it worse. Reliving the moment he lost his brother was too much.

He already lived with the constant memory during the day. He didn't need the dreams.

It was like some cruel joke. There was no comparison. The children in the pickups still had a chance to live a full life. The boys at Handan did not get that chance. They were cut down like dogs by the Stewards, killed without a chance.

Much like young Liam's brother.

His head pounded. Outside voices cut through the drumming, piercing his skull. It was so hot. The confines of the tent pressed in on him, smothering him. Struggling to breathe, he shoved his way through the flap, nearly running into Crue, who took one look at his face and faltered.

"I-I'm sorry, sir! I wasn't watching where I was going."

The apprehension the teen displayed gave Mason pause, and he let out a sigh, his anger cooling. "Nay, it's not your fault. I'm just a bear right now."

Still looking uncertain, Crue retreated so Mason could step outside.

It was well past midday, the sun high in the sky, but the site was shaded by the wall of the Slate Mountains on one side, and surrounded on all other sides by either the thick forest or towering bluffs. Everyone in the camp was busy with their everyday tasks, their pace upright and strong. Whereas Mason felt like he had dragged himself into camp on his hands and knees.

Bruin had sent him back to camp to wait on Jader's messenger, but Mason could not help but wonder if these new orders were a result of his outburst at the last pickup. At the moment, he didn't care, glad to be free of Stonehard.

"Is there anything I can do?" Crue asked, his voice tentative.

"Aye. You could bring me my horse." A ride in the woods might be just the thing to clear his head.

Looking relieved to have a task, Crue hurried off and returned in a short time with the roan saddled and ready to go. Mason watched as the boy patted the horse with genuine affection. Something squirmed within him. Crue wasn't much older than Liam's brother.

"Crue, where did you come from?"

His head came up. "Sir?"

"I mean, before you came here. What brought you to serve in Bruin's camp?"

Crue stared at the ground. "I used to live in Ginny. Then when my folks...were gone, I went looking for work. I heard Commander Bruin's army was always needing servants, so I joined up."

Mason's brows furrowed. "How old are you?"

"Fifteen."

"How did you lose your folks?"

Crue licked his lips and kept his voice low. "My father lost his land when...it was needed for...I mean..." He sighed. "My father lost his property to the Dark Army."

Mason tilted his head. "How was that?"

"Emperor Jader needed land to house his growing army," Crue replied matter-of-factly, stroking the roan's mane. "Papa couldn't find work after he lost the farm, so he turned to...other activities. He was killed in a tavern fight one night. My mama sort of gave up on life after that and died in her sleep a few months later." He took a deep breath and forced a brave smile. "It wasn't their fault, and no one else's either, I guess. Just the changing times."

Mason stared at his servant boy. How long had Crue worked for him? How could he not have known about his sad past?

Because you were wrapped up in your own problems. Feeling rather small, he breathed in deeply through his nose. "I hope you didn't mind me asking."

"Nay, not at all. Will there be anything else?"

Sensing he was ready to end the conversation, Mason took the reins. "Nay, thank you."

Crue ducked his head and entered the tent.

Mason mounted and exited the camp at an easy pace, Crue's story playing out in his head.

It was unfortunate, to be sure, but Crue's situation was not the norm. Jader's reign was for the good of the people, their freedom. Civilians were not often uprooted for the army, but sometimes sacrifices had to be made.

But where does most of the sacrifice fall?

The question turned his mind to the Jayeses, a hardworking family with physically fragile parents who were both forced to work to cover Jader's war tax.

The Jayeses are just one family.

But an uneasy feeling snaked down Mason's spine as he recalled the economic state of the towns he had ridden through. Worn, tattered clothing. Steep prices of food items. Never had he seen the toll the taxes took on the families. It was rather disconcerting to see that Jader's rule may not always bring about the best outcome for his people.

Startled at the direction of his thoughts, Mason shook his head and clicked his tongue, urging the horse to a trot.

It's the nature of this job and the season. Once Jader had what he needed, he would be able to break through the Gateway and unseat the Passions.

Things would get better for the people when the Stewards were gone.

32

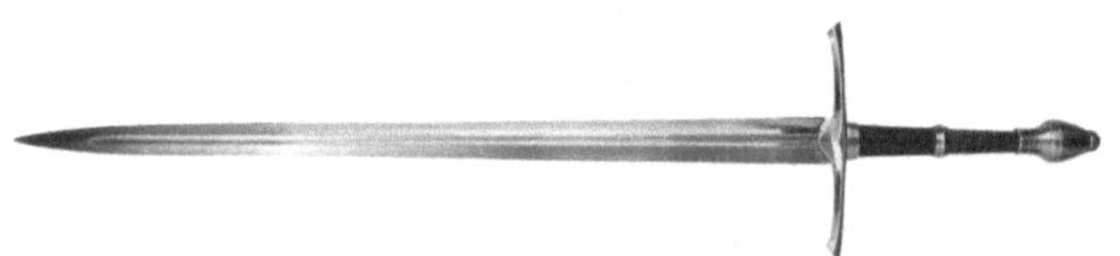

As soon as Eric gave the call to stop, Seria lowered herself to the ground with a dull thud and leaned against her horse's round side, trying not to groan at the aches in her joints.

While many of the Stewards began to make camp in the woods under Ollen's direction, Eric remained in his saddle. "I'm going into town to speak with our contact." He gave Seria a compassionate smile. "And I'll get you a room."

She gave a tired nod and watched as he and Braylee rode away. Then she took a deep breath and went to see what she could do in the camp. But everywhere she offered to help, the men assured her things were well in hand. Determined to do her part, she found a bucket of water and went looking for dirty clothes. One cadet let her take his sweaty tunic, and she knelt by a wagon to scrub.

Ollen found her a little while later. "What are you doing?"

"Laundry," she grunted. *Again,* she added to herself.

"Seria." Ollen stopped her. "We sleep in our clothes out here. There's not much need for cleanliness." He took the sopping wet tunic and flung it at the cadet with a frown. Then he took her arm and led her back to the wagon. "You're not used to riding such a long distance, especially in one stretch. You're going to be in agony later if you don't rest a bit. We can handle things here." He waited until she sighed in compliance before walking away.

Seria sat on the end of the wagon and watched the busyness around her. The men did know what they were doing. The tents were set up quickly, and a fire soon crackled in the center of the site, its smoke drifting lazily toward the sky.

The sights and smells carried her back to the times she used to fish with Sanjo. It had been so long since she had slept outdoors. Some women would be turned off by it, she was sure, but Seria enjoyed it. Her father had taken her camping and fishing sometimes when she was a girl. He was the one who had instilled in her a love for the outdoors.

Her throat ached at the memories. How she missed her family and wished their lives had not been cut short. All because someone wanted her father's land. It couldn't have been worth much, but the law was loose in that area. People took what they wanted without fear of consequences, and in the end, that's what happened. Those who wanted the land took it. At the expense of Seria's entire family.

That is the land Emperor Jader rules over.

The realization dawned over her, stealing her breath. Was this the freedom Jader promoted? That anyone could take what was not theirs?

Just like the children in the Gateway.

Seria squeezed her eyes shut, not ready to deal with the idea. Maybe she was being too quick to judge. Maybe there was a huge misunderstanding here, and the Stewards would find that the situation was not as dire as they feared.

She was not sure how long she sat there, wrapped in worries, when Eric and Braylee rode back into sight.

"You look at a loss," the prince said, as they both dismounted.

Seria shrugged and slid down off the wagon. "I tried to help, but there was nothing they needed."

"They're trained for this sort of thing," Braylee assured, waving a private over to tend to their horses.

"I secured a room for you," Eric said. "I'll have someone escort you there directly."

Before she could reply, they were converged upon by Ollen and Lionel.

"Any news?" Ollen asked.

"I talked to a man who said a lot of the pickups are happening up north," Eric said, his face sober. "The army is hitting random towns with seemingly no plan to their strategy. But I have trouble believing that Jader does not have a plan."

"Up north how far?" Lionel asked.

"At the very edge of the Gateway," Braylee answered. "Some of them have never even labeled themselves as Gateway towns."

Seria kept quiet and listened, wondering if they had forgotten she was there.

"So Jader is still keeping his distance."

"Somewhat." Eric crossed his arms and leaned on the wagon. "Rackson is the closest he's ever ventured."

Ollen narrowed his eyes in thought. "Didn't Rackson claim allegiance to him for a while?"

"That's right. And when they went back on that, he attacked."

"Perhaps that's his focus then," Ollen said. "He's hitting towns that are resisting his control."

"That's my thinking." Eric stood up straight. "I think we should visit some of the towns that have already been hit, see if we can get a feel for how they're working."

Braylee nodded. "I agree."

"We'll go first thing in the morning. In the meantime, Sgt. Lionel, get ready to escort Seria to her hotel room."

Seria swallowed, trying to ignore the scowl Lionel turned her way before he left. Heat crept into her cheeks.

"I'm sorry, Prince Eric," she said once they were alone.

He waved a hand. "We've already discussed this. It can't be undone, but there's no point in you continuing to apologize. Once was enough."

She bit her lip. "How many towns were hit?"

"So far? Five. But there will be more."

Seria tugged on the frayed hem of her father's tunic. "I suppose people have gotten hurt?"

"I'm afraid so. Few are willing to hand their children over without a fight. Many would lay down their lives." He gave her a direct look. "A few did just that."

"Can I go with you?" The question came out low and hoarse.

"I'm not sure that's a good idea."

"Please, Eric. I know I acted out of foolishness, but there may be people who need medical care. I can at least give them that, even if I can't promise them their children back." She waited with bated breath when he hesitated.

"All right," he said with a nod. "I expect it's safe enough, since they've already been hit, and I'm sure they could use your help. But it won't be easy."

She licked her lips, her pulse racing. "I know. I never expected it to be."

Eric left her then and called for a meeting, laying out the plan for the next day. One platoon would split, with one half to follow Braylee and Ollen east to a town called Jixon and the other to go with Eric up north to Marsels.

Ollen appeared before she was to leave for the night with Lionel. "You take care tomorrow," he said. "Stay close to Prince Eric or Lionel. They'll keep you safe."

She chuckled in an attempt to lighten the mood. "Are you sure Lionel won't toss me to the wolves?"

His attempt at a smile did not erase the shadows in his eyes. "He won't let anything happen to you."

"I'll be fine, Ollen," she assured. "I'm more worried about all my Stewards. You're the ones facing the enemy."

Something flashed across Ollen's face too fast for her to identify. Fear? Dread? Before she could nail it down, he was smiling at her again.

"I'll see you soon."

As she left the camp behind, a sudden yearning for Mason swept over her, taking her breath away. How she needed to feel his arms around her at that moment, to be captured in his intense gaze, to hear his words of assurance that everything would work out.

Because in that moment, she was not sure it would. Somehow, she knew that whatever was ahead would change her. She wasn't sure she was ready for that, but she had gone this far. She could not go back now.

33

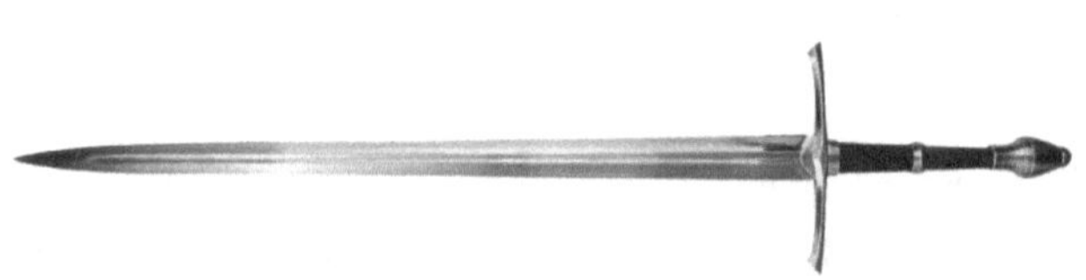

Seria and Eric arrived in Marsels early in the day, and he led the way to the meeting hall. The weather was perfect, warm and bright. But the sunshine brought to light the devastation Marsels had undergone a day ago when six innocent children had been snatched from the streets. The very air was charged with tension and fear.

Seria's heart skittered in her chest. Very few children under the age of thirteen roamed the streets. The ones that were about were held tightly by their parents. A grief-stricken silence choked her as they dismounted outside the hall and tied their horses before entering. There they found dozens of people of all ages.

"What are they all still doing here?" Eric asked their guide, a solemn man with a lined face and gray hair.

"Many fled here the night of the seizure and are afraid to go out into the streets alone," the man said. "This is where we've been tending to the wounded as well."

Seria caught Eric glance her way, but she could not move from her spot. In one corner, a young mother clutched a small girl to her breast, as if terrified someone would take her right out of her hands.

While Eric and the guide continued to talk quietly about the details of the pickup, Seria forced her gaze around the room, noting the beds where the wounded were kept. A few adults moved about, tending to those who needed them.

In one corner sat a huddled group of a dozen or so, all sharing the same tragic look. A sickening pang shot through her. These were the parents of the stolen children, waiting, albeit hopelessly, for news of their safe return. *Oh, Lambient.*

"A young boy was killed during the abduction." The guide's words floated to her ears. "He was trying to protect his younger brother."

Seria's throat went dry, and her heart dropped to her stomach. Surely Mason would not take part in such a tragedy. Not after losing his brother in a brutal act of violence.

Though she fought it, her mind conjured images of Darkmen sweeping in, snatching vulnerable boys and girls, cutting down anyone who dared cross their paths to stop them. And in the midst of it all, she saw Mason, following Jader's orders without question.

A deep trembling started at her very core, spreading its way to her limbs. She wrapped her arms around her middle.

"Seria, are you all right?" Eric's voice sounded far away.

Not able to answer, she turned away and fled the miserable scene, back outside where she slumped against the wall, gulping for air. She had come here to see firsthand what Jader's army was executing. To be able to help in any small way. But she could not.

Shaking violently, Seria stared out at the dusty, quiet street. Tears flowed down her cheeks. Again, she saw the faces of the parents who had lost their offspring, maybe forever. The pain of those wounded in their fight against the brutal Darkmen. The loss of those slain—including a young boy trying to save his brother.

It's terrible. It's ugly, cruel, and it's happening because of Jader.

Eric found her a few minutes later. "I was worried about you."

"I'm fine." She sighed. "I apologize for running like that. I guess I wasn't as much help as I thought I'd be."

"Don't be too hard on yourself. It's not a pretty picture."

It was true. Her stomach still turned every time she thought of it.

"Are you ready to go back in?"

Nay. She could never go back in there. What had she been thinking? She didn't belong out here in the Gateway. All she wanted was to go back to the safety of the fort.

"Marsels has no healer. They could use your help."

Shame flooded her. There were hurting people, and here she stood, hiding from the ugliness of it all. Swallowing against the lump in her throat, she pushed herself off the wall and nodded. "I'm ready."

Eric left Seria at the makeshift infirmary, where she got right to work, her face pale, but her chin firm. He strolled through the rest of the room, talking to a few witnesses here and there, trying to get a full picture of how the Darkmen did their work.

"Prince Eric?"

Surprised to hear his name, as he had been careful to withhold it for the time being, Eric sought to find a familiar face. A middle-aged man with long, shaggy hair pushed himself up to a sitting position on his corner cot, his eyes wide. "By the moon, it is you."

Recognition was slow, but then chills ran up and down his arms, and memories stabbed at his mind. "Sgt. Mavis?" The very man who had taken Eric's orders so long ago that led to the Handan tragedy.

Eric's shock was mirrored in Mavis's gaze as he bobbed his head and tried to stand, a difficult feat with one leg wrapped in bloody cloths.

"Please, don't stand." Eric hurried to sit on the empty cot beside Mavis. "It's been a long time, my friend. I never expected to see you here."

Mavis settled back against the wall. "I found that *here* was where I needed to be, especially after the Dark Army brought their bloody pickups to the Gateway."

Eric glanced down at the bandage. "I'm not surprised you fought back."

"Commander Bruin himself led this attack." He frowned. "I was sure he would regroup and come back to finish me off, but he met up with his other Darkmen on the other end of town and rode out."

Eric stiffened. "He may very well come back for you. Jader has made a mission of seeking out what few Stewards are left out here."

At that, Mavis gave him a startled look. "How many?"

"I'm afraid I don't know for sure, but too many."

Mavis let out a sigh. "I am sorry for that."

"I'll leave some of my men behind until you are well enough to leave Marsels. Neither Jader nor Bruin will give up until they know you're gone."

Stubbornness lifted Mavis's chin for a moment, then he deflated. "Aye, I suppose that's true. I don't want to bring more trouble here than I already have."

"I doubt that is the case," Eric said. "I'm guessing you helped ready the people here."

The Steward's face darkened. "Seeing as we still lost children, it did little good."

"It could have been more."

"Mayhap." Mavis shifted and winced, his hand massaged his wounded leg. "I'll leave town as soon as I can walk."

"I've a friend who can look after your leg."

Mavis waved a hand. "Let her see to the others first. I can wait."

Eric clasped his hands between his knees and looked at the floor. "I'm ashamed to say I've only recently learned that you and your men chose to serve out in the New Realm and Gateway. I'm deeply humbled and proud of the work you'e doing."

"I'm honored to still be able to serve, Your Highness," Mavis said. "And I'm truly glad to see you leading the Stewards again."

Swallowing past the lump in his throat, Eric focused on the man before him. "Unfortunately, there's an even greater risk. Jader has a very powerful Reader in his Shadowmen ranks."

Mavis's brows went up. "Mercies. That explains a lot."

"How so?"

The sergeant scratched his head. "There are reports of a man ordering parents to give their children up. And without a thought, they handed them over to Darkmen hands. Now they're berating themselves that they could do so to their own kids."

Eric's eyes slid shut. It did not surprise him, but it did make the situation all the more difficult. "They may be relieved to know they had no control in the matter, but I'm afraid it gets worse."

"How so?"

"The Reader is a survivor of Handan."

Mavis's face went white. "I thought there were no survivors."

"Only one. And now he has a vendetta against all Stewards for the death of his brother."

"Skies above," Mavis murmured, running a hand over his tangled hair. "How are we supposed to fight against that?"

"With Lambient's light, Sgt. Mavis." The words planted themselves deep in the cracks of Eric's worries. "That's the only way how."

Mavis stilled. After a moment, his expression cleared, and he nodded. "Aye. You are correct in that."

Silence fell, and Eric's mind went back to a chilly fall evening, a young, headstrong prince, and an order that resulted in tragedy. Though there was so much he wanted to say, he was bereft of words. Finally, he pushed out a hoarse, "I'm sorry, Mavis."

Mavis's gaze deepened in comprehension. "You weren't the only one responsible, Prince Eric. I led the charge."

"But I stepped back and let your squad take the fall."

"We never thought that, Sire. Paladin needed its prince."

"Nonetheless, the situation was handled poorly, and for that, I do apologize."

Mavis regarded him for a long moment, then nodded. "And I accept."

"Come to the fort, Sergeant," Eric urged. "As soon as you are able. It is no longer safe for you out here alone. Come back to the army and fight with us."

The man seemed to wrestle with the choice but finally shook his head. "Nay, Prince Eric. My place is here for the time being. Maybe not in Marsels anymore, but in the Gateway."

The steadfast peace that shone from Mavis's expression arrested Eric's argument. He gave a nod. "Very well, then. Regardless of where you are, I feel the time will come that we will be called upon to fight together."

"When that time comes, I will be more than ready to fight by your side."

34

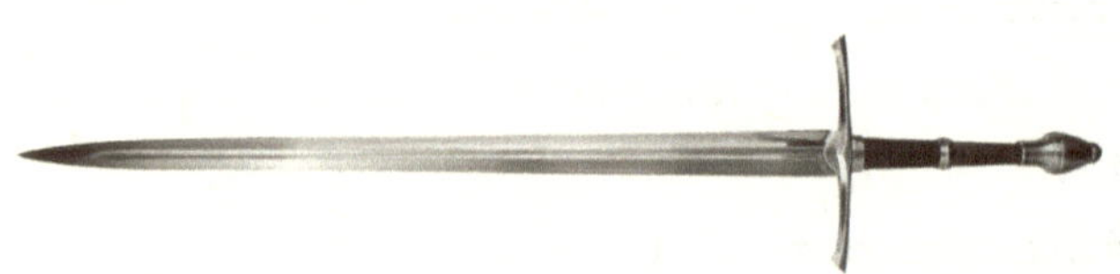

"Hey, Mason!"

The voice jerked Mason from a sound sleep. Irritation simmered that someone had the nerve to wake him, especially when sleep was so sporadic these days.

"Come on, lazy bones!"

He blinked, trying to place the familiar call. Jumping up from his cot, he flipped the tent flap back and stared at Shon. "When did you get here?" He grabbed the other man in a quick, exuberant hug, a move that surprised even himself.

Shon laughed but returned the hug. "I just got in with a message for Bruin."

"Wait, you're the messenger I'm waiting on?" Mason grinned. Bruin must have known this. "So, what's the message?"

"I can't say much, but he's coming."

Mason's brows rose. "Jader is? Why?"

"Wants to check on the progress."

"Why didn't he use the Shadowstone to say so?"

Shon patted the canvas bag hanging on his shoulder. "Because there's more that can only be delivered in person." He hesitated. "And because I requested joining up with your outfit."

"Really?" It wasn't like Shon to make such a bold request of Jader. Mason studied his friend. He looked thinner and worn out, which was to be expected after such a long ride, but upon closer look, Shon looked preoccupied. "Everything all right?"

"Hmm? Oh, fine. Here's Emperor Jader's approval."

Mason took the parchment from Shon and skimmed it over. "Well, it seems you've been approved, so I guess that means I have to put up with you."

Shon grinned.

"How 'bout a drink to perk you up before we go?"

"Now? Isn't Bruin expecting us?"

Mason shrugged, more thrilled than he should be to have his friend along. "Bruin doesn't know when you're supposed to arrive. He won't miss us for a few hours."

Shon's face lit up. "Sounds good to me."

Though Shon seemed glad to be there, it did not take long for Mason to acknowledge the niggling suspicion that something was off. When Mason inquired about the trip, Shon's answers were vague and brief. At times, he fell uncharacteristically quiet during their visit, and he stared down into his mug as if seeking answers.

"All right, what's eating you, Shon?" Mason finally asked as they made their way back down to Mason's tent.

"Nothing, man." He kept his gaze conveniently averted. "I'm just ready to put the past few weeks behind me. All that riding can mess with your head, not to mention your body."

There had to be more, but Mason would not push. Nor would he take advantage of his Gift to read what was troubling his friend. Shon was not ready to share, and he could be more stubborn than Mason, so for the moment, he let it drop.

"Well, I'm glad you're here." He smacked him on the back. "It's been a bit dull with you gone."

"You mean you missed me?" Shon flashed him a wide grin.

"I did."

Shon arched a brow towards him. "Getting soft?"

The question gave him pause. He wasn't getting soft, was he?

"It was a joke, Mason."

"Not a very funny one," he quipped, trying to mask the uneasiness it had generated.

They had their horses saddled and were ready to mount when an excited horseman galloped into the camp. He passed the two of them, heading for the quarters of the lieutenant in charge.

"What's that all about, you think?" Shon asked.

"Not sure." Mason squinted after the rider. "Maybe I should wait a few minutes before leaving. Just in case there's more news for Bruin."

They didn't have to wait long. The news spread like wildfire throughout the soldiers, prompting cheers and laughter after more than a week of boredom and inactivity in the main camp.

The Stewards were back in the Gateway. Just as Jader had predicted they would come.

Upon hearing the words, Mason's heart jumped, then beat with the steady thrum of expectation. He could feel Shon's gaze, waiting for his reaction. Indeed, the exhilaration of what was coming swept over him. But he had expected more. More anger and heat rushing into his veins. More excitement about the potential of seeing his vow executed soon. But instead, he felt flat. Tired.

"I guess we have something else to tell Bruin then?" Shon asked.

Mason nodded and pushed a smile. "I guess so. He'll be glad to hear it."

Shon quirked a brow, but to Mason's relief, said nothing more.

Once mounted and turned toward Joshun, Mason mulled over the news again. Everything was going as Jader had planned. Which meant Mason would soon see the Stewards fall. Maybe even have a hand in it.

The Shadowstone hummed against him, warm and comfortable. Suddenly his mind went back to the day he watched the Stewards kill his brother and the other boys at Handan. Even his friend Baris, standing to the side trying to keep a young, distraught Mason safe, fell at their bloody hands.

He ground his teeth, the expected rush of anticipation now flooding him, heating his blood, coloring his vision. Sitting up straight, he let it surge through him, his mind inundated with images of victory. Of justice.

Of vengeance.

"I want a squadron to hit Marsels before nightfall," Bruin growled as he stalked the cool, dark halls of Stonehard. Sgt. Greggor walked beside him, nodding in acquiescence.

Bruin stopped at the door of his suite. "They will have settled down, lowered their defenses by now, since they've already been hit. And I don't care what else you have to do to see it done, just make sure you take that Steward out."

Greggor bowed his head. "We'll see it done, sir."

"Good. I'll expect a positive report when I return."

"Understood, sir."

Bruin dismissed him and started for his suite when his name was called again. Not bothering to mask his irritation, he spun to the messenger. "This better be important."

The skinny man blanched and took a step back. "Sgt. Mason has returned."

Tightening his jaw, he waved the messenger off and entered his room to sit at his desk. A moment later, Mason walked through the door, followed by the courier Bruin had been waiting for. "I expected your message sooner," he said.

Shon stopped before the desk and bowed. "I beg your pardon, sir," he said. "I was delayed over the course of my assignment."

Turning his glare to Mason, Bruin leaned back in his chair. "What were you thinking of bringing him here? You know the emperor is to approve anyone to know this location."

Shon spoke again. "This will address that concern, Commander." He held out a parchment.

Bruin accepted the missive and read over the request. He shrugged and handed it back. "Makes no difference to me," he said, even as resentment grew. Jader catered to anything that had to do with Mason these days. "Where's the official report from the emperor?"

The young man handed that over next.

"You may go." Bruin loosened the string around the rolled parchment. "I'll let you know if I need anything else."

Mason cleared his throat then, bringing Bruin's gaze back up. "Is there something else?" he asked, his voice hard.

"Eric's Stewards are here, sir. As is the prince."

That stopped him for a moment, and he leaned back again. "Is that so?"

Mason nodded. "The word came directly from Larence. Lt. Laggens made sure I would pass it on to you."

For the first time that day, pleasure blossomed through Bruin's chest. His lips lifted in a smile. "So it begins." He looked to Mason, who stared back with a dark flame burning in his eyes. Hope rekindled within him that Mason would not let him down after all. "I have new orders for you, Sgt. Mason."

"Aye, sir?"

"Go into Shales and scope out the situation. Make contact with Larence so he will stay on his toes. I don't want him to have any doubts about his loyalties. Keep an eye on things. And maybe get a little more information. Don't worry about reporting back to me. Jader is already on his way. You can meet him at the campsite when he arrives."

Mason gave a calm nod, his jaw tight.

Bruin sobered. "Remember some of those Stewards have seen your face. We don't want to announce that the Reader is nearby. But if you happen to cross paths with Passion..." He shrugged. "I'll leave you to make that call."

Mason's face reflected the eagerness that he tried to control. "I'll be happy to, sir."

35

Seria lost track of time tending to the injured. Her feet and back soon ached with the same intensity as her heart. As she worked, the stories drifted over her, piercing through the numbness.

Stories of the imposing commander who rode in as cold as stone. Of the Darkmen who ripped sons and daughters from their parents' arms. The teen boy who was killed in cold blood because he dared to fight back for his little brother. A man who gave orders no one could refuse.

After that, she stopped listening.

By the time evening came, she felt like a shell of the person who had ridden into Marsels. She stood at a window of the meeting hall and watched the sun descend. The shadows sent a chill through her. What was it about the darkness that drew Mason?

He's a Darkman, Seria.

As much as it pained her now, even more sorrow awaited her if Mason grasped the opportunity to do what he had vowed to do for years: kill the prince of Paladin. Would she stand aside and let it happen?

The sound of horses drew her gaze to the street. Braylee and Ollen had arrived in Marsels with their company. A few minutes later, they entered the hall and sought out Eric. Ollen looked in her direction, but something about his expression froze her to her spot.

The men spoke in low tones, their expressions so grave that her stomach flipped, and she turned back to the window, not ready to face what they discussed. A few minutes later, Eric joined her.

"Are you all right?"

She shook her head, not looking at him. Fear turned her blood into ice, but she forced herself to speak. "He was here, wasn't he?"

There was a long silence. "Aye, Seria. Mason has been a part of the pickups."

Seria's heart shattered. Afraid to reveal how deeply the revelation hurt her, she stared out at the street, unable to see anything for the tears. A cold band tightened around her chest, making it difficult for her to breathe. She kept her back straight, her chin up, and fought for control, scared to death Eric would see through her.

There was a long pause before Eric spoke again, his voice heavy with compassion and regret. "I know this is difficult for you, Seria. But you must know what Mason is, what he's become. I know you would never consider bowing yourself to Jader's rule, but Mason has done that very thing."

She spun around. "And you know why, don't you?" She regretted the words as soon as she spoke them. Covering her mouth, she stifled a sob and sniffed. "I'm sorry."

Eric's lips twisted to the side for a moment. "So am I. You have no idea how sorry. I wish I could go back and change the past, but I can't. All I can do is decide what to do in the here and now." His firm gaze snagged hers. "Mason has made his decision, as well. He is a Darkman and a Shadowman. He's let Jader's influence blacken his soul and his conscience so that he will do anything for the man, including destroying the lives of innocent children. He's the enemy."

Every word was a blow, smashing every hope into shards that pierced her very soul. Because no matter how much she wanted to fight them, to strike out at him at how unfair he was being, she could not.

Because they were true.

They prepared to leave Marsels not long afterward. Seria hovered near the back of the caravan, unable to pull herself from her daze to uphold a decent conversation.

She watched Eric shake Mavis's hand, urging him to use all caution in the days ahead. Seria had treated his leg earlier, and the man would make a full recovery.

They set out, the soft hum of chatter and hoofbeats fading in and out of her awareness as the buildings passed by her. A cool evening breeze blew over her skin, but she was too numb to appreciate it. Scattered images and memories floated through her mind in no sense of order or time.

Mason teaching her to use a sword. Eric pleading her pardon from the Council. The mother in Jixon clutching her small child. Mason's eyes when he looked at her. The battle in Rackson. Eric's face as he admitted his part in Handan. Mason fighting the Stewards.

She closed her eyes in misery, even as her conscience smote her. What had she been thinking? Mason was a Darkman. A devoted Shadowman who chose to carry out Jader's orders to the fullest. And Jader was a tyrant.

Seria had been fooling herself. She let her feelings for Mason cloud her judgment and beliefs. Her parents had tried to teach her about the Sacred Code. She may not know much, but she still knew what it stood for, what it represented. And she believed in it with her whole heart. Her desire to be important, to do something great, had influenced her to go against what she knew to be right.

To uphold what is right, preserve what is good, protect what is pure, honor what is just, accept what is true. She heard Eric's fervent voice as he quoted the vow. He meant it with his whole heart and was willing to give his life for it. As would all of the Stewards.

Bowing slightly under the weight of her revelation, Seria gripped her horse's mane.

The Stewards defended the weak, even at their own risk. They stood for justice, peace, and freedom. They swore to serve the Sacred Code and to uphold the Lambient. The sincerity of their vow was proven by the light rods, their Beacons of virtue, channeled by the Lambient itself. Their life was spent fulfilling their oath.

And the Darkmen? Seria trembled, but forced herself to continue.

The Darkmen stole children from their families and then forced them into a life of service to Jader. They sought to destroy the Stewards and spread a message of rebellion against the Sacred Code. Advocators of chaos rather than peace, they carried out orders of taxation and intimidation over the people.

That was what Mason stood for. He had proven it time and again with his actions and his words. She had been too naïve and foolish to believe what he truly was. But she was wrong to continue making excuses for him, to turn a blind eye to all he was.

Dropping her head so that her hair hid the tears threatening to spill, she bit her lower lip in a feeble attempt to control her emotions. Waves of sorrow washed over her. How was she supposed to pick up the pieces? All she cared about and held dear was jeopardized. She felt so alone.

A hand covered hers, startling her. Ollen sat on his horse beside her, both at a standstill. No one else was around, though she could hear the sound of hoofbeats up ahead. The genuine caring on his face was too much for her. With a sob, she covered her face and let the tears flow.

Ollen dismounted and reached for her, pulling her off the horse and into his arms. Unable to stand on her own any longer, she leaned against him.

In her mind, she pictured Mason as she last saw him, his eyes full of love, his hands so gentle on her face. How could this same man devote his life to doing Jader's bidding? How could she have been so wrong about him? An unexpected rush of anger filled her, consuming the grief. She gritted her teeth and slapped her open palm against Ollen's solid chest.

"Why, Ollen, *why?*" she cried. The words could not be held back. "How could he do this? He could be so much better than this. There's good in him, I know it. How could I be stupid enough to fall in love with a Darkman?"

Just as quickly as it had come, the rage was gone, leaving her exhausted. With a start, she realized what she had said and looked up, expecting to see shock or disappointment. Instead, Ollen offered her a sad smile.

"I'm sorry, Ollen." She leaned back. "I didn't mean to carry on."

"No need to apologize." He slid his hands up to her shoulders, as if to lend her his support.

Awkwardness filled her, and she could not look at him. What must he think of her blatantly admitting she loved the enemy?

Ollen's fingers squeezed, drawing her attention back up. "There's a lot I could say right now, but I don't think it's my place, nor the right time. But I do know this." His gaze deepened. "You will get through this. And you're not alone."

She inhaled deeply, letting his words sink in. "Thank you, Ollen. For being here when I needed you."

Ollen stared back at her, his eyes darkening. "I'll be here for you as long as I am able, Seria." The words came out low and husky.

Seria caught the unspoken meaning in his words, and something inside of her ached. Ollen was a better man than Mason. Why could she not have seen that before it was too late? Now her heart felt sliced through and bleeding.

He released her then and stepped back. "We should probably catch up before they leave us behind."

They had not ventured far from Marsels. Seria could still see the two rows of buildings lining the street when she looked over her shoulder. Homesickness tugged her heart to her little boarding room in the fort. "It already seems so long since we've left."

"It often feels that way when we're away from home. But we'll be back there soon."

"I hope so," she murmured. "I have a lot of people I need to make amends with. I only hope they forgive my actions." At the forefront of her mind was Lena's hurt face when Seria accused her of not caring.

Ollen snorted. "Please. They'll probably hold a parade to celebrate you coming back home safe."

It was her turn to snort. "Led by none other than Ira Dankton, I'm sure."

He smiled, but his expression turned thoughtful. "Did you know he used to be a professor in the New Realm?"

She gaped at him. "*Ira?*"

"Apparently a well-respected one, too."

Seria pictured the heavy-set man, his eyes always glazed over in drunkenness. "What on earth happened?"

Ollen did not answer right away. "He lost his wife and daughter in an epidemic that hit their hometown. After that, he lost the will to live and turned to drink. He ended up losing his home, his job—everything."

Seria had no words. She could not imagine Ira as a family man, but that was because she had never seen him as anything other than a drunk. "I never would have guessed," she murmured.

"Just goes to show you never really know why a person does what they do until you get to know them."

"But that doesn't make them right." Memories of Ira threatening and belittling her came to mind.

"You're right," Ollen agreed without pause. "Wrong is wrong, no matter the reason behind it."

Shame filled her as she thought about her relationship with Mason. She had been willing to overlook his wrongs, even when she knew he wanted to kill the men she claimed to call friends.

"Sometimes, though, people just need another chance to change."

A deep sigh deflated her. "But they have to want to change."

He glanced over at her. "That's true. And it doesn't mean we subject ourselves to abuse in the meantime."

She shook her head. "I never really tried to see Ira as anything but a drunk." And yet she still managed to see past Mason's Darkman exterior to the good man he could be. Even after he had taken the Shadowstone.

"No one expected you to put yourself in harm's way," Ollen said. "I think Ira needed to see himself at rock bottom in the brig for a while before he was willing to admit he needed help."

"I'm glad you were there for him." She sent him a smile, thankful again for this gift of a friend.

Braylee waited for them down the path. Ollen moved his horse over, giving the captain space to ride between them.

"How are you, Miss Seria?"

"Feeling very weak and pitiful," she admitted with a smile.

"A human response. These are hard times we're facing. But you are stronger than you feel."

"I feel like a scared little girl."

The captain braced his fist against a thick thigh, looking very at home on the back of the bay stallion. "Courage doesn't mean you never feel fear. It means you do what has to be done in spite of it. Sometimes that means sacrifice, but when you're doing the right thing, it's always worth it."

She swallowed. Nothing was said about Mason, yet Seria was positive Braylee knew what was on her heart. She took a deep, cleansing breath, even as a great wave of pain washed over her, leaving her feeling raw and exposed. She knew what needed to be done, what *she* needed to do.

But did she have the strength to go through with it?

They had almost caught up to the rest of the party, even in their relaxed stride. Then Braylee stiffened, his head going up. A whistle cut through the surrounding woods. He reached for Seria's reins. "Lieutenant, get on her other side now."

Ollen obeyed without question, his face stiff. Seria's mouth went dry at the change in their stance.

Then Eric's voice rose over the sounds of travel. "At arms!"

36

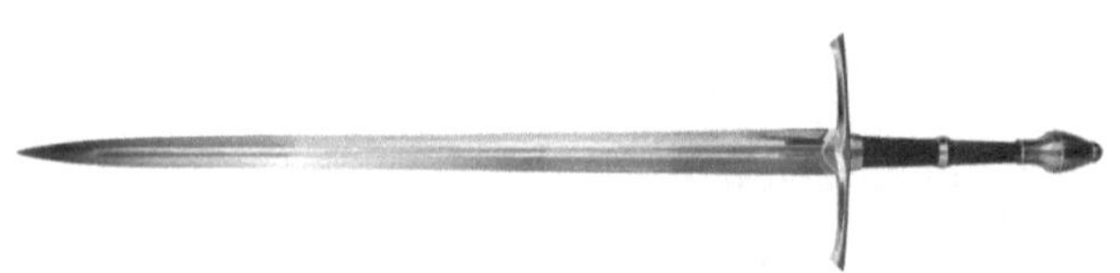

Seria held tight to the saddle horn, her breath stuck in her windpipe, as Braylee kicked Beast to a canter and led her horse to the middle of the company. Ollen stayed right with them.

A sharp *twang* sounded just before an arrow shot out of the woods, knocking a Steward off his horse.

Eric yelled out, though Seria could not make out what he said, and a Steward responded with his bow. There was a grunt as someone in the woods fell over.

Then the air filled with shouts as men emerged from the woods and advanced toward the Stewards. Braylee tossed the reins back to Seria. "Stay low!"

The hiss of metal surrounded Seria as the knights pulled their swords. Eric galloped back to where they stood in the middle.

Before Seria could take another breath, fighting broke out on all sides. She kept her head low and a tight grip on the reins to keep her horse from bolting. Blood pounded in her eardrums, and she gasped as dark-clad swordsmen drew nearer. She gripped the hilt of her sword with white fingers, like she thought it would help.

Eric wielded his blade with a fierceness Seria had never seen from him before. His eyes sparked like blue fire, and he utilized his Gift to knock men to the ground and wrench their weapons from their hands.

Braylee moved with a speed that defied his size. Seria ducked with a grimace as a blade came within an inch of his ear. But the seasoned knight swiveled, and the Darkman was soon left dead on the ground.

On her left, Ollen was pale and sweaty, but his movements were sharp and focused. Behind her, Lionel fought to keep his position.

Sobs rose in her throat. *Lambient, please keep everyone safe.*

A Darkman broke through Braylee's side, his wild gaze falling on Seria. His eyes went wide in surprise, a grin twisting his lips.

Seria tried to scream, but Eric was already there, driving the man back. Then he spun and put a hand on Seria's shoulder, pushing her down. She felt the whoosh of air as he swung his sword over her back, stopping another advance on the other side.

Lionel drew closer, putting his opponent on the defense. Another Darkman approached him from the back. Clutching at the slim sword hanging at her side, Seria brought it up and gave a clumsy swipe, barely nicking the man in the side. The blade slipped from her damp hand.

The man snarled and turned his surprised glare on her. But in his preoccupation, he missed Ollen's appearance. Ollen jabbed his sword, and the Darkman fell with a heavy thud.

Seria's pulse thrummed wildly, and she bit down on her tongue, filling her mouth with the salty taste of blood. Would it ever end?

But the fighting did indeed wear down. And soon, the last of the Darkmen fled back into the woods, the sounds of their retreat all that was left of them.

"Gather the wounded." Eric's order was sharp. "Lt. Ollen, send more men back to Marsels. Those men were not here by happenstance. Make sure Mavis and the civilians are safe."

Ollen quickly gave the order to a young sergeant while other Stewards helped their comrades mount. And then they all took off at a brisk pace back to their campsite outside of Shales.

Seria's heart struggled to return to its normal rate. She gave the horse its head, unable to concentrate on guiding it. Fortunately, the animal was content to keep pace with its fellow mounts.

She glanced over the men around her, checking them over with a healer's eye. Lionel had a rip on his sleeve, but there was no blood. Braylee and Eric, though streaked with dirt and sweat, looked none the worse for wear. Ollen worried her, though, with his white face and stiff posture. She prayed he was not hiding an injury.

After an hour or so, Eric called a halt. He sent scouts out to check the area, then ordered a rest.

Seria slid to the ground and hurried to those who were being helped down. There were five men with injuries that ranged from an arrow wound to the shoulder to a gash in a leg. But none of them were life-threatening, to her relief.

Busying her hands and having something to focus on went a long way in calming her frazzled nerves. After she had bandaged the last wound, she looked around for Ollen. He stood off to himself with the horses, his back to the group. She pushed herself off the ground and dusted her hands as she approached.

"Ollen?"

His shoulders shuddered, and alarm rocketed through her. "Are you hurt?" she asked.

He shook his head but gripped the saddle on his sorrel as if it was all that held him up.

"Ollen." She drew nearer and touched his arm. "What's wrong?"

"I'm fine," he managed, pressing his face into one arm. "Just fine."

"Nay, you're not. Are you hurt?"

"I'm not hurt." He finally raised his head so she could look into his face. His eyes were dark in his stark white face. He shook his head again, trying to catch his breath. "Trying to convince myself..."

Awareness filled her. "That everything is all right?"

His face twisted. "I just...realized." He gulped for air. "Almost everyone I care about...was here."

"And we're all still safe." She moved closer, trying to get him to look at her. "No one was lost. We're fine."

"I can't..." His eyes widened, and his mouth gaped. "I can't breathe."

She ducked under his arm to stand right in front of him. "Ollen, look at me." She gave the order curtly, trying to cut through the panic that threatened to swallow him.

Sweat poured from his skin, and he shook like a leaf. He pressed a hand against his chest.

"Ollen." She caught his face between her hands.

His eyes finally wandered to her face.

She drilled her gaze into his, keeping her voice steady. "Breathe out."

His body quaked with the effort.

"That's it. Now take another breath." She stroked his cheeks with her thumbs to calm him.

Gradually, the shaking lessened. His eyes cleared and regained their focus. Color returned to his face.

"Good." She gave him a smile and lowered her hands. "That's better."

He released his grip on the saddle, his brow creased. "I'm sorry."

"Don't be. You were there for me. It was my turn to do the same for you."

He turned away, avoiding her gaze. "I don't know what came over me."

She grabbed his arm. "Ollen, not all wounds are on the skin. There's no shame in being hurt. Even if the wound can't be seen."

He drew in a deep breath through his nose and looked back at her. "Thank you for being here."

"I will always be here for you, Ollen. For as long as I'm able."

He started to say something, then stopped and nodded. Seria gave him space and moved away to her horse, held by Lionel, who stared at her with an unreadable expression. When he did not hand her the reins, she raised her brows in question.

Lionel shifted his jaw back and forth. "I appreciate what you did back there."

For a moment, she wasn't sure what he referred to. Then she remembered her clumsy attempt to use her sword. She laughed at herself. "What I tried to do, you mean?"

"It was enough to keep me from being stabbed in the back."

She cocked her head. "Well, I owed it to you for trying to keep me safe."

He held something out to her.

"My sword." She took it in her hands. "I thought I'd lost it back there."

"I came across it just before we left. You don't want to lose something like this."

"Thank you, Lionel."

He shrugged and handed her the reins. Seria took pity on him and said nothing more. As she settled on the saddle, she glanced over at Ollen, once again at her side. He gave her a strained smile but looked much more like himself.

She took a deep breath, in shock at how much had transpired in such a short amount of time. How much she had learned and gained since leaving Cadence.

And even how much more she had lost.

37

Areem was assigned to join Mason and Shon on their excursion to Shales. Mason was anxious to head out right away, so after Bruin and his company left for another pickup, he wasted no time getting ready.

They rode into Shales that afternoon, dusty and watchful. He kept his hood low over his head and rode straight for Larence's house, all the while staying alert for a glimpse of a murderous prince.

The three men dismounted in front of the modest cabin owned by Bruin's longtime source. Areem knocked loudly. The door creaked open, revealing a teenage girl with fair hair and cheeks. Her face drained of color, even as Larence bustled to the entrance and welcomed them all in.

"I daresay, your arrival does not come as a surprise." Larence rubbed his hands together. "I figured Bruin would've gotten my message by now."

"That's right." Areem held his head up high and gave the girl a cocky grin.

Larence smacked his daughter's arm. "Julia, quit standing there gawking!"

Julia jumped and went to the hearth, stirring something in the pot, all the while flicking quick glances over her shoulder.

"Bruin said you were to give us a place to stay." Areem acted emboldened by the obvious intimidation he held over the people in the room. He looked over at Julia and sneered. "That won't be a problem, will it?"

She shook her head rapidly, clutching her spoon with white fingers.

Mason swallowed. This girl could have been Seria. She even sported the same long blonde hair and bloom of innocence. But her eyes nearly swallowed her face in her anxiety.

His stomach soured. Had Seria not found him that fateful night in the Gateway and pushed her way into his stubborn heart, she would have stared back at him with the same fear and dread as this girl.

"Of course not," Larence said with a greasy smile. "We have plenty of sleeping space in Julia's room. She'll be happy to sleep elsewhere."

"That won't be necessary." Mason cleared his throat. "We'll take a room in the village."

Areem blinked at him. "Bruin said we would be given a room here."

"There's no reason to run these people from their beds."

"It's no bother." Larence bobbed his head, oblivious to his own daughter's terror.

"We appreciate the offer. I just wanted to make you aware of our presence, should you come to any new information."

"Of course."

Mason gave him a slight nod, already reaching for the door. He looked once more to the girl, who looked only slightly relieved that they were leaving. She became aware of his look and lowered her gaze.

"Let's go, Areem."

The young man pounced as soon as they had stepped back outside. "What was that?"

Mason shrugged. "I don't think everyone was thrilled with the idea."

Areem threw his hands out. "So what? We would've had it made there! Did you see the way those people looked at us? They would've given us anything we wanted."

"We're not here to capitalize on people's fears, Areem." Mason ground the words out.

"Aren't you the one who told me to use whatever means necessary to get to the end?"

The words echoed in Mason's head, stunning him to momentary silence. Areem was right. Mason had taught that very lesson in his training.

Through it all, Shon stood by without a sound, unusual for him. His eyes flitted back and forth between Areem and Mason, his expression unreadable.

"Come on, Mason." Areem huffed. "There's no reason we should pay for a room when—"

"That's enough, Areem."

"But this is nonsense!" The young man's face flushed.

"I said that's enough, Private!" Mason took a quick step forward into his student's face. "It would do you good not to forget your place."

Areem glared back at him, his jaw clenched. "Aye, *sir.*"

Mason took a calming breath. "Good." He pulled a small pouch from his belt. "Here. So you won't have to pay for your room. There's a pub down the street that favors Jader's men." He tossed the bag to Areem, attempting to ease the sudden tension between them.

Areem caught it, gave Mason a tight-lipped nod, and stalked away.

Mason let out a tense chuckle to conceal his turmoil. "That's a hot-headed one there."

Shon grunted, his arms crossed in front of him. "Hope you're planning on paying for mine, too."

Mason rolled his eyes. "Sure. I'm used to having to cover for you."

They stepped away from Larence's door, out into the dusty street. Areem was already long gone, likely to stew over rum all night. Mason kept his head down as he led the way to the pub, but his eyes up. Stewards could be staying in Shales even now—maybe even the prince. Mason would not be caught off guard.

The trip back to the Steward camp was quiet, everyone too tired or troubled to talk much. Ollen certainly did not have the endurance to carry on a conversation. Weariness weighed his limbs down, and he was too drained to think.

Seria was quiet, her expression contemplative. Her usual sunny disposition was darkened by the cloud dimming her eyes. He wished he had the words to lighten her spirit, but he couldn't control his own anxiety, much less ease hers.

His young sergeant, newly promoted Kleff Jaycobs, rode at his right, his squad in formation behind them. Kleff's squad was made up of fifteen men, young but well-trained and focused. They had responded quickly to the threat in the woods.

"Your men did well back there, Sgt. Kleff."

Kleff straightened in his saddle. "Thank you, sir. And I want to say, I am glad to be a part of your company." He waved to the squad behind him. "We all are."

Ollen let out a tight chuckle. "I haven't had much time to get used to the idea, much less be a lieutenant."

It felt strange to lead his own platoon. He wasn't much older than the men he was supposed to lead. He should have had time to work with his new men and get to know his sergeants. But the process had been cut short. Braylee and Dudley had worked together, with Ollen's input, to install the new company. And before he knew it, Ollen was riding out behind Captain Braylee and Prince Eric into the Gateway with his platoon, which included this new sergeant and a squad of very capable, very green men.

"You may not realize it, but you've made quite an impression on the lower ranks," Kleff said. "You've earned a lot of respect, due to your character, as well as your skills. We look forward to working with you in the future."

Though Kleff's words were meant to encourage him, and Ollen was humbled, they also stirred up a whirlwind of anxiety. These men depended on him to be strong in the middle of battle. What if he could not hold up?

They soon broke through the woods and into the clearing where dozens of tents were set up. An almost audible sigh of relief rose and fell. Prince Eric trotted Oakley to the center. "Thank you, men, for all you've done. Let's get some rest now." He gave everyone a nod, then turned away, followed by Braylee, who waved Ollen to join them.

Ollen led his horse down the short path to Eric's tent, where the two older men were already dismounting. When they entered the tent, he hesitated. Was he supposed to join them?

Braylee's face appeared in the opening, his dark eyes twinkling. "Come on in, Lt. Ollen."

Unable to hold back a sheepish grin, he followed Braylee inside.

There was no missing the strain on Eric's face as he paced the confines of his quarters. "They know we're here now. And I somehow missed it."

Braylee frowned. "What do you mean, you missed it?"

Eric shook his head. "How did they get that close without my realizing it? I should've known. I should've sensed something was wrong."

"Prince Eric, you're not omniscient. No one expects you to know what's happening before it happens."

"But I've always been able to tell. What's wrong with me?" Eric stopped and ran a hand over his face. "Now that I'm here, I can't seem to get a feel for what I'm supposed to do."

Ollen waited by the exit, feeling more and more awkward as the conversation turned personal. Surely the prince did not mean for him to be privy to his airing out his worries.

Braylee stood as unruffled as ever, his arms crossed, and remained quiet, letting Eric talk.

"I thought it would be a safe trip since it had already been hit and no one knew we were here. I never dreamed we'd find a Steward spy there. And I shouldn't have allowed Seria to go."

"What's done is done," Braylee reminded him.

Eric nodded. "True. But still." He drew in a deep breath. "It's time we make some plans, take the initiative," Eric said, his voice stronger. "I did not come all the way out here to be sent into hiding. Not again."

The statement reminded Ollen of the years the prince had stayed in Paladin while Uralis Faunt led the Stewards. There had been a lot of questions and resentment about the silence from the royal house. A lot of conspiracy rumors that the commander staunchly shot down.

An ache formed deep within at the thought of his old mentor. Uralis would've been proud of his promotion, but Ollen wondered how the veteran commander would've responded to his panic attack earlier.

Eric clenched his fists, his brow bunched. "Bring me a map."

When the charts arrived, all three men bent over the diagram of the layout of the area, trying to find something, a clue to the Darkmen's strategy. Nothing was said about the Reader, but Ollen had no doubt his presence weighed heavily on Eric's mind. The reports had made it clear that Mason Grey had had a hand in the pickups.

"Five towns." Eric mused over the layout of the nearby towns. "No particular order or direction, other than that they're all northern Gateway towns."

"And they entered every town from both ends, not giving any hint as to where they came from," Braylee added. "Yet, they left together, usually heading northwest."

Eric traced the areas with his finger. "I have to figure this out." He stood and crossed his arms, scanning the map again. "How far is Thaylor from here?"

"Half a day's ride." Braylee looked at him. "What are you thinking?"

Eric scratched his jaw. "Not sure." He moved closer to the map, but his gaze drifted again to Thaylor. His features hardened. "We need to ride to Thaylor."

Braylee narrowed his eyes. "Why?"

"I can't explain it, but I think it may be next."

"We'll get on it right away."

Eric turned his attention to Ollen. "Lt. Ollen. I'd like for you to stay in town while we're gone. Keep in contact with our source."

"Aye, sir."

"We'll take two of your squads, including Sgt. Kleff's. They did well."

Ollen knew the compliment was directed at him, as their officer, but he did not feel he had earned it. Not yet. "They're good men."

Eric started to say something else, then stopped. Braylee excused himself at that point, leaving Ollen alone with the prince.

"Are you all right, Ollen?" Eric asked, his voice soft.

Ollen stiffened. Had Eric witnessed his breakdown in the woods earlier? "I'm fine, Your Highness."

Eric took a deep breath and faced him. "War can do a lot to a man. Inflict a lot of damage."

Warmth spread up Ollen's neck even as a new fear mounted. What if he lost all he had worked so hard for? His title? Was this the reason he was directed to stay behind?

"I wish you would've said something sooner," Eric went on. "Or I should've noticed. Maybe I could have said something to ease your mind."

Ollen swallowed. "Sire?"

"You're not the only one who's experienced anxiety after a terrible ordeal, Ollen. I'm the one who went running back to hide in my castle and left Uralis to take my charge." A pained look crossed his face, evidence that Ollen was not the only one who missed the Grand Marshal.

Eric's humble admission alleviated some of the shame that climbed up Ollen's spine, but he still wondered if his position was on the line. A soldier who could not do what was expected of him was a useless soldier, indeed. "I will do my job, Sire."

"Oh, I have no doubt, and I hope I didn't imply otherwise. All I meant to do was reassure you that you are not alone. I do not ask you to remain because I think you weak, quite the opposite. I trust you to watch over the town, as well as keep Seria safe." His eyes darkened. "The people of the Gateway are in distress, much like what I saw in Danyon. Their welfare is suffering at the hands of Jader's thirst for power."

Ollen had sensed it as well. A heaviness settled over this part of the Gateway.

"I want to learn more about the people of the Gateway. See what tactics Jader is using on them to keep them under his control. I feel you are a good man to earn the trust of the people of Shales."

Relief eased Ollen's tension, even as respect for the prince mounted. Not many men would be willing to share their struggles to give a lower officer peace of mind. "I thank you." It did not take his anxiety away, but it did help.

38

If darkness reigns in your heart, how great that darkness will be.
-The Sacred Code

By the time they arrived at the inn, the sun had made its descent, and Seria was exhausted, her eyes dry and gritty, her muscles stiff and sore. Ollen helped her from her horse in front of the small building at the end of town. She nearly stumbled into him in her weariness.

"Are you all right?" His arm was steady as she regained her footing.

"Honestly, I don't know. And now Eric and the others are leaving again." Her voice caught. Visions of the recent skirmish flooded her mind.

"Hey." He reached out and clasped her hand. "I'll still be here."

"I know." She squeezed back. "I'm glad of that." Her respect and admiration for Ollen had grown. He was sensitive and kind but also strong when he needed to be.

At his silence, she looked up to see him watching her, his expression unreadable. "I think you need to get some rest."

She nodded. "You're right. I don't know when I've been so tired." Her whole body drooped.

Ollen gave her hand another squeeze and stepped back. "You go on in. I'll see you in the morning."

The promise did much to lighten her heart as she bid him good night and closed the door. Her world may be falling apart, but it comforted her to know that Ollen was near.

A storm raged in Mason's chest. The world froze around him in the alley where he stood, everything silent and tense while the blood roared in his ears.

Seria was here. She was *here*, in the Gateway–in Shales.

The sight of her, so close but so unreachable, sent a physical ache through his body. His heart pulled him toward her, the longing almost overpowering his reason. She had consumed the majority of his thoughts since he had left her. And now that she was here, it was almost too good to be true.

Almost.

Something within him quivered at the warmth that had passed between Seria and her escort. The man stood where he was for a long moment after Seria had gone inside, staring at the ground before leading his horse around the corner to the barn behind the inn. Mason moved back further into the shadows as he neared, his jaw tight, his blood seething. He was not concerned with being seen, not with the stone around his neck—buzzing and heating at his emotion. But he would take no chances.

His suspicions were confirmed as he got a glimpse of the man's face. He wore simple homespun clothing instead of a knight's garb, but Mason was not fooled. This was one of the Stewards at Eric's side the day Jader attempted a negotiation. The one who had escorted Jader's company out of the stronghold. Mason recalled his name.

Ollen.

His hand dropped to his sword as heat surged through his head. What was he doing here with Seria? Taking advantage of her in a weak moment? He trembled with the urge to attack.

A huge knot settled itself in his stomach like a rock. What was she doing here? The question screamed itself at him time and time again. The arrival of the Stewards came as no surprise. Jader had been counting on it, and Mason was ready. He could take to the battlefield against the Stewards. He could face off with Eric, all in the name of justice for his brother. But knowing Seria was here rocked him. Why had she come?

And how could he do what he had to do when she was so close?

Anger at Seria then swept over him. How could she do this to him? How could she have any kind of regard for a Steward, all the while knowing what they had done to him?

But then the memory of her appearance filled his mind. The spark he so loved about her and the quick smile that lit every dark corner of his heart were gone. Instead, she looked beaten down, defeated. Was he the reason?

Letting out a heavy sigh, Mason leaned his head back against the rough wooden wall behind him. *Seria, what am I doing to you?*

Fear that she knew too much, that she had changed her feelings, left him breathless. He couldn't lose her. She was the only good and beautiful thing in his life. If he lost her, what would there be but darkness and emptiness?

Following the Steward with his eyes until he disappeared into the barn, Mason considered his options. Maybe he could get close enough to overwhelm him and take his Beacon. Then he could control him into helping Mason get in to see Seria.

Taking care to stay out of sight, Mason eased his way out of the alley and eyed the inn where Seria stayed. His whole being yearned to go in and see her, but he held back. This was not the place or the time. But he had to see her soon, before this Steward wormed his way into her heart. For now, the Steward would bear watching.

39

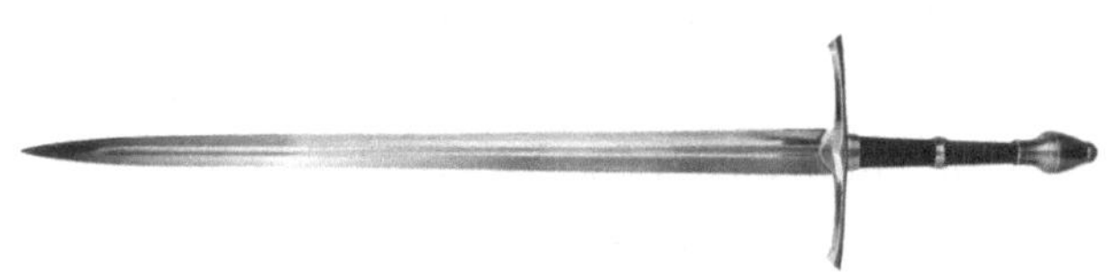

Thaylor, the Gateway

Bruin stood on a hill overlooking the little town before him in the dawning light. His riders were nearby, the horses chomping at the bit in eagerness. A confident grin slipped past his lips. For the most part, the pickups had run smoothly, other than a couple of minor hiccups—both of which involved Mason.

The subjects were still housed at Stonehard. According to Dreeya's last report, some were already more willing to do as they were told. For others, it would take longer. A few nights of sitting in pitch darkness went a long way in making them more submissive.

He expected at any time to get the report that the Steward in Marsels had been dealt with. The emperor would be more than pleased to learn that Bruin had eliminated another of the Gateway spies.

Looking over his shoulder, Bruin slid his gaze over his men. The other half was on the opposite side of town, awaiting his signal. The young man who had taken Mason's place was not as competent, but he got the job done. This was a smaller area than the others; it would be a quick job.

"Let's go." Instantly, the sound of pounding hooves filled the air. They had not even hit the town's edge before the screams could be heard. The people knew what was coming.

The other riders rode from the opposite direction. A few kids had already been targeted. Bruin kept a firm hold on his reins, overlooking the action around him. He watched one of his men grab a young girl by the arm, ready to haul her into his saddle.

An arrow flew through the air, catching the Darkman in the chest and knocking him to the ground. The girl scrambled away into her mother's arms.

Outraged, Bruin turned to see who had dared to fire. A trio of men stood on the porch of the general store. As one, they raised their bows again and let the arrows fly.

There was a shout on the other side of the street. He watched as another small group emerged, their swords already flashing. The ground vibrated as still more appeared on horseback, charging at his Darkmen.

This was no civilian resistance.

"Fall in!" Bruin spun his horse in a tight circle. The Darkmen released the kids as their objective shifted to that of defense. "Come on! Get it together!"

His horse stumbled just then, losing his footing and hitting the ground. Bruin rolled out of the way, his sword already in hand. Shock and rage exploded through him. Another man caught his attention, stepping off a porch on the other side of the street. His blood boiled at the familiar figure.

The prince of Paladin.

Bruin's lips curled. Curse the man's intuition.

Eric Passion met his look head-on. Moving out into the open, he headed straight for Bruin, his famed sword held firmly in his right hand. He was stalled briefly by one of Bruin's men, but with little effort, left him behind and moved on, boldly challenging Bruin.

More than ready to meet him, Bruin advanced. His breath quickened as they approached one another, their swords raised. The loud clang of metal against metal rang, drowning out the chaos around them.

Moving in unison, they came at each other full force, their eyes locked, matching swing for swing. It seemed time had frozen for the pair locked in a death duel. The madness around them continued, but all that mattered was the here and now and the man across from him. He sneered as his blade missed Eric's face by a mere few inches. He pulled back in time to miss Eric's steel. Visions of victory danced in his head as he struck again and again.

But the prince was quick and agile, his face lit with determination. Not a word passed between them, but there was no lack of communication as the swords did the talking. Their blades locked at one point, their faces mere inches apart. Bruin overpowered the prince, knocking him back.

A panicked horse bolted between them. Bruin took the chance to survey the battle around them, incensed at how many of his men had already fallen or fled. The Stewards had gained the upper hand. This time.

Not about to let himself fall into Steward hands, Bruin turned and grabbed the reins of a riderless horse, swinging up smoothly and quickly. With a savage kick to the ribs, the horse shot forward, leaving the prince and many of Bruin's men behind.

Eric jumped on Oakley's back and bolted forward, gripping the saddlehorn. Bruin was already several yards ahead. Thaylor's structures flew by in the chase, soon left behind completely.

Gritting his teeth, Eric kept going, one hand holding the reins, the other clutching Lavrynth's hilt. Eric bent down low over his horse's neck. "Go, Oakley!" The big gray surged forward, his hooves pounding the dirt. They were gaining ground.

A cold wind hit him in the face, making him gasp with its sharpness. Oakley tossed his head with a snort as an icy chill surrounded them. The sun disappeared behind a thick cloud, driving the temperature down even further. Eric's fingers froze around the leather straps of the bridle, and his eyes smarted at the cold air.

Bruin was pulling ahead. Still, Eric kept going. It was not until a frosty fog rose, completely concealing Bruin, that he knew it was hopeless.

His body shook as he pulled his horse to a stop, his breath frozen in the air. With one last look into the fog between him and Bruin, he turned Oakley back towards Thaylor.

Braylee met him at the town's border. "What happened?"

Thankful the cold snap had not gotten as far as Thaylor, Eric had to clench his jaw to keep his teeth from chattering. "B-Bruin p-pulled one of his w-weather tricks."

Braylee sighed as he helped the prince down. "We were so close."

Tucking his stinging hands under his arms, Eric looked around. "At least we stopped this one."

"A few got away, but we don't think they had anyone. We're still trying to make sure all the kids are accounted for."

"Good," Eric grunted as warmth began to steal back into his body. He gave a shake of his head at how quickly Bruin managed to change the weather. Traces of the thick fog hung outside of town and remnants of the cloud drifted around the sun. "He's a hard one to pin down."

"But you sent him running. Few can boast of that."

"Aye, I sent him running. Running straight back to Jader." Eric looked around, appeased to see that the fighting had ended. Seven Darkmen were on their knees in the street, their hands bound. Four others lay covered nearby. The rest had scattered.

Unfortunately, their side had suffered casualties as well. Three Stewards had lost their lives, their bodies already wrapped and draped over their horses. Eric sighed, his heart breaking at the loss. They had accomplished what they had set out to do, but it came at such a cost.

"Thank you."

The husky voice at his side drew his attention. A bearded man with dusty clothes stood there. In his arms, he held a boy of six or seven. The child's arms were wrapped tight around the man's neck. "Willem is all I have. If I'd lost him…" His voice broke.

Eric reached out and clasped his shoulder, his throat too tight to reply. The sound of applause rose from both sides of the streets. Men and women, many of them with children at their sides, showed their appreciation with their ovation. The children clapped too, looking at the prince and his Stewards with huge smiles.

His vision blurred, Eric raised a hand in acknowledgment and moved to join them. He walked down the line, shaking the hands outstretched to him, speaking with many of them, hearing their stories. Tears flowed freely down the faces of many of the parents.

The rest of the Stewards were thronged as well, the citizens praising them for rescuing their children. Young boys and girls stared up at them in awe, delighted beyond words when a knight spoke to them.

After several minutes, Eric met up with Braylee again. The big man looked moved as well, having gotten his share of handshakes and even hugs. He looked to Eric and shook his head in wonder.

Eric's eyes found the bodies of the Stewards again. The fight had come at a loss. The Stewards knew the risk every time they picked up the sword. But he knew his men, and if they could make the choice, he was sure they would do it all over again.

The people of the Gateway were suffering at the hands of Jader's thirst for power. But there was a hint of hope now that the Stewards were here, fighting for them. The few people he had talked with in Marsels, and now Thaylor, spoke of their desire for change, for new leadership. No longer did they wish to cower under Jader's hand. They wanted the full security of the Stewards and the Sacred Code.

This was just a small sample of the people living between the New Realm and the Old, but Eric hoped it meant the time for Jader's terror was drawing to an end.

He had yet to continue his search for the Shadowpit, but he was not giving up on it. In the meantime, he had taken up the yoke of protecting the children. It grieved him to think of what Jader planned for them, the way he would take them and turn them into cold, hardened soldiers willing to do anything for him.

Like Mason.

His shoulders tensed. The day was coming he would face Mason again. And now that he was here in Hashore, the time may be sooner than he dared to hope.

Thaylor did not have a facility secure enough to hold the Darkmen, so the Stewards would take them back with them. Eric called for Lionel.

"Ride ahead and let Ollen know we'll need a place to secure the Darkmen."

"Aye, Sire." He sounded out of breath.

Eric gave him a long look, noticing for the first time Lionel seemed a bit pale. "Are you all right?"

Lionel nodded. "I'm fine, sir."

"You're sure? I can ask someone else."

"I can ride, sir. I'm fine."

Not wanting to insult him by pressing him further, Eric agreed. "Be careful. Stay out of the open as much as possible. Let Ollen know we'll be in Shales before nightfall."

Lionel nodded and mounted his horse without hesitation, his cape draped around his shoulders.

Eric watched him ride out at a brisk trot, hoping he was not pushing himself too hard. He had proven to be a dependable knight, and Eric could not afford to lose any more.

40

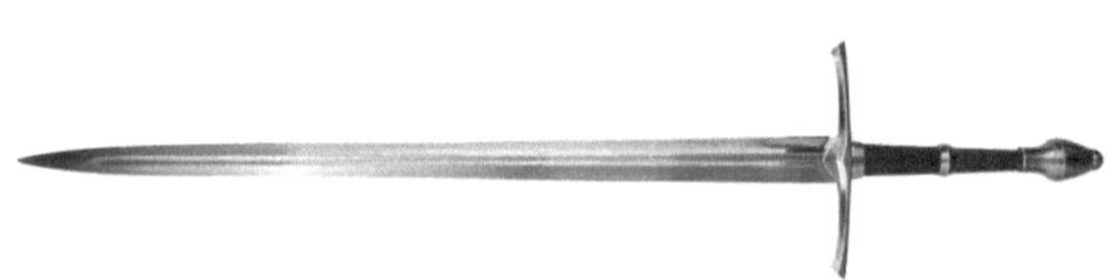

Seek peace and you shall find it.
-The Sacred Code

A chill clung to the early morning air as Ollen strolled the quiet streets. The breeze drifting down from the nearby Slates made him appreciate his cape. His sword was in his room, but he carried his Beacon hidden under the cape.

As he made his way through the sleepy town, he wondered if Eric and his company were on their way back from Thaylor yet. The rest of Ollen's men were camped a few miles outside of town. A part of him balked at being left here, but for now, this was where he needed to be.

He approached the far end of Shales, taking in all he could about the layout of the streets. This was not a large town but should have been fairly prosperous, given its size and location. But Ollen could not help but notice the impoverished state of many of its citizens. Small, rundown shacks lined both sides of the streets, and even most of the businesses looked worn. It seemed Shales was amid an economic decline.

Jader's rule certainly did not seem to be in the people's best interest. So how could anyone continue to be loyal to him?

A young man suddenly appeared in front of him, staggering out of one of several pubs the town boasted of. "Hey, watchit!" the man yelled as they collided.

"Excuse me, sir." Ollen steadied the man as he stumbled.

The man jerked away. "Who are you?" His speech was slurred.

"Just a visitor." Ollen offered a smile. "My name is Ollen."

Turning to face him, the man eyed him up and down. Ollen inwardly winced at how his well-tailored clothes contrasted with the man's worn and roughly-patched garments.

"I meant no harm."

"Sure." The man glared. "Yer one of those well-to-do fellas that think you own the street. You wear yer fancy clothes and talk like one of those edjecated folks and think we gotta clear the street for ya."

"That's not the case at all, sir." The man's loud speech drew spectators from the pub.

"What's goin' on, Teddy?" one big man with protruding eyes asked. "This man giving ya trouble?"

"None I can't handle," Teddy said with a grin. He crossed his arms and glared at Ollen. "I've seen his kind afore."

"Sir, I merely bumped into you, and I apologize. I'm not looking for trouble." Attempting to avoid the confrontation, Ollen started to turn back the other way. The big man blocked his way, an eager grin on his ugly face. Ollen's pulse quickened at the malicious looks of the onlookers. This was a crowd looking for a fight.

Teddy went on. "Betcha think yer too good to buy me a drink."

Ollen set his jaw, wishing now he had his sword with him, but he had not wanted to draw attention to himself. Foolish move. The mere sight of it might have discouraged the animosity. "I think you've had enough to drink."

"Ya see?" Teddy threw his hands up.

The big man spoke again. "Seems to me you oughtta show 'im the error of his ways, Ted."

"Yeah, Teddy, give him what fer!" A woman called out loudly from the porch of the pub.

"Let's see who the bigger man is!" Other loud voices chimed in.

Surprise rippled through Ollen at how quickly the situation had turned ugly. What goaded these people's need for a fight? Boredom? A bent for violence? They stood back and cheered Teddy on, laughing every time he made a move.

"I'm not interested in a fight."

"Well, ya found it anyway, sonny!" someone else yelled. "Ted ain't gonna let ya push him around!"

"Go on, Ted," the big man goaded. Ollen caught the gleeful gleam of anticipation in his bulging eyes.

Teddy stepped closer. "You good enough to fight me?"

"I don't want a fight."

Teddy's fist shot out and met Ollen's jaw, sending him stumbling backward a step or two. Stars exploded in his head.

"Come on, pretty boy!" Teddy sent the crowd a cocky grin. "Afraid to get blood on those pretty clothes of yers?"

Ollen straightened, the right side of his face throbbing. "I have no reason to fight you."

Teddy swung again; this time Ollen ducked and moved aside.

"Ooh, nice move, pretty boy!"

"Here, Ted, this'll make him fight!" Someone tossed a rusty sword out to him.

Ollen stiffened as Teddy grasped the handle and turned to him. "Now, maybe you'll take me seriously, pretty boy."

Mason heard yelling ahead, where a crowd formed outside the tavern. He hastened his step, but before he could be seen, he slipped back into the shadows between the pub and the dilapidated shack next to it. Trotting around the back, he came upon the scene, still staying out of sight.

About twenty people stood around two men in front of the pub, one of whom was the Steward, Ollen. The crowd urged the men on, seeming to enjoy the show. The young instigator was drunk, as well as most of the spectators.

Looks like the Steward's got himself in a fix.

Ollen backed away from the other man, his hands help up in a show of passivity. "You don't want to do this."

Mason grimaced. So he was a coward, too.

"Sure he does!" a woman called. "Teddy's gonna show us what kind of man he is!"

Teddy grinned at the woman and nodded. "That's right!" He raised his arm, holding a scuffed-up sword high.

Ollen stepped back in time to miss the blade slicing through his shirt. Teddy had no skill with the sword, but as the Steward was unarmed, Teddy had the advantage. They slowly circled one another, Ollen careful to stay out of reach of the sword's tip. The crowd cheered and hollered the whole time.

Teddy took a few quick steps forward, slinging the sword around, forcing Ollen into a fast retreat.

"Here, let's be fair about this now." The big man stepped closer, tossing another rough-looking sword the Steward's way.

Ollen caught it easily, then raised it to meet Teddy's blade in midair. The clash of metal rang in the air. Mason straightened. The odds had tipped.

"Now we've us a fight!" The big man hollered.

Ollen spread his feet out, his lips flattening. Mason caught the flash of uncertainty on Teddy's face at the change in his opponent.

"I don't want to do this." Ollen ground the words out.

"Come on, pretty boy!" The woman yelled at him. "Let's see whut ya got!

"Get him, Ted!"

"You got him! Keep going!"

Teddy scowled and tightened his grip. He lifted his sword and aimed it at Ollen's head. Ollen blocked him easily. Teddy tried again and again but could not get near him. Finally, Ollen advanced, his sword flashing as he swung it back and forth in quick, perfect arcs. With little effort, he knocked the sword out of Teddy's hands. An instant cheer rose from the crowd.

Angry at being bested in front of his people, Teddy roared and ran at Ollen, throwing them both to the ground. They rolled mere feet from where Mason stood in the shadows. Ollen released his sword and wrestled with the man, writhing his way out from underneath him, his cape discarded on the ground. Teddy struggled, but Ollen ended up on top, straddling him.

The crowd erupted as Ollen slammed his fist against Teddy's jaw. The young man's eyes glazed over, and his body slumped. He was done. Ollen pushed himself to his feet, panting.

A reflection from the sun drew Mason's gaze to the ground. His heart jumped at the tip of the light rod sticking out from under the cape. The Steward was without his Beacon.

The big man with the swollen eyes tossed him Teddy's sword. "Go on, pretty boy! Finish him off!"

Ollen stared at him, his face unreadable. Then the rest of the crowd chimed in.

"You got him now! Get 'im while he's down! He won't bother you again!"

"Take him out! You earned it!"

Ollen peered down at Teddy, still on the ground, his fingers curling around the hilt. His expression darkened, and Mason braced for the final blow. *This is how they do it.*

Instead, Ollen slung the sword to the ground. "You people are shameful!" His outburst caught everyone off guard, including Mason. "To turn on one of your own who only moments before, you cheered and goaded on. It's despicable." He waved his hand towards Teddy. "This man's life is not to be toyed with to satisfy your own callous needs."

Still trying to catch his breath, he met their gaze head-on, his face flushed in his fervor. "Is this the legacy you would have? That of senseless violence? And for what? For entertainment? You would sacrifice a human life just for a show?"

He inhaled deeply. The onlookers did not look as brash as they had moments ago. A few ducked their heads.

"If that is the way you wish to be remembered, then so be it. But I'll have no part of it." With that, he turned and offered his hand to Teddy. The young man looked up at him in surprise, then hesitantly stretched his hand out. Ollen grasped it firmly and helped him stand, looking him straight in the eye. "There are more worthy things to fight for than pride and rank, my friend. I would suggest you find something you can fight for without shame."

Teddy dropped his head with a nod. "I apologize, sir. And...thanks fer not killin' me when ya had the chance."

Ollen reached out and slapped his shoulder. "No hard feelings, then?" He shook his head.

Distaste filled Mason's mouth at the hidden agenda the Steward carried under those pretty words. Flowery words to win the people, then betrayal and tyranny.

An awkward silence fell as the crowd began to disperse. It was not clear if most were ashamed or insulted. The big man spat in disgust as he passed.

Ollen bent down to get his cape, then paused, slowly lifting his head to peer into the alley. Mason stiffened when Ollen's gaze raised to his, and, for a moment, they stared straight at one another. But then Ollen looked away, clueless to what he could not see in the shadows, and retrieved his cape and Beacon. Mason stayed where he was, his mind churning, as the Steward stood and walked across the street, disappearing in the crowd.

41

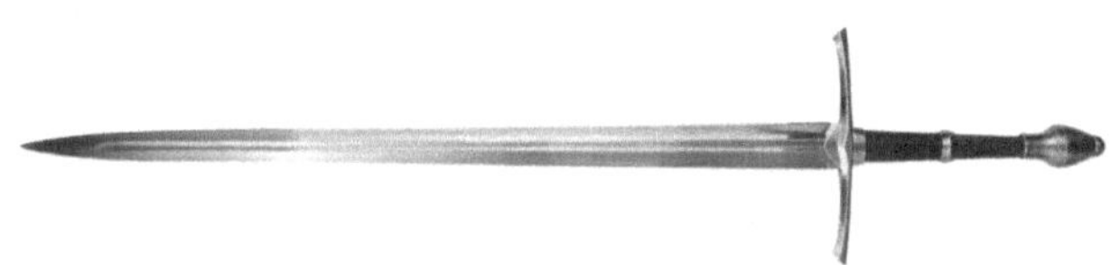

Seria stepped out onto the porch, surprised by how late it was. She had slept fitfully the night before and spent the morning in her room, but she could not hide from the world forever. A sigh escaped her lips as she viewed the citizens of Shales strolling up and down the streets, all wrapped up in their agenda for the day. No one seemed concerned about a band of soldiers barging into their town, taking their children. She wondered if they were even aware of what Jader's men were doing in their neighboring towns and villages. If they even cared.

She leaned against the post, her mind going to where Eric and his men must be by now. Were they able to stop another pickup?

A wave of remorse hit her as she considered how rocky her friendship with Eric had been in the last few weeks. How could she have been so cold toward him? He had only ever wanted the best for her, even risking his reputation to save hers. She was a hypocrite, one who did not deserve his friendship. For weeks, she hid her relationship with Mason, a noted enemy of the Stewards with plans to kill them. She had no call to get angry at Eric about Handan. And she could not lay the blame at his feet for how Mason turned out. Mason had chosen his own path, just as she had done.

Pushing herself away from the post, Seria took a deep breath. The sun steadily moved its way up the sky. A breeze teased her hair as it blew past her, chilling her skin as she moved to go back inside. The sound of a galloping horse pulled her attention to the town's border, where Lionel approached.

"Seria, where's Ollen?" he asked, pulling his horse to a quick stop.

Her heart jumped. "I don't know. What's wrong?"

"I need to give him a message." He swung off the saddle, but as soon as his feet hit the ground, his knees buckled, and he went down hard.

"Lionel!" Seria gasped, hurrying to his side.

Footsteps hurried to her side, and an unfamiliar civilian man crouched down to help him sit up. "Easy now."

Lionel sucked in a breath and tucked his arm close to his side. "I'm fine. Just lost my footing."

Seria got a good look at his pale, sweaty countenance and frowned. "You're not fine. You look about done in."

The stranger offered him a canteen; Lionel winced as he reached for it. A large, dark spot stained the sleeve of his upper arm. "You're hurt!"

Looking down at his arm, Lionel frowned and tried to shrug it off. He took a long swig from the canteen. "I'm fine, Seria." He moved to stand, and the stranger helped him to his feet. Lionel gritted his teeth once he was upright.

She gave him a dark scowl, noting the way his damp hair clung to his forehead. "Tearing into town like a fool, wounded, and I would wager with very little rest or food in the past two days. It's a wonder you're still on your feet."

The other man spoke up. "He may not be for much longer." Lionel's face washed out, and he swayed. The man steadied him before he ended up in the dirt again.

"Come on, Lionel. You've got to get that arm taken care of." She pressed him toward the inn.

He tried to pull away, his movements growing weak, and leaned on his horse. "I can't. Prince Eric is returning with—" He cut off shortly and shot a glance at the man beside him.

Seria got her first good look at the stranger. His clothes were simple but of quality cloth. He had a thick head of dark red hair that hung around his face. "Thank you for your help, sir," she said with a smile.

The man shrugged and looked over his shoulder. "It was nothing."

"An act of kindness is never nothing."

A muscle jumped in his jaw. "It was just a drink."

Lionel swallowed hard and handed him the canteen. "I didn't catch your name."

The man grew more tense, casting another quick glance around. "I didn't give it. I best be going." Instead of walking back down the street, he headed for the alley beside the inn.

"Who is he?"

She turned back to the injured knight, puzzled by the brief exchange. "Honestly, I have no idea."

Lionel's mouth twisted. "I shouldn't have spoken so freely with him standing right there."

"There's no use worrying about it now. Right now, we've got to get you to bed before you fall."

He argued all the way inside, but his face was growing paler by the minute, and he looked ready to collapse again. Seria enlisted the help of the elderly innkeeper to usher the knight to the spare room and wasted no time in cleaning his wound. It was no wonder he had collapsed. Despite his assertions that it was nothing but a simple nick, a blade had cut deep into the muscle. The danger was past, barring infection, but he would be sore for a while. Throughout the entire process, he insisted he didn't have time for her fussing.

She wrapped a strip of clean cloth around his bicep, ignoring his complaints.

"Confound it, Seria, this is serious," he said, sucking in a breath. "I need to talk to Ollen."

"You're not going to be able to talk to him at all if you bleed to death," she said, tying off the end. "Besides, I've already sent the innkeeper for him, so quit carrying on."

"Well, why didn't you tell me that in the first place?" he asked, pulling his arm away from her when she was done.

"Because you wouldn't be quiet long enough for me to tell you." She pushed him back against the pillow. "You rest while I get some food."

"I don't have time to rest."

She paused on her way out the door to give him a glare. "If you get out of that bed, so help me, I'll have Ollen help me tie you to the bed. Believe me, it wouldn't be the first time."

Lionel stared back at her, his stubborn jaw shifting from side to side. But he did not look too sure of whether or not she was bluffing, so he said nothing as she left him alone.

Retreating to the small kitchen to the side of the main entrance, she fixed him some stew and tea, all the while listening for Ollen to arrive. She was on her way to the stairs when he came through the door, his clothes dirty and torn.

"What on earth happened to you?" she asked, pausing at the bottom of the steps.

He stopped and glanced down. "Oh. A little misunderstanding with a local." He slapped at the dirt. "Where's Lionel?"

"He's in the spare room across from mine."

His movements stopped, and his head came up. "What happened?"

She hurried to reassure him. "He's all right. But the fool rode all the way here without realizing he was wounded. You might as well come up. He won't rest until he talks to you." She turned to go up, and Ollen fell into step behind her.

Lionel scowled at them as they entered. "It took you long enough."

"What happened to you?" Ollen demanded as Seria set the tray on the bedside table.

"Got a little too close to a Darkman's sword, that's all."

"Is it serious?" Ollen directed the question to Seria.

"He lost some blood and is completely drained, but he'll be fine, so long as he stays in bed today."

"I'm fine. Just overdid it." The way Lionel cradled his injured arm contradicted his own argument.

Ollen put his hands on his hips. "Where's everyone else?"

"On their way back with prisoners." Lionel winced as he pushed himself into a more upright position. Seria tucked another pillow behind him.

"Prisoners? Did you prevent another pickup?"

"We did, though we lost a few."

Ollen grimaced, and Seria bit her lip. Those were his men out there. She could only imagine his concern.

"They're bringing prisoners back here?" Ollen asked.

"Aye, there was no place to hold them in Thaylor. Prince Eric wants you to secure a place."

"All right. Any idea when he should arrive?"

"Sometime tonight."

"I'll take care of it." Ollen reached over and smacked Lionel's good shoulder. "You rest up and do as Seria says." He sent Seria a wink. "And you let me know if he gives you any trouble."

Lionel huffed at him. "Wouldn't dream of it."

42

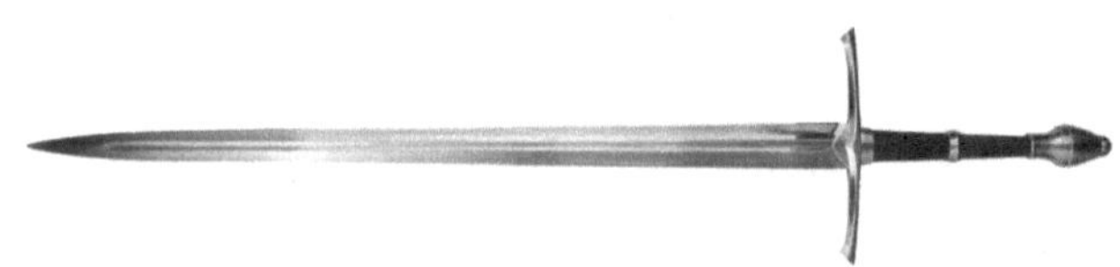

The truth brings light.
-The Sacred Code

Mason emerged from the shadows of the alley beside his boarding house to find Shon standing on the stoop, his arms crossed.

"You sure been spending an awful lot of time in alleys lately," Shon said, his features hard.

Mason gave him a sharp look. "What's that supposed to mean?"

Shon moved for the door. "There's no time."

Mason grabbed his arm. "What's going on, Shon?"

"You can tell me yourself as soon as we get out of the street." Shon pulled his arm away. "But for now, I can tell you that the prince and a troop of Stewards are due to arrive in Shales anytime."

Mason's heart jumped. "How do you know?"

"Heard a couple of locals talking about it."

Mason caught the hesitancy in his reply, along with the way he glanced over his shoulder, as if concerned about being seen.

"All right, Shon, out with it. What's going on?" Mason asked once they were safe in his room.

Shon glowered at him. "Out with it? You disappear without a word to anyone, and then you want me to spill my guts?"

Taken aback by his anger, Mason gave a quick shake of his head. "Something's been bugging you since you got here."

"You're one to talk, aren't you?" Shon jabbed a finger at him. "You haven't been the same since you disappeared months ago."

He ground his teeth. "We're not talking about me, Shon."

"Of course, we're not! You gotta put it off on someone else instead of manning up to your own problems!" He turned away, but not before Mason caught a flash of fear on his face.

Forcing himself to calm down, Mason watched as Shon paced, all the while not looking at Mason. "What happened while you were delivering Jader's message, Shon?"

"You mean you haven't figured it out just by looking through me?"

"Nay, I don't want to do that. But I will if I have to to figure out what's got you so jumpy."

Shon sighed and dropped down on the bed, his elbows on his knees, all the fight gone. Mason was startled at the change. He looked defeated, resigned to whatever fate the next few minutes would bring him.

Mason took the chair. "Talk to me, Shon. What happened?" His stomach tensed as he waited.

Shon stared at him a long time, as if willing him to understand. "I was jumped."

Mason's brows rose. That was it? "Jumped? By who?"

"By five thugs who didn't take too kindly to seeing one of Jader's Darkmen in their parts." His tone was dry. "Apparently, not everyone out in the New Realm thinks as highly of Jader's regime as he would like to think."

There had to be more. "So, then what?"

Exhaling deeply, Shon dropped his head forward and interlocked his fingers together. "They caught me by surprise and knocked me off the horse. That alone took my breath away, and then they were on top of me, about did me in. I couldn't get to my sword, and I really thought I was done for."

"But you weren't," Mason stated the obvious. "You must've managed."

"Nay, I didn't." He stood and walked around again. "This...man showed up out of the blue. I couldn't make out what he said, but it got their attention. He was a gray-headed old coot, but they clearly didn't want to cross him, and they all split. I was half-dead, but he got me patched up. By the time he got some food and water in me, I thought I may actually see another day."

It took a lot not to read Shon's thoughts, but Mason waited for him to get through it.

"He had this old, ratty cloak, so he looked more like a bum than anything. But I saw it hanging on his belt." There was a pause. "His Beacon."

Mason narrowed his eyes. "His Beacon?"

"He was a Steward."

His heartbeat echoed in his eardrums. This had to be one of the Stewards Jader had referred to. Maybe even one of the ones who had taken part in the Handan massacre.

"He knew what I was, Mason," Shon said. "Just like those thugs that got me down. I wasn't exactly trying to hide it. Had too much pride. But while they were ready to kill me for it, this guy, a Steward of all people, intervened. He could've killed me right then and there, believing it his duty, and not a soul would be wise to it. Or at the least, he could've let those guys finish the job. So, why didn't he?" He stared at Mason, as if expecting an answer.

"He's just one man, Shon." The statement sounded lame to his own ears.

"Sure, one man." Shon nodded. "But still a Steward. I mean, we've been led to believe Stewards were the ruthless ones. Yet, the motto of our own army is 'No Mercy.' And we've more than lived up to it, all in the name of so-called freedom and justice."

His throat went dry. Shon's argument rocked him. Even more troubling was that he had no answer.

"I don't blame you if you hate me after this." Shon lowered himself on the bed again. "I just..." His words faded, and he shrugged. "I don't know what to think. Maybe I'm overthinking. But I can't help but wonder if...maybe the Stewards are not the monsters we've been led to believe."

Mason swallowed, aware of Shon's scrutiny. His mind flashed to Ollen, and his refusal to kill the man who had goaded him into a fight. Even Mason's glimpse into the Steward's mind had not hinted at an ulterior motive. He rubbed the back of his neck. "Maybe not all of them."

Shon gaped at him, then let out a relieved laugh. "I figured you'd be ready to turn me in for even suggesting it."

"I wouldn't do that to you, Shon. You should know that."

"I also know how you feel about the Stewards, and with good reason."

Mason had never made a secret of his animosity towards the Stewards. But it bothered him that Shon had felt the need to hide what had happened to him for fear of Mason's rage.

"It's your turn now."

The statement pulled him back. "What?"

Shon looked back at him expectantly. "It's your turn to tell me what's been going on with you since you disappeared those few weeks."

Mason stirred. "I don't know what you mean."

Shon frowned at him. "Don't go there, Mason. I know you. The news that Eric Passion was in Shales should have had you chomping at the bit. This is what you've been waiting on for years. But you act like something else is taking precedence."

Tension mounted within him at the questions. He now understood Shon's earlier hesitance. The last thing he wanted to do was open up and share all that he had done behind Jader and Bruin's backs for weeks.

"I met the girl."

Mason's breath left him in a rush as he pinned his gaze on Shon's. For the first time, he allowed himself to see past Shon's eyes and saw the truth. Shon had met Seria.

"How'd you find her?"

Shon flashed him one of his characteristically cocky grins. "Hey, I may not be a Shadowman, but I'm still a scout. One of the best, I might add." He sobered. "I can see why you think so much of her. She seems the kind of girl that would make a guy want to change."

Still shaken, Mason gripped the arms of the chair. "I never said I wanted to change."

"But you have." Shon's brows lowered. "I can't put my finger on it, but you're not as driven as you used to be."

Pursing his lips, Mason looked away, not ready to accept that. He was still driven, still committed to seeing Jader to victory, still set on seeing his brother's murder vindicated. That had not changed.

But at the same time, there was a trace of truth in it. While his goals had not changed, his priorities had. The fact struck him for the first time since learning Eric was in Shales. Here the prince was within reach, and he found himself more concerned for Seria than for his own long held agenda.

"I meant that as a good thing, Mason," Shon said. "For years, you couldn't feel anything but hatred. It's about time you experience something good for a change." He paused. "And it doesn't hurt she's cute."

Mason let out a single chuckle, as some of the tension left him. He shook his head slightly. "I'm afraid it's a little more complicated."

"I figured as much." He bent forward, clasping his hands together. "What are you gonna do?"

The question reverberated in his mind, echoing in his subconscious. What was he going to do?

One thing became clear in the midst of the turbulence in his spirit. He had to find a way to see her. And he knew who could help him bring that about.

Drawing his tired mount to a stop before the little inn on the west end, Eric met one of Ollen's men, who directed the others to go on down the road to where Ollen had arranged a holding cell for the prisoners.

Eric was glad the sun had begun its descent, casting deep shadows over the town. He wanted as few spectators as possible. As it was, when morning came and the news got out that some of Jader's men were being held, there would be mixed responses. He had tried all this time to stay as inconspicuous as possible, but this would be enough to bring their presence to light.

Braylee was still with him as they dismounted. The big man looked ready to drop, much like he felt. Together they entered the inn.

The only person in the foyer was Seria.

"You're back!" Her face lit up, and she rose from the stuffed bench by the wall, then hesitated, her eyes flitting to Eric's, then back to Braylee. "I've been trying not to worry. You both look beat."

"Not beat." Braylee sighed. "But ready for bed."

"Have you seen Lionel?" Eric asked.

"Aye, I did. He came in earlier today, about dead on his feet. I don't suppose you knew he was wounded when you sent him, did you?"

"Nay." Eric exchanged startled looks with Braylee, who shook his head. "Is he in a bad way?"

"Not anymore, but he will need to rest. I put him in one of the extra rooms."

"I'm sure he hasn't been an easy patient," Braylee said dryly.

"Well, he argued something fierce about being put to bed." Seria smiled. "But I've had worse patients." She froze for a split second, as if the reminder was a painful one. Then she went on with a rush. "My father was the worst. Mama used to get on him all the time when he would not let her take care of him. He'd get hurt in the woods and insist he did not need her fussing over him. And when he got sick, he'd have to very nearly pass out with fever before my mother could do anything with him. She even tied him to the bed once. I threatened to do the same to Lionel."

Eric lowered his head, hiding a smile. She was rambling in her attempt to be casual. He sympathized with her, but it was nice to hear her going on in her usual rapid-fire pace. It had been a while.

Braylee chuckled and shook his head. "A man's got his pride."

"Too much sometimes." Seria rolled her eyes. "My mother used to wag her finger at him and tell him, 'Your pride is gonna be the end of you, Shasta Gayle!'"

The name arrested Eric's attention, and he straightened, even as the same shock crossed Braylee's face. At their reaction, Seria fell silent. "Am I talking too much?"

"I thought you said your father's name was Tug," Braylee said.

"Tug was more of a pet name. No one called him Shasta, except when my mother was frustrated with him. What's got you both so frazzled?"

Eric shook his head in wonder. "I never put two and two together." He directed his words to Braylee. "Even with the last name."

She put her hands on her hips. "What are you talking about?"

Braylee urged him on with a nod.

Eric took a deep breath and met her confused gaze. "Seria, your father was a Steward."

43

Seria would not have been more shocked if he had thrown a bucket of cold water in her face. "My father was a farmer."

Braylee shook his head. "Shasta Gayle was a Steward, and a good one."

It was too incredible to believe, and Seria let out a breathless laugh. "Surely you're thinking of someone else."

"Not if your mother's name was Helena."

Seria gasped. She had never shared her mother's name. "How could you know that?"

"Because Helena Gayle was known by the Stewards as one of the best healers in the Gateway," Braylee told her. "There's more than a few Stewards alive today because they found their way to their house."

"What were they doing in the New Realm?"

Eric took her elbow and led her to a bench. "I only learned of this recently. He was a part of a company of Stewards that was the first to experience Jader's manipulation. While they never strayed from their devotion to the Lambient, they were deceived and used by him during Calla's War."

Seria brought her trembling hands to her face. It was too much to take in. Her father had fought in the war?

"Those Stewards moved to the New Realm, hoping to see the land turn back to the Sacred Code. He lived a life of obscurity, believing he could do more if no one knew his true pursuit. He was one of our most dependable contacts." Eric's voice was soft with feeling. "It was a great blow to learn he had been killed, along with his wonderful wife and children."

She swallowed past a dry throat. "There was a landlord who wanted our land."

Eric reached out to take her hand, as if bracing her for another shock. "Nay, Seria. He was killed because someone found out who he was and what he had been doing."

A shudder went over her. The sorrow she had lived with twisted within her, cutting her raw. She thought of her father, the way he lived. He was a simple farmer, yet he still taught his family about the Sacred Code. He had attempted to teach his children how to defend themselves, even if he had to hide his own skill. Even the escape games they used to play were his way of protecting them. "All this time..."

"Are you all right?" Braylee's deep voice cut through the fog.

"I'm...in shock. I always thought..." She could not seem to pull her thoughts together. "Are you sure?"

"Very. I can't believe I never made the connection, especially since you talked about your mother's healing ways."

"We knew nothing about Shasta's family," Braylee added. "When we sought to find out what happened, we learned Shasta and his wife were killed, along with his children. We assumed it was the whole family."

Seria's memory slipped back to that day when she found her loved ones laying scattered in the field. Her father died in her arms only moments after she found him. "So, Jader...?"

"Was responsible." A muscle in Eric's jaw tightened. "Your father was so careful in how he worked and sent his messages, but somehow, someone figured it out."

"But why kill my mother? And three innocent children?"

Eric had no answer, not that she expected one. She breathed in deeply, feeling a new sense of grief at the loss of her family, but also a great deal of pride. Her father had been a Steward! He had put his own safety aside for the cause of the Code. And her mother had worked at his side for years.

"I can't tell you how sorry I am that it happened at all." Eric's face was dark with feeling. "But I must say I am overjoyed to know his daughter survived and that I can call her a friend."

Tears blurred her vision, and she blinked rapidly. Braylee looked down at her with a smile of wonder. She was finally able to give him one of her own. "I can't believe it." Her voice shook in her awe. "My father, a Steward."

"A fine one," Braylee said. "He was a good soldier in the Old Realm, and when he moved to the New Realm, he became a great asset to the people still clinging to the old ways."

Seria fell silent, trying to process all she had learned.

Braylee and Eric left her to her thoughts to go check on the prisoners, so she retreated to her room and sat in the single chair, still reeling. She thought back to her childhood, searching for a clue that would have hinted at the secret work her father was involved in. But there was nothing other than his own good character.

Never would she have suspected he was one of the famed Stewards she had long admired. To her, Tug Gayle had been a kind, devoted husband and father, a good neighbor, and honest man. But he was so much more than that.

She was not sure how long she sat there when a soft knock interrupted her musings. Wiping moisture from her eyes, she opened the door to find a small boy with bare feet.

"Byron!" She gaped at him, then gave him a warm hug. "What a delightful coincidence. I didn't know this was your town. How is everyone doing?"

"Fine." As was common, he had nothing more to say, but she could tell something was on his mind.

"Would you like to sit down for a minute?" To her surprise, he nodded in agreement.

Delighted to be able to touch base with her young friend, Seria perched on the edge of the bed and invited Byron to sit next to her. She smiled at him, ready to launch into their usual one-sided conversational format. But he spoke first this time.

"I need to tell you something."

"Of course, Byron." She gave him her attention.

The boy stared up at her, his brows bunched over his eyes. "Mason's here. In Shales."

The floor tipped beneath her. Her fingers went numb, yet her skin tingled. "How do you know?" she whispered.

"I talked to him. Today."

Seria's mouth came open. Struggling to control her reaction in front of the boy, she willed herself to breathe again. Her lungs seemed to have forgotten their function. The thumping in her ears made it difficult to attend to what Byron was saying.

"He wants to see you."

Her eyes snapped back to Byron. Anger rose within her, though she fought to hide it. "Byron, did he tell you to come see me?"

Byron shrugged. "He didn't make me."

Again, surprise took her. "You mean...?"

"I know he can read my thoughts and make people do stuff."

She inhaled. "But he didn't make you come here?"

He shook his head, shoving aside the hair falling into his face. "He asked me to. I didn't mind, cause..." He lowered his head. "He's my friend."

Seria closed her eyes in regret. Byron had always held a strange fascination with Mason. "Is that so?"

"I got lost in the woods, and he helped me get home and met my folks."

"Byron..." She hesitated. "You know he's..."

He ducked his head. "A Darkman. I know. I didn't tell my parents." Then he looked up at her, his eyes full of hope. "But I don't think he's as bad as the rest."

A streak of pain went through her. Knowing what she did about Mason, how he felt about Eric and the Stewards, how he had been a part of snatching children from their families, her heart broke at his innocent assumption.

"He needs to see you."

She hesitated, suddenly pulled in so many directions. Part of her wanted to refuse to ever see him again. She was also terrified that if she did see him, she would not be able to go through with what she knew she must.

The discovery of her father and all he had stood for was still heavy on her mind. He had lived for the Lambient with his whole heart. And it had cost him his life.

Byron still watched her, waiting for her response. With a heavy sigh, she rested her hand on his head. "Where am I to meet him?"

Bruin sat alone at the large table in what used to be the main dining hall of Stonehard. His fingers tapped on the smooth, worn table top as he played again and again the botched pickup in Thaylor. His anger churned every time he saw the self-righteous face of the prince. What men had escaped the fight were still filtering back to Stonehard, but in the end, only a fraction would make it back.

They had underestimated the prince. While Bruin knew the Stewards had arrived in Shales, he had not counted on Eric getting the jump on him. He had known of the keen perception of the Passions, and now he had finally witnessed it.

After losing Eric in the wintry fog, Bruin had arrived back at Stonehard, livid. It was not often he was beaten, and when it did occur, he did not quickly forget it. He would meet Eric again, and when he did, the outcome would be far different.

The door opened without invitation, and Bruin looked up, ready to chew up the fool bold enough to barge in on him. He held his tongue, however, when Areem approached, his young face beaming with importance.

"You were right, sir," Areem began without preamble. "The girl's in Shales."

Bruin clenched his jaw against the fury that already threatened to overtake him. "You're sure?"

"Saw her myself." Areem crossed his arms and tilted his head cockily. "She came with the Stewards."

Sitting back in his chair, Bruin studied the young man before him. Areem had shown nerve and skill in the field, despite his inexperience. He held nothing back in his drive to be the best. Already he was proving to be someone Bruin could rely on.

"Where is she staying?"

"At an inn on the end of town. Looks like it would be easy to get into it."

"Good job. Get some rest and be ready to move out early."

Instead of moving to follow orders, Areem scratched at his jaw. When Bruin raised a questioning brow, he spoke again.

"There's something else you should know."

44

Mason waited in the shadows as Seria dismounted her horse in the alley beside an abandoned building across the street. He held his breath as she stepped to the door and held up a lantern, casting a cautious look around before entering. Pride swelled at the way she carried her sword in her hand. His pulse thrummed in his neck, his arms stiff with the ache to hold her. But he held himself in check. Just a little longer.

After what seemed like an eternity, Shon appeared at his side. "It's all clear."

Mason nodded and licked his lips. That Seria had come at all did much to ease his mind, but it did not erase the doubts that had etched themselves into his spirit.

"You better go if you want time."

"Right." He forced himself to move forward, giving the street another careful sweep up and down. Shon would keep watch and signal at any sign of trouble, but Mason held on to hope that his time with Seria would be uninterrupted.

He took another slow breath before he pulled the door open. His vision cut through the shadowed edges of the room and found Seria on the other side, holding her sword up before her. The lantern sat on a large, dusty table in the middle of the room between them.

Her eyes found his, just as green and deep as he remembered, and she lowered the sword. "Mason." Her voice was soft, breathless.

He strode forward and caught her up in his embrace. After a brief moment, her arms slid around his waist. There was no describing the emotions sweeping over him at the feel of her in his arms again, where she belonged. He held her close and breathed her in.

One thing became very clear in his mind then. He needed her. More than any vow he had ever uttered, more than any desire for justice.

He pulled back so he could look down into her face. "I've missed you."

Her smile was strained, her eyes moist. "I've been thinking of our first days in the cabin. It seems like an eternity ago."

He rested his forehead against hers in a familiar move. Had it only been a few months ago? He was not sure how, but in the time apart, something had changed him. A whisper of fear blew into his mind. What if she had changed as well?

Not giving the question any room to grow, he put her sword on the table, took her hands, and drew her to an old bench. They sat, turning slightly so they could face one another. "You look wonderful."

She pulled her hands to her lap and dropped her gaze. "I feel completely drained and as weak as a wet slipper."

"Well, you look better than a wet slipper."

She seemed at a loss for words, which was unusual for her, but he attributed it to the moment. He reached out and caressed her cheek. "Hey, I owe you an apology."

Her head came up, and her expression brightened. "You do?"

"About Byron and his family." He gave her a grin. "Turns out, I had no idea what I was talking about. I've never met anyone who earned my respect so quickly."

She smiled, though her shoulders sagged a bit. "I admit, I was surprised when Byron said you were his friend."

"He actually said that?" His chest warmed. "He's not one to give away a compliment."

Seria shook her head with a soft laugh. "Nay. I could tell he meant it."

"Well, I mean it, too. I can see why you thought so much of him. He's a good kid."

"I'm glad you realized that."

Something was off. Seria was too quiet. He wanted to reach for her hand again, but her reserve kept him on edge, afraid to say the wrong thing, lest he reveal too much. And he could not inquire too deeply after her, for fear she would press to know about him.

Her gaze met his and locked, as if trying to read his thoughts. Her scrutiny sent ribbons of alarm through him. Unable to bear her stare any longer, he leaned forward and kissed her. He slipped his arm around her, trying desperately to cling to the moment and relive the closeness they had shared in the woods.

But she did not respond like she used to, her body stiff in his arms. Then she pulled away and walked to the other side of the room, putting distance between them. A long silence fell, one that weighed on him like a pile of stones.

She faced him, her cheeks pale. "Mason, my father was a Steward."

Her words rattled in his head, landing in his gut with a thud. "What?"

"I found out a little while ago."

"How do you know it's true, then?" Someone was toying with her. A Steward, perhaps. Maybe Eric. Or Ollen, in an attempt to win her heart.

"I have no reason to doubt it," she said. "Not with what I already knew. He was working to preserve the Code in whatever way he could, and that got him killed, along with the rest of my family."

A sick feeling hit him, and he stood. "You don't think..."

"Nay, I don't believe you had anything to do with it. But the fact remains that they were killed. At Jader's order."

He drew in a shaky breath at the revelation. Her father was one of the Stewards Jader sought out. "Seria...I don't know what to say."

She turned from him. "It got me to thinking. We both claim to be so steadfast in our beliefs but selfishly hold on to our own wants and desires, despite the way they conflict with what we stand for." She sounded so resigned and resolute.

"We're making it work."

"But we're not," she said. "We're living a lie. I'm living a lie, and—" Her shoulders straightened. "I can't go on like this anymore."

He narrowed his eyes. "What are you saying?"

"I came here to the Gateway because I needed to see for myself what was going on. Foolish as it was, I took a huge leap of faith, hoping that maybe something would convince me that what I had been doing would be justified. That I hadn't been wrong about us."

"And?" The single word ripped from his throat, leaving it raw.

"Everything about us is wrong."

It was as if someone had driven a sword through his chest. "You're not serious." But he could see that she was, more so than he had ever seen her before. His heart plummeted.

"I'm afraid I am." Her answer was so quiet, he almost missed it. "I just came to say goodbye."

"You've already tried once to leave me. And yet, you still came back."

"That's true. But I came back for the wrong reason. I thought I could save you."

"I don't need—"

"I know what you've been doing here."

The air left his lungs. Even without reading her thoughts, he could see the truth on her face.

Her lips pinched at his silence. "You're not going to try to deny it?"

He clenched his jaw. "I'm just following orders, Seria."

"I know. It's the fact that you carried them through that I can't get over."

He moved closer, desperate to explain, to make her see why he had to do it. She stepped back, her expression cool.

"Is this about the Steward?" The question came out harsh and cold. "Is this about Ollen?"

Surprise flashed across her face. "Nay, it's not about Ollen. This is about the path you've chosen. And the path I must now take." She clasped her hands in front of her. "We're both survivors of a tragedy, Mason. But we each took vastly different paths from that point. I chose to cling to the Lambient, whereas you went down the path of vengeance."

His lip twitched into a sneer before he could stop it at the mention of the Lambient.

Seria raised her chin. "I know you don't believe in Him. But it doesn't really matter one way or another. Because when I reach the end of my life, if I find that I was wrong and Lambient really doesn't exist, I won't regret the choices I made in living for Him."

"I don't regret seeking justice, Seria."

"You kidnap children, Mason," she snapped, her eyes sparking.

The statement was a barb that pierced the wall holding back the shame he had tried to ignore. Heat rose to his face, scorching and stifling. "Those kids are still alive, at least," he shot back.

"What about the boy who died trying to save his brother?" Her cheeks reddened. "What about *Liam's* brother?"

Blades.

The name was a knife to his chest, and the image burned into his mind again. He turned and walked a few steps, raking his hand through his hair.

"What if it had been Byron?"

"I wouldn't have let that happen."

She advanced on him, her brows slashing. "But it's acceptable for others to be taken or killed?"

"That's not..." He clenched his teeth, robbed of any argument that would erase the anger, laced with deep hurt, from her face. A hundred tormented thoughts and feelings swirled about in him so that he could not think straight. He moved to stand in front of her. "We both know we have some...differences. But we can—I can overlook that. They don't matter to me. I only care about you."

"The differences matter to me, Mason." Tears dimmed her eyes. "I always believed there was good in you. But I never expected you to go this far. All because of hate."

"Then let's leave." The words came out before he could stop them. But as soon as they were out, he clung to them.

"Leave?"

Mason nodded, taking her hands in his. "Just the two of us. I'll give it all up. We'll go somewhere far away from here and forget all about Stewards and Darkmen, Beacons and Shadowstones. We'll live our lives the way we want to. Together." Hope sprang anew within him as he watched the emotions flit across her face.

"It can work." He pulled her closer. "That's what we need."

Then she tugged her hands free, and his heart sank.

"It won't work."

"Why not? Isn't this what you've been wanting from me all along?"

"Our beliefs would still come between us."

He clenched his fists. "They don't have to."

"There's no future for us." Her calm rationale was maddening in the face of his desperation.

"Is that what *he's* told you?" He wasn't even sure if he was referring to Eric or Ollen at this point.

She gave a frustrated groan. "Mason, this is about me. I've been fighting the truth for some time, but I have to do what's right. Especially since learning about my father."

He gave her a dark scowl. "So, you're doing this because it's what your papa would want you to do?"

"In part, aye." She jutted her jaw out. "Finding out about him only confirmed what I already knew. What was already in my heart. I will not compromise my belief in the Lambient. The hatred you have for the Lambient and the Stewards will eat you alive. You've got to come to peace with yourself, with what's happened in your past. And I can't wait for that."

There was a loud hammering in his mind, and a sharp pain bit into his temple. Seria murmured something about having to go and started to leave. Panic reared its head, and he grabbed her arm. "Wait a minute." He looked her in the eye, ready to say what he must to get her to stay. Even if it meant controlling her.

"Mason, I took a big risk coming here to see you." She looked up at him boldly, her admission taking him off guard. "You could control me into doing anything you wanted. Or at the least, you could know everything on my mind. But I came anyway because I believed you cared too much to hurt me."

Mason's world shattered as she stepped out of his hold. He closed his eyes and exhaled, long and deep. "Seria, don't do this. Don't leave me like this. Not after everything I've already lost."

"I'm sorry." Her shoulders straightened as she stood to her full height. "You should leave town before someone learns you're here."

Pain ripped through him. "You're threatening me?"

Tears spilled down her cheeks as she shook her head. "Nay. I'm choosing where I stand." Her voice caught as she breathed her last words to him. "Goodbye, Mason."

He stood there like a statue as she took her sword and turned and walked away. Everything in him screamed to go after her. She did not have the power to resist him; they both knew that. All he had to do was catch her gaze one more time, speak a few words. And she'd be his again.

But he could not. He would not. So, he stood there, his head pounding and his heart splintering. The hole grew and swallowed his very being as he watched her leave.

And this time, he knew she would not come back.

It was late by the time Eric and Braylee arrived back at the inn after checking over the temporary holding cells for the Darkmen. Pleased with the security of the location behind the general shop, Eric had set some guards for the night and left it to their hands.

He glanced over at his captain as they entered the quiet foyer. "How are you holding up, my friend?"

Braylee took a deep breath. "Trying not to fall asleep on my feet."

Eric nodded. "Things are secured for the night. We should both be able to sleep. And I know better than to bother you in the morning."

The teasing earned him a light glare, and he chuckled. Weariness weighed his limbs down as he looked to the stairs, envisioning the bed waiting for him. But before he could make the first step, the door opened up behind him, and Ollen entered the inn with their source, both looking serious.

"What is is, Ollen?" he asked, dismay tightening his voice more than he intended. Why couldn't he just go to bed in peace?

Ollen motioned to the man beside him. "Larence has news."

Eric looked to the thin shopkeeper who had fed them information about the Gateway for years. "What is it, Larence?"

The man's lips turned down. "I received an anonymous report a little while ago about a potential pickup in Wyxel."

Eric frowned. "Where did the report come from?"

Larence shook his head. "I don't know. I found this parchment on the counter when I was closing up." He handed it over to Eric.

"How far is Wyxel?"

"A day's ride, thereabout."

Trying not to let his frustration show, Eric thanked him, and Larence nodded and took his leave. Eric motioned for his captain and lieutenant to follow him and led the way to his room, but stopped at Lionel's door first.

The young knight was still awake, more worried about what he was missing than his injury. "Have the Darkmen been detained?"

Braylee answered him. "They're under guard now, so don't be fretting."

Lionel tugged at the blanket, a scowl etched on his face. "I don't need to stay in bed. It was only a—"

Eric put his hand up. "I've learned that you don't argue with a healer. Seria knows what she's doing, and if she says you need rest, then you see you get it."

Lionel sighed. "Aye, sir."

Hiding a smile at his eagerness, Eric promised to check on him on the morrow and left him to his rest. Gathering around the small table in his room, he and Braylee discussed the message while Ollen listened quietly.

Eric braced his elbows on the wooden surface and waited for some kind of leading. There was nothing. No hint or pull in any direction. "I don't feel any urgency about this."

"Do you think it's a false report?"

"It just seems too easy." His knee jiggled as he waited for his usual sense of intuition to kick in. There was nothing. "I don't feel the need to pursue it."

"Are you sure?" Braylee asked.

Too tired to explain his reasoning, Eric assured him he was and sent his officers to find their own rest.

He could not run all over the Gateway without a solid lead. Larence had never steered him wrong, but he needed more than an anonymous report. Especially with the Dark Army knowing they were here.

His stomach twisted at the thought of the Reader being so close, as the reports pointed out. Mason could be anywhere and would soon seek him out, he had no doubt. They both walked away the last time they had faced off.

He wasn't so sure that would happen this time.

45

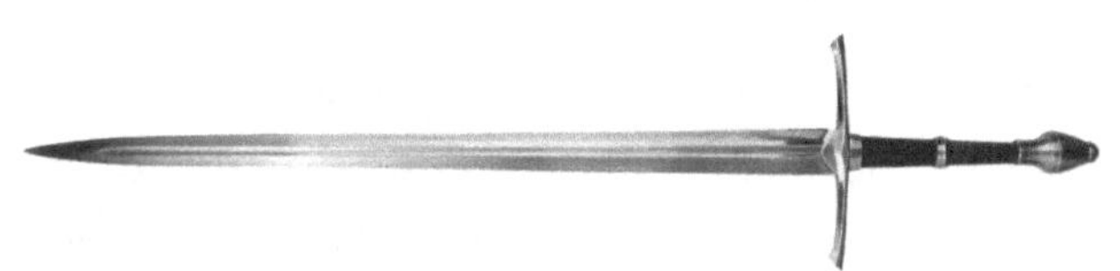

Seria passed the night in tears until she had nothing left to cry. By morning, she felt drained and empty, like a pitcher after the wine had been consumed. There was nothing good left.

It was in those early hours that she cried out to Lambient in repentance. In the beginning, her feelings for Mason were real, but her motives had been selfish and prideful. She had continued their relationship, fully aware of what he was, believing she was the one who could change him. Her desires for significance had tainted her actions. But she could not change Mason or anyone else. Nor was she responsible for the choices he made. She could only answer for herself.

Her prayer was short and broken, but sincere. "Dear Lambient, I'm so sorry for going against what I knew to be right." She sucked in a shaky breath. "Please, forgive me."

In her sorrow, a measure of peace whispered to the tattered edges of her spirit. More alone than she had ever been, separated from the man she loved, and deceitful to the friends she had gained, Lambient drew near, wrapped her in arms of comfort and forgiveness. A small flame of hope was kindled that it was not too late. She could never go so far that the Lambient would not find her or receive her back into His fold.

Tears formed and rolled down her cheeks, dampening the pillow at her head. But this was not a cry of despair, but rather release. Peace stole through the jagged pieces of her heart. Despite the grief, she knew she had done the right thing.

When Ollen called through the door a little later, she was ready to wash her face and join him at a little pub down the street to break the fast. He did not press her to talk as they ate but as they walked back to the inn, she said, "Thank you so much, Ollen." Gratitude for the kindhearted Steward swelled. How many times had he stepped in with a word or deed that touched a place in her heart that needed it?

He searched her face. "I guess this trip has not been easy for you."

"Nay, it has not, but much of that was my own fault." She looked up at the sky. "It brought me face-to-face with my own mistakes and made me realize that it was time to let go."

He stopped at the door of the inn, his regard serious. "That's not always easy."

"It's never easy, especially for someone as stubborn as I can be." She laughed a little. "But I'm learning that the Lambient meets us where we are. And despite how hard it is to surrender my own will, it's better in the end to trust His own."

Ollen was quiet for a moment. She looked at him to see his gaze was on her, and she smiled at the warmth in it.

"You are right," he said, his voice low. "There's no better one you could trust."

The morning was far spent by the time Mason stirred from a restless and troubled sleep. He groaned as he shook himself free from the blankets of the cot. The sounds of a busy camp could already be heard outside the canvas of his tent. He gave a soft grunt. Had Bruin been here, Mason would never have gotten away with sleeping in.

After Seria's warning, he and Shon had left Shales and arrived at the Darkman camp in the wee hours of the morning. Areem had gone out without letting them know where he was, so Mason left word with Larence of their whereabouts.

Swinging his feet to the floor, Mason braced his head in his hands. The memories of his parting with Seria flooded him. How could she turn on him—even threaten him? Did she have any idea what he had gone through for her? Deceit and lies to the ones he served under, always putting himself at risk each time they met. And she shrugged it off as if it meant nothing.

Mason's hands trembled slightly. The temptation to turn his torment into the same kind of anger and rage he had felt for Eric all those years pressed on him. It had to be better than living with the pain of the loss. But despite how much she had hurt him, he could never hate her. Part of him even admired her for what she had done. Mason was selfish enough to want both—Seria and his convictions—but she had shown herself to be the stronger of the two.

Maybe it was for the best. It was wrong to fraternize with a known accomplice of the enemy. He had seen what had happened to Hepp.

Angry with the direction of his thoughts, he stood. Crue was already gone, busy with his daily chores. The boy had been asleep when Mason arrived the night before, for which Mason was thankful. He had not felt up to Crue's cheerful greeting.

After dressing and hanging his sword at its usual place on his belt, he stepped outside, squinting against the sunlight. By the energy level in the camp, Jader must have already arrived.

Reluctance to speak to the lord tugged at him, which was strange since Jader was the one person who had remained Mason's constant support in the last few years. But he would want a full report, and Mason had nothing to tell him. His pickups with Bruin had ended in disaster. He had yet to lay eyes on Eric, had no idea where the Stewards camped because he had not gone looking. And he had lost Seria.

Mason turned for the roped-off corral at the southern end of the camp. Sure enough, Crue dutifully tended to Mason's tired horse.

"Good morning, Lord Mason!" Crue greeted him with his usual smile. "I wasn't able to bed your horse down last night, so I thought I'd give him some extra attention this morning."

Stopping to scratch the roan's long nose, Mason tried not to be annoyed at the teen's constant cheerful disposition. "Thanks."

Another young boy approached with a message for Mason. Jader requested to see him. Though his heart sank, he did not waste any time in following the lad to Jader's tent. The emperor bid him to enter as soon as he was announced. Mason stepped in, feeling like it had been a year since the last time he had spoken with the busy emperor.

Jader mumbled under his breath as he motioned Mason to a seat on the other side of the small table at the center of the tent. He shook his head in exasperation. "I cannot imagine how these people have managed to remain in my army as long as they have." He frowned. "Bruin is gone but a few days, and everyone forgets how to carry on without him."

Not sure how to reply, Mason gave a small nod.

"Now then." Jader folded his hands and sighed, ready to move on. "It has been a while, my boy. You look a bit peaked."

Mason fidgeted. "I got in late last night and didn't get much sleep."

Jader's face darkened. "This comes as no surprise," he said. "I am sure you are very distracted, knowing Eric Passion is in the area."

He swallowed the knot that had suddenly formed in his throat. "I have every intention of tracking him down, sir. But...there've been some delays."

Leaning back in his chair, Jader regarded Mason with his one good eye. "I can see this has been difficult for you."

Mason's brows furrowed. "Sir?"

"You have been driven with the need for justice these past years, fixed on having a hand in the Passions' demise. However, you are but human, and I suspect knowing you are so close to reaching your goal has brought back all the pain of losing your brother." Jader leaned forward. "It is good to let yourself feel. You suffered greatly watching those Steward butchers massacre those boys. It is that emotion that will drive you into fulfilling your goal."

Letting the images flash though his mind again, Mason felt that familiar stirring of anger. "Aye, sir."

A small smile appeared on Jader's thin lips. "Good. Now, I have a task for you. I do not trust anyone else in this inept camp to carry it out, and it is of utmost importance."

"Of course."

Pulling out a rolled-up piece of parchment, Jader handed it to Mason. "This is for Larence. It contains instructions that will lay out the next phase of our plan. Give it to him personally." An ominous gleam lit his eyes. "Now that Eric Passion and his Stewards are in the Gateway, we must ensure they do not leave."

The thought of going back to Shales made him ill. But duty called, and he would not let himself get sidetracked again. "Aye, sir."

The message was urgent, so after the meeting, Mason headed straight for the corral. Crue had moved on to his other duties, leaving Mason to saddle his own horse.

"Where are you off to already?"

At Shon's question, Mason looked over the back of his horse to see the other man approaching. "Got to get a message to Larence."

Shon looked doubtful. "You sure that's a good idea?"

"Duty calls."

"You need me to tag along?"

It was tempting; Shon's company was always welcome. But Mason shook his head. Jader had requested he go alone. "It shouldn't take long. You've been on the go since you came back. Take it easy today."

"All right, then. You be careful."

"Aye, mother."

Shon made a face. "Man, I ain't yer mama!"

Mason mounted and urged the horse on. When he glanced back, Shon still stood where he left him, his hands on his hips and a disgruntled look on his face. "See you in a little while."

Shon gave him a salute. "I'll be here."

Jader remained in his seat even after the sounds of Mason's horse exiting the camp faded. A frown settled on his brow.

Something was amiss. Mason had not once looked him in the eye, which said something, considering his Gift. He seemed preoccupied, troubled, reverting to the days after his absence in Cadence.

Steepling his fingers in front of him, Jader considered all that had been accomplished in the last few weeks. Things were going according to plan, and that included Mason's development. The prince was within reach. Even now, his army advanced on the Gateway. The Old Realm would soon be his.

He would not let anything or anyone interfere with his plan, but for the first time, he was concerned about Mason. His zeal was missing. Something else had taken precedence over his need for vengeance.

Jader glanced down at the thick canvas in front of him, where only moments before, Bruin's cryptic message had appeared in purple shadows. Though the words had already faded, Jader could still see the words in his mind.

We've got a traitor.

46

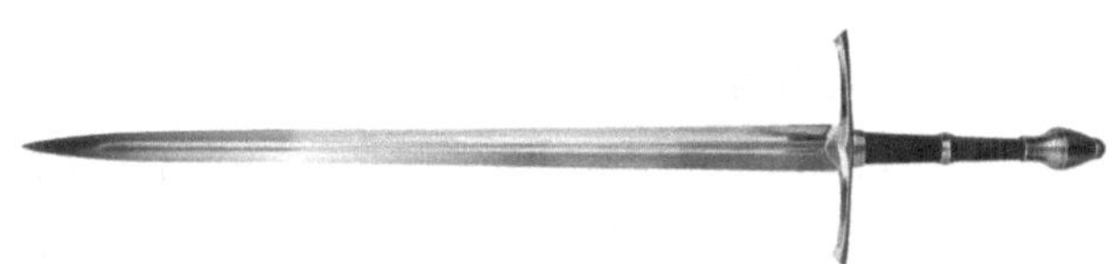

Bruin rode into the main camp with a small company behind him, the afternoon sun beating down on his head. He dismounted in front of Jader's tent and motioned for the others to wait.

Jader met him at the door. "I trust things are well in hand in Stonehard."

"Greggor is on his way to Wyxel as planned." He did not express his unhappiness at leaving his work to someone less competent. But the matter of a double-crosser could not wait.

The emperor raised his head. "Then let us proceed."

Bruin bowed his head, then exited, his steps swift and sure. He summoned his company to fall into step and led them to a tent at the edge of the site. He paused for a heartbeat, then ripped the flap back and stormed inside.

Shon Larson jumped to his feet, the bridle he had been treating falling to the ground. He blinked at the sight of the Darkmen filing in behind Bruin. "What is this, Commander?"

He cocked a brow. "Surely you already know."

Shon's face paled before he made a grab for the sword hanging from his cot. Bruin's men were on him in an instant, forcing him to the ground.

"What're you doing?" Shon growled.

They wrenched his hands behind his back and shackled them, then jerked him to his feet without an answer. He stood before Bruin, panting for breath. Not a word was said between them, but Shon lifted his chin in defiance.

Bruin tipped his head to the door, and they hauled Shon outside, half-dragging him all the way to Jader's tent. The scout's face was stoic as they jerked him to a stop before the emperor. He stood tall, his dark eyes meeting those of his commander, jaw tilted defiantly.

Jader looked on with calm interest in front of his tent. A crowd of Darkmen had already gathered, tense and eager at what was about to transpire.

"Shon Larson," Bruin spoke, his voice little more than a snarl. "You've been charged with treason."

Shon's expression did not change. He did not flinch, did not try to explain or even deny it. The very fact made Bruin angrier, and he stepped forward, his fists clenched.

"It's been reported by a reliable eyewitness that you offered a Steward aid."

A loud murmur rose from the spectators. Shon, however, was silent. He lifted his chin slightly, his gaze never wavering.

"Have you nothing to say?"

"Am I not entitled to a trial?"

Jader stepped forward. "A trial is not necessary." The lord talked in smooth tones, as if talking about the weather. "We have a witness, and you know the consequences for such an act. There is no need to hash it out further." He handed a coiled rope to Bruin.

Satisfied at the flash of apprehension in Shon's eyes, Bruin stepped close enough to slip the noose around his neck. "Now, do you want to talk?"

Shon narrowed his gaze, taking in Jader and Bruin with his look. "Only that I'm glad I figured out who the real monsters were."

Mason spotted the large crowd when he entered the campsite after delivering his message to Larence, but with the mood he was in, passed it on by and dismounted in front of his tent. He tethered his horse, his attention flicking back to the crowd. Had Jader called a meeting in his absence?

Crue ran toward him, distraught and pale.

"Crue? What's going on?" Dread gathered in his gut.

"A trial, sir." His voice came out shaky. "It's...Master Shon."

His heart slammed in his chest. "Not Shon." He took off at a run, the distance stretching endlessly before him.

A large roar erupted just then, sending his blood pounding in his ears. His boots beat the dirt. He could stop it. Jader would listen to him.

The crowd had lost control, jumping, yelling, and cheering, everyone's concentration riveted to a spot beyond Mason's field of vision. A desperate urgency overrode every other sense as he reached the outer ring of spectators.

"Wait! Stop!" Another cheer sounded, drowning out his voice. A riderless horse barreled through the middle of the crowd, and panic clawed at his throat as he shoved bodies out of his path. "Get out of my way!" A few immediately complied. Others ignored him, slowing his progress. "Move!"

The tree loomed over their heads. The outstretched limb. The taut, thick rope slung over it. *"No!"*

He pushed his way through the front and stumbled to a stop. Everything else around him faded away.

It was over. The rope swung slightly, the weight of Shon's lifeless body pulling it from side to side. Cold shards pierced Mason's heart. His legs gave way, and he sank to his knees in the dirt, staring up at his friend. He was too late.

Everyone began to make their way from the scene, their momentary thrill satisfied. Mason looked around in a daze. Shon had been one of them, a friend. How could they have turned on him like that?

Feeling a gaze on him, Mason looked up at Dreeya, her expression cold, almost gleeful. Dark rage overtook him, and he stomped toward her. "How could you, Dreeya?" he grated. "Shon was a friend. *Your* friend!"

She rolled her eyes. "Nay, Mason. He was a scout. Same as you and me. He had a duty, and it did not include offering his canteen to a Steward."

Mason clenched his fists to keep from smashing one against her face.

"There was no question about it. Areem saw it all. He was guilty and executed, simple as that. If you have a problem with that, take it up with Jader." She gave him a smirk and sauntered off.

Mason stared after her. Did she have such little regard for the people she spent her days with that she would dismiss their lives so easily?

The limb creaked, drawing Mason's attention again. Grief and rage battled within him. Dreeya's last words echoed in his mind.

If you have a problem with that, take it up with Jader.

Mason gritted his teeth as he spun around and barreled through the entrance of Jader's tent.

Bruin blocked him. "You have no business marching in here, Mason."

"Get out of my way, Bruin."

Bruin's posture went rigid at Mason's insubordination, but Jader spoke up before he had a chance to retaliate. "Give us a moment, Bruin."

Bruin's eyes narrowed as he took a step back, his glare promising that this breach of protocol would be dealt with later. Mason waited only until he had stepped out before lashing out at Jader. "*Why?*"

"Because he broke the rules, Mason, and could not be trusted."

"For giving a guy a drink? That's hardly anything to be executed over!"

Jader shook his head and walked away. "I can see I have coddled you too much," he said. "You expect me to bend the rules for you, just because Shon was your friend. He received the same judgment Hepp did, which you supported at the time. What makes this any different?"

The question was a punch in the gut.

Jader faced him again. "We are not your enemies, Mason. It is the Stewards we are fighting. And we cannot tolerate any compassion toward them, or they will overtake us."

Mason clenched his jaw, confusion knotting within.

Jader pressed harder. "The Stewards are the ones who have taken so much from innocent people. They are the ones who kill those who stand in the way of their *righteousness.* They are the ones that took the lives of every boy at Handan, including your own brother."

The Shadowstone hummed against him, fueling Mason's rage. But he struggled to distinguish where the rage was directed. Faces flashed through his memories like paintings in the wind. Liam. Hepp. Shon.

Jader stared back at him with his good eye, his features sharp and intense. A cloud draped over Mason's mind, warm and heavy, making it hard to remember why he was here. Jader's voice rose and fell in fragments, cutting through the fog.

"*...how it was that Liam died...point him to the prince...the one responsible...ever learning the truth.*"

Mason blinked slowly. "What truth?"

Jader straightened, puzzlement darkening his gaze as he turned away. "Truth? I am afraid you will have to clarify."

Alarm slammed through Mason's body, and the cloud lifted. Surely he had not gotten a glimpse into Jader's thoughts. A sharp jolt cut through his head, cutting his reply short. He sucked in a breath and pressed a hand to his temple.

"Are you all right, son?"

Mason gave a quick shake of his head, already backing his way out. "Aye, I'm fine." Without waiting for permission to leave, he spun on his heel and escaped the confines of the tent. He didn't bother with going back to his tent but fled the camp for the nearby woods. The constant sound of birdsong needled at him, and the shards of sunlight that cut through the foliage pierced his vision. He braced himself against a tree trunk as another streak of pain sliced through his head. Then it faded, leaving him weak and gasping.

Questions and fears poked at him, but one fact overrode them all, draining the oxygen from his lungs.

Shon was dead.

The words barely registered in his head, but his heart bled with the loss of his best friend. His only friend. The one who was never afraid to speak his mind, never hesitated to put Mason in his place if need be. Unintimidated by Mason's abilities, he had pushed through the resistance Mason had erected.

And why had it happened? Because he had shown compassion towards a Steward.

Mason gritted his teeth, grasping at Jader's reminders of the Stewards' blame. Once again, they had robbed him. Had they stayed in the Old Realm, where they belonged, Shon would still be alive.

And so would Liam.

With a groan, Mason covered his face, gripped by the emotions trying to strangle him, and focused all of the hurt on the one man who had taken everything from him. His brother, his friend, his home. Even Seria.

Clenching his fists, Mason shook with renewed resolve. He would not leave Shon's body hanging from the tree all day, but come nightfall, he would find the prince. And when he did, it would be over. That man would not be able to take anything from him again.

Tonight, Eric Passion dies!

47

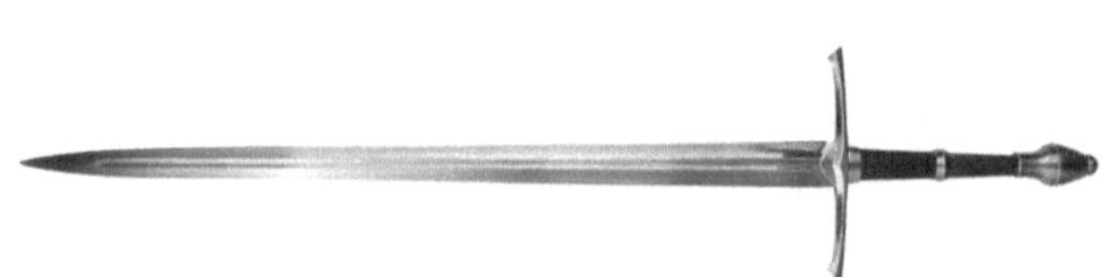

Steward Camp, the Gateway

Word arrived from Larence in Shales right before sundown. Wyxel had
been hit and fifteen kids taken.

Eric turned away from the messenger, sick to his stomach. He had
failed. Again. Clenching his jaw against the emotion that threatened to
burst from him, he stalked for the shadows of the woods that hid them
from unwelcome eyes.

What am I even doing here? He grabbed his hair with both hands,
trying to catch his breath. "Lambient, what are You doing? Why have
You left me to do this on my own?"

Lambient had pulled away from him. His own Passion intuition had
failed him. He had no idea what to do next, no direction.

Lowering himself to a fallen log, he propped his elbows on his knees
and dropped his head.

Fifteen kids taken. And he could have prevented it, had even gotten a
tip, but he dismissed it, all because he did not feel led to follow through.
And now those kids were being held like all the ones before them. Held

hostage in a prison that he was no closer to finding than when he first arrived in the Gateway.

He had come here with such grand intentions. He, the prince of Paladin, would put a stop to Jader's pickups. The people of the Gateway would see him as a leader they could trust. His Stewards would find Joshun, that famed prison where Jader hid his young captives. And just maybe, Eric would find the Shadowpit while he was here.

Instead, he had floundered, walking around like a man lost, waiting for a sign.

Like he had in his very early days of leading the Steward Army.

"I don't understand," he whispered, looking up. "I did what You moved me to do. I faced the demons of my past. I stepped back into the role I had walked away from. I led my Stewards against the darkness that threatens the land. I have served You. Why do You not help me?" He shouted the question, but there was no answer from the sky, mocking in its silence.

Braylee found him a little while later. "Are you all right, Eric?"

Eric gave a bitter laugh. "Sure, I'm all right. Can't say the same thing for those kids, though, can I?"

"It's not your fault."

Shooting to his feet, Eric waved the statement off. "Nay, Braylee. I got the message. Someone warned me. And I shrugged it off." He rubbed his face. "This is Handan all over again."

Braylee crossed his arms. "These kids aren't dead."

"Not yet. But when word spreads that I deliberately ignored a call for help, we'll be forced back to Paladin. Just like before."

"So, what will we do next?"

Eric scoffed and turned away. "Don't you get it, Braylee? I don't know what I'm doing out here. I can't seem to get anything right."

"You kept Thaylor safe."

"One town. But I let Bruin slip through my fingers. And the Darkmen are still gallivanting about, kidnapping children. The Shadowpit is still out there, creating more Shadowstones. I haven't accomplished anything I set out to do."

Braylee's lips twisted in concentration. Then he drew his sword. "Come on. Spar with me."

Eric frowned. "Spar with—nay, Braylee, I'm in no mind to spar."

Not even acknowledging Eric's refusal, Braylee tossed him a gum sleeve, then slipped a second over the sharp blade of his weapon. He had come prepared. "Let's go."

"I said I'm not sparring."

Braylee's jaw jutted. "You need to busy your mind with more than feeling sorry for yourself. Get yourself ready because I'm striking shortly regardless."

For the first time, irritation smoldered at his captain's obstinance. Fine. Braylee wanted a match, Eric would give him one. With the mood Eric was in, it would not take long.

Jerking the gum sleeve on, Eric joined the ever-patient and smug Braylee in the clearing. He gritted his teeth and held his sword up. Braylee crossed it with his own, and then they were off.

Anger pulsed through Eric as he swung his blade, surging through his veins and adding strength to every move. He ducked and blocked Braylee's offensive strikes, taking every advantage offered him.

But Braylee was not to be taken for granted. The big man met his blows with hard ones of his own. His dark eyes never left Eric's face, his look penetrating.

Eric parried another swing and went on the offense, pushing Braylee back. But a few steps later, Braylee had Eric retreating again.

His grip tightened around Lavrynth's hilt. Heat wrapped itself around his body. He would not allow himself to be bested by his own captain. Braylee must already see him as nothing but a foolish young prince, always stumbling over his own choices.

Eric panted for air as he sidestepped the tip of Braylee's blade. He let out a grunt as his sword was blocked again.

He had to do something right. If not here, how could he succeed at anything else? He had to win this. Eric's heart pounded in his chest as determination became a roar in his head. He had to stop these pickups and find the Shadowpit. He had to beat Jader.

If you can do it all on your own, why do you need the Lambient?

The question stopped him in his tracks.

Braylee did not miss the chance. One quick, familiar move, and Eric's sword went flying into the air.

Eric stood there, gasping for breath, realization slapping him in the face. "I can't do this."

Wiping sweat from his brow, Braylee regarded him silently.

"I can't do any of it." Eric shook his head. "I can't stop Jader. I can't rescue the kids. I can't." Release loosened Eric's limbs, cleared his mind. "I've been trying to do it all on my own. But I can't do any of it without Lambient."

Braylee took a deep breath and pulled his gum sleeve off.

Eric put one hand on his hip and pinched the bridge of his nose with the other. "Braylee, I've been so wrapped up in trying to make up for my mistakes in the past, convinced I had to fix it all myself. I never even asked for Lambient's leading. Just relied on my own ability."

"I suspected that was the case," Braylee replied. "I wasn't sure, so I figured the only way to know for sure was to beat it out of you."

A bark of laughter escaped him, letting in a sweet rush of peace. "Nothing like a lesson in humility to put a man back on track."

"So, what will you do now?"

Eric hesitated. "I still don't know."

Braylee cocked a brow. "But?"

"But I know Lambient will lead us from here on out."

He walked with Braylee back to the main camp, more tired than before, and yet his mind was more rested than he had felt in weeks. His revelation did not erase the obstacles that lay before him, but he did not face them alone.

Braylee seemed to sense his need for solitude at that moment, for he waved the men off back to their duties and then moved away himself. Eric stepped into his tent and sat on his cot, pressing his hands together. "I can't do this on my own," he whispered. "Forgive me for ever thinking I could. I need Your guidance. Not for my sake but for the people of the Gateway."

He swallowed and forced his tightly knit fingers to loosen. Taking in a deep breath, he exhaled slowly, letting his body relax, his mind clear. This was not his fight. This battle belonged to the Lambient. And He would see Eric through it.

As he considered his next move, awareness flooded his senses. That same familiar sense of foreboding that took root in his gut every time something was about to change.

Mason was coming after him. He knew it with as much certainty as if Mason had sent him a direct message.

His heart constricted at the thought. Handan would forever be a scar on his soul. He closed his eyes as he thought of the rage Mason had held against him for the last twelve years. At Mason's lowest point, the only person to whom he had been able to turn had been Jader. And thus, his whole life and soul had been consumed with hatred and vengeance.

"Prince Eric?" Braylee's soft call drew him out of his thoughts and back outside. It was time to act.

"I think you and Ollen should take a company to check out Wyxel tonight," he told Braylee. "See what you can find out there."

The slight lift of Braylee's brows was all that spoke of his surprise. "Without you?"

Eric gave a single nod. "There's something I have to deal with here."

He was done running from the past. It was time Mason knew the whole truth.

48

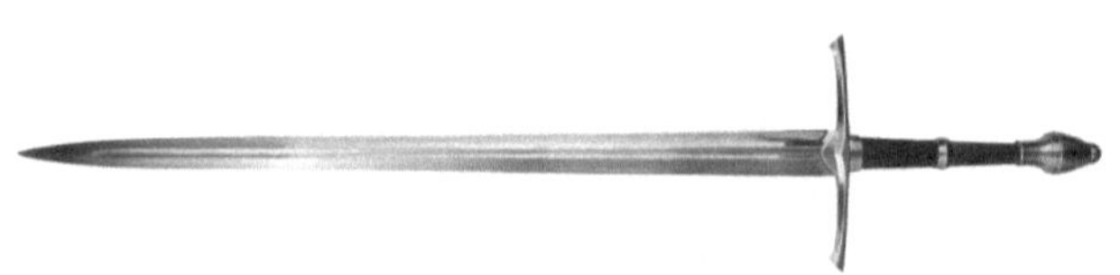

Let the light of the Lambient shine through you.
-The Sacred Code

Ollen accepted the prince's orders without complaint, though his insides squirmed. He had grown comfortable working in Shales, keeping close to Seria. But Eric would stay here, and Ollen had a job to do.

The town of Wyxel had experienced the worst number of losses since Jader's pickups began. Prince Eric speculated it was intentional, especially after Marsels and Thaylor. If so, then the Dark Army would be looking to strike hard from here on out. It was hoped that in doing so, they would make a mistake.

Ollen readied his company of four squads, making sure to include Sgt. Kleff. The young sergeant had an easy way about him and a good command of his even younger privates.

They rode out of the camp in formation under a full moon and halted outside of Shales. Ollen directed them to wait and went into the town, where he was to meet Braylee. First, he stopped by the inn.

Seria was already standing outside the door, watching him approach. "I hear you've got new orders," she said, her cheeks pale.

He swung down to her level. "Aye. We hope to find a trail we can follow at Wyxel."

She looked as if she wanted to say something, but stopped. Then she took a deep breath and looked out over the town, her look contemplative. "I'll be glad when this whole ordeal is over."

Ollen took advantage of her preoccupation to study her. Silver moonlight lit the golden strands of her hair. There was a new maturity that marked her fair countenance. Her eyes were shadowed with sorrow, but it did not erase the peace that emanated from her now.

Her acknowledgment of her mistakes from the day before had stuck with him. He knew better than to believe it meant he had any kind of place in her future, but a stubborn hope persisted anyway.

"It'll all be over soon," he said. "With the Lambient on our side, how can we lose?"

She smiled. "That's a good reminder, thank you."

His throat ached to say more, to tell her all that was in his heart, but he resisted. She wasn't ready, and the time wasn't right. Maybe someday.

But all reasoning nearly failed him when she surprised him by stepping closer and offering him a sweet hug. For just a moment, he indulged himself and held her, cradling the back of her head with his hand and resting his cheek against her hair. His heart throbbed at her nearness.

She drew back too soon, but her smile was sweet and hesitant. He returned it and stepped back lest he betray his feelings.

The door opened behind her, and Ollen lightened his tone. "Watch out for Lionel, all right? He can be a handful."

Lionel snorted as he stepped out, rubbing the bandage on his arm. "I'll watch out for myself, thank you."

Seria laughed, not put off by Lionel's surliness.

"Don't be sore," Ollen said. "You'll be back on duty soon."

His friend responded with a short nod.

Ollen looked over his shoulder at the livery a few doors down. "I better let the captain know I'm ready."

"You'll be all right?" Seria asked, and he caught the underlying meaning. His palms were moist and his back streaked with sweat, but he would do what he must. The Lambient would see him through the anxiety that tried to cripple him.

"I'll be fine."

She gave him a long look, seeing past his façade, he was sure. "I'll be praying for you. For all of you."

"I appreciate it."

"You better get before Captain Braylee comes looking for you." Lionel's voice was brusque, reminding him of his presence.

"I'm going, I'm going." Ollen chuckled and climbed back in the saddle. "You two stay out of trouble while I'm gone."

Lionel leaned on a post with a scowl. "Can't get into too much trouble here."

The night's undertaking was heavy on Braylee's mind as he saddled his bay stallion. Seeking out a troop of Darkmen was always risky, but doing it after dark in unfamiliar territory brought with it extra dangers. And always at the forefront of his worries was the chance that they could walk into a trap. Jader knew they were here, after all.

Beast reached out for a nibble from a stack of hay. "Stop that, you overgrown pony," Braylee scolded, pulling the bay's head back around. It was fortunate the horse was so dependable in a pinch, or he'd be tempted to retire him to the fields to eat to his heart's content.

Maybe I'm the one who needs to retire. Though he never bucked at an order, travel did not come as easily as it once did. He was tired, ready for the war to be over so he could be home with his family.

He stopped and sighed, convicted of his grumbling. *Forgive me, Lambient.* He was a Steward first, so he would do what he must. And right now, that meant traveling to Wyxel.

He was tightening the last strap on his saddle when Eric joined him in the barn, his face drawn. Sending his men without him seemed to almost pain him. "Are you sure you won't go along with us?"

For a moment, Eric seemed to consider the idea, but then he sighed and shook his head. "Nay, I'm afraid not. I have another pressing matter to tend to."

Braylee held his tongue, wishing he felt better about leaving Eric behind. He had a strange feeling this pressing matter had something to do with the Reader.

Eric reached over a stall door to stroke Oakley's neck. "I wish we were home."

"We will be soon enough."

The sound of hoofbeats drew their attention outside, where Ollen rode up, his shoulders straight, his chin set. Braylee led his horse out to meet him, Eric at his side.

"We're ready, sir," Ollen greeted. "The men are waiting just outside town."

"Thank you, Lieutenant." Braylee held his hand out to Eric. "I'll see you soon."

Eric clasped his wrist with a nod. There was no missing the shadow of unease hanging over his brow.

Braylee mounted and turned Beast to stand beside Ollen's mare. Eric stepped between the horses' heads, rubbing their long noses. "Take care, friends."

"You too, Prince Eric," Ollen returned.

Eric stepped aside so they could ride out. Braylee raised a hand and tapped his horse's sides to round the corner of the inn, where Seria and Lionel waited out front. Both responded to his wave as he passed.

Lionel looked out of sorts to be left behind, but Eric wanted to give him more time to rest before he resumed his regular duties. Besides, Seria still needed a guard, especially with the Reader being nearby.

Braylee met Ollen's sober gaze, then led the way out of Shales to where his men waited for him.

49

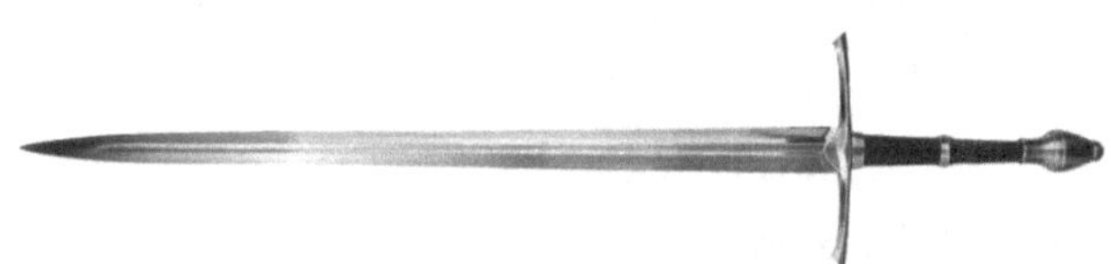

Outside Shales, the Gateway

Eric sat on a stump before the small campfire, his muscles tight and his senses on high alert. The moon hung low in the sky, just above the treetops. A few stars were scattered here and there. Dawn was a few hours out.

He closed his eyes and drew in a deep breath, trying to slow his sprinting heart. Mason was looking for him. And he would not stop until he found him.

Lambient, I believe I am here at Your bidding. Guide me in what is about to happen.

He had chosen the site carefully. It was a safe distance from Shales, and the circular clearing was surrounded by thick woods, where Oakley was tethered nearby. His small campfire sent a thin tendril of smoke skywards, easy enough to be spotted if someone was looking. Someone with a Shadowstone.

A whisper of a sound reached his ears, and Eric raised his head, his nerves humming. It was not loud enough to be footsteps, but he sensed that someone was out there. From the darkness, a black shape emerged into the dim light of the fire, though his Shadowstone kept him swathed in shadows. Eric stood to his feet.

Mason stepped into view, his jaw clenched at the sight of him, his sword already in his hand.

Eric moved around the ring of light so that the fire did not stand between them. "I've been waiting for you."

"A mistake on your part." Mason's eyes blazed. I don't know what you're trying to pull sitting out here without your Steward guard dogs, but you should've stayed in Paladin. 'Cause you're not leaving here without a fight."

"I'm not fighting you."

"Oh, you *will* fight." Mason took a step closer. "You've taken everything from me. The only home I ever really had. My brother, my friends. Everything I've ever claimed and lost, I can lay the blame at your feet." Mason continued with a low voice. "So don't stand there so pompous and self-righteous and say you're not going to fight me." He gritted his teeth and raised his sword. "I'll make you fight."

Just as Mason took another step, Eric raised the hand holding his Beacon, his pulse racing. Mason halted as the rod lit up angrily between them.

Neither of them moved or spoke. Eric tried to wrestle back the doubt and fear trying to strangle him. *Lambient, be with me.* Then, with a deliberate move, he opened his fingers and let it fall, his eyes never leaving Mason's. The light hit the ground, flickered, and went out.

Mason watched it fall, his face twisted in bewilderment. But it did not take long for him to recover, and when he did, his gaze drilled straight into the thoughts and will Eric lay bare before him.

There was a long moment, chilled with shock and tension as Eric waited with bated breath. Then Mason's face blanched, and he took a quick step back, his blade dipping. "You *what*?"

Eric drew in a deep, shaky breath, knowing which memory he referred to. "I buried the boys of Handan."

The Darkman shook his head in denial.

"We laid each one of them in his own grave." Eric kept his gaze steady so Mason could see the truth. "I stood over every one of them and gave them their moment of respect."

"*Why?*" Mason asked through clenched teeth. "Why would you have them slaughtered like animals, and then go back and bury them like you had any thought for them at all?" He was shouting by the time he'd finished the question.

Eric dropped his head before Mason could see the answer. Shame drew a tight band around his throat, but he forced himself to say it out loud. "It was my fault. We got...a report. I thought they were a band of Darkmen, readying for an attack against a nearby village that stood against Jader. If I'd have known...that they were just boys..." Eric sighed and raised his head. "I've lived with the regret ever since."

Mason glared and raised his sword again. "And I've lived with the loss."

"I know. Your life was destroyed that day with all of the others, and I would do anything to go back and change it. I came here to tell you that I'm sorry."

The words hung between them like a bird caught in a trap. Eric felt release in having said them, but he watched the struggle play out before him. Anger, grief, confusion—all of them cut across Mason's hard face like broken pieces of glass. That Eric had dropped his rod at all, allowing his thoughts to be laid out like a book, had rocked the other man. And now, Eric stood before him, unarmed and vulnerable. This was the moment Mason had hoped to see one day—justice served for his brother, for all the other boys at Handan. And now that it was here, he did not seem to know what to do with it.

He won't kill me.

With that assurance planted firmly in his mind, Eric stepped forward. "I have a duty to my kingdom, Mason, and I will do what I must to protect it from Jader and his army." He kept his voice firm. "I will fight him with every ounce of my being. I will *not* allow his dominion to extend into the Old Realm."

Mason stiffened at the challenge. But Eric was not done. He sensed a greater presence within him, pressing him on.

"This moment here, however, is between you and me." He lowered his voice. "This must end now. We both know what you've been after for the last twelve years, Mason. Me. My blood." He raised his palms slightly. "Here I am."

"You trying to go down the martyr?"

"Nay." Eric shook his head. "But if taking my life will turn you from your course of vengeance and save my people, then so be it."

A muscle in Mason's rigid jaw jumped. "You deserve to die," Mason ground out, bringing his other hand to grip the hilt.

"Aye, I do. I don't deserve the grace and mercy Lambient offers any man willing to accept it. Under the law of man's justice, I deserve to die." Eric swallowed. "If you think killing me is going to bring you the peace you lack, then you cut me down where I stand. Just leave my kingdom alone."

Mason's brows crashed over glittering eyes, his nostrils flaring. Eric could see his limbs quivering from where he stood.

"Don't back down now. You can end it all right now. It's your call." Eric pushed harder. "Or you can control me into taking my sword and fighting to the end, if that's the way you want it."

His face twisting, Mason tensed, as if to take a step. But his feet seemed frozen.

"Come on." Eric took another step so that the tip of Mason's sword nearly touched the base of his neck. His blood pounded in his ears. "This is what you've wanted all this time—recompense and justice."

The war continued. Mason's knuckles were bone-white, his face wracked with emotion and streaked with sweat.

"What are you waiting for?" Eric raised his voice.

"*Shut up!*"

"What's holding you back? Isn't this what you wanted to fill that hole in your soul?"

Mason jerked back and dropped his sword, grabbing his head and letting out a guttural scream.

Something snapped in Eric's head, and he was knocked off his feet. Rolling over on his hands and knees, he wondered briefly if Mason had somehow hit him over the head with his sword without him seeing. Hearing another cry, he blinked his vision clear.

Mason stood doubled over, writhing in agony, his face bright red with the exertion. Mystified, Eric pushed himself up, ignoring the pounding behind his eyes.

"Mason?" He took a tentative step.

Mason put his hand up. "Stop!"

It was like hitting a wall. Eric's feet were nailed to the ground, and he could not take another step. He watched, speechless, as Mason let out another yell, his face contorted. The Darkman cast a wild look around, picked up his sword, then stumbled back the way he had come from, one hand still holding his brow.

Eric let out a shaky breath, his own headache receding. Rubbing one hand over his mouth, he peered into the woods where Mason had disappeared. He had envisioned many outcomes to their confrontation, but this was not one of them.

A growing dread settled over him as one thought took precedence over all others. He was still alive, although he suspected he would feel the effects of being controlled in a few hours. But that was not what bothered him. In that last moment when Mason gave his command, Eric had obeyed without thought or hesitation. And Mason had not had to look him in the eye when he did.

50

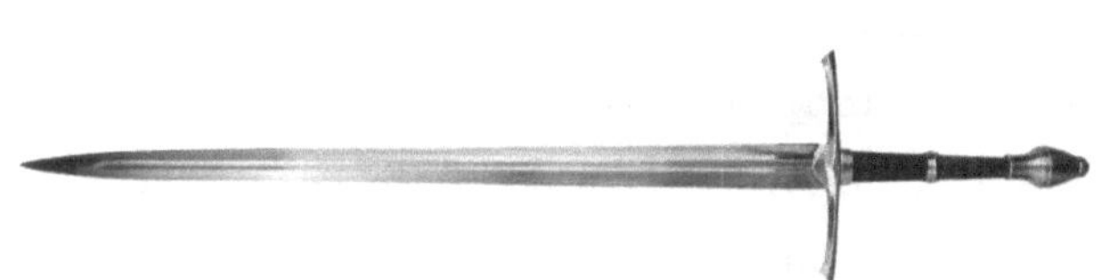

What's happening? Mason gripped his head between his hands as he
fled. His whole body convulsed as wave after wave of pain crashed over
him. Fire lit through his temples, while everything in between was being
ripped to pieces. Not even taking on the Shadowstone had hurt this
much.

He had not gotten very far when the pain became too much to bear.
He sank to his knees, groaning with every jolt. Images flew through his
mind uncontrollably. Dozens of faces flashed before him, many he had
never even seen before. Voices rose and fell until he thought his head was
going to explode.

Then it was over. Mason gasped as the pain lifted, leaving him breathless and exhausted. He fell forward on his hands and dropped his head to
the ground. After a long moment, he raised up and pushed his hair off
his brow with shaky hands.

What was happening to him? Fear rose within him as he considered
the possibilities. Was he going mad? After all he had gone through, was
this how it was going to end? Losing control of his own mind?

Never had he felt so lost and vulnerable. And there was no one he could turn to. Seria had left him. Shon was gone. He thought of going to Jader but quickly dismissed it. No one could help him, or cared to. He was completely alone.

With nothing left to do, he found his roan and led it back into camp, his legs too shaky to even make it up on the horse's back. Disappointment, shame, and confusion pounded on him. He had failed again to take out the prince.

It was dark and quiet, with only the night guards out and about. Mason took the roan to the corral and painstakingly pulled the saddle and bridle off, dumping all of it on the ground, and retreated to his tent to collapse on the cot.

How he missed Seria. Her upbeat, chatty spirit enlivened him, gave him hope in a future where he could find some peace when he felt his life was spinning out of control. But now she was gone from his life, and he didn't even have Shon's friendship to fill the emptiness.

Anger still burned within him at the way Shon's life was taken by his own comrades. Despite everything Jader said to defend the move, Mason questioned a system for killing a man for showing mercy, even if it was towards an enemy. Even Eric had offered Seria a pardon when she had been convicted of nursing a Darkman back to health.

Mason frowned as the prince of Paladin came to mind. Everything he had believed about the man was shaken to its very core. He had seen the truth with his own eyes. For reasons he could not fathom, Eric had gone back to care for the bodies of the slain boys. Not only that, but he had lived with the deep lasting regret ever since.

Not that it should make any difference to Mason. No mercy to his enemies; that was how anyone made it in this world. But then again, was it not that belief that had gotten Shon killed?

The questions, all without answers, left a thudding ache in his skull. Which brought him to perhaps his greatest problem yet. Something was wrong. Splitting headaches at random moments, uncontrollable pictures and voices in his head. As if he could see and hear the thoughts of people nowhere near him. But that was impossible, wasn't it? His abilities only came through eye contact. So, what was going on?

The hours passed, and he did not move. His mind and body were numb and heavy.

But with the morning came a runner announcing an assembly ordered by Jader. Mason swallowed a groan and pulled himself to his feet. The last thing he wanted to do was stand in a crowd of people and listen to more plans by Jader.

He caught himself. This was his job. He had not worked his way to become one of Jader's most trusted Shadowmen by dragging his feet at the duties given him. *Snap out of your doldrums, Mason.* Wallowing in self-pity was not going to get him where he wanted to go. Even if he did not know where that was anymore.

The assembly passed in a blur. Mason heard very little of Jader's speech. Something about a faction moving out with Bruin that night. Getting closer to their goal of trapping Eric Passion and his Stewards. Mason might as well have stayed in his tent for all he got out of it.

Jader caught him after the assembly, putting his hand on Mason's shoulder. "I am truly sorry, Mason. I understand that Shon's treason is difficult to accept."

Mason bristled.

"I wish I could take away this pain you have lived with," Jader went on. "I can only imagine what you go through day in and day out, living with the memory of Liam's murder."

At the mention of his brother, Mason frowned, noting for the first time how often Jader brought the loss of his brother up. Mason had always appreciated his empathy, but now, it seemed almost forced.

Eric's voice filled his memory. *I buried the boys at Handan.*

"Are you all right, son?"

Mason's eyes snapped to Jader's, the man he had trusted and confided in for years. The one man who seemed to understand him better than most. He hesitated, then forced himself to ask the question. "What happened to the body?"

"The body?"

"My brother's body and the rest of the boys. What happened to them all?"

Jader sighed heavily, his face darkening. "I hoped you would never ask." He turned his head, his brows drawn low. "Their bodies were destroyed by the Stewards."

Mason inhaled sharply as Jader continued.

"After I knew you were safe, I sent some men back. Apparently, those... butchers were not satisfied with the job they had done. They went back at some point and hacked the bodies into pieces. Then they burned them beyond recognition. By the time my men returned to the site, the bodies had...." A shudder went through him, as if he was horrified by the picture.

A chill went over Mason, and his throat went dry. *He's lying.* Every word that came out was a lie. Mason did not have to read his mind to know. He had already seen it in Eric's.

"Is that what has been bothering you?"

"You could say that." He cleared his throat. "I, ah...I never knew."

Jader moved to look him straight in the eye. "Those men are wicked beyond imagination, Mason. I do not know how they could have committed such an atrocious act, or how they could live with themselves afterward."

Mason's mind went back to the sincere regret Eric had carried with him all these years. No one felt any regret for Shon's death.

Another pain hit him behind the eyes, scaring him. He felt Jader's hand on his shoulder again. "But rest assured, son. The day will come when you bring Eric to justice. You will destroy him and everything he stands for."

The voices were beginning to grow in volume again. "Aye, I will."

Jader tilted his head. "Are you sure you are well?"

"It's a lot to take in," he said, running his hand over a bracer.

"It is," Jader agreed. "But we must not let ourselves be so caught up in the moment of our emotion so that we cannot fulfill our duty." He straightened the folds of his robe. As he moved, Mason's gaze was drawn to the Shadowstone around his neck. As long as he had known Jader, the emperor had never needed to wear the stone.

But if Mason had read into his thoughts, Jader might suddenly feel the need. The realization rocked him.

Jader spoke again. "I would have liked to have sent you with Bruin last night, but I somehow did not feel you were up to it."

Trying to ignore the drum in his head, Mason stared back at him, an apology locked behind his gritted teeth.

"Take it easy today," Jader said. "Get your bearings. I understand you have had some harsh blows lately, but it is time to get our focus back on our goal."

"I understand." Before Jader had a chance to say anything more, he gave a quick bow and turned away.

As soon as he was alone, Mason let out the breath stuck in his throat. Sweat broke out on his forehead, and his heart hammered in his chest. Bypassing his own tent, he headed for the roped-off corral.

Crue appeared at his elbow. "Would you like me to fetch your horse, sir?"

"Nay."

"I'd be happy to."

"I said, nay!" The pain in his head was almost unbearable. Crue took a quick step back, a hurt expression on his face.

"Take a break, kid," he said, his tone only slightly warmer.

Crue nodded. "Aye, sir." He quickly took his leave before Mason barked at him again.

Frustrated now, Mason slipped a bridle over the roan's nose and jumped on bareback.

Why would Jader lie to him? What purpose could he possibly have for convincing Mason of the despicable acts he claimed the Stewards had done?

Mason gave the horse his head, letting him pick his pace. Unsurprisingly, the gelding took off at an eager canter. As he rode, Mason's memory carried him back to all the times Jader spoke with him about the massacre, constantly reminding Mason of what was done, feeding his anger, encouraging his hatred, pressing him towards revenge.

Revenge. Mason pulled the roan back to a trot. That was all he had thought about for the past decade. Revenge against the Stewards, against Eric. And that was what Jader wanted.

Mason was no fool; he realized what an advantage his Gifts brought to Jader's army. As long as he was driven for vengeance, he was an asset to the Darkmen. *He's been using my anger for his own benefit.* Using Liam's death to keep Mason committed. It did not matter how many years it had been, Jader kept it fresh, as if it had just happened.

Maybe it's time to let it go. The thought came unbidden.

"Argh! This is ridiculous!" One exchange with Eric, and he doubted everything he had stood for for years.

"I gotta get out of here." He knew he should stay close to the camp but was not ready to face Jader again. Did not want to be reminded of Shon's absence. He had his sword, so he was not concerned for his own safety. But he had no idea where he was going.

51

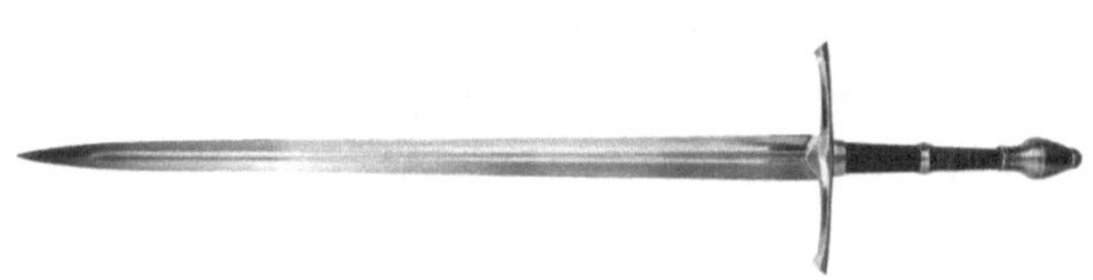

Every bone in Eric's body protested as Oakley trotted into Shales. After Mason's abrupt departure, he had waited around in tense expectation, but the Reader had not returned. So Eric had returned back to his tent in the Steward camp, where he attempted to grab a few hours of sleep. But the remainder of the morning was spent tossing and turning.

Despite the way his meeting had ended, he felt a peace about what he had done. He had followed Lambient's leading and confessed his role in the Handan massacre to Mason. Whatever happened from here on out, he had resolved his part. He would no longer let his guilt for Handan hold him back from what he needed to do, even if it meant facing Mason on the battlefield again.

But under that peaceful resolve, anxiety rumbled like a gathering storm. It wasn't the unsettled confrontation that kept him awake or even the awareness of the Reader's growing power. There was something more.

A heaviness hung over him, making it difficult to breathe. Almost like grief. So strong was the feeling, he arose before dawn to summon his father's palace, but Captain Jervis had reported that all was well in Calla.

Still the feeling persisted as he went about his morning, casting his worry to the Stewards out on mission. He had not heard anything from Braylee since he had left the night before.

It was almost noon by the time he gave up trying to be productive at the camp and headed for Shales. Stifling a groan at the dull ache that throbbed between his ears, he dismounted in front of the inn. His head swam, and he braced a hand against the saddle. Mercies, he would be glad when the effects of Mason's control would fade.

He stepped into the lobby, where both Lionel and Larence stood at the counter, talking. The diminutive shopkeeper gave Eric a quick bow. "Good day, Your Highness."

"Larence brings more news," Lionel said.

"Aye, that is correct." Larence's thin face sobered. He held out another small parchment. "This one's rather cryptic, though."

Eric took it and read the brief script.

I know where Joshun is. You know where to find me. – Kullen

Eric sucked in a breath at the name at the bottom. "Thank the Lambient," he murmured. "When did you get this?"

"A traveling mercenary I'm familiar with brought it to my shop this morning," Larence explained. "Said a cloaked man stopped him on the road and asked him to deliver it here on his way through."

His ears humming with anticipation, Eric slowed down to consider his options. He did not want to rush and make another drastic mistake.

Very few people would know the name of Jader's secret lair. And there were only three men who would know the whereabouts of Kullen—Eric and his two captains. He read the note again, trying to slow the thrumming in his veins. His emotions were in such a state of turmoil, he would have to be careful. *Only You can lead me in this, Lambient.*

He was in no shape to take on a long trip at that moment, but the answer throbbed clearly in his heart. As soon as he was able, he would ride out to Kullen's location.

"Sire, I am plenty well enough to join you," Lionel objected as he followed Eric to the livery where Oakley was stabled.

"I do not doubt that." Eric did not slow his pace and pulled the saddle from its place on the wall. "But I still wish you to stay behind."

"But, sir—"

Eric whirled around. "I need you to quit questioning me, Sergeant."

Lionel snapped his jaw shut, his neck reddening, but he gave a small, submissive nod.

Drawing in a sigh, Eric calmed himself. "I truly need you here. Someone needs to keep a watch over the town, and I don't want to leave Seria without a guard. I trust you to keep her safe."

The younger man's face hardened at the mention of Seria, and Eric stepped closer. "The Reader is close by, Lionel."

At that, his eyes widened. "He's here?"

Eric resumed his task, remembering again the tense standoff the night before. "I don't think he will risk coming to Shales, but I can't guarantee he won't."

The news sobered Lionel, and he sighed. "I apologize for my insubordination, Sire. It's just, I wanted to be of use when I came."

"And you have been. Still are." Eric tightened the girth around the gray's belly. "Larence has a couple of men he trusts keeping an eye on things, but I need a Steward here."

Lionel stood a bit taller. "Very well, Sire. I will not let you down."

Wyxel, the Gateway

Wyxel was a town battered and beaten. Braylee and the Stewards had traveled all night and arrived by midmorning to find its citizens grieved, angry, and frightened. More families had been impacted by this pickup than any other town ransacked by the Dark Army. One family lost all three of their children to the Darkmen. Sixteen people had been killed.

"They really went on a rampage here, didn't they?" Ollen muttered when he met back up with Braylee in the town square after scouring the area.

Braylee shook his head. "This was a statement, to be sure."

Sgt. Kleff rode up to them just then at a trot. "Captain Braylee, one of my privates has picked up a trail."

"How far?" Braylee tried not to read too much hope in the statement. The Darkmen always left a faint trail when they left, but it was short and untraceable.

"Zakkias is about a mile out, sir."

Braylee exchanged looks with Ollen. That was further than anything they had found before.

"He says they were very messy with this one, Captain," Kleff added.

"All right, we'll follow it as far as we can. Lt. Ollen, leave a squad here to assist the recovery."

Braylee rode tall in his saddle as he led the rest of the men northeast out of town, his eyes and ears seeking out anything amiss in the woods around them. As time passed by, nothing changed, except the landscape. More bluffs and cliffs rose up around them as they neared the base of the Slate Mountains. The forest floor deepened and darkened, untouched by the sun. Ollen rode beside him, looking wary but not anxious.

Zakkias kept his scrutiny on the ground, his face a study in concentration.

"What are you noticing, Private?" Ollen asked at one point.

The young scout shook his head. "It's strange. One would think they had given up all attempt at covering their trail."

"Could be trying to lead us into an ambush," Ollen said.

"Maybe," Braylee agreed. "That's why we need to stay alert."

The men behind them were quiet as they followed. Braylee was impressed with the lot. Most were young—younger even than Ollen. But they showed awareness and caution as they went along, keeping their noise and movements to a minimum. Ollen had prepared them well.

Braylee wrestled with his optimism as the afternoon dragged on. This was the first time they managed to track the Darkmen so far, but he knew better than to trust it meant things would go their way.

Zakkias returned from scouting up ahead.

"Something's not right," he said, keeping his voice low.

"How do you mean?"

"It's too quiet the further you go. As if every bird and creature has fled the place."

Braylee's skin crawled as the silence became very heavy.

"What would cause something like that?" Kleff asked.

"Something they see as a threat," Braylee answered. "A big threat." Dread poured down his spine, and he reached for his Beacon. Before he could give an order, there was a loud crash in the distance and an ear-piercing bellow.

Ollen's gaze crashed into his. "It's grizlons."

"Beacons up!" Braylee roared, whipping his rod out. Where there were grizlons, there were sure to be Shadowmen.

Lights flickered up and down the ranks. The horses danced about in agitation at the approaching commotion. The noise grew louder until three grizlons tore through the woods and into view, their snouts already snapping.

"Keep the lights bright!" Braylee directed, holding Beast steady between his legs. Experience had taught him that these monsters were near impossible to kill. Their only hope was to blind them with the light from the Beacons, so long as the men could hold steady.

One grizlon slid to a stop, already blinking and snarling at the light. He stood atop his long, muscular legs, his shaggy fur making him seem even bigger.

Another one, enraged by the lights, let out a deafening roar and charged. Braylee yanked the reins to the side, urging his horse out of range of the flashing fangs. Screams met his ears, however, as the grizlon ran straight through the company behind him.

Lambient above, help us! Braylee prayed desperately that he had not led these young men to their deaths.

Ollen whipped his crossbow up and fired into the woods. Seconds later, a Shadowman fell out of the dimness and into the light of the Beacons.

Two grizlons stood together before Braylee, their stances menacing. Arrows would not pierce the thick hide of these creatures enough to kill them, and swords required close distance, which was too dangerous.

Braylee gritted his teeth and tightened his hold on the Beacon. Pulling in a deep breath and bracing himself for the energy it would take, he drew his Beacon back and then slung it forward like a whip. The flash of light stretched and snapped towards the beasts. There was a loud pop, and both grizlons collapsed, the weight of their fall shuddering the ground beneath him.

One did not move again, but the second rose up on all fours and lumbered off, grunting and growling in pain.

Braylee slumped over his saddle, panting for breath. His strength gone, he could barely raise his head to see Ollen give a shout and ride for the woods, his sword up.

The remaining grizlon had reached the end of the ranks, but instead of raging its way back through the broken lines of scattered men, it circled around them and loped off into the woods with the other.

There was a brief sound of fighting as Ollen and his men sought out enemy soldiers hiding in the woods. Braylee ground his teeth, straightened against the jolts running down his back, and took the Beacon in the same hand as his reins. Then he reached for his own sword and followed his Stewards into the woods.

Ollen's heart battered his ribcage as he faced the mounted Shadowman before him. Shrouded in night, the man attempted to avoid the Beacon's light, but Ollen continued the offense until his horse was alongside the other. Then their swords met.

Blood pounded in Ollen's ear and flowed from a small cut over his eye, but still he fought on, meeting every swing of the other man's blade. The clang of steel rang out again and again until finally, the man pulled back in an unguarded moment so that Ollen could reach him.

As soon as the man hit the ground, Ollen looked around, but the chaos had lessened. The grizlons could still be heard in their loud departure, and Ollen's men searched the wooded area around them for more Shadowmen.

Braylee trotted his horse over to Ollen. "Well done, Lieutenant."

Ollen swallowed and gave a nod but did not trust himself to speak without his voice wavering. He turned to check on the status of his men.

A few had been injured by the charging grizlons, but miraculously, none had been killed. Only one was serious enough that Braylee ordered him to be taken back to Wyxel and their healer.

"Someone should track those grizlons while the trail is still fresh, sir." Zakkias's quiet voice fell on Ollen's ears.

"What's that?" Ollen turned to find him standing nearby.

He licked his lips, his face pensive. "Those grizlons headed in a different direction than the tracks are leading. Same as what few Shadowmen we managed to spot. That seems a bit coincidental."

"You think they were heading for a specific location?"

Zakkias nodded. "If we could track them, maybe we can see how they're domesticating the grizlons."

Ollen considered this. "We would have to split up to cover both trails. Not sure how safe that would be."

"I'll go after the grizlons." Braylee's voice cut into Ollen's contemplations.

"You, sir?" Zakkias asked.

Braylee gave a chuckle. "You're not the only one who can sniff out a trail. I used to track bears back in my youth."

Zakkias blushed. "I never meant to imply—" He cut off when Braylee slapped his shoulder.

"No offense taken, Private." He then addressed Ollen. "But I do think you should take Zakkias with you to continue on the path of the Darkmen. They're a little more likely to cover their tracks than those beasts are."

"Are you sure we should separate?" Ollen asked. "Could be risky."

"I'm sure it will be. But we've gone too far to turn back. We need to push on."

Ollen could see the truth in the statement, but a part of him wavered at being in charge of his men. What if he wilted when they needed him the most? "Aye, sir."

The squads soon formed behind their respective leaders. Braylee looked over at Ollen, his expression calm and confident. "This may be the break we need."

Ollen straightened his spine and responded with a dip of chin. "Here's to the end of the pickups."

52

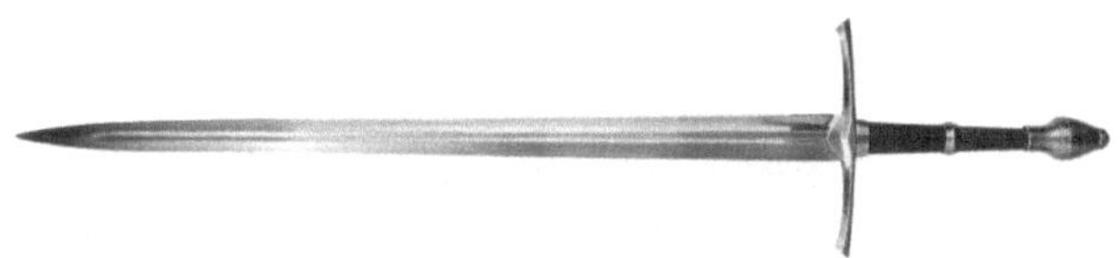

The Lambient is light, and in Him there is no darkness.
-The Sacred Code

Mason stared up at Stonehard as his horse trotted up the dirt-packed path. His legs were sore from the long bareback ride, but the ache was a good reminder that he was still alive. For all the good that did him.

He had not meant to aim for Jader's secret little location of Joshun. But it was the only place he could count on not running into anyone he did not wish to see. Jader and Bruin were back at the main camp, as well as Dreeya. And Seria was in Shales. There was nowhere else he could go.

The roan's back was slick with sweat by the time Mason slid off, his damp trousers covered with red hairs. He tied the reins around a post, not sure how long he was staying. His steps were heavy as he climbed up and trudged through the doors.

The coolness of the stone building hit him as soon as he stepped in, raising chills on his arms. A small block of late-day sunlight peeked into the room, afraid to reveal itself in the darkness. Mason stared at the beam for a moment. All it would take was a word from Jader, and that light would be snuffed out. Engulfed by black shadows.

Much like his mind.

He wandered around aimlessly through the halls. What was he even doing here? Where was he going? The last question struck him deeper than his current destination.

Where was his life going?

He knew the layout of the castle, that there were a lot of small rooms, or cells, in the deepest part of the building, separated by foyers and halls. The gray stone walls were streaked with condensation, adding to the chill in the air. This was certainly not a place meant to keep one comfortable.

His feet moved of their own accord to the steps leading to the lower floors. Descending the winding stone stairway felt like he was sinking into the very depths of the earth. It got darker and colder the lower he went. His stomach soured. He had never cared to see this part of the castle before.

A commotion rose from the bottom of the stairwell. He made out a gruff male voice and a younger distraught one. Rounding the last corner, he encountered a Darkman wrestling with a skinny boy with pale skin and tattered clothes.

"What's the problem, Benkis?" He kept his voice calm as he took in the scene. The man was obviously flustered and irritated, one hand gripping the boy's shirt and the other fending off his clumsy fists.

"Aw, this kid tried to run as I was taking him back to his cell." Benkis shook the boy, who looked back at them with a defiant tilt of his chin. He looked to be about twelve. His eyes were too big for his thin face, and his hair hung in limp mats over his forehead. Even from where he stood, Mason could see the boy shivering.

He frowned, not recognizing him. "Is he from one of the pickups?"

"Nay." Benkis readjusted his hold on the boy's shirt. "He's been here for a while. Still doesn't know how to respect authority."

"I want to see my sister!" the boy snapped.

"What's your name, kid?" Mason asked.

There was a long, insolent silence.

"Answer him, kid!" Benkis yanked on his shirt.

He scowled but answered. "Dalton Stattler."

Stattler. Why did that name seem familiar? "How did you come to be here, Dalton?" If he was not from the pickups, he had to have been surrendered by his parents.

Dalton's eyes flashed. "The Darkmen took me after they killed my father for being a Steward," he spat out.

Understanding dawned, drying Mason's lips. Jader spoke of Nebb Stattler, one of the Stewards who had remained in the Gateway to spy on the Dark Army.

"And then they got my sister, but they won't let me see her!" Dalton continued, his voice strained and weak.

"That's because you haven't earned it," Benkis snarled. He sighed and looked to Mason with an eyeroll and a smirk before shoving Dalton back down the steps.

Mason followed, slower now, until he reached the lower level, which forked away into four tunnels. Taking the first one on the right, he entered a long, narrow room. The smell of human waste and stagnant water hit him in the face, and he almost gagged. Two rows of cells lined the walls on either side of him, enclosed with thick, wooden doors. A square barred window of about six inches was cut out high in every door. The hall and all the cells were pitch black.

He stepped close to one, letting his Shadowstone enlighten his vision. A girl sat inside, hunched in a corner, shuddering and sniffling. The next one revealed a smaller boy, about the same age as young Liam from Marsels. The third cell held an older boy who paced the small four-by-four enclosure, occasionally smacking the wall with the side of his fists.

Any one of those kids could have been Byron.

Bile rolled around in Mason's stomach. A nasty tasting lump settled in his throat, and he backed away.

This was what he had been a part of?

He spun away, almost stumbling for the door.

"Help me!" the girl cried out when he bumped by her door. "Please, let me go!" Her pleading ended in a sob.

Blaze, get me out of here. He pounded up the stairs, trying to block out the images and sounds and smells.

Bursting through the upper floor, he sucked in the cleaner air, but it wasn't good enough. It was too cold, too wet. Too dark. His lungs seized, his muscles cramped, and he searched for the door that would lead him outside, away from the children and the awareness of the role he had played in putting them there.

Shame sliced through him, leaving him raw and bleeding. What had he done? All those years he had blamed the Stewards for taking the lives of the Handan boys, and the Darkmen were no better. *He* was no better.

Those kids did not deserve what they had been put through. It was unnecessary. Inhumane. Cruel. And he was a part of it.

The door finally appeared before him, beckoning him to escape the prison he had walked into, to leave the shadows that flooded his mind until he could not think. The Shadowstone warmed against his chest, a reassuring sensation when all else seemed intent to drown him. He grabbed for the cold metal doorhandle and wrenched the heavy door open.

Once outdoors, he jumped on his horse and fled, leaving the castle and its prisoners behind.

The further Ollen went, the more optimistic he felt. Whoever Zakkias was tracking, they were careless. Zakkias pointed out several areas where it looked as if they had stopped for a bit, leaving too many signs and hoofprints. They even found some empty, discarded flasks.

It could be a trap. The risk had to be acknowledged, but Ollen somehow doubted it. It was almost like this group was playing by their own rules, feeling too confident. And in doing so, they may lead the Stewards straight to Joshun.

Sgt. Kleff rode at his right, always alert and looking. The woods were quiet and still around the soft clopping of hooves, save for an occasional flutter of wings or a bird's call. Above them to their right, the Slates stood like tall, proud kings of the east. Immovable and impenetrable. The sun began its slow descent; daylight would soon fade.

Zakkias jogged his horse back, looking excited. "Sir! I think I've found it!"

Ollen's heart jumped. "Show me."

He and Kleff followed the young scout to a sparsely wooded area where the last shards of evening sunlight broke through the trees and allowed him to see distant bluffs spilling out from the Slate Mountains. A wooded hill rose before them.

Ollen directed the rest of the ten men to wait at the bottom of the hill, while he and Kleff followed Zakkias up the slope. They rode until it got too steep for the horses, then dismounted and tied them securely to a tree to go the rest of the way on foot. Once at the top, he found that the hill bled into the top of a cliff. Zakkias led them out onto a rocky overhang, where they crawled to the edge. Ollen's breath caught in his throat at the view.

Below them, a wide valley stretched before them, shadowed by the Slates and bordered by thick woods. A large, ancient-looking castle stood at the base of the mountains, nestled among more crags and timber, concealing all but the front of it. Dark figures walked here and there around the castle. Guarding it.

"Would you look at that," Kleff murmured.

Exhilaration soared through Ollen's chest, and he grinned at the sergeant. This had to be it! It was the perfect spot to hide children from the world, secure and hidden.

"Good work, Private." Ollen clamped a hand on Zakkias's shoulder, keeping his voice down.

Zakkias beamed as he stared down at the sight, his face flushed with victory in the glow of his light rod.

Ollen chewed his lip, mulling over his next steps. There was no way they could take the place with his small squad, and he had not passed a pool or stream that he could use to contact anyone else. Which meant someone needed to go back for the other Stewards. But he did not like the idea of leaving the place unmonitored.

There was an abrupt shout, then more yelling and metallic clangs erupted from below. His limbs went rigid, and he met Kleff's stare for a brief instant before they both dashed down the slope, where their horses were tethered. From there he could look down into the clearing.

Darkmen poured from the woods, penning his men against the cliff below them. Ollen's blood chilled, and he pulled his sword, his mind already moving to what had to happen next.

A Steward let out a cry and hit the ground. Ollen gritted his teeth. There were so many of them. "No one knows where we are." He gave Kleff a pointed look.

The sergeant clenched his jaw. "I won't leave you or my men."

Ollen had expected nothing less. "Zakkias." He waited until the young man dragged his stricken gaze to his. "We need someone to know where these kids are."

Grim understanding dawned, and Zakkias swallowed, grabbing the reins of his horse.

"We'll cover you," Kleff said, his face stark white but resolute.

"Wait until we ride out, then circle around us," Ollen said, his heart clanging against his ribs. "And ride hard."

They mounted and Zakkias got into position, looking over his shoulder at them one more time, his eyes dark with emotion.

Awareness flooded Ollen's senses as he mounted alongside his sergeant, but there was no question in his mind, no hesitation in his movements. No fear holding him back. He exchanged sober looks with Kleff, then kicked his horse's flanks, racing down the short slope to where his men fought. His sergeant let out a war cry as they plunged into the midst of the bedlam, catching the Darkmen off guard with their sudden, bold arrival.

53

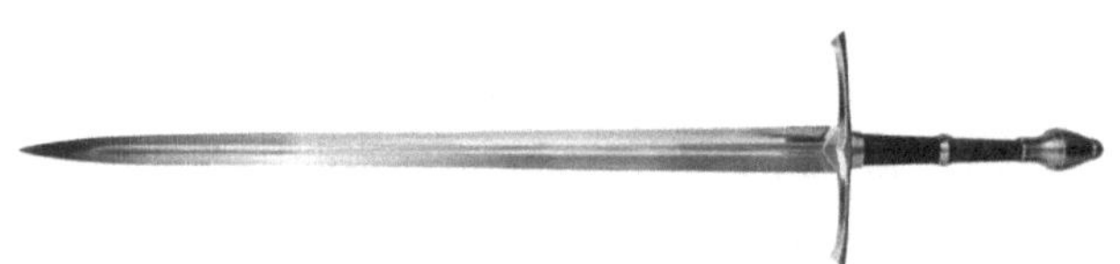

"The flame is soon extinguished, and the candle runs out. But the darkness will always last."
-Pre-battle speech given by Graulik Jader during Calla's War

Braylee peered through the trees at the camp spread out before him. Darkmen meandered about among the tents. A roped-off corral held at least a dozen horses at one end of the site, with a few others saddled and staked out at various tents.

At the edge of the camp a circle of cairns butted against the bluffs spilling from the Slates, creating a natural corral. Thick wooden posts lay horizontally between two large boulders, barring the single entrance into the enclosure. Snarls and growls filtered over the rocks surrounding the animals within.

Braylee looked over at the sergeant at his side. "I'd say we've found where they've been keeping the grizlons."

Sgt. Fleming nodded, his face lit with eagerness. "So, what now?"

He didn't answer right away, taking in the layout of the camp. There were not a lot of men down there, but there were sure to be Shadowmen included. No one would be able to control the animals without their cover of darkness.

Braylee glanced up at the sun already sinking in the west. Time was against them. The Shadowmen would have the advantage if night fell.

But these grizlons had been used to control and terrorize the Gateway long enough.

He set his jaw and turned back to the younger officer. "I'd say it's time the grizlons head off to their hibernation grounds."

Taking advantage of the cover of trees and rocks the place afforded, the two men crept closer to the grizlon pen. Braylee pointed out a bored-looking guard, and Fleming nodded and moved away. A moment later, Fleming struck, and the guard fell unconscious to the ground.

Another Darkman leaned against a boulder. Braylee sidled up to his side, grabbed him in a chokehold until he stopped struggling, and dropped him.

He was only a few yards from the barred entrance. His blood pumped hotly through his body as he scanned around. Then he bolted for the stone corral.

There was a shout somewhere, and the sound of hooves rumbled through the air. Braylee clenched a fist in satisfaction and flattened himself against the wall of the pen as the Darkmen's horses ran free through the camp.

Curses and yells resounded as everyone scrambled to retrieve the horses. Braylee took that chance to approach the opening. One man stood there, his attention fixed on the chaos in the camp. He turned just as Braylee approached, his mouth opening in surprise. But he had no time to call for help before Braylee's rock-hard fist plowed into his cheekbone, knocking him out. Braylee dragged him away.

The wooden logs were thick and heavy. Bracing himself, Braylee lifted the top log and slung it out of its hold. A growl met his ears as a large grizlon caught sight of him and advanced from the inside, his fangs flashing.

"Leave me alone, you big brute, and I'll get you out of here," Braylee muttered, already lifting the next log out.

Other beasts were starting to rouse now and looked his way. The first one struck out at him, his claws almost catching Braylee's face.

"Fine." Braylee pulled his Beacon and aimed it at them. They all roared in outrage but retreated from the light. Braylee struggled with the last post, his biceps straining against his sleeves, his ears buzzing with the anticipation of his discovery.

And then it came. "Hey! He's letting the grizlons out!"

The shout was picked up by others until Braylee found himself the focus of attention of a half dozen soldiers.

Fleming let out a call, and half of his squad burst through the woods on horseback, cutting the Darkmen off.

There was bedlam all around. Horses ran about with no riders, some long gone. Darkmen on foot fled or attempted to take a stand from the ground. The few who still had their horses swung up and faced off with the Stewards.

Braylee resumed his task, sweat dripping into his eyes and slickening his grip. With a loud growl, he flung the last log up and out of its restraint. Then he backed away, keeping his light before him.

It took a moment, but one grizlon soon stuck his nose out, testing its freedom. It snarled at the fight, tensing to pounce. A few others crowded their way out.

Another band of Stewards appeared, all raising their Beacons. The grizlons reacted in a cacophony of shrieks and bellows, but they swung away from the men and fled the light. All of them streaked from the pen, the ground vibrating beneath their massive weight. They veered away to the north, free at last to leave the heat of the summer for the cooler lands of their hibernation grounds.

Braylee let out a breath before dashing for Beast, tied to a tree and stamping his hooves in fury.

"With me!" Braylee called as soon as he was safely astride. His Stewards disengaged and rallied behind him.

The Darkmen also regrouped, those on horses cutting off their exit. The men on foot ran for their weapons. Braylee set his jaw and pulled his sword, acutely aware of the sun sinking lower. It mattered not to him how he had to see it done. Those grizlons would not be used by Darkmen again.

Ollen ducked a blow and stuck the tip of his sword into a Darkman's gut. There were still seven or eight more gathered around him. One already lay on the ground. Two more had blood dripping from their arms. The rest still came at him.

His horse had fled. About half of his men still fought. Kleff lay lifeless on the ground, his cape soaked with blood.

Unable to grieve his fallen men, Ollen panted heavily, his back to the cliff, his face streaked with perspiration. His shirt clung to him, save where a Darkman blade had sliced the front. His arm screamed at him, and his legs felt ready to buckle. And still, he fought on with the hope that Zakkias had made it through.

Adrenalin pulsed through him as he sidestepped another jab, shifting further from the rock behind him. And just like that, Ollen was surrounded.

He gritted his teeth. His mind went to Seria. His mother. Lionel. Eric. Braylee. All those who meant so much to him. If Zakkias did not make it, no one would even know what became of him or his squad. But there was no fear. Only boldness and determination to take as many with him as he could.

Lambient, my life is yours.

Another one of his men let out a cry and fell. Four Darkmen stood around him, their faces alight with the nearness of their win. Ollen raised his Beacon, letting the bright light blind them momentarily. He jumped forward, knocking one man to his knees. Another braved the light and swung at him. Ollen blocked him, then spun around to counteract another jab from behind.

The Beacon slowed them down, but it did not stop all of them. Ollen had just slashed his blade across one man's stomach when something cold and sharp pierced his side. Letting out a guttural cry, he looked to see one of the soldiers standing close, a malicious glint in his gaze as he jerked his sword back.

Another one took advantage of the moment and came in at the other side. Shock radiated through Ollen's body as he slumped to the ground, unable to catch his breath. He braced his arms against the fire in his sides and looked up through bleary eyes. Three Darkmen stared down at him in triumph. One raised his boot and gave a savage kick. There was a blast of pain, then it faded into merciful blackness.

54

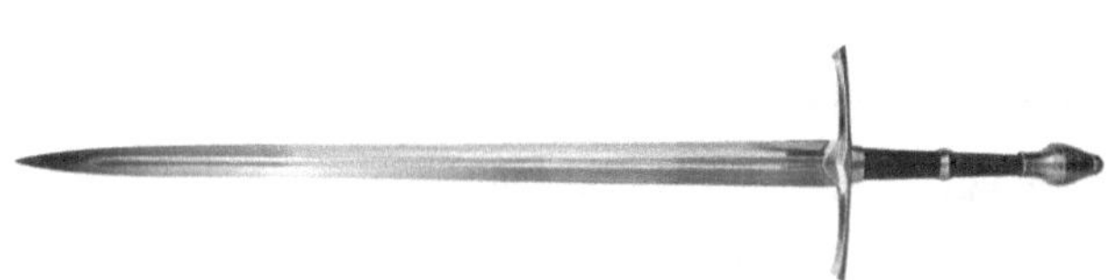

Chest heaving, Mason pulled the roan to a stop at the base of a rocky precipice in the woods beyond Stonehard. His head pounded, sharp streaks buzzing through his temples and down his tight neck. *Not again. Not now.*

The voices returned, interspersed with the cries of children. Eric's steady timbre cut through the chaos, his words inaudible. And Seria's sweet, sunny tone, broken by tears. Over it all, the sounds of battle—swords ringing and voices shouting—echoed until everything mixed in a jumble that made no sense. Anxiety tightened across his shoulders. It was as if his Gift was exploding, bringing random voices and thoughts from afar.

The headache began to ease, but the noise continued to reverberate within his consciousness. Swallowing the dry knot in his throat, he slumped in the saddle and wiped sweat from his face with a trembling hand.

He had no energy to fight the wave of despair threatening to drown him or figure out what he was supposed to do now. All he knew was that he could not stay here in the same building with those kids. The kids he had helped imprison.

How had things fallen so completely apart? For years, he had his purpose, knew what he wanted. Now he was lost in a raging sea, adrift without a course for his life.

When he was a boy, Liam had led him. After he was taken from him, Jader was there to guide him. For a little while, Seria had filled the missing pieces of his heart. Now, she had turned from him, and the trust he had in Jader had been shaken.

There's no place for me.

The voices faded into silence, though the constant sound of battle seemed permanently etched in his mind. Then it hit him that the sound came from without. He frowned and raised up, searching for the source of the fight. The echoes drew his gaze to the bluff above him, silhouetted against the darkening sky.

His breath hitched, and he glanced around for a way up, not even sure what his motive was. A grassy slope wrapped up on one side to the top of the bluff, so he guided his horse up. The roan's hooves dug deep into the dirt as he lunged up the hill until going on foot would be faster. Mason slid to the ground and climbed onward, ignoring the twigs reaching out to grab him, scratching his face and arms as he brushed by them. He slipped and slid as he climbed, pulling himself over the ledge to the top and peering through the woods.

About twenty Darkmen walked around in the middle of a mess of trampled shrubs, broken branches, and discarded weapons. And bodies.

The men looked rough, their clothes dirty and torn, but they laughed and cheered. One man stopped a few feet from him and stood over a motionless, blood-stained figure on the ground. The Darkman spun his sword, pointing it down over the body. The man on the ground raised a feeble hand.

"Stop!" Mason shouted, too late to prevent the blade from dropping.

But all the Darkmen froze in their tracks, their expressions melting into compliance. Mason stared at them, bewilderment overshadowing his dismay for a moment before hurrying to the man on the ground. The face staring sightlessly up at him sent a strange shock through him. He was a Steward, and he was young, no more than a year ot two older than his brother, Liam.

"Get out of here," he growled.

"At once," the Darkmen murmured, filing past him silently.

Mason gritted his teeth and scanned the still forms. There were several others—fresh-faced, smooth-cheeked boys who had joined an army and died because of it. About two dozen dead men from both armies lay scattered around him. The Stewards had almost reached Stonehard, but outnumbered, they had not stood a chance.

Just like the boys at Handan.

A bad taste filled his mouth, souring his stomach, and he turned from the gruesome scene, tried to deny that it resembled Handan in any way. But once the thought took shape, he could not erase it.

There was a moan, and Mason jerked back, skimming the forms until he spotted movement. Recognition made his heart jump.

"Ollen." Mason hurried to his side, eyeing the large red stains spreading over his torso.

The Steward's face was gray, his short hair limp with sweat. He blinked slowly up at Mason, then flinched and turned his face away, closing his eyes. "Nay, don't," he murmured.

"Blades, man, I'm not gonna..." He pulled his vest off, wadded it and pressed it over one of the wounds.

Ollen looked down at Mason's hands. "What are you doing?" His words slurred.

The vest was instantly soaked, and the bleeding continued, staining Mason's hands. Alarm roughed his voice when Ollen stiffened. "Take it easy. I'm just trying to help."

"My men first."

The soft request drove a knife through Mason's chest. He looked around at the dead men. "They're fine."

Ollen groaned and squeezed his eyes shut again. "Lambient, be with them." Then he whispered so faint that Mason almost missed it. "My life is yours."

"You're gonna be fine." But the truth pounded through him. It was too late. Ollen was going to die right here in front of him, and for some reason, Mason wanted to fight it.

Ollen ran his tongue over his dry lips and gulped in mouthfuls of air. "I'm not afraid to die for Lambient."

Without warning, anger overtook Mason, burning through his chest like fire. The heat surged to the Shadowstone, and it reacted with a hum and spark. "No one should have to die for a light that doesn't exist," he spat out, his muscles constricting. "I've seen nothing but darkness from your Lambient. He wasn't there for my brother, just like He's left you now. I owe Him nothing but hatred."

Growing still, Ollen forced his eyes to Mason's. "How can you hate Him if He doesn't exist?"

A chill chased away the flames raging through Mason's veins. Ollen's gaze grew so intense that he felt exposed, every act of violence and selfishness he had ever committed laid out for the dying man to see.

Ollen winced. "Darkness fades when light...is allowed to shine."

Mason adjusted his position and pressed the wound harder to stay the constant flow of blood, all while avoiding the pensive stare of the dying man. "It's too late for me."

Ollen made a noise that sounded strangely like a snort. "Never too late." A shudder passed over him, and his head lolled to the side.

"Look at me, look at me." Mason grabbed Ollen's face with his free hand, trying to distract him from the agony rolling over his body. But Ollen's focus slid to the darkening sky above him, and Mason cursed under his breath. The fact that he could not maintain control over the man told him this was a losing battle.

Something inside him twisted until he was sure his ribs would crack. His throat tightened as Ollen's breathing grew more labored. He hesitated, then allowed himself to look past Ollen's glassy stare, into his last thoughts.

He had no thoughts for himself. Instead, his mind moved to those he loved and held dear. His mother. His fellow Stewards. His prince. Seria.

Ollen's selflessness in these last moments struck Mason like a battering ram, and he ground his teeth until they hurt. This man loved Seria, even knowing it was not returned. It shone from his pain-clouded eyes. They could have had a good life. Ollen had shown himself to be brave and honorable. So why was he on the ground, fighting to breathe?

Ollen turned his head, looking for something. "My...Beacon."

Swallowing, Mason glanced around and spotted it a few inches from where Ollen lay. Without hesitation, he took it and placed it in Ollen's hand. A weak smile lit the Steward's face, and he brought it to his chest, where the rod began to glow with a soft, steady light. For the first time, Mason was not repulsed by the sight.

There was nothing but peace on Ollen's face. In these last moments, he had no remorse for the life he had lived. He accepted his death with dignity, not bitterness at what he had lost.

"Ollen..." He waited until the man looked at him once more. "I'm ...sorry I didn't get here sooner." A few minutes earlier and he could have stopped it.

Ollen shook his head slightly in reply, too tired to say anything more. Struggling to focus, he raised his hand, and Mason gripped it with his own.

Taking a shallow breath, Ollen forced himself to speak again. "Don't be afraid...of the light." His words faded. Then his face relaxed, and his eyes slid shut one last time. The faint grip he had on Mason's hand slackened, and a moment later, the Beacon went dark.

Emotion swept over Mason, hard and fast, catching him by surprise. Dropping Ollen's limp hand, he pushed himself up on his feet, staring down at the young man, his mind spinning. How could Ollen display such peace in his final breath?

Unable to stay there, Mason stumbled away, leaving him behind. He went to the edge of the cliff and fell to his knees, panting for breath. He dropped his head and started to rub his face, but the sight of the blood on his hand stopped him. Ollen's blood.

Shutting his eyes, Mason was slammed with the reality of how wrong he had been. About everything. From the Lambient to Handan and Eric to his own assumption of the Stewards' lust for blood. Even his opinion of Byron and his family had been skewed. And the pickups. How had he allowed himself to believe, even for an instant, that it was all for the good of everyone involved?

His life had become nothing but lies. Lies about his brother's death. About Jader's role in his recovery. About Eric's involvement. Mason had lived for nothing but revenge for years. With nothing to show except a trail of violence and fury.

Gripped with a crushing sense of regret and sorrow, Mason thought again of the Steward lying a few yards away. And of Shon. Two men, so different, whose lives had been taken too soon. And for what?

No one save Mason would mourn Shon's death. The truth pierced like a jagged blade. His friend's life would not count for anything, having spent it to further Jader's cause. And in the end, it was Jader's cause that had gotten him killed. His life had been wasted.

Whereas Ollen had served a cause that left him with no regret. He died a hero, seeking out the very children Mason had helped take. He died with honor and even pride, and his loss would be grieved by many.

Mason lost track of time as he sat there, unmoving. He stared out into the dark valley, not really seeing anything. Numb.

The cramp in his legs pulled him back to the present, and he shifted, hanging his feet over the edge as he gazed out at the valley. It was so dark. His Shadowstone allowed him to see through the gloom, but still it surrounded him. Even the stars were hidden, casting an inky black blanket over the vale.

Dark. Black. Empty. Just like him. The night stretched out before him, unending and ever-reaching. How many sunsets had he watched in his lifetime, reveling in the sight of darkness overtaking light? Light always fell to darkness. He had witnessed it time and time again, confident in his belief.

Now the darkness seemed suffocating. Blinding. Deceitful. Ugly.

Closing his eyes again, he braced himself against the ground, feeling wearier and weaker than he ever had. Not even the death of his brother had left him feeling so low. His anger had fueled him, given him purpose, but that purpose had failed him. Now he was left with nothing.

Seria. Shon. His trust in Jader. Even his vow against Eric. All of it gone.

He wasn't sure how long he sat there, lost to the darkness within him. With a heavy sigh, he dragged his eyes open again. The faintest hint of pink teased his vision on the eastern horizon. He sat still and watched it grow, splashing its fragile bits of color across the black sky. Purple. Red. Gold. Rolling from the horizon as if powered by some unseen source.

The valley began to transform before him. The shadows were cast to the side as glimpses of life appeared in the growing amber light. Green foliage. Strong, sturdy tree trunks. Even a shy deer stepping out of its hiding place. A small pool of water he had not noticed glistened. And the birds! The air abruptly filled with song as they awakened with the new day, soaring in the air with weightless energy.

The shadows lost ground as the sky lightened. The colors spread over all the heavens now, chasing away the last little bit of darkness. And then the sun made its first appearance, a great, big, golden orb of fire, peeking over the horizon. Majestic and powerful, it climbed the heavens easily, flinging its beams across the last of the dimness.

And just like that, the night ended, beaten back with nary an effort by the dawn of a new day.

Mason sat transfixed through it all, stunned by the transformed view. Light spilled all around him, warming the ground and his chilled body, caressing his upturned face.

He had seen it backward all this time. Darkness did not overcome light. The opposite was true. The dark lost all power when the sun appeared. Even a small candle was enough to light one's way through the blackest of nights.

Jader's power of darkness could snuff out any lamp or illumination, save for the Stewards' Beacons. The Lambient's pure radiance outshone and outlasted any other source. The very light the Stewards fought to protect. Light brought life and truth.

"You are real," he breathed. He pushed himself to his feet, mesmerized. As he rose, the Shadowstone swung slightly on the chain, bumping his chest and flooding him with heat. Doubts gripped him.

Was he seriously considering stepping off the path he had trod for so many years? He was committed to Jader, to darkness. The Shadowstone proved it.

A whisper breathed past the walls erected in his mind. *"Don't be afraid of the light."* Ollen's last words.

Mason gritted his teeth, wrestling with his next choice with a fervor that brought an almost physical ache to his body.

Gripping the Shadowstone in his fist, he pulled the chain off his neck and stared down at the purple-black rock, remembering his gratification in receiving it. How it infused him with the dark power resting in Jader, assured him during his dirty work. Now it seemed to mock him, reminding him of the years he had lost to Jader's lies.

No more. He clenched his fist. Taking a step back, he flung the stone over the ledge as hard as he could. All the anger and bitterness that had been bottled up in him for years drained away, leaving a cleanness he did not expect.

He inhaled deeply and stared up at the sky for a moment, letting the impact of what he had done sink in, as well as considering his next course of action.

Pulling his gaze from the sunlit valley, back to the woods behind him where a brave Steward lay among his fallen comrades, Mason made up his mind. He would return to Stonehard. But first, there was something he had to do.

55

It felt strange walking back into the Darkmen camp, looking for all the world as if he belonged there. He returned a few greetings, even cracked a smile or two. All the while, Mason's heart raced in his chest, afraid someone would know by looking at him that something had changed and he was not the same man who had ridden out the day before. Or that his Shadowstone was missing.

Twelve horses remained out of sight in the woods, each bearing a dead Steward. It had taken some effort to get them here safely, but he could not leave any of them behind. The men he had controlled to help with the task were gone, sent on a random trip away from Stonehard. Mason hoped the effects of his control would last long enough for him to do what he needed to do.

Crue was, thankfully, at his tent, tending to the laundry in his usual competent way. For the hundredth time, Mason was glad he had given the boy a chance after Dreeya had threatened to have him removed. Crue had proven his worth over and over.

"Master Mason!" Crue called when he saw him, genuine concern darkening his eyes. "I'm glad you're back. I wasn't…I mean…I've been…"

Mason lifted a hand to halt his stammering. "It's all right, Crue. And I apologize for being so hard on you lately."

"Oh no, not at all." Crue shook his head. "I understand, what with…" Again, he stumbled to a halt.

Mason finished the sentence for him. "Shon."

Crue relaxed. "I know it's been difficult for you."

"Aye, it has," Mason said with a frown. "It shouldn't have happened."

Crue's brows rose slightly. "Um, Lord Jader is gone," he said, with no idea how relieved Mason was to hear that. "He went to meet Commander Bruin somewhere. The whole camp is getting ready to move to a new location."

Mason could see it was true. Many of the tents had already been taken down. The pack animals were tacked up and ready to go. All his belongings were already packed, thanks to Crue. Mason regarded the boy. It hit him how difficult his next move would be.

"When we leave here, there's something I want you to do for me."

"Sure." Crue looked back at Mason, open and earnest.

"I want you to stay behind."

A confused frown settled on Crue's young face. "Sir?"

"I think it's time you settle down somewhere." Mason lightened his tone in an attempt to make it sound like an opportunity. "Stop following us all about and make your own way in the world."

Crue looked distressed. "Have I done something wrong?"

"Not at all." Mason was quick to reply. "But you're too smart for this way of life. I want you to do better for yourself. Find a decent job. Learn all you can. You deserve more than what I can give you."

"But, sir. I can't. I have nobody."

A pang went through him at the admission. "I understand. I was younger than you when I found myself in that same place." He hesitated, unable to believe what he was saying. "I think if I could do it over again, I'd be a little more careful of the decisions I've made."

Crue still looked upset, so Mason stepped closer and cupped one hand behind Crue's neck, surprising the teen with the unusual display of affection. "You've done nothing but good by me, Crue, and I could not appreciate you more." His voice was hoarse. "That's why I'm doing this. Someday, you'll understand." He looked directly into Crue's eyes. "You will not follow."

The expression of distress fell away. "At once."

Seria paced the confines of her room, ready to tear her hair out in frustration. Braylee and Ollen had been gone for two days, and now Eric was gone on a different mission. There were too many things to worry about. Too many weights on her exhausted spirit.

After a while, the pacing began to grate on her nerves, so she left her room and found Lionel in the lobby. The Steward had been none too pleased when Eric insisted he stay behind. He glanced up when she descended. "You, too, eh?"

She nodded, catching his meaning. They were both restless, wishing there was more they could do. Instead, they paced and waited.

"Have you heard...?" She did not finish the question, already knowing what he would say.

He shook his head before she finished. "Nothing. Not from anyone." He sounded as uneasy as she felt.

With a sigh, Seria moved to the window and glanced up and down the street. Business in Shales went on as usual despite her turmoil. People worked, shopped, and visited as if all was well in their world. And for the moment, it was.

A young boy, about fifteen or sixteen, appeared on the street leading a horse. Across the animal's back was draped a large bundle, carefully wrapped and secured. Seria took a closer look. The saddle and bridle were trimmed with the same silver as the standard Steward tack. The sorrel mare looked familiar.

Her heart stalled. "Lionel!"

He hurried to the window and gave a quick look out. "Stay here," he said, his voice strange.

"Lionel—"

He was already out the door. Seria moved to stand in the entrance, her heart in her throat, afraid to draw any closer. Lionel spoke to the boy, then reached for the bundle. He pulled back the cloth, his face contorting. His stricken gaze drew Seria from the inn.

"Nay, Seria, don't."

She shoved past him. With trembling fingers, she drew back a corner of the canvas and saw a familiar white-blond head. She gasped and sank to her knees, her whole body trembling. Blood pounded in her ears, silencing everything around her as she cradled the cold face in her hands.

Not Ollen. Please, not Ollen.

Someone—she assumed it was Lionel—reached for her and pulled her to her feet, turning her to the inn.

"I have to go." Lionel's strained voice cut through the roar and drew her gaze up. "There are more outside of town."

Seria looked to the end of the street, where she could just see another horse waiting, with yet another bundle over its back. Her body shook with the impact. How many more were there?

"Seria?"

At Lionel's hoarse murmur, she whispered through stiff lips, "Go."

He stared into her face for a moment before he nodded and walked away, taking the teenager with him.

Seria stumbled back inside on trembling legs, her mind trying to comprehend what her eyes had told her.

Ollen, her dear friend, hanging lifelessly on his horse. Gone. How could that be? What would she do without him? No more would she know his constant support or see his boyish grin. His laugh was forever silenced, his goals for the future ended. His service to the Stewardship over. What would Lionel do, his closest friend? And Eric, who always felt things so deeply?

She collapsed on the bench, strength bleeding from her limbs, and attempted to breathe. Her heart lodged in her throat, her lungs hollow blocks of ice. She took several uneven breaths as she tried to process it, to make the truth real in her mind. Ollen would not be returning.

Nay, that was not true. A sob escaped her, and she covered her face with her hands, releasing the torrent of grief. Ollen had returned. For the very last time.

56

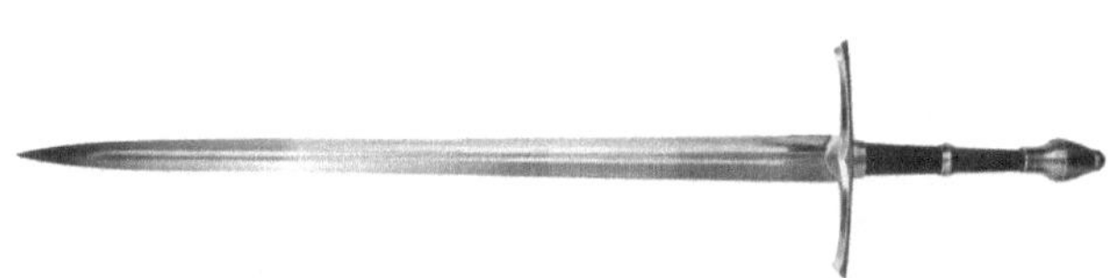

The next few hours passed in a numb fog. Lionel had dispatched the rest of the bodies and put them in a safe place in the inn's stable until they could be taken home.

Standing in front of the single window in her room, Seria wrapped her arms around her middle and swallowed past a raw, achy throat. Her face was swollen, her eyes gritty, but there were no more tears. They had all been spent. Silence enveloped her, thick and heavy, laced with a sharp cord of grief.

She could not grasp the truth that Ollen was gone. Guilt held her in a cold grip for all the times she had taken him for granted. He had loved her, though she had missed the signs in the beginning and then tried to pretend they weren't there. Yet he never pushed her or made her uncomfortable, but stood to the side, always there when she needed him.

He was a man she could have loved if given the time and chance. But that would never be.

Loud male voices drifted up the steps, shaking her from her daze. A quick dart of hope that Braylee or Eric had arrived shot through the painful fog, and she dashed downstairs.

But it was an unknown group of men who congregated at the front desk. She descended the last step, searching for a familiar face. It took a moment before she noticed the innkeeper's strained expression and the way the darkly-clad men turned to watch her.

"That's her," one of them murmured.

Her stupor shifted into alarm when two men approached her, their faces twisted in malice. With nowhere else to turn, she turned to run back up the steps. An arrow whizzed by her face, burying its tip into the wall inches before her.

"Come on back, missy, unless you want to see the old man hurt," the frontman spoke, his voice hard.

The innkeeper stiffened. "Leave her alone. She's no concern of yours."

One of the men raised a crossbow and released a dart into the man's chest. Seria cried out as he dropped behind the counter. Two men grabbed her arms and jerked her toward the door. She fought them every step of the way, kicking, elbowing, even biting at them, attempting every trick her father had taught her to slow them down.

Footsteps sounded on the steps before Lionel appeared, his sword already in hand. "Let her go!"

The crossbow came up again and fired. Seria screamed when Lionel was thrown back with the impact and hit the floor with a thud. *"Lionel!"*

"Make sure he's dead." One of the men headed toward him with a dagger.

"No!" She jerked an arm free and raked her nails across the face of one of her captors. He yelped and backhanded her. Pain and panic blinded her as they dragged her away.

The door flew open, hitting the wall with a crack. "Stop!"

Every man in the room froze, riveted on the man in the doorway.

Mason turned blazing eyes on the men holding her. "Get your hands off her or so help me, I'll rip you apart."

They complied, with soft murmurs of "At once."

Seria stumbled back, rubbing at her hurting wrists. Her eyes locked onto Mason, who stalked into the room, holding his sword with white knuckles, consumed with a fierceness she had never seen.

"What are you doing here?" Mason demanded through tight lips.

"Following Bruin's orders to get the girl," one man answered, his expression blank.

Seria's chest caved. Bruin had sent them? To get *her?* She looked to Mason, who looked as thunderstruck as she.

Mason clenched his jaw until the muscles popped. "Get out," he growled, his brow knotted.

One man blinked slowly. "But, sir—"

"I said get out!" The words exploded from him, making Seria jump. "And don't come back!"

The six men all chorused their compliance and hurried out. A moment later, the sound of hoofbeats sounded and drifted away.

Mason lowered his sword, breathless. "I heard you scream."

A harsh sob broke through her, like a dam released. Her body shook as she looked about her wildly, trying to rein in her terror. Upon seeing the Steward at the bottom of the stairs, she cried his name and ran to him. She fell beside him, his still face cutting what was left of her spirit into ribbons. "Nay, not you, too." She ripped at her dress, trying to tear a piece off to stay the blood flowing from his head. So much blood. Her fingers trembled, and tears flooded down her cheeks, making her task difficult.

"Seria." Mason crouched beside her and pressed a rag into her hands.

She wept as she pressed the cloth to the wound on Lionel's temple. "Please, Lambient, not another one." Her shoulders shuddered with every breath, and her pulse pounded in her ears. "Don't die, don't die. Please, Lionel, don't die."

Warm hands covered hers. "Seria." His voice finally cut through her panic, and she raised her eyes to his. He leaned closer, capturing her attention. "It's just a graze. He'll be fine."

It took a moment for the words to pierce the panic, but she could see that he was right. Lionel's breathing was steady. "H-head wounds always b-bleed a lot." She stated the fact out loud to further convince herself. She looked behind her, to where the innkeeper lay. "Th-the innkeeper?"

Mason hesitated, then shook his head.

She focused on Lionel again. "It's my fault."

"Oh, sweetheart." Mason tried to pull her to him, but she pushed him away. He was a part of this army, served under the very man who had sent these men to attack an innocent innkeeper and her Steward guard.

He sat back on his knees and sighed. "I'm the one to blame. Bruin is trying to use you to get through to me."

She sent him a sharp look. Why would Bruin need to get through to Mason? He already had his loyalty. Had Mason staged this attack to win her trust again?

"You have to get out of here, Seria. Bruin knows you're here, and he won't quit after one botched attempt."

There it was. He was using this incident to scare her into leaving, maybe running away with him. She hardened her heart and focused on Lionel's wound. "I already told you. I won't leave with you."

"*Blades*, that's not what I meant."

Lionel moaned and stirred slightly, the motion washing over Seria like a cool breeze of relief on a hot day. But Mason looked ready to bolt for the door. When the Steward slipped back into unconsciousness, he leaned closer.

A small piece of her heart ached for his touch again, but her resolve held firm.

"I'm sorry, Seria." He reached out for her hand, drawing her gaze to his. "Where's Eric?"

She pressed her lips together, refusing to tell him anything about the message from Larence. But Mason's face paled. "The message." He smacked his thigh with a fist and punched to his feet, moving for the door. "I'm the one who gave it to him."

"What?" She recoiled. "You read my thoughts!" Hurt and anger rose within her, sharp and piercing. Mason had resorted to using her. "How could you?"

Mason hesitated at the door. "I had no choice."

The statement chilled her. What was Mason about to do?

Lionel groaned and pushed himself up. Mason whirled away and slipped through the door, but not before Lionel caught a glance of him.

"Stop!" Lionel pressed a hand to his head and glared at her. "What have you done?"

Her heart pounded as she stared out the empty doorway. Mason was gone, chasing after Eric.

She looked down at Lionel, who still glowered up at her. "Lionel, we have a problem."

Mason stood at the edge of town, within the outside edge of the trees bordering Shales, wrestling with his next choice. Fury colored his vision that Bruin had targeted Seria. His fingers brushed the hilt of his sword as part of him hoped he would see his commander again so he could end the threat to her life. Another part doubted he would walk away from it.

But his plans for getting help had been disrupted by the prince's absence. Thanks to Larence's message—a message Mason had delivered to the store clerk personally—Eric was miles away leading his men into a trap. Mason was sure of it.

Familiar drums pounded in his head, and he squeezed the bridge of his nose, trying to ignore the spell. But the voices chimed in again—voices he knew this time. Seria crying. Ollen gasping out his last words. Eric calling orders to his men.

Don't do it, Eric. Mason pressed his palms over his eyes, focusing on the prince's voice in an attempt to overcome the pain. *It's a trap. Turn back.* If only he could reach him before it was too late.

The headache and voices faded. He sighed and rubbed a hand over his jaw as the gravity of his situation weighed him down. There were too many problems, too many pressing concerns. Too many wrongs he had committed to ever make them all right. But he could start with one.

Mason would have to go back to Joshun alone.

57

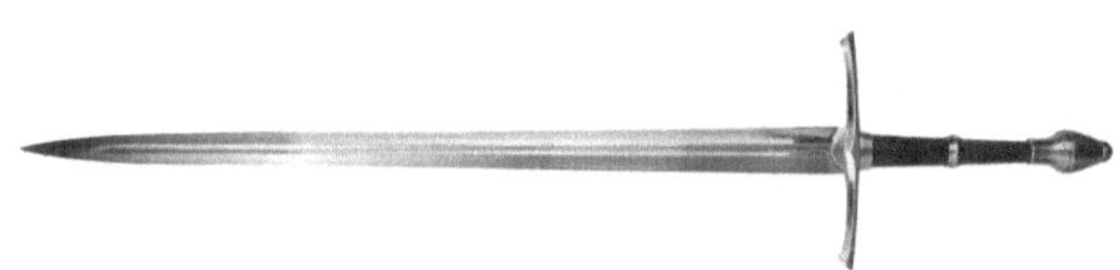

The shop was quiet as Seria entered. Her heart jumped when she spotted Lionel standing at the counter with Larence. He sent her a dark look, said a few words to the shopkeeper, and headed for the door.

"Lionel, please."

"Nay, Seria. I'm done."

She put her hand on his arm. "But—"

He jerked his hand away. "You're not to be trusted. Letting him go was the last straw."

Seria watched him slam through the door and gave a huff. "As reasonable as ever." Her eyes darted to where Larence watched her. "I'm sorry you had to see that." She let out a weak laugh.

Larence gave her a grin. "No worries, my dear. I hope everything's well?"

She frowned and approached the counter, her pulse racing. "Not really. But I can't really blame him," she said. "I've lost his confidence."

"Oh, come. It can't be as bad as all that."

She gave him a steady look. "I'm an ally of the Reader."

His brows went up a fraction, and he swallowed. "Oh. I...was not aware of this."

Glancing over her shoulder, Seria let out an uneasy sigh. "I couldn't let Lionel...hurt him." She swallowed past a dry throat. It was vital that Larence believed her. "I've loved Mason since I first met him. Despite what the Stewards think of him."

Larence narrowed his eyes but said nothing.

She took a deep breath, casting another quick look at the door. "I need to get out. When Eric comes back, Lionel will have me arrested. Again."

Larence licked his lips, turning his attention to wiping his counter. "I'm sorry, miss, but I can't help you."

"Mason told me he's working with you," she whispered.

"That's not true." The shopkeeper frowned but kept his focus on his rag.

Seria tried again. "I know about the messages." This time, Larence's eyes flew to hers. She swallowed. "The last one you gave Eric was from Mason."

Larence stared at her for a long moment, his face set like stone.

"He said it's not safe for me here, but he had to leave to join Bruin. Unless the prince finds him first." She let her voice quiver.

A slow smile spread across Larence's face. "I would fear no such thing, miss."

She blinked at him. "Why not?"

Larence shook his head, his hands again busy with wiping the counter. "Even now, the prince is walking into a trap. Soon, he will no longer be a nuisance. Jader will see to that. And you...?" He gave her a grin. "You will be safe to be with your Reader. Without the prince or the Stewards looking over your shoulder, forcing you to live a life according to their righteous standards."

There it was. Something cold slid down Seria's spine, and her hands began to shake. She stepped away from the counter, her eyes never leaving the deceitful shopkeeper. "Did you hear?"

At the volume of her question, Larence stopped and frowned, until Lionel's voice sounded just outside.

"Aye, I heard."

The door opened, and Lionel stepped in, his glare fixed on Larence. "Our source is a fraud."

Larence's jaw unhinged. "Nay, y-you misunderstand me! I am loyal to the prince." He pointed a finger at Seria. "Sh-she's the one who is a traitor! She let the Reader go! She even admitted it to me!"

"Save your breath, traitor." Three other Stewards filed in behind him. "I already know what Seria's done. She's revealed your true loyalties." He gave her a long look. "And her own, as well."

Seria stepped out of the way as the other knights led Larence out, yelling curses as he went. The Stewards would not be able to legally imprison him, as he was free to choose where his loyalties lay. But they would detain him so that he could not send any more messages.

Something within her shriveled and died at what Mason had done. She had known he would kill Eric when given the chance, but the deceit hurt her deeply. The man she had fallen in love with was truly a Shadowman.

Lionel moved to her side, chewing his cheek. "Now I know why there was no one around when Darkmen showed up at the inn. But I don't like what this could mean for the prince."

"Is there anything you can do?" she asked, desperation clawing at her. "Some way you could reach him?"

"I already tried after the attack at the inn." Lionel clasped his hands behind his neck. "Skies above, they're going to be ambushed, and I can't do a thing."

Seria crossed her arms over her rolling stomach. "Don't you know where he went?"

"He was meeting a Steward friend who wished to keep his location unknown."

All Seria could see was Ollen's lifeless body hanging over his horse. Visions of more death, more bodies flooded her with terror. "Lionel, we can't just sit back and do nothing!"

"I don't know where he is!" Lionel held his arms out in defeat. "I have nothing to follow. No message, no map." He stopped short, his eyes widening. "Map."

Seria stared as he dug into the pack hanging at his side. "What is it?"

He pulled out a small torn piece of canvas. "I found this... with Ollen."

She nodded for him to go on. He unrolled the parchment to reveal a hastily, crudely drawn map. She pressed against his shoulder to get a closer view. "What is that?"

"I don't know." He scowled at it. "It's the only thing I have to go by, though. Maybe it was something Ollen wrote."

It didn't look like Ollen's handwriting, but she did not refute it. She pointed to a small label. "What's Joshun?"

Lionel's gaze sharpened. "That's what we've been looking for," he whispered. He stared at it a moment longer, then straightened his spine. "I'm sending you back to the fort."

"What?" She jerked her attention from the map.

He rolled it up and put it back into his bag. "It's not safe for you here anymore. Those soldiers could come back for you."

It was the same thing Mason had told her, more or less.

"Besides. I need to get our men home." Lionel's voice fell, and as he led her from the shop and back to the inn to prepare for the journey, Seria did not argue.

58

When the darkness closes in, still I will trust in Him.
-The Sacred Code

Mason descended the dark steps of Stonehard, sweat beading his forehead and stinging his eyes. He started to grab a torch to guide his way but found the stairwell illuminated enough for him to see.

The castle was empty of the Darkmen guards. Some stood watch in key locations, at his command, and others he had sent away. The control would only last overnight, and then they would be back. But if all went well, he would be long gone by then. He had not come across any Shadowmen, which was fortunate, but also strange.

Benkis met him at the bottom of the steps, swinging a keyring back and forth in his hand. Two more large hoops hung on his belt. "Hey, Sgt. Mason. What are you doing down here?"

"Killing time." Mason glanced around. "Anyone else down here?"

"Besides all these whining kids? Nay, just me." Benkis leaned against the wall. "My shift is over, but I'm still waiting on Malcom to show up." He grumbled a bit about the other man's tardiness.

Mason nodded absently. Malcom was probably somewhere out in the woods by now. "I'll cover for you."

Benkis cocked a brow. "You want to take my shift?"

"Nay." Mason looked at him. "I want you to help me get them out."

The man pulled the rings off his belt. "At once."

Mason took the other two rings and called out. "Dalton Stattler?"

There was no answer, so he went further down the hall and hollered again. Finally, a young voice responded at the end of the hall. Mason dashed to that door and peered in the small window. A dirty, thin face blinked up at him. "Are you ready to get out of here?"

"Shut up, you lying Darkman."

Mason responded by trying a key in the lock. After three keys, he found the right one and swung the cell door open. "We don't have a lot of time." Bruin could return at any time with more men.

But Dalton still eyed him suspiciously. "How do I know you're not just trying to trick me?"

"It's a chance you'll have to take." He pointed back to Benkis, who had already opened two cells. "I need your help getting the rest of the kids out." If at all possible, he did not want to control the kids. He held a key ring out. "Make sure you find your sister."

Dalton's face creased in surprise, and he accepted the keys. "I'll get everyone, sir." He hurried to the first door and started working through the keys. Already nearby voices were clamoring for him not to forget them. They cut through Mason like blades.

He moved to another hall lined with tiny dark chambers and began working through the keys. With every one that didn't work, a noose tightened around his neck. The process was painstakingly slow, and always he listened for the sound of discovery. He had no idea where Bruin was or when he planned to return. The last time he saw him was days ago. At Shon's execution.

How he wished his friend was here to help him. Somehow, he had no doubt that Shon would have been with him in this. But he had to do this on his own. Just him, a few controlled guards, and around fifty scared, hungry, exhausted kids.

Questions plowed through the resolve in his mind. How was he going to get that many kids out of here to safety? Where would he take them?

He flattened his lips and pressed on. The answers would come when he needed them. For now, the important thing was getting them out of here, away from the clutches of Jader's men.

He worked his way down the hall, and then the next one. The dark hall soon echoed with cautious whispers and the soft pad of bare feet. The ding of keys sounded every few moments as Benkis and Dalton released more kids. Some of the older kids took charge of the younger ones.

CLICK! The last lock sprang, and he opened the door. After one more sweep to make sure no one was missed, Mason moved back to the stairwell. Benkis waited for him, as did Dalton, gripping the hand of a girl younger than him. Mason looked out over the crowd of kids, his eyes falling on the small, smudged face of little Liam, clutching the skirt of one of the older girls. A stone formed in the base of Mason's throat.

"Let's go."

"It's too dark."

The words from somewhere in the crowd of youngsters stopped him in his tracks, one foot positioned on the bottom step. The kids all squinted through the darkness, many of them grasping a nearby arm or bracing the wall. He looked back up at the steps, laid out before him clearly, despite the deep shadows, and grabbed a torch off the wall. "Just follow the light." The absurdity of his own statement hit him.

There were a few nods and murmurs of acquiescence, so he moved on, with Benkis bringing up the rear.

The large foyer was silent and empty. Two rows of thick pillars lined either side of the long room, reaching all the way to the high ceiling. It was still dark, but a few streams of weak light poured through the closed shutters. Mason set his torch in its sconce and led the way to the long room. The kids were not very quiet, though he sensed they tried to be. The dozens of footsteps grew in volume until it buzzed in his ears like bees' wings. A few fearful whimpers escaped some of the young ones, quickly hushed by others putting on a brave face.

They approached the double doors, but Mason tensed. Where was his doorman? He paused, his ears humming, and waited. Nothing stirred, except for the youngsters behind him. It was too late to go back. He had to go on and hope the controlled doorman had just wandered off with the others.

He made it to the doors and held up a hand to hush his followers. Moving ever so slowly, he inched one door outward and peeked out. The courtyard lay out before him, empty and bare, save for the tall, ancient trees planted decades ago in strategic formation.

"Come on." He led the way through the large portico and down the steps, his sights set on the surrounding forest beyond the courtyard. The outside walls had fallen and decayed long ago, making their exit easier. If he could just get them through the bailey of Stonehard, within the cover of trees, he could breathe a little easier. Then he would go from there.

Bruin stepped into his path, his hands resting on his sword hilt and his face as black as a thunderstorm. Mason stopped short, his heart slamming into his chest, and held his arms out, as if he could shield all the kids from Bruin's view. Gasps and soft cries sounded from the young captives.

The commander's jaw shifted, his glare stabbing Mason where he stood. "I knew as soon as you reacted so irrationally to the fool traitor's execution that you could no longer be trusted."

Mason gritted his teeth. *Stay calm.*

Bruin walked forward, his pace unhurried and casual. "You should've known your actions would be reported. Every last one of them. Starting with the disappearance of the dead Stewards from the cliff who have rendered this location useless." He sneered. "Along with your heroic rescue of that peasant girl."

"You keep your hands off her," Mason growled, heat pouring down his spine. "She has nothing to do with this."

"On the contrary. She's fully responsible for the trouble you've caused recently." He waved a hand to the crowd of silent onlookers behind Mason. "Unfortunately, you've only made things worse for our targets."

"They're children," Mason ground out, dread pricking at him. "Not tools to be used at your disposal."

Bruin shrugged. "Thanks to you, you've disrupted their training and those *children* can no longer be used."

"I'll die before I let you harm them again."

"I'd like nothing better." Bruin glowered and pulled his sword. "Unfortunately, Jader still has use for you."

Darkmen poured into the courtyard. Others emerged from the shadows of the wall, their stones swinging against their chest and eyes alight with the thrill of the challenge.

"Get back to the castle!" Mason pulled his sword and backstepped, keeping himself between the Shadowmen and the kids fleeing for the terrace. Benkis led the way, silent and compliant.

"Come, Mason." Bruin moved forward. "You'll only prolong the inevitable."

A blast of cold wind hit Mason in the face and slammed the doors of the keep shut. Cries erupted as the kids panicked and cowered behind the pillars and railing.

"Keep the kids safe," Mason ordered, but before Benkis could make a move, a dagger hit him square in the chest, and he fell in a lifeless heap.

For the first time in his life, Mason faced his commander with fear. Bruin would stop at nothing to gain the advantage, even at the expense of his own men. Mason had led these kids straight into more danger.

He gripped his sword, his knuckles white and his muscles tight. Images of everything he had done wrong flipped through his mind like a tome caught in Bruin's windstorm. Living in hate. Using his Gifts for Jader's dark purposes. Taking the Shadowstone pledge. Kidnapping children. Killing Stewards. Turning away from the Lambient.

Darkmen and Shadowmen drew closer. Bruin raised a fist, and lightning struck the building somewhere up above. The children screamed as blocks of stone tumbled down around them. Mason dove out of the way of a tree that succumbed to the wind. He jumped to his feet and faced the soldiers.

"Stop."

A few did, their feet stuck to the ground and their faces blank. The Shadowmen continued on without a pause.

Mason tightened his grip and stood before them. No one fired at him, which made their advance worse in a way. Why not kill him and get it done with? They would have to before he let them get their hands on those he had sworn to protect.

The terrace was surrounded by Shadowmen now, all with weapons glinting in their hands.

Lambient, I don't deserve anything from you, but please, help me get them all out.

The appeal shook him. It was the first prayer he had uttered since he was twelve, but he had no doubt that it was heard.

Spreading his feet out, he readjusted his hold and went on the offense, swinging at the first Shadowman who reached him. Their swords crossed briefly before Mason overpowered him and kicked him out of the way. Then he turned to face another one. And another.

More Darkmen neared, passing those who still stood where Mason had controlled them. A rock shot out from behind him, hitting one of the soldiers square in the head and knocking him flat on his back. Mason swiveled around just as Dalton scooped another stone and flung it.

"Nay, don't!" Mason blocked a jab.

More rocks soared through the air as other kids joined the onslaught. Dalton grabbed another one, his chin jutted. "We'll fight."

Another blast of lightning hit the building, raining debris all around them. A crack drew Mason's attention upward at the crumbling roof of the terrace. *Blazes.* Their fight would do little good if they were buried under rubble.

Wind roared around them, whipping their clothes and tossing their hair. Clouds darkened the sky as Bruin sent another bolt shooting through the sky. Part of the building crumbled in on itself.

The ground beneath them reverberated, and another sound joined the fray. Despair rounded Mason's shoulders. What now?

But Bruin's soldiers also paused and looked around at the noise. Some even broke away and dashed for their horses. Others turned from the castle and readied their stance for another attack. What was happening?

To the left of the courtyard, Eric Passion broke through the woods astride his gray stallion, an army behind him, their crimson breastplates flashing and beams of light shining from their upraised hands. From the other side, Eric's broad-shouldered captain appeared with another troop, catching Bruin's army between them. An enraged roar rose as the Dark Army ran to meet the Stewards.

Liam jumped up and down from behind a pillar. "The Stewards are coming! The Stewards are coming!"

"Go!" Mason yelled, pointing to the woods to their left, where the Stewards swarmed. "Get to the trees."

The kids bolted from the terrace, some jumping over the rails, others ducking beneath. The littler ones were helped along until no one was left behind. Breathless, Mason watched as a band of Stewards veered away at the sight of them. One by one, the men reached down, pulled the kids up on the saddle with them, and galloped for the safety of the woods while others shielded them from the Darkmen.

Weakness invaded his body, and he slumped against a pillar. He looked over his shoulder at the battle that had erupted around him. He got a glimpse of Bruin, turning away from the castle to meet a Steward head-on. Then they were lost among the throngs of his Darkmen.

A shout drew Mason's gaze back to the fleeing children. Areem stepped into view, his bow up and aimed at Dalton, at the back of the pack.

"*No!*" Mason couldn't get the word out fast enough.

The string snapped. Dalton went down, an arrow protruding from his shoulder.

Mason charged, pulling a dagger from its strap. Areem spun to face him, blanching as Mason plowed into him. Mason grabbed the front of his shirt and shook him, rage boiling. "You have *no* idea what you've done!"

He jerked Areem close to his face, the tip of his knife poking his stomach. "I should kill you on the spot like you tried to do that kid. Just like they did *Shon*."

Areem's dark eyes reflected dread, stunned at his own actions. Mason froze, his fingers itching to plunge the blade forward. But a few short years ago, Areem had been one of those kids. Until he had been taught and trained in the ways of the Dark Army...

By me. Mason was as much to blame for letting that arrow fly.

Behind Areem, Dalton struggled to his feet and kept running. Another Steward swept him up in front of him and carried him off. Mason let out a harsh breath and shoved Areem to the ground. "I ruined you, kid." His words came out low and hoarse, thick with shame and anger. "Now, get out of here. Don't come near me again."

Areem nodded. "At once."

59

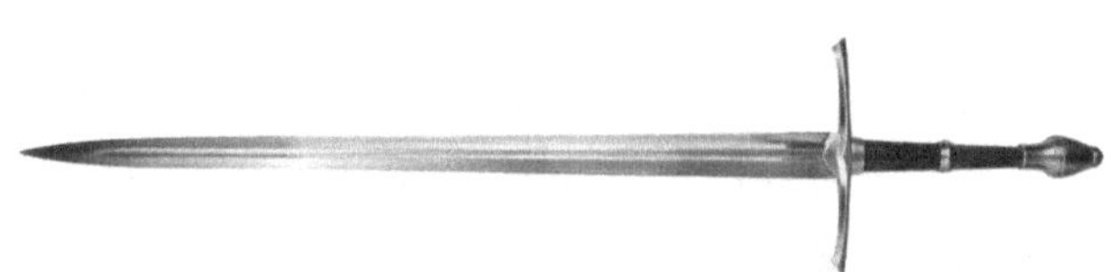

"We fight a battle in the war that has already been won by the Lambient.
We will overcome!"
-Pre-battle speech given by King Aden Passion during Calla's War

Triumph bloomed in Eric's chest as his men swept the kids into their grasp and away from danger. The question of how the young victims were already outside of the castle walls would have to be answered later.

A swarm of fighters cut off his view, and he raised his sword and met his opponent, disarming him and kicking the man from his saddle. Oakley sidestepped beneath him and tossed his head.

All around him, the air filled with dust, angry shouts, and the echo of steel against steel. The wind had died down for the moment, but Bruin was still close by. Men from both armies were already falling, horses bolting to safety.

It was getting dark. Too dark for this time of day.

"Stewards—" Oakley reared just as harsh wind caught him by surprise and slammed him to the ground, knocking his breath from him. His sword and Beacon flew from his hands, out of sight in the growing shadows.

There was bedlam all around. A thick fog formed, making it hard to distinguish who was who, save for the Beacons the Stewards wielded. Their lights spilled over the ground, giving it an early morning luster.

Stunned and breathless, Eric gasped for air and rolled over, scrambling for his weapons. It fell strangely quiet where he crouched, the fighting shifting away from him. There was no sight of Bruin. The sun barely hung on.

The many lights of the Beacons glinted off something a few feet away. Lavrynth. He coiled himself to dive for it, but someone's boot was suddenly there, blocking him.

Eric's eyes shot up to meet Mason's, and his heart stuttered. Mason reached down and picked up the sword as Eric jumped to his feet. Reason screamed at him to turn away, but something in Mason's gaze held his.

Everything around them faded as they faced each other once again. Mason's jaw shifted as his mouth came open. His brows pinched together in an inward struggle. He then set his chin and held out Eric's sword, hilt first. "You're going to need this."

Eric hesitated. Mason looked as intense as ever, but there was something missing.

"Take it." Mason drew in a deep breath. "It's time to fight."

Mason's words held no command over him. Eric slowly reached out to take the sword, still eyeing the Shadowman warily.

And then it hit him. Mason's Shadowstone was gone.

Before he had a chance to dwell on that knowledge, Mason moved, and Eric tensed. But Mason circled him, his attention fixed on someone behind Eric. A group of Darkmen approached from the shadows. Mason positioned himself between them and Eric and spoke.

"Stand down."

The whole group stopped in their tracks. Mason ordered them all to leave, and they obeyed amidst a chorus of, "At once."

Dumbfounded, Eric waited until Mason looked at him again. "What are you doing?"

"Righting some wrongs." His soft voice was almost lost in the midst of the fighting.

A tangle of Darkmen and Stewards broke between them, swords clashing. Eric lost sight of Mason and found himself back in the heart of the skirmish. He had just dropped another Darkman when a violent blast of wind hit, driving everyone else away. Steadying himself, he looked up in time to catch a glimpse of Bruin approaching, his face a thundercloud. Eric's Beacon was still lost somewhere in the fray. He caught sight of a shadow and lunged back in time to miss Bruin's sword at his neck. He grunted as Bruin jabbed him hard in the ribs with his elbow. The two men spun out of reach of one another, then faced off again.

His blood pounded in his ears as he searched for the Shadowman within the black clouds of fog. Flashes of Beacons around him were all that allowed him to make the tall man out as he approached.

"It's over, Bruin," he called out. "You can't hide children here any longer."

Bruin's low words drifted through the fog on his left. "Stonehard served its purpose. It drew you here so you could die."

Eric smirked. "I don't think so." A spark of silver streaked at him from the side, and he blocked Bruin's sword. "I don't think all of this was in your plan." Mason's unexpected appearance earlier stood out in his mind.

Bruin reacted with a growl and a hard strike. Eric parried and back-stepped, his feet tangling beneath him. *Stay focused!*

"Don't think you're going to walk away from this." Bruin's voice sounded from behind. "I will not miss the second chance to kill the prince of Paladin."

Eric sidestepped and missed the tip of Bruin's blade. Spotting a thick limb a few yards away, he reached his hand out and lifted it in the air, swinging it full force at Bruin. A blast of wind sent the branch right back at Eric, catching him straight in the chest. He landed hard on his back and gasped for air. He pushed the limb off and stumbled to his feet, holding Lavrynth with trembling hands. The hilt warmed his fingers, but he stood in nothing but darkness.

Bruin was nowhere in sight.

Mason hated what was happening. He wasn't sure where he belonged. Did he kill those he had only days before fought alongside? Or did he join an army of men he had hated for half his life?

Eric had disappeared in the crowd. Mason searched for him in the blackness, while attempting to stay out of the way of slinging blades. Unable to bring himself to fight against those he had up until only recently been allied with, he used his words instead, sending Bruin's men away from the fighting.

Then he spotted Greggor, walking straight for him with a cold sneer. Several men flanked him, all bearing Shadowstones. His blood ran cold as he faced them.

"We don't have to do this."

"After what you've done?" Greggor returned, his voice hard as flint. "Aye, we do." He lunged for him, his companions following his lead.

Before Mason could take a breath, they were on him, the wind of Greggor's sword hitting his face. He moved quickly, knocking one man flat on his back before he could even take a swing. Kicking one man hard in the knee, Mason ducked another sword. His lips stretched tightly across his teeth as he thrust his weapon forward, straight into one man's stomach. Unable to stand still for even an instant, he rammed hard against another man, breaking out of the circle they had entrapped him in. A few seconds later, it was just him and Greggor.

The Shadowman stared back at him coldly. "You've betrayed Emperor Jader."

Mason struggled to catch his breath. "I've learned a few things."

With an ugly leer, Greggor attacked again, too confident in his speed. Mason deflected the blade and came back around with a hook, catching Greggor across the chest. The man gaped at him for a heartbeat, his sword falling from limp fingers before he slumped to the ground.

Mason stared down at the man he had worked alongside with for years. Then he stepped away and searched for Eric. Bruin's fog made it difficult enough, but just then, darkness spread over him, dousing what little light the sun offered and announcing Jader's arrival.

Mason's heart hitched as he peered through the inky blackness surrounding him. The Darkmen had all disappeared, as helpless in Jader's darkness as anyone else. But the Shadowmen came on, and the Stewards tried to keep up with the help of their rods. Mason's skin prickled as he pictured his Shadowstone at the bottom of a gorge, out of reach and use.

So why could he still see?

Braylee stood back-to-back with Zakkias, their swords in constant motion. The young Steward held up remarkably well after his long ride from Stonehard and back again. He wielded his sword and Beacon with a pale face but sure movements.

Ducking a wild swing, Braylee flipped a Darkman over his shoulder and squinted through the heavy mist.

Where was Eric?

A grunt beside him drew him back around to where Zakkias faced off with two men, his steps faltering in his exhaustion. Before Braylee could get to him, Zakkias buckled and fell to his knees, holding his Beacon up in defense.

Braylee forced his way between the Shadowmen and Steward, sending them back a few paces. His sword swung left and right as he fought them back, his chest heaving with the exertion. He struck low and sank his blade deep into the upper leg of one, but that move cost him valuable seconds against the second. He turned as the other man's sword came down and braced himself for the blow.

But the man never struck. He gave a violent jerk and froze as the tip of a sword appeared under his breastplate. He fell at Braylee's feet, and Zakkias pulled his sword from the body, breathing hard.

Braylee exhaled. "Nice work, young man."

Zakkias swallowed and nodded. "I already lost my lieutenant and sergeant, sir. I'm not ready to lose my captain."

The grief Braylee worked to suppress knocked against his heart. "You made them proud, Private."

The younger man's Adam's apple bobbed. "Thank you, sir."

For the moment, the fight had shifted further in the fog, so Braylee took the moment to look around, desperate for a sight of Eric. Dozens of Beacons offered him snatches of images. His men fought hard against the Dark Army.

Finally, his eye caught a blond head standing before the tall form of Bruin Pralus. Eric held his sword before him, but his Beacon was nowhere to be seen.

Would that prince ever learn to hang on to his light rod?

A black shroud draped over them, slowly surrounding them, and more Shadowmen appeared. His vigilance shot up, and he held his Beacon up, scattering light through the thick darkness that could only mean Jader was nearby.

Just before the darkness covered the prince, Braylee caught a glimpse of the Reader, diving into Eric and slamming him into the ground.

60

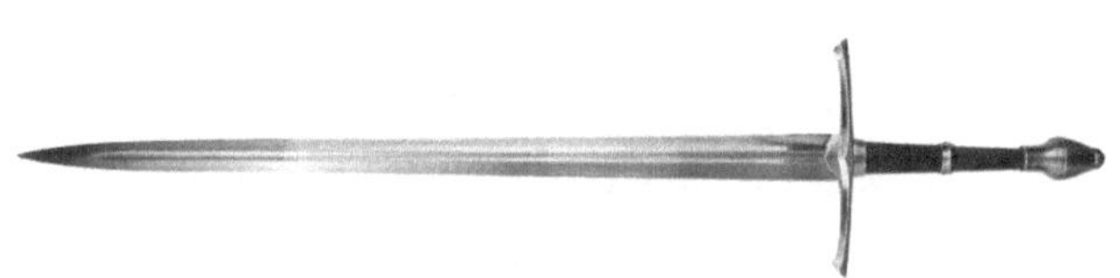

Mason landed on top of Eric, rolled off and jumped to his feet, hoping Eric wouldn't blindly stab him in the back. A bolt of lightning pierced the ground where the prince had stood seconds before.

Eric gaped. "Thanks."

Bruin appeared under the flickers of the retreating bolt, his face black with rage. "I'm going to kill you, Mason. I don't care what Jader says. I'll kill you both."

Eric stepped to Mason's side just before Bruin came at them with a roar, his broadsword spinning with greater speed than Mason thought possible for a man his size.

He struck at the prince first, hitting the blade so hard it sent the smaller man stumbling to the side. Mason braced himself and caught the brunt of the attack, straining to keep the blade from reaching his face. He deflected, spun, and swept another strike away. Just as Eric jumped back in, Bruin forced Mason into a hasty retreat and flipped the sword out of his hands.

Bruin turned to redirect Eric's swing while Mason reclaimed his blade. Bruin kicked Eric in the stomach and aimed the tip of his blade for a killing shot. Mason intercepted, sweeping the sword and going on the offense.

Eric recovered, but before he could assist, Bruin raised his hand, and a blast of wind knocked them both off their feet. Mason gasped and rolled to his side, peering through the fog. Standing tall against the black haze around him, Bruin skewered him with a hate-filled look and raised a hand. Lightning gathered above his head, crackling and shimmering. A streak shot from the sky, racing too fast for Mason to move.

He threw his arms up over his head, but the bolt never reached him. The area lit up in white-hot light, energy hissing. Mason opened his eyes, holding his breath. Eric stood over him, his sword in front of him, the silver blade capturing the bolt. His face contorted as he struggled to hold the power. The sword glowed from tip to hilt.

Mason pushed himself up and out of reach. Eric grunted and swung the sword forward like a club, directing the current back at Bruin.

There was a flash, and then the lightning disintegrated. Bruin still stood there, his lips curling upward on his craggy face. His fingers reached for the stone hanging from his neck.

The air cooled, and shadows seemed to press in from all sides. Eric sucked in a breath and hunched over, his face twisted, gripping the gold hilt with white knuckles.

A chill gripped Mason. Emptiness and fear wrapped themselves around his lungs, smothering what little air he had left. Awareness of what was happening flooded him. This was the Shadowstone's power being turned on him.

A sharp pain hit his sternum, right where his stone used to hang. He cried out and gripped his chest. A web of darkness wrapped itself around his spirit, pulling him deeper into the bottomless pit he had carried around for years.

He dropped to his knees, gasping for breath. The darkness tightened, sparking the drum to sound in his head and voices to scream in his ears.

A desperate grunt brought his heavy head up. Eric still faced off with Bruin, but his body shuddered under the weight of the stone. Other Shadowmen appeared around Bruin, their eager stares fixed on the prince, multiplying their power.

The blackness deepened, shooting a dart of cold fire through Mason's core. He slumped forward, catching himself before he hit the ground face first. Every move sent daggers through his body, rendering him powerless.

This was his fault. The blame for every life lost here would be laid at his feet.

Forgive me. It was a simple request, but those two words were like a cork unplugged. Purpose—righteous purpose—flooded his spirit. If he had to die in recompense for his sins, so be it. But he would serve the Lambient with his last breath.

His fingers bumped something. He dragged his eyes open and blinked until it came into focus.

A Beacon.

He dragged in a shallow breath and looked up. Eric was still on his feet, but his face was white, his features slashed with agony as he resisted the multiple attacks. Mason gritted his teeth and grabbed the light rod.

"Eric!"

In the blackness, the prince turned blindly in his direction, but his eyes quickly found him and widened, stopping Mason in his tracks. What was wrong?

A glimmer drew Mason's gaze down. The rod in his hand lit up, softly at first but grew in intensity. It hit him like a battering ram. The Beacon was glowing. For *him.*

A warmth enveloped him, starting from his hand. Healing. Truth. Light. It was as if dawn had broken through his spirit, chasing the shadows back into the pit and sealing it off. A strange weight lifted off him, and suddenly, he could breathe.

This can't be right! The rod waxed hotter in his hand, startling him from his bafflement. He drew his arm back and flung the Beacon at Eric.

Eric used his Gift to draw the light rod to him, exhilaration pumping through his blood, and whipped it out in front of him. A harsh grunt ripped from him as a lash of white light zipped from the Beacon straight for the men facing him. There was a loud burst, and several men slumped to the ground.

Eric's heart skipped a beat and then drummed rapidly as the Beacon whip recoiled back into the rod.

Bruin flinched, his stone clenched in his fist, but he recovered swiftly, poised to charge again when a distant trumpet sounded. The shadows lifted suddenly, and Eric's Stewards seemed to suddenly gain new strength.

Reinforcements were coming.

"It's over, Bruin." Eric's body ached, but his spirits soared as the thunder of approaching hooves increased.

A vein in Bruin's forehead twitched, his eyes almost white in the glow of the Beacon. He turned to glare at Mason, standing a few yards away. Eric caught the revulsion on his face.

"I think not." Bruin raised his hand, and another blast of wind hit both men square in the chest, knocking them flat on the ground.

Eric rolled over in time to see Mason struggling to stand.

Bruin was gone.

Eric groaned and pushed to his knees. More Stewards poured into the courtyard. Darkmen, now caught in the middle, fled into the woods. Gentle sunlight took the place of Jader's shadows.

Mason turned to leave.

"Mason!"

He stopped and turned warily. His face and arms were cut up and bruised, his clothes ripped. But there was a new awareness in his expression. Something had changed.

Eric painstakingly stood and approached him. One thing stood out above all else in his mind. Mason had lit a Beacon. Which could only mean one thing. Somehow, like every Steward before him, Mason had surrendered to the Lambient.

Mason spoke first. "How did you know to come here?"

Eric thought back to what had driven him here. It had been a strange turn of events, but it made sense now. "I heard your voice in my head."

At that, Mason frowned. "What?"

"I know it sounds impossible, but I was on my way to see an ally, when I heard you telling me it was a trap."

Mason's gaze drifted to the side, his jaw shifting.

"So I turned another way. A little while later, I came across Captain Braylee after he had released the grizlons."

That grabbed Mason's attention. "The grizlons are gone?"

"Back to the north where they belong."

A sigh relaxed the tense lines of Mason's shoulders. "That still doesn't explain how you found us."

"One of our young scouts tracked us down and led us back here." His brows bunched. "Though it may have been too late to save some of my men."

"Ollen?"

Surprise that Mason even knew the name made Eric hesitate. "Aye."

Mason gave a sober nod. "I'm afraid so."

It was as he suspected, but it did not stop the sharp stab of grief. What did surprise him was the sorrow that darkened Mason's countenance.

Eric cradled an arm against his aching ribs. "You freed those kids, didn't you?"

A grimace passed over the Reader's face, and he looked ready to bolt. "Get them back home."

Eric nodded. "We will."

"All of them."

"Mason, my men are seeing to it even now. They'll get home." He marveled at the dramatic change in the other man in such a short amount of time. "What happened?"

Agitation twisted Mason's face. "I don't-I don't know." He gestured with his sword at the Beacon in Eric's hand. "I don't see how..."

Eric started to reply, but movement a short distance behind Mason caught his eye. Alarm slammed through him when Braylee leveled a crossbow on Mason and fired.

"Watch out!" Eric threw a hand up and deflected the bolt as Mason jumped behind a tree.

"I guess not everyone's happy to see me," he grumbled, sounding much more like the angry Darkman Eric had known. "My cue to leave."

"Where will you go?" Eric asked. Jader and Bruin would not let his betrayal go unpunished.

Mason hesitated, his expression flickering from uncertainty to resignation. "I don't know." He turned to go without another word.

"Mason, wait!"

"And let your men shoot me in the back?" Mason called back over his shoulder. "Nay, thank you." He ran into the woods, and a few moments later, Eric heard a horse take off.

"Prince Eric!" Braylee rode up, leading Oakley behind his bay. "Are you all right?"

Eric stood motionless, wondering if he had imagined the whole thing. "I'm fine." To Eric's surprise, Lionel followed the captain. "What are you doing here, Sergeant?"

Lionel swallowed, urgency tightening his face. "I apologize for breaking your orders, Sire, but some things have happened. Larence is a traitor."

"Larence?" Shock mixed with clarity now. "I don't know how I missed it."

Braylee shot him a sharp look. "Because you're human."

"Aye." He sighed. "But it doesn't make the betrayal any easier." Their allies in the Gateway seemed to be dwindling.

But then he remembered what had happened with Mason. Bewilderment battled to reign in his mind, but he pushed it aside. He doubted anyone would believe what he had seen, but if the Beacon had glowed in Mason's hand, that was enough for him.

61

The Lambient leads the way. Follow Him and His path shall be light for you.
-The Sacred Code

When the first gates of the lower courtyard leading into the Gateway Stronghold appeared ahead, Seria almost wept. All was calm and serene. She rode with a small company of six Stewards, all dressed in civilian garb to mask their identity. They had had no trouble on their journey, much to her relief.

Turning to look over her shoulder, Seria checked on the wagon at the back of the line, bearing the precious burden of fallen soldiers, carefully wrapped. Her throat ached that this was Ollen's last return to the stronghold. No more would he ride out with his prince to defend the innocent from Jader's clutches.

Crue, the boy who had brought Ollen and his comrades back to Shales, rode at the front of the wagon, looking drawn and uncertain. He was very close-lipped about how he had come across the bodies. Seria was more than a little interested in learning his story when she could handle it.

The tall gates closed behind them, shutting off the view of rocky ledges, thickening woods, and a few open fields. Still no sight of an army, no sign of danger.

Turning forward again, Seria's brows furrowed. Eric was still back there somewhere, along with Braylee, Lionel, and the rest of the Stewards.

And Mason.

Grief and anger twisted within her. How could she have been so foolish?

"We're almost there," said the Steward leader, a kind man named Gann.

Seria lifted her head. The gates of the inner wall rose before her. They had made it. She was almost home.

Her eyes burned with sudden tears, borne by intense relief and worry. Would the rest reach the Gateway safely as well? Or would she lose them as she had Ollen?

The gate swung open to let the caravan in. Gann was greeted by Dudley on horseback, who looked the group over with a somber eye. "Looks like we lost a few."

"I'm afraid so, sir," Gann replied.

The simple statement slapped at Seria's composure, and she bit her lip hard.

Dudley nodded. "Let's save it for the debriefing. King Aden will want to hear it himself in the Council Hall."

Surprise rippled through the soldiers. "The king is here?" Gann asked.

"That's right. Said he felt an urge to come." Dudley turned his horse to lead them in. "We learned long ago not to argue with the Passion intuition."

Seria tried to conjure up some interest in the arrival of the king but was too drained to care at the moment.

As soon as the caravan came to a stop in the inner bailey, she slid from her horse and handed the reins off, turning down any offer for an escort.

"I'm fine, thank you," she said, her voice wobbling. Then she stumbled toward the barn.

It was dark and blessedly quiet. She lit a lantern and closed the door behind her, so as not to disturb the livery keeper from his nearby home. Oakley's and Beast's stalls were empty, which did nothing for her turbulent emotions. The donkeys all crowded in a corner, dozing. One gray donkey jerked his head up at the sight of her and let out a snuffle before leaving the warmth of the group and ambling her way.

"Oh, Sanjo," she whispered, hugging his scruffy neck over the bar. "I'm so sorry I've neglected you."

He set his chin on her shoulder and let out a contented sigh, prompting a shaky laugh. "I should've known you'd forgive me." She leaned back and rubbed the spot between his eyes. "You're just the forgiving type, aren't you?"

The door swung open, and she turned, stopping short upon recognizing Lena's slight form.

"Oh, Seria," Lena breathed.

Seria met her in a hug halfway, both of them weeping into each other's shoulders.

"I'm so glad you're back safe," Lena said, squeezing her tight.

Seria gulped back a sob and leaned back to face her friend. "I am so sorry, Lena, for everything I said to you. I was so wrong." She wiped tears from her cheeks.

Lena led her to Oakley's clean stall, and they sank down into the sweet-smelling straw. "Are you all right?"

She answered with a sniff. "My heart is shattered in so many pieces, but my eyes have been opened to some pretty hard truths." She clasped Lena's hands. "You were right, Lena. I was in this for the wrong reason. It took me so long to see that."

Lena wrapped an arm around Seria's shoulders. "You're human, Seria. The good thing is, Lambient is very forgiving of that."

"But are you?" Seria blinked back more tears and met Lena's gaze. "I took advantage of you, treated you awfully, and left you without a word as to where I went."

Lena smiled, her eyes sparkling in their moisture. "I do forgive you, Seria. How could I call myself a follower of Lambient if I hold on to a grudge?"

Seria leaned into her. "Oh, Lena, I've missed your words of wisdom. If I'd have listened, I wouldn't have made such a fool of myself."

"You had to see things for yourself. I can't make those kinds of decisions for you." She tilted her head to look into Seria's face. "I'm guessing you saw Mason."

"Aye." Seria scrubbed at her wet cheeks again. "I was so wrong, Lena, to continue that relationship, knowing what he was. For so long, I wanted to do something important, and I got it in my head that I could be the one to change Mason." She shook her head, her lips trembling. "But I can't. So I had to let him go."

Lena did not try to fill the space with empty words but simply nodded in understanding.

Seria drew in a deep breath, feeling the cracks in her heart widen. "But it doesn't change the fact that I truly loved him." Her whisper turned into a sob. "And I'm so *angry* at him!" Ollen's death throbbed in her heart, but she could not bring herself to say it out loud. Lena would find out soon enough.

"I can't imagine what you've been through," Lena said. "But rest in the fact that you did the right thing. Even if it doesn't feel like it now, Lambient sees the sacrifice you made, and He will bless you for it."

The reassurance did not settle as deeply as Seria would have liked, healing the scars that were there to stay. But they did soothe the wounds of her heart. She found some small solace in the fact that no one had discovered her deceit. "Thank you, Lena, for always understanding."

"You look exhausted."

A single laugh broke through her tight throat. "In mind, body, and spirit."

"Then you need to rest tonight. Tomorrow's a new day. Deal with it when it comes."

Seria allowed the smaller woman to help her up from the thick bedding and lead her from the barn, but not before she stopped to give Sanjo another hug.

They trudged through the quiet streets back to Mallie's boarding house. Seria's body yearned for her soft bed, but her heart turned a different way.

Eric had not returned yet with the rest of the Stewards. Jader's army was still coming. And Mason was somewhere out there, caught in the fray.

What would the new day bring?

Darkness flooded the land, the moon hidden by a wisp of a cloud. Even the stars seemed sparse and dim. The nearby woods cast their deep shadows, adding to the inky blackness.

Mason guided his roan through the dark, his vision still cutting through it easily. That fact alone troubled him. Why was his night vision still intact? Had he not cast the shadow of Jader's hold off his spirit like he had thought?

He wandered without a plan, though he kept to a familiar course. As the night passed, his mind went back multiple times to what had happened at Joshun. He had aided the very man he had sworn to kill for years and turned on the man he had faithfully followed for the same amount of time. How could his allegiance change so quickly?

The answer took shape in his head. Because he had learned the truth of Jader's far-reaching deception.

But he never expected the light rod to glow in his hand. He could not wrap his mind around it even now, but the memory of how it felt could not be shaken. And despite the myriad of emotions churning inside him, a sense of assurance pulsed through his chest. He had been right to do what he did. No more would he be used for Jader's dark purposes.

But that did not make his future any clearer. Mason's path was hidden before him, with no clear direction. The Dark Army was no longer his to claim. Bruin would kill him the first chance he got. He had no idea where he was headed or where he wanted to be.

A pang cut through him. That wasn't true. He knew exactly where he wished he could be. His arms physically ached to hold her. He needed to hear her voice, lifting his spirits, assuring him that she was there for him.

But she wasn't, and he could not blame her. Not after everything he had done. He swallowed hard at the thought of never seeing her again, but it was better this way. She deserved better.

Stirring, he looked around him to get his bearings and straightened at the sight of the bluffs straight ahead. Cadence was just on the other side. He had made it all the way to the narrow valley.

Seized with a desire to lay eyes on the fort, to ensure it was still safe, Mason urged his horse right up to the crags. Seria's shortcut was close by, so he slid off the saddle and searched through the deep shadows for the opening, glad, for now, he still had his night vision.

His heart jumped when he finally spotted it, and he led the horse in. It was narrow and short, yet allowed for a comfortable walk.

Until they reached the fork, where heat blasted from the left. He paused to look back, curious about that side of the passage. A strange desire pulled at him, urging him to come closer. Staring down into the tight walkway, he almost gave in. With a reluctance that surprised him, he forced himself onward to the right. His roan snorted and tossed his head, not liking the tight quarters.

"Come on, we're almost there," he whispered, patting the arched neck.

Finally, the heat passed, along with the strange pull, and he stepped back out into the open. The Gateway lay before him, the Slate Mountains stretching out on both sides of the valley. All was peaceful and quiet.

Cadence looked the same—small and vulnerable. Yet, Mason did not have the same adverse feelings toward it. He had always thought its people weak and foolish, stubbornly resisting Jader and all he had to offer them. Instead, they chose to reside in the Gateway, mere yards from the Steward fort, subjecting themselves to their rigid ways. Pathetic and ignorant, not worth wasting his time on.

But that was before he met Seria.

Mason swallowed as he peered out at the now-vacant town. Seria had changed him. More than he had ever realized. Had it not been for her, he would have never given a boy like Crue a chance or seen the true value of people like Byron's family. He would not have been so willing to forgive Shon for expressing his doubts about Stewards. And he may never have learned the truth about Eric.

And the hole. Mason marveled as he searched for the bottomless pit that had threatened to swallow him. It was gone. Filled by the Beacon that had lit his soul, chasing away the shadows.

His heart yearned to share with her what had happened, but he would not disrupt her life again. He wished he could see through the walls of the fort, however. Was she safe inside? How long would it take for the Stewards to arrive?

Rather than moving closer to Cadence, Mason climbed back into the saddle and guided the horse up onto a rocky slope that curved away from the gap. From the vantage point on a high cliff, he could see much of the western valley, stretching out for miles before him. The mountains, fields, and woods. A long, thin stream to the left. And a slow-moving band of knights winding its way to the fort.

Tensing, he rose in the stirrups for a better look. Even from this distance, he could tell they did not wear the colors of the Stewards.

Gathering his reins, Mason prepared to descend the hill. He could not stop a whole army, but he could control as many as he could, create a commotion, disrupt their carefully laid-out plot. It would not hold them forever, but it was all he could do. They were but a few hours from the Gateway, still out of sight from anyone watching from the fort. He could not stand by and let them reach the unsuspecting people of the garrison.

The gelding picked its way down the rocky slope. They made it to the bottom before Mason was hit with a jolt of pain so sharp he couldn't breathe. He grabbed his head in his hands and let out a groan. The horse sensed his sudden tension and danced around nervously. Mason leaned forward, trying to keep his seat. Painstakingly, he swung his leg off and slid to the ground. His knees immediately buckled, and he pitched forward, barely catching himself before his face hit the dirt.

Dots danced before his eyes; his ears pounded mercilessly. The voices were deafening in their roar. His heart raced in his chest as his lungs desperately pulsated for air.

I can't…make it…stop! The pain left him helpless. Would it kill him this time? *Not now!* Not before he could reach that army. It was the least he could do.

There was a snap in his head, and the pain lifted. He gasped for breath, still on his knees. With his sleeve, he wiped the perspiration from his face. His heart beat too fast, making it hard to relax.

He heard a twig break behind him and looked over his shoulder. Five Stewards stood there, their arrows and blades trained on him.

"Don't move, Darkman."

He tried to shake his head, but a wave of dizziness overcame him. "Nay, wait." He struggled to breathe.

"Silence!"

"Dark Army...coming."

The Steward's face darkened. "Your threats will do you no good, Darkman."

Two men strode for him, grabbing him by the arms and lifting him from the ground. He was still too weak to fight against them, not that he would try. As they half dragged him to where several other Stewards waited, all looking alert and ready for anything, he could only hope Eric would make it back to the fort before the approaching army reached the gates.

The next few minutes were a blur as he was led into the inner bailey and made to stand before more Stewards.

"We found him sneaking around in the western bluffs." The voice seemed to fade in and out.

"Looks like he had a little too much to drink," another one said.

Mason struggled to focus on what was taking place before him. He stood between two pointed swords, his hands bound behind him. Blinking furiously, he tried to make out the man before him. Gradually, the grizzled features and the sharp eyes of the older knight became clear.

"He was alone?"

"Aye, Captain."

The man pursed his lips. "Could be a setup. Wouldn't be the first time he's managed to get inside."

Mason sensed the others exchanging confused looks. "Sir?"

"I take it you boys don't realize who this is?"

"Who?"

The man pinned a shrewd look on Mason. "This is the Reader."

Mason felt the instant change in the air, but he kept his focus fixed on the knight before him, partly because he could not deny what he had said, and partly because he needed something to focus on to keep the world from spinning.

"Captain Dudley!"

Mason watched as the captain turned slightly to acknowledge the newcomer.

"They're ready, sir."

Dudley nodded, his face stern. "Good. Then we won't waste any time." He turned back to Mason but spoke to his men. "Be on the lookout. I doubt they would send him alone."

Mason could have told him they did not send him at all, but it would do no good. He had given these men no reason to trust him.

Dudley rested his hands on the hilt of his sword, looking every bit the seasoned knight. "I don't know what your game is, young fella, but I can tell you that I'm not in the mood. And I'm not taking any chances with you, either. Not after what you pulled the last time you were here."

With that, someone stepped forward and wrapped a long cloth around Mason's eyes, plunging him into darkness.

They may have anticipated a struggle, but he had none to give. He knew what to expect. The Council would have no reason to do anything but convict him. His past deeds had caught up to him.

62

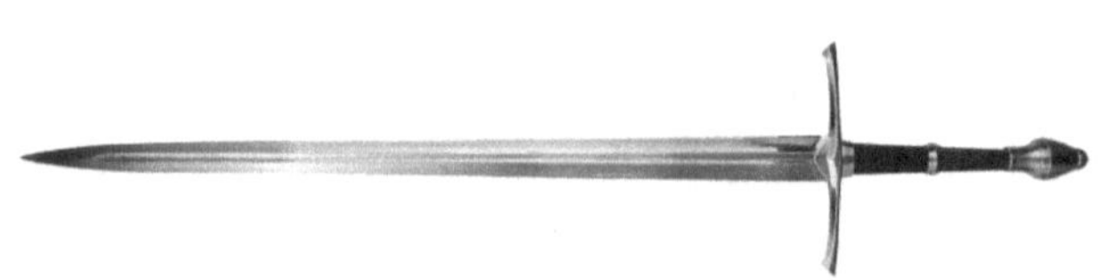

Darkness breeds fear, creating monsters that can only be conquered by the light of truth.
-The Sacred Code

"Seria!"

Lena's panicked voice cut through Seria's troubled dreams as a loud knock drove sleep from her. She rolled out of bed and plodded to the door. One look at Lena's somber face, and she was wide awake.

"What is it, Lena?"

"It's Mason. He's on trial before the king."

Mason! The king! "What? How did that happen?" She pulled Lena into her room so she could pull her clothes on over her shift.

"I'm not sure. The rumor is that he was found just outside of Cadence last night. A group of Stewards brought him to Captain Dudley, who put him under arrest."

Seria tied a clumsy knot in her belt, grasped Lena's hand, and then the two women dashed down the steps and through the winding paths to the Council Hall.

A large crowd had gathered under the second-story balcony, murmuring and restless. Seria caught a few hard glances her way. Some still remembered the part she played in allowing the Reader such close access to the fort.

The double doors of the balcony swung open, and the king stepped out, his blue robes sweeping the floor behind him. The golden crown on his white head caught a gleam of morning light. He rested his hands against the rail and looked down at the people. A captain with dark brown skin and deep-set eyes stood to his right. The Councilmen of the stronghold gathered to the left.

"I have already heard from many of you who feel you should be privy to this trial, considering the widespread havoc caused by the Reader," King Aden said. "Therefore, I will heed your requests. This trial will take place right here. Bring forth the accused."

Seria's blood ran dry as two lieutenants exited the hall beneath the balcony, leading a blindfolded Mason between them. She gripped Lena's hands with bruising strength as the man she had loved stood in the middle of the crowd, his hands tied before him and his head down.

"Oh, Lambient," she whispered, not sure what she was praying for. Mason had fought against the Lambient's Stewards for years, all in the name of Jader's brand of justice. By the standards of the law, he deserved death.

A young soldier named Timothy told the account of Mason controlling him into attacking his own men in Rackson. Three more reservists stepped up to tell how Mason had ordered them to keep anyone from following him out of the fort. The gateman, Frakes, described the night of the storm, when he was overpowered and ordered to keep watch, which led to him nearly killing Captain Braylee.

Attempted assassination of the prince. Smuggling Shadowmen into the Old Realm. It went on and on until the verdict was more than clear. Her heart clenched with the reality. There was nothing she could do about it.

Mason stood there, silent and slumped. Gone was the proud set of his chin and the straight line of his shoulders. His eyes were hidden from her, but his mouth sagged. There was no resistance, no fight. He looked resigned, defeated. Nothing like the fiery man who had frightened her with his intensity. He was broken, a shadow of the strong man she had known.

Her bleeding heart ached and throbbed in her chest. She could not argue against the wrongs he had done, had witnessed some of them herself. But was she not guilty as well?

I knew what his intentions were and chose to be silent. The truth blazed across her mind. She had deceived the Stewards. Would she let Mason be executed without admitting her own blame?

King Aden raised his hand at one point when the shouts grew loud and raucous. As soon as a hush fell, Seria stepped forward.

"Your Majesty." Her voice cracked, and she cleared her throat while Aden searched the crowd to see who had addressed him. She raised her chin to meet his probing stare. "I'm afraid I must admit my faults concerning Mason Grey."

Mason's head shot up and began to shake. "Seria, nay."

She clasped her hands together and went on, acutely aware of every eye fixed on her. "My name is Seria Gayle, and I admit to fraternizing with this man, knowing he was the enemy."

The king gave her a kind look. "I understand, Miss Gayle, that you took this man in not knowing what he was. There is no fault in that."

She licked her lips and stiffened her spine. Her next words would most likely isolate her from almost everyone in the fort. "I continued to see him after that, knowing full well what he was."

Aden's face grew grave. "Do you realize what you are saying, miss?"

Mason protested again. "Nay, she's not responsible."

Seria sucked in a shaky breath. "I do, Your Majesty." Peace cooled the flames of fear that threatened to consume her. Her admission may change the course of her life, but it was the right thing to do.

The king started to speak when Lena called out. "King Aden, I am responsible for facilitating their association."

Seria gasped and spun to where Lena stood at her side, her head held high. "Lena, nay!"

Lena pursed her lips. "I am no more guiltless in this than you are."

The white-haired king looked angry now. "You admit to doing this of your own free will?"

"I do."

Mason went rigid, prompting his guards to tighten their hold on him. "They've done nothing. It was all on me."

"Silence," Aden demanded, giving a stern look out at the people around them. "Does anyone else wish to confess their ties to the Reader?"

Lena's fingers grabbed her own, and Seria clung to them in despair. What would happen to her friend now?

Aden stood tall and looked down his nose at the two of them. "I suppose, then, that I must give out three verdicts."

"Prince Eric!"

Eric stirred from the monotonous rhythm of hoofbeats. The fort was little more than a mile away, but the nightlong ride had been tiresome, especially after the whirlwind that had happened at Joshun. Braylee and Lionel both rode toward him after conferring with one of their scouts. Both looked grim.

"There's a large army on the other side of the cliffs," Braylee informed, waving westward. "They're sure to see us if we keep going as we are, and we don't have the men to fight them here."

"So, what are you suggesting?"

Braylee looked him straight in the eye. "We make a run for it."

Eric chewed his cheek. "Is there any way to reach Dudley?"

"There's no water around here," Lionel answered.

"We can send an alert through the Beacon," Braylee said. "But that won't tell them what to prepare for."

Seeing no other way, Eric sent the word along his ranks, stressing that once they started running, to keep going and make as much speed as possible. It was their only chance of making it back to the fort in time before being cut off by the Dark Army.

Everyone seemed to hold their breath, waiting for the signal. Eric stood in the stirrups and looked out at the lines, all watching and waiting. The responsibility for their lives weighed heavily on him, and he gripped his Beacon.

"Let us make it," he breathed. "To the very last soul."

He raised his hand, a small red flag held high. With a snap, he lowered it, and the air filled with the sound of thundering hooves. The ground shook as his men took off at top speed. He had to fight his horse to keep it in place.

Braylee was at his side, as always, alert for the first sign of trouble. Neither could see what was happening on the other side, but there were too many of them for their flight to go unnoticed.

"Let's go." Eric took position with Braylee at the flanks. As soon as they passed the protective shield of the bluffs, Eric looked over his shoulder.

There they were. A large mass of darkly-clad soldiers already giving chase. They outnumbered Eric's men three to one at least.

The dust rose thick in the air from the galloping horses, filming Eric's damp face and coating his throat.

Braylee looked over and gave a short nod. Eric checked Oakley's speed and turned slightly in the saddle. With a wave of his hand, he gathered a large cloud of airborne soil, creating a veil between them and the others. Then he sent the cloud back, traveling with the wind and his mental force until it met the other army, mingling with what they had already stirred. It created a thick haze, difficult for anyone to see through.

"Let's go!" He spurred his horse on.

He did not know how long the dust storm would hold them—hopefully long enough for them to pass through the gates. That was all he needed.

The fort was just ahead. His front lines were already passing through Cadence. He slowed enough to ensure his men all made it before him and looked back; the dust was not as dense as before, allowing their pursuers to pick up speed.

Then a black cloud formed over the heads of the approaching army, roiling and swarming. Eric stared into it until he could make out shapes. Monstrous bodies. Claws and fangs. Wicked-looking horns and cold, black eyes.

Mercies. Jader's shadow creatures.

Eric reined Oakley around, searching through the dust and smoke for a sign of the emperor.

There. Standing on a tall precipice out of reach of arrow or Beacon. Graulik Jader stood there, watching him. Even from there, Eric could feel his cold stare boring into him. He reached for Lavrynth.

An arrow whizzed by, finding its mark high on the shoulder of a Steward passing by. The man cried out and lost his reins. Braylee immediately spurred his horse to his side.

"Hang on!" He grabbed the flapping reins. "We're almost there!"

Eric gritted his teeth, the wind stinging his face. He could hear the Darkmen getting closer, could feel the ground vibrate with their approach, could see that cloud growing. Labyrinth's hilt warmed in his hand.

A cheer rose from the front of his company, and relief flooded his senses.

Captain Dudley led a charge through Cadence, straight for the Dark Army. Most of the men with Eric turned their mounts around to join them.

But it was unnecessary. The black cloud dissipated, and the Dark Army pulled back at the sight of the charge and retreated. Once again, a cloud of dust rose until it covered their departure.

The men let out a thunderous yell, raising their fists in their triumph.

Eric looked up at the precipice. Jader was gone.

Braylee turned the wounded soldier's horse over to someone else and waited with Eric for Dudley to join them.

"I am thoroughly glad to see you," Eric said with a smile, his insides still quaking at what he had witnessed.

Dudley squinted at Eric. "How did things fare with you?"

"The children are safe and on their way back to their homes."

"Wonderful." Dudley beamed. "And I have more good news. The Reader's been caught."

His heart skipped a beat. "What? When?"

"He was found prowling not far from here early this morning. Fortunately, your father is also here, so we were able to gather what information we needed for a speedy trial."

"When?" His voice came out sharper than he intended, causing Dudley's brows to go up. "When was the trial?"

"It's in progress now. Last I heard, the verdict was about to be given."

Which meant Eric did not have much time. His breath quickened as he tapped Oakley's sides with his heels, spurring him into a gallop. His horse thundered through the gates, and he prayed he was not too late.

63

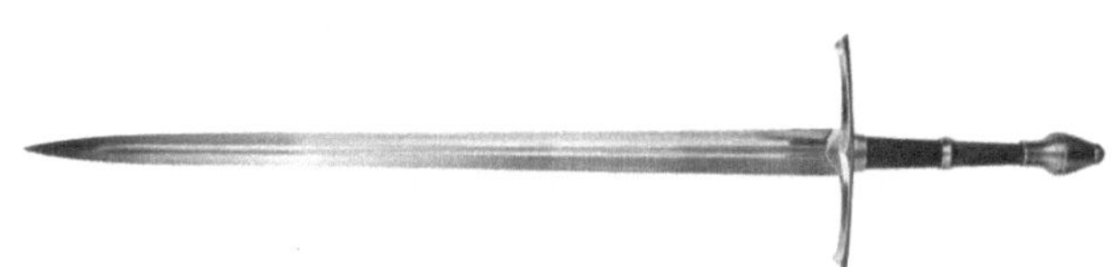

There is nothing more pure or true than the Lambient. His judgment is right, His power lasting.
-The Sacred Code

Mason stood stiffly, the soft dirt mashing beneath his boots. He could sense the cold stares, hear the whispers. He had no idea how many people were in the courtyard. His Steward escorts stood nearby, ready to act should he try anything.

He was too tired of fighting for himself. Tired of being controlled by his anger and running from the past. He was ready for it all to end, even if it meant execution. What was there left for him? Seria would never look at him the same, not after everything he had put her through. Shon was gone. He had lost Liam so many years ago. He had even let Crue go. There was no one.

But the possibility of Seria being punished for his wrongdoings sent nausea rolling around in his stomach. Why on earth had she openly admitted to seeing him? Did she not realize what that would do to the life she had built for herself? Her dream of being a healer would be ended.

And if that wasn't bad enough, Lena had also claimed her guilt. While Seria's attempt to defend him did not surprise him, Lena's admission did. Why would she do such a thing?

Someone cleared his throat in front of him. Silence fell as the king spoke, his voice gravelly with age and tinged with steel.

"Regardless of what these young ladies acknowledge about their roles, your list of crimes against the Gateway is quite extensive. Not to mention the attempt on the prince's life. My son." His tone hardened.

A quick flame of anger stirred within him. He would've never had a reason to go after Eric had it not been for the Handan massacre. But just as quickly, his anger drained from him. He could not blame Eric for Handan anymore, nor could he blame the king for his animosity.

"You have the floor, young man," Aden said. "This is your one chance to have your say, to offer a defense."

"I have none to give for myself." His words came out strained and scratchy. "But these women do not deserve punishment for my actions. I am solely responsible for everything they committed against you."

There was a brief silence, and then Aden cleared his throat again. "I have no desire to become a tyrant." He seemed to change the subject. "I would never assert my authority anywhere that was not mine to give. I respect that the New Realm is Jader's jurisdiction, and had he been content to live there and allow us to live in peace, I would have left it at that."

Mason tried to swallow. For so long, he had assumed the Passions wanted nothing but more power for themselves. But all along, Jader was the one seeking supremacy. And revenge against the Passions.

Just like me.

"However," Aden continued. "That was not to be. Through the acts of his Dark Army, Jader is threatening the people of my kingdom and the innocent civilians of the Gateway. You, in particular, have managed to get into the Steward stronghold, where you allowed Shadowmen into the Old Realm and very nearly killed the future ruler of Paladin."

Mason squeezed his eyes shut, though the blindfold already shielded him from being able to see anything.

"You've endangered the lives of every man, woman, and child in the fort, as well as Paladin, now that the Shadowmen are spreading Jader's brand of justice. People have died at your hands, as well as due to the indirect acts you've committed."

Breathing became difficult, and his head throbbed with the familiar jolts of pain. His chest tightened as voices started to rise in his mind again. *Please, leave Seria and Lena out of it and get it done!* Anything to end this turmoil.

"Therefore, you are to be sentenced to death."

A few cheers resounded, but Mason did not care about himself. What about the girls?

The sound of hoofbeats overrode the chatter, echoing through his head, and a familiar voice cut through the air.

"Father! I must ask you to stay your sentence."

There was an instant rumble as everyone began murmuring. Shock rolled over Mason.

"Eric, what is the meaning of this?" Aden asked.

Footsteps approached and stopped beside Mason. "This man is guilty of the crimes you sentence him for," Eric said, his voice breathless. "Justice must be meted out, but I also believe there is a place for mercy."

"To one who would see us and all we stand for destroyed?" Aden questioned.

"Nay," Eric said. "To one who has been deceived."

"Eric," the king said, a warning in his voice. "I would advise you to think about what you are doing."

"I have." The swish of cloth met Mason's ear before Eric spoke to the crowd around them. "I do not make excuses for this man's actions, but I must also confess my own."

Mason's chest caved in. First, Seria and Lena, now the prince was stepping in for him?

"I've hidden the truth too long, but it must be known before this man's sentence is carried out." Eric paused, as if gathering himself. "Years ago, a group of teenage orphans were killed by my foolish, blind order. It was not intentional, but that did not erase the outcome of the Handan Massacre. This man was the only survivor."

Eric moved away, closer to the balcony where the king stood. "My actions created a ripple effect that caused more harm to my kingdom and the Gateway. I gave up the leadership of the Stewards, which was taken up again by Grand Marshal Uralis Faunt. I quit searching for the Shadowpit, which only allowed Jader's power to grow and spread. The marshal was killed because I hid myself for years. Noble Stewards were shamed and forced into a life of secrecy and are now being hunted and slain by Jader. And Jader tightened his hold on the people of the Gateway, even taking their children as payment."

The silence cut through the air, sharp as a knife. Mason's mouth went dry at Eric's list of confessions, his willingness to lay his faults out for everyone to see.

Eric continued, his voice thick. "Furthermore, I made things worse by hiding behind the secret of my mistake, cutting myself off from my Stewards and creating division and distrust. You and the Steward Army were willing to give me a second chance. I believe we should offer the same to Mason."

"Eric, this man tried to kill you. He despises everything about the Stewardship and the Lambient!" His tone sharpened. "He's a Shadowman!"

"He did try to kill me, but he also saved my life against his own commander." He paused as the crowd murmured again. "And he's the one who freed the children from Jader's hold. Today, I am a witness that even a Shadowman can change. That he stands before you so humbly is a testimony to that. Because the fact is, the cloth covering his eyes cannot stop him from controlling anyone who does not carry a Beacon."

The blindfold loosened and slipped over Mason's head, and he met Eric's intense gaze. Over the prince's shoulder, he caught the apprehensive looks of the Steward captains. Beyond that, Seria's wide, tearful eyes snagged him.

"Isn't that right?"

Eric's quiet question pulled him back to the moment. A myriad of emotions settled into his bones, making him heavy. Wariness. Surprise. Pain. Shame. He inhaled deeply and gave a short nod.

Eric turned back to his father. "I believe there's something else that needs to be brought out, Father." He reached down and took his light rod, which responded by glowing softly. "The Sacred Code tells us there's nothing more pure or true than the Lambient. His judgment is right, His power lasting. I think we can all agree on that, aye?"

"Of course." The king looked as if he was growing impatient.

"I have put my faith in the Lambient since I was a boy," Eric continued. "As I know you have. I still choose to believe that He will never lead me astray. Can you say the same for yourself?"

Aden frowned. "You know I do, Eric. Where are you going with this?"

Eric looked back at Mason, his gaze telling him to trust him. Mason's heart jumped as Eric slowly stretched his hand out, offering the rod to him. Sudden fear gripped him at what Eric attempted to do. What if it didn't work for him again?

But Eric's stare was steady and patient, as if aware of the struggle going on within him. He dipped his chin.

Mason let out a long breath, his attention riveted on the Beacon before him. Feeling like he was in a dream, he reached out, hands still bound, and took it. The light dimmed for what felt like an eternity as it passed from hand to hand. Then it began to glow, growing brighter with every second.

The reaction from the people was instant. Aden's posture straightened. Seria gasped, and Captain Dudley let out a low, "Skies above."

Mason stood stock-still, staring straight into the light, still amazed at the feelings it gave him. Warmth. Peace. Forgiveness.

"The Lambient does not lie. So, if you don't go by my word alone or by the merit of this man," Eric pointed to the Beacon, "then go by the virtue of the Lambient."

But Mason still grappled to believe what he held before him, afraid the moment would pass. The rod's heat radiated through his skin, and he shoved it back to Eric, lest it stop glowing. But even as the warmth passed from his hand into Eric's, the reassuring sensations lingered.

And his headache was gone.

Eric spoke again. "Mason Grey has left the ways of the dark and turned to the light."

Seria stared at Mason, her heart a wild thing flapping around behind her ribs. She could hardly believe what she had seen, but the truth of it landed in her awareness with the boom of a cannon blast.

Mason had not used his Gift on her for his own purpose. Mason had rescued the kids from Jader. Mason had *saved* Eric's life. There were so many questions, but the Beacon shattered any doubt that had lingered.

Lambient be praised!

Eric stood beside him, his countenance firm with resolve. Mason, looking rather haggard, fisted his bound hands and made eye contact with her, his stricken expression begging her to understand. Her body leaned forward, as if to run to him, but the Stewards who had taken position on either side of her and Lena barred her way. All she could offer him was what she hoped was an encouraging smile, though her mouth trembled.

The king leaned heavily against the railing, looking stunned. He gave a small frown and turned to confer again with the Councilmen and his captain.

Fear chased resignation around in her chest until she couldn't breathe. What would happen to Mason now? The Beacon would not erase his past. Would it save his life?

She had no regrets in admitting her part. It was the right thing to do, though the unknown made her almost sick. Overshadowing her fear, however, was wild, unbelieving joy. Mason had changed.

Beside her, Lena was composed as usual, but her face shone white. Her mother stood behind her, her hands clasped under her chin. Seria hated the turmoil she had brought her dear friends.

A hush fell as the king turned back out onto the balcony. He looked out at the people, his face unreadable. Seria's breath lodged in her windpipe in a painful knot. She reached for Lena's hand again.

King Aden took a deep breath before he spoke, his shoulders bowed with the weight of his responsibility. "My son is a brave, honest man. Maybe braver than I have been. He is right in exposing the secrets that bound him for so many years. I see now how wrong it was to hide the mistakes of the past. The truth is, my son is not the only one who has hidden from the upheaval Graulik Jader brought within our midst."

Seria glanced at Eric, who stared up as his father straightened his shoulders, bracing himself to keep going.

"Jader's pursuit of darkness began when he was a young reservist in my militia army in Paladin."

A collective gasp sounded. Seria exchanged looks with Lena, seeing the same surprise that rocked her.

"He gathered his own army of followers, all under my nose, and started a civil war. One in which Stewards were deceived and misled into fighting one another." Aden sighed. "Eventually, it came to a head in Paladin, and he was expelled into the New Realm. I spent the next few years covering the truth of what had happened and allowed the mortified Stewards involved to leave the Old Realm in other pursuits. And so, here we are today."

Seria squeezed her eyes shut at the truth that had sent her father to live in the New Realm for so long. Jader's love for darkness was further reaching than she had ever realized.

"I tell you that story to acknowledge that, aye, hiding those past mistakes was wrong. And to declare here and now that it will not happen again. Darkness thrives in lies and secrets. Truth brings the light." Aden raised his head. "But that truth also means accepting responsibility for one's wrongs."

Seria's breathing failed her as the king seemed to grow in stature, his face resolute. A sinking feeling chained her spirits down.

Aden peered down at Mason, who seemed to have lost all his fight. "While I acknowledge your change of heart and loyalty, it does not take away the harm you have brought—all with a full comprehension of what you were doing. Therefore, you must face the consequences."

Her heart broke at the resignation on Mason's guarded face, but he only nodded.

"But."

What little fragments of hope remained grabbed hold of the single word.

"I will rescind my sentence of execution."

64

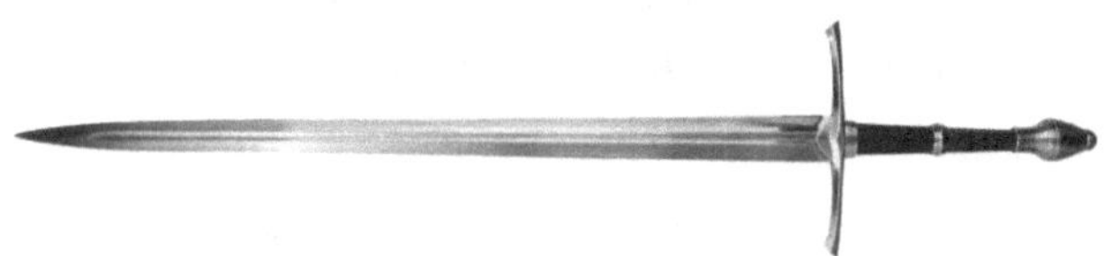

"We will hide in the shadows no longer."
-Pre-battle speech by Graulik Jader during Calla's War

After determining for years that he would never see the inside of a Steward prison, Mason sat on a narrow cot and stared at the cell walls around him, numb to anything but the shock chilling him to his bones.

Aden's words drifted in and out of his subconscious. A fortnight of imprisonment, while divulging his full insight on Jader and his Dark Army. Then service to the fort and its citizens under constant supervision. Placement in the lowest rung of the Steward army. And absolute submission to his superiors. Failure to do so would result in lifelong imprisonment.

But not death. And deep below the layers of humiliation, he was relieved. He wanted to live—*needed* to undo all the wrongs he had done. Hoped to honor the memory of his brother who had wished to become a Steward himself.

A Steward. Mason huffed a little at the thought. He still did not see himself as a Steward, and wondered if he ever would, but the irony was not lost on him. He was now an accomplice of the Stewards. And that also made him a target of every man in the Dark Army, especially Bruin Pralus.

Mason straightened his aching back, thankful his headache had rescinded for the time being, and looked around at his new living quarters. Stone walls surrounded him on three sides and a torch outside the barred door lit the space within. It was small and held nothing but a cot in one corner and a wooden pail in the other. But it was leagues better than the cells the children at Stonehard had been forced to dwell in.

He had no call to be upset at anyone but himself for the position he was in. And unlike the other Shadowmen imprisoned down the hall, Mason had a chance of getting out. A second chance for a new life.

In truth, none of his stipulations bothered him for himself. Though he did not look forward to living in a fort surrounded by people who despised him, he had survived worse. But it was Seria's sentence that upset him the most. She was being sent to the Old Realm, away from the fort, forbidden to associate with him.

He sank back against the wall beside his cot. All the time he was in the Gateway, it was with the hope that he would finish his job and be free to return to the girl who lit his heart brighter than any flame. And now he was here, and she was leaving, with no guarantee when he'd see her again. Or even if.

He kept waiting for the rage to overcome him, the habitual hatred and desire for blood to override what little good sense he had left. But he was tired of those negative feelings chaining him down. Instead, a sharp hunger twisted his stomach. Hunger to see things set aright. To see Jader's lies turn inside out and for truth to prevail. Hunger to wash the land from Jader's darkness and destroy the hold he had on the people.

And a desire to do the right thing for once. Even if it meant losing Seria.

It was different from the vengeance that had fueled him for so many years. This felt right. Pure. Maybe it was the Lambient's touch. He didn't know, and he didn't care.

It was strange, really. The girl he loved more than anything had not been enough to heal him. It was not until he had given up the Shadow-stone and that Beacon flushed out the remnants of shadows clinging to him that he experienced real peace. The kind of peace that filled him.

Braylee could not hold back his frown as he walked alongside Eric, taking the street in long strides, his mind still churning as it had since he had ridden at top speed back into the fort behind the prince.

"Talk to me, Braylee."

He pursed his lips as he reflected on the trial. He had seen the Beacon light up for Mason with his own eyes, but it still left him unsettled. It was not that he doubted the Lambient's authority, but it was all too much to take. How could Mason suddenly switch sides? How could he transfer his loyalties that quickly?

"I can't deny I have my concerns," he finally said, masking his deeper feelings. "I saw him attack you at Joshun."

"I do not blame you for reacting as you did, but it was not what it seemed."

"I worry this is going to affect the unity of the Stewards."

"They saw the same thing I did."

"Aye. But that's oversimplifying it."

Eric frowned. "How so?"

"Because this is going to shake the faith of many of them." Braylee stopped to face the prince. "They may question how Lambient could accept a Shadowman who same as sold his soul to Shreil to destroy the light of the Beacon. A mere few days ago, that Shadowman was fire-bent on killing every Steward here and anyone else who got in his way. You can't expect them to welcome him with open arms."

Sobering, Eric sighed. "Do you think he even has a chance here?"

Braylee put his hands on his hips, studying the ground in front of his feet. "Your father knows that everyone is going to need time to accept this, including Mason. The layers of the sentencing will help, give everyone a chance to get used to the idea of him being around and for him to gain their trust. But even so, it may be that some never accept him."

"Like Lionel?"

Braylee nodded, picturing the stone-cold face Lionel presented at the end of the trial. He wasn't sure of the king's decision to put Mason under his direct charge, but trusted Aden's wisdom. "And he won't be alone."

They resumed their walk. Eric looked preoccupied, and Braylee let him keep his silence, trying to process through his own feelings.

In all his years as a Steward, Braylee had never struggled with laying aside his own feelings and ambitions for the sake of the Beacon. He had been asked to leave his family for months at a time, to spend grueling hours on the field, to fight with his very last breath in battle. But this? How was he to accept this? This was the man who had tried to kill his prince, and would have, had Ollen not intervened.

The clench of pain at the reminder of Ollen's death did not help. They had become more than captain and subordinate, but friends. Braylee had watched him grow as a Steward, had looked forward to seeing what the future held for him.

And now he was gone, while Mason was alive and well. A very poor exchange, in Braylee's opinion, and he found it all very difficult to swallow.

It was an uncomfortable feeling, being at odds with the very Source he promised to serve. The Lambient had only ever been a spring of purity, goodness, and peace. Mason had served the exact opposite. How could He redeem such a man?

But the Lambient extended His hand of grace and mercy whenever He could. And He would look for Braylee to do the same.

Jader stood on a balcony overlooking Ignadon when Bruin arrived. He did not move, but stared out at the brightening sky, fixated on a spot in the horizon. He refused to speak, even when his commander stepped to his side.

Finally, Bruin let out a sigh, disturbing the silence. "Mason has joined with the Stewards, my lord." Bitter rage lanced every word.

Jader did not respond, only lifted his head slightly. Bruin took that as an invitation to continue.

"He cleared every cell in Stonehard."

Jader's eyes narrowed. "Seems he accomplished quite a lot for one man," he said cooly.

"I assure you, Lord Jader," Bruin growled. "The first chance I get, I will kill Mason Grey. I promise you that."

"I do not want him dead, Bruin. Surely you have not forgotten my plans for him."

"After this? You mean to overlook all he's done?"

Jader huffed as he moved away from the balcony. "Honestly, Bruin, sometimes I wonder how you can still be so clueless."

Bruin schooled his features, but not before Jader could see the flash of indignation. It amused him. Let Bruin stew for a while. It would keep him sharp and focused. "His true power is only beginning to develop. I am not about to let him go now."

"I'm afraid I don't understand, Master," Bruin said bluntly. "He's a defector."

Jader shrugged nonchalantly as he moved to his throne. "He is playing pretend."

"But it's not an act," Bruin insisted. "I saw the Beacon in his hand."

"That means nothing."

"It means his loyalties have ch—"

Jader spun around, his robe billowing out around him, and snapped, "Darkness begets submission."

Bruin's face blanched, and he took a step back, his gaze going distant.

"Submission begets power," Jader continued, approaching the motionless man. When Bruin dipped his head, his expression acquiescent, Jader stepped to his side, murmuring in Bruin's ear. "Have you so easily forgotten the power of our Shreil, Bruin? The moment Mason took on the Shadowstone, he was infused with the same darkness that powers each one of us. You know as well as I do, once that happens, it cannot be shaken. It matters not how many light rods he can get to glow. The Shreil does not release his subjects." His voice grew whisper soft in his fervor. "Mason may be having an emotional experience, but I assure you, Bruin, the darkness is there to stay."

Bruin blinked and nodded. "Aye, Master."

"Good." Bruin's resentment for Mason ran deep, but Jader cared little for Bruin's feelings. His thirst for power was still unsatisfied. He would stop at nothing to get what he wanted. And he was not about to let one setback sway him now. At least not for long.

"Let him play now, Bruin," Jader said, settling on his throne. "In due time, we will have him again. He is what he is. A Shadowman. And in the end, he can do nothing to change that."

65

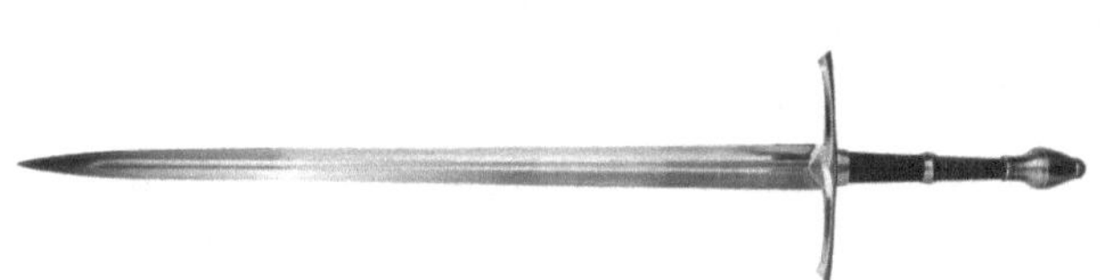

"We'll leave at first light tomorrow. That will give the ladies a day to rest before they move on to their new respective destinations."

Eric acknowledged his father's decision with a nod, trying to ignore the little ache that flared. He had laid no claims to Lena's heart, had not even spent more than a few minutes at a time with her. But always at the back of his mind, he had hoped to return from the Gateway and get to know her better. That would be hard to do if she was sent to a distant city to serve in some unknown fashion.

Aden fell silent, his look pensive. "You look tired, son."

Eric forced a smile. "It's been a busy day. The drain that comes after an adrenaline rush is very real."

"You should rest tonight," Aden directed. "You and I both know that the days are only going to get harder."

The truth was a heavy rock settling down in his gut. Jader would not take the loss of his Reader passively. Nor would he accept the defeat at Stonehard. There would be a price to pay.

After bidding his father good night, Eric paused in the narrow hall outside the door to rub his eyes. The last few weeks were catching up to him. His mind, body, and spirit were exhausted, drained and twisted like a wet cloth through the wringer. He was still reeling from the recent turn of events, still bracing himself for the turmoil to come.

Instead of taking his father's advice, he went to the small room down the hall where Seria had been taken. A single guard stood outside her door, an unnecessary precaution—one that Eric suspected even his father was aware of. But protocol required it. A second guard stood in front of another door, but Eric could not bring himself to look in on Lena. He had spoken to her after the trial, but it was brief and awkward.

Nodding to the guard, Eric gave a short knock, confident Seria was still awake. His heart ached for the girl on the other side of the door whose world was about to be uprooted again.

Seria rose from her seat on the bed and cleared her throat. "Prince Eric." Her trunk sat by the door, ready for the journey to the Old Realm the next morning.

He smiled in an attempt to ease the strain on her face. "How are you holding up?"

"I haven't been honest with you."

"So I've heard."

Her lips trembled, and she curled her fingers into her palms. "I am truly sorry for that, Prince Eric. I was wrong to deceive you and maintain ties with the enemy of the Stewards, especially one who had vowed to kill you."

Her words flew almost too fast for him to understand, but he let her talk, sensing she needed to get it all said before she left.

"It was also wrong to go against the Lambient and try to do things my way. I fully admit my faults and accept the consequences of my actions." She raised her chin. "I will serve in whatever capacity King Aden asks of me and try to make up for causing you nothing but trouble since the day I found Mason in the woods."

"Do you regret that you saved his life?"

She blinked at the question. "Nay, not at all," she said. "I would do it again. For anyone."

"I believe you. You stepping in to care for an injured man was not wrong."

"But I was convinced I had to be the one to change him, that he would not get the truth any other way. But in reality, it was when I got out of the way that it became clear to him." She lifted her gaze to the ceiling. "I was so foolish."

"But not beyond Lambient's forgiveness. He can take our feeble attempts and still work His will."

Seria sniffed and nodded. "I sure hope so." Her spine was ramrod straight, her shoulders set, as if determined to face whatever fate befell her without complaint. Eric admired her courage.

Uncertainty traced her brow as she studied him, and he stepped forward to take her fisted hands in his own. "I forgive you, Seria."

Her chin quivered, and she clung to him with cold fingers. "Thank you, Eric. For the grace you've shown me so many times. And for doing the same for Mason." Her voice caught. "I will forever be grateful."

He pulled her in for an affectionate hug. "I will miss the spark you bring to this place, Seria. But I believe you're going to be fine." He stepped back and smiled down at her. "Try to get some sleep. I'll see you in the morning."

Too keyed up to sleep, Eric took to the outdoors for a walk to clear his head. Despite the sorrow of those who had gotten tangled up in their mistakes, wonder filled him. The Reader who had served Jader now stood with the Stewards. Eric had no fantasies that the transition would be smooth. He already dreaded the clash of personalities, and resentment was sure to flare. His leadership may take another beating over the fact that he chose to intercede. It wasn't the first time he had done so, and most likely it would not be the last.

The sky was just beginning to darken, the day having passed in a current so swift it took his breath away. Night would soon fall. But it would not endure. There was always a dawn.

And he chose to believe it would be the case now. With Seria and Lena's departure. With Mason's conversion. Things would be rough for the moment. His Stewards may challenge his authority. There may be division in his ranks. And on top of all that, Jader's Dark Army was still out there.

But Eric's faith in the Lambient was strong. He had no doubt it would bring the truth to light. The Stewards would emerge stronger.

The morning would come.

Seria followed Eric through the dirt streets of the stronghold in the stillness of the early morning hours. Her trunk had already been taken from her room and loaded into the caravan. She wore the sword Mason had given her on her side. Unable to leave her father's old sword behind, it was tucked safely in her trunk along with her few clothes and camouflage cloak.

Numbness had settled into her spirit as she took one final look at the fort that had become so familiar to her. She was unsure she would ever see it again, and she faced moving from this home and all the friends she had made here to start all over. Again.

She had no one to blame but herself. She was the one who had put aside her sense of right and wrong to be with someone she knew was an enemy. Lambient was merciful to forgive, but that did not mean there would never be consequences.

For one brief, surreal moment, while Mason held the Beacon, a faint dream had been rekindled. But as soon as that fragile spark ignited, she dashed it away. It was selfish to think of herself at a time like this. There was so much more at stake here than her own happiness.

If only she had not dragged Lena into this mess. There was no guarantee they would serve in the same location, so she could not even comfort herself with that possibility. And Lena's plans for her bakery would once again be delayed—if they ever came to pass.

Her mind was in such a quandary that it took her a moment to realize Eric did not lead her to the gates where the caravan waited to leave. Instead, he headed for a small room at one end of the Steward quarters. Two guards stood outside the door.

"Where are we going?" she asked when her curiosity became too much.

Eric paused and looked over his shoulder before he gave a short knock, then stepped aside so she could enter.

Seria managed one step before her heart stuttered, then raced within her.

Inside the room, Mason shot to his feet, knocking his stool over. "Seria."

"I can only give you a moment," Eric said. Then he left, closing the door behind him.

Now that she stood before Mason, Seria wasn't sure what to say. He seemed to be at a loss as well and avoided her gaze. Her heart bled at the state he was in. His clothes were torn and a few cuts and bruises lined his face. What had he endured to get to the place he was at now?

"Are you all right?" she asked.

He nodded and adjusted one of his bracers. "I'm fine."

A strained silence fell, one that made Seria's throat tight.

But then he sighed and looked at her. "I'm sorry."

In those two words, Seria knew what he could not say. There was a lot of meaning hidden behind the simple statement, so many weeks' worth of regrets.

"What happened?" she asked.

"I was wrong. About everything." A line creased his brow. "There were too many signs that pointed to the truth, though I was so stubborn about it for too long. Once it became clear, I didn't want to subject myself to Jader's lies or his mad thirst for power. Not anymore."

Looking into his face, Seria was amazed at the difference. Questions still shadowed his eyes, but there was a hint of peace that rested on his countenance. "You're the one who drew that map to Joshun, aren't you?" She swallowed the tears in the back of her throat. "And you made sure Ollen got back."

His face twisted, and he gave a short nod.

"I'm proud of you."

"Nay." He shook his head, the lines deepening on his brow. "I've done too much to be proud of."

"I'm not proud of what you used to be," she said. "But you're different now. A new man."

The words seemed to agitate him more than comfort him. "I never expected..." He motioned in the air.

"The Beacon?"

His hand fell at his side. "I still don't get it. I'm not a good man."

Seria gave him a shaky smile. "The Lambient believes you can be."

"But do you?" He gave her a desperate look.

"I always did."

He pressed his lips together for a moment. "And do you think someday you'll be able to forgive me?"

A painful vice squeezed her chest at the longing in his voice. "Of course, Mason. How could I not when the Lambient forgave us both?"

He let out a breath, his eyes moist. After a moment, he rubbed his hands together and nodded. "I, um." He cleared his throat. "I know I have a lot to answer for, and I certainly didn't expect a second chance. Not here."

Seria detected his uncertainty, despite the way he tried to hide it. It broke her heart. He would be surrounded by soldiers he had hated only a few days ago. And they would be hard-pressed to accept him as one of their own, despite the Beacon.

"But it won't matter to me what anyone else in this fort thinks of me, Seria, as long as I know you don't hate me."

"Oh, Mason." Her voice broke. "I could never hate you."

In three steps, Mason reached her, pulling her to him and burying his face in her hair. "I'm not sure I can do this, Seria," he whispered. "Not without you."

His vulnerability broke her, and she held him tight. "You already did it without me."

He tried to shake his head, but she pushed him away to catch his face between her hands, willing her tears back. She needed to be strong for him.

"You can. Lambient believes in you, or He would never have let that Beacon shine. Eric believes it, too."

His Adam's apple bobbed, and his fingers pressed into her back. "But what if I can't?"

"It doesn't matter. You made the decision to surrender, and Lambient responded. You don't have to be strong enough, Mason. You just have to let Him be strong for you."

He released her with a sigh. "I'm sorry you're leaving."

Seria drew in a ragged breath. "It seems we're always saying goodbye. And I'm usually the one walking away."

His face hardened. "You had every reason to walk away from me. Do not take the blame for any of this."

"We both know it was wrong to keep a relationship and deceive those we claimed to serve loyally. In that, I am at fault as much as you."

Mason frowned and opened his mouth, but she cut him off. "Don't argue with me. It doesn't do any good."

A weak chuckle escaped him, the sound of it disintegrating a bit of the gray cloud over her head. But it could not sponge away the knowledge that things had changed between them. She missed their closeness before, but it was for the better. Mason had a new purpose, and she would not stand in the way of it.

"King Aden is right to send me away." She crossed her arms in front of her. "You need to start a new life here, helping the Stewards. And I think it would be better for all involved if I am not a part of it."

Again, he looked as if he wanted to argue, but resignation drew his head down into a single nod.

Eric would return any minute, so Seria gathered what was left of her control. "I need you to do something for me," she said.

"Anything."

She swallowed, her chest tightening. "Sanjo is too old to make the trip with me."

"I'll take care of him, Seria. I promise."

His gentle assurance broke the dam, and the tears came in a torrent as she wept for all she was leaving behind. He wrapped his arms around her, and she leaned on him one last time. An occasional tremor passed over his form as he stroked her hair and let her cry.

But even through the tears, a confidence that this was right flowed through her. This was what she needed. What Mason needed. Even if it broke her heart to leave. The Lambient would see them through whatever the future held.

The door opened again, and Eric's soft voice filled the small space. "It's time."

Mason's arms flinched, but she straightened and looked up at him. "Goodbye, Mason. May the light of the Lambient guide your way." She kissed his cheek and made herself turn away and follow Eric from the room.

66

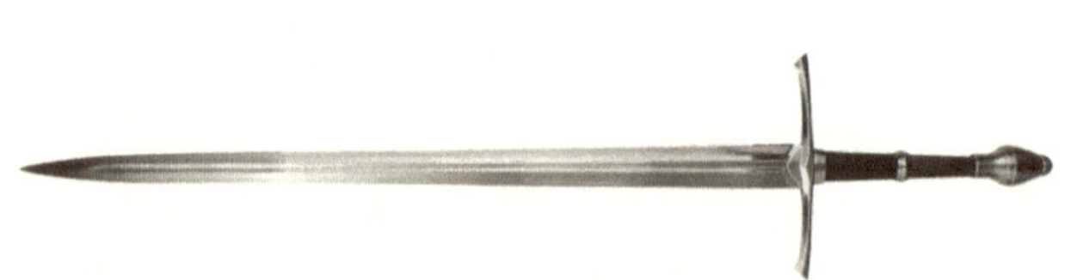

The Lambient makes straight and true the path that was broken.
-The Sacred Code

Mason stood at the top of the back wall facing the Old Realm. To his surprise—and the guards' disapproval—Eric had put off his return to the cell so he could see off the caravan of horses, particularly the carriage at the end that picked its way through the rough path. Leaving the Gateway. Leaving him.

This is for the best. The words pulsed within him, but with every step of the horses, his heart cracked a little more. He wasn't good enough for her. Not after everything he had done. She deserved someone who could freely love her without dragging chains of guilt and shame behind him. Someone like Ollen.

A blonde head turned to look back at him, her arm in the air. He lifted his hand high so she could see the rag he waved. He braced himself against the stone wall, his spine ramrod straight, afraid to bend lest he break under the weight.

The caravan drifted around a hill and was gone. The impact of her departure sank in, making the days ahead more bleak than ever. He could face Bruin and Jader's wrath. He would tolerate the Stewards who despised his presence. But the idea of Seria being gone from his life filled him with despair.

Eric spoke behind him. "Mason."

Gritting his teeth, he turned to face the prince, expecting to be led straightaway to his cell.

But Eric did not motion for the guards. His regard was steady, piercing through the wall Mason held up between them. "That Beacon lit up in your hands because you made a commitment to the Lambient. Did you mean it?"

The question burned through the ever-present anger that struggled to release itself, but the answer rose above the flames. "I did."

"Then I need you to hear this." Eric's gaze sharpened. "I have repented to you, and I have defended you. What happens from this point on is up to you."

"I can't be a Steward." The admission slipped out before he could stop it.

"With Lambient's help, you can."

Mason turned away to look out at the distant hills of Paladin. The assurance was nice and all, but how deep did it run true? Especially when the only light he had ever known had left him?

Eric stepped beside him and rested his elbows on the wall. "Seria brought a light into your life, but that Beacon did not glow for her. That came from the light of the Lambient dwelling in you."

Rubbing the back of his neck, Mason exhaled and bowed his head. *Please, help me.* The prayer formed almost without thought, but as it ascended from his fractured spirit, it left a scent of assurance that he would not be forgotten.

Silence reigned for several moments before Eric sighed. "There's something else you need to know about Jader."

Mason brought his head up. "What's that?"

Eric straightened and looked Mason straight in the eye. "I believe he was behind the Handan massacre."

Something clenched inside him. "What do you mean?"

"In looking back, there were too many coincidences, though it took me a while to see them." He shook his head, his face grim. "Someone knew exactly where those boys would be. They knew where we were and made sure we got the report. And the rainfall was so thick, the Stewards could not see clearly who they were attacking until it was too late."

Everything clicked into place. The unusual storm clouds the day of the attack, undoubtedly provided by Bruin; the way Jader's men showed up so soon after it was all over; even Jader's strange comments through the years, keeping Mason's attention diverted from the truth.

"All this time," Mason murmured. "All the years I spent with him, and the whole time he knew... I feel like such a fool."

"Jader's the king of manipulation and deceit, Mason," Eric reminded. "By using the Stewards in such a brutal act of violence, he was able to keep us out of the Gateway."

Mason's blood chilled, and he gripped the stone wall. "He was after me. My Gift."

Eric nodded once. "I suspected as much when I learned the Reader was a survivor."

The same old rage that had fueled Mason for so long swept over him, dimming his vision. A twinge of pain formed in his temples, and he curled his hands into fists. For a moment, he wanted to lose himself in his anger again, to turn it all on Jader, the one who had been the cause of his grief all along.

"Hate will destroy you, no matter who it's intended for."

For a brief moment, Mason wondered if Eric could read his mind. But he was right. Vengeance was not the answer. Mason knew that now, though the lesson had been long and painful.

"Are you all right?" Eric asked.

"Not sure at the moment." Not ready to divulge his feelings, he deflected the question and waved a hand at the empty path. "But thanks for letting me see her." He had needed the chance to resolve where their relationship had left off before he could move forward into this unexpected new life.

"You're welcome."

The moment struck him as surreal. He was standing shoulder to shoulder with the prince of Paladin, whom he had opposed and despised for most of his life. Now they stood on the same side against the man who had been a mentor for so many years.

"I, um." Pride reared his head, but he had already been too humbled to ignore what needed to be said. He cleared his throat and forced himself to go on. "I want you to know that... I'm sorry. For everything." There was so much more he should have said, but the words locked up inside him.

Eric gave him a long look. "I forgive you, Mason." He crossed his arms and tapped the wall with the toe of his boot. "I've cleared the years of guilt from my conscience. Now you have the chance to clear yours."

"I'm not sure how to do that."

"Start by learning to trust in Him." Eric smiled. "You've spent the past twelve years realizing Jader's plan for you. Now it's time to learn the Lambient's."

For the first time, a seed of hope sprouted. He took a deep breath and let it out, releasing the toxic hatred that threatened to stain him again. This battle was the Lambient's. And Mason would do what he could to serve.

The next few weeks would not be easy, but he relived in his mind the pureness of the light of the Beacon those brief moments he held it. The way it cleansed and filled him. The grace extended to him. And Mason knew he would never turn away from it.

The prince's voice sounded again, fervent and confident. "You do not face this new future as one who has no hope. You're a child of the Lambient now. You are a Steward."

AUTHOR'S NOTE

Dear Reader,

It's a bit surreal for me to think that I made it to the end of another book. And that you, my reader, finished reading it. In many ways, Lightshed was more challenging to bring to print than Shadowcast was. I had written an early draft years ago, but since Shadowcast went through so many changes over the years, of course, things had to be adjusted in Lightshed as well. And I found the *rewriting* stage to be just as daunting as writing the first draft.

But I am thankful for what I learned and how I grew through the making of this book. Writing a book is very much like a journey, and God was right beside me through every step and every page. And now it's complete and in readers' hands.

Even with all the struggle in the writing process, in some ways, I've been more excited about releasing this book in the series than the first book. I really love this powerful story and the way my characters grew. I hope it speaks to you and encourages you to grow and learn, just as they did. Just as I did in the writing of it.

If you enjoyed this book, or its predecessor, Shadowcast, please consider leaving a review!

God bless you, friend!

Until we meet between the pages again,
Crystal D. Grant

ACKNOWLEDGEMENTS

Helen Keller once said, "Alone we can do so little; together we can do so much." And it's so true. The making of a book does not happen through the author's work alone but through a team of people. And I am so thankful for my team.

Mom and Dad: thank you for an upbringing rich in words, books, and faith-based learning. I'll always attribute my love for reading and writing to the way I was raised. I love you!

Richard: thanks for all the encouragement, support, and patience as I worked to get this book done. And for another fabulous title!

Holly: thank you for the many conversations, rereads, and brain-storming sessions that helped shape Lightshed into the cohesive story that it is.

Emily: thanks for your beta reads, suggestions, and overall support as Lightshed came into being!

AJ: I'm so glad I've had the chance to work with you these last few years. Thank you for your patience and enthusiasm. And thanks for believing in this story. I'm blessed that I can call you not only my publisher but also my friend.

Meghan and Sarah: Lightshed would never be as shiny and clean without your input. I appreciate all the work you put in!

C.A.V.A. girls: you'll never know how much your friendship has meant to me these last few years. May we always lift one another up and support each other. Amber and Vanessa, thank you for the extra reads and time you spent helping polish it up. Anna, thank you for helping me with all the promotional stuff that you're so good at.

The Quill & Flame family: I'm so glad we have such a supportive group of people, all cheering each other on and celebrating every book release and success story. Thank you and God bless each of you!

The Gateway Keepers: Oh my goodness, you guys are the best street team ever! I never expected such enthusiasm and excitement. You filled this author's heart with so much joy and appreciation. Thank you for sharing my story with the world.

My local ACFW chapter: For years, I wished I had a local group of like-minded authors to get together with. I am so thankful for our group and our time together. You are truly a blessing to me.

Nadine Brandes: Your course on self-editing came at just the time that I needed it. I can't tell you how much I appreciate the time and personalized support you took with me during that time. It made such a difference in getting this story complete.

A big thank you to all the following ladies for submitting epigraphs for chapter headings! I loved all of them and made sure each found its place in the Sacred Code. *Bex, Brittany, Jessica, Suzanne, Rachel, Elisabeth, Ashley, and Holly.*

Lacey Scott: You did it again! I'm convinced you're a magician who can take my pitiful chicken scratch and turn it into a beautiful map.

Emilie Haney: You are a master. I'm still in awe of the loveliness you created for Shadowcast. And now I can say I've had two beautiful covers created by THE Emilie Haney. Thank you.

And to the Creator of *my* story. Thank You for all this and so much more.

ABOUT THE AUTHOR

Crystal Grant is the author of Shadowcast, book one of The Gateway Trilogy, along with multiple short stories and poems. As a hearing-impaired, home-school graduate, she found her voice in writing about characters fighting to overcome their obstacles. A self-described daydreamer who adores freshly-baked cookies and anything with fur or feathers, she strives to instill a love of books and learning within her young students. When she's not reading or writing stories that sweep her away to another time and place, she watches classic movies and TV shows that do the same. Or she works on jigsaw puzzles. Crystal currently resides in smalltown Missouri, where she is always looking for space for another book or scented candle.

DISCUSSION QUESTIONS

Unlike many main female characters in fantasy, Seria is not adept with a sword or bow. How do you think that affects her character? Do you feel that she is still a strong female character? Why or why not?

Both Eric and his father hid secrets in their past concerning mistakes that were made. Do you think it is ever right to hide a past wrong? If they had been open from the beginning, how do you think the story would have changed?

Seria is forced to leave her home and move to a new location for the third time. How difficult is it to start a new life in a strange town? What difficulties do you think Seria will have to face in the Old Realm?

Mason showed his true conversion when the Beacon glowed in his hand, but he still had to face consequences for his past wrongs. Do you think that someone who shows genuine remorse for a wrong should still be punished? Why or why not? What circumstances would change your opinion?

Was Seria right to think she could change Mason? Have you ever experienced or witnessed a similar situation?

Which character did you find the most relatable? Explain why.

In book three, Mason will be facing new challenges as a member of the Steward army. What kinds of unique challenges do you think he will face as a former Shadowman of the Dark Army? How do you think the Stewards and militiamen should receive him?